I0700809

THE SOUL COLLECTOR

AUDREY STEVES

THE SOUL COLLECTOR

AUDREY STEVES

This is a work of fiction. The names, characters, and events in this book are either the products of the author's imagination or are used fictitiously. Any similarity to any real persons living or dead is coincidental and not intended by the author.

Copyright © 2022 by Audrey Steves

Cover by Whimsy Book Cover Graphics

Interior Design by Audrey Steves

All rights reserved.

No portion of this book may be reproduced in any form without written permission from the publisher or author, except as permitted by U.S. copyright law.

ISBN (Hardcover) 979-8-9874431-1-8

ISBN (Paperback) 979-8-9874431-2-5

e-ISBN 979-8-9874431-0-1

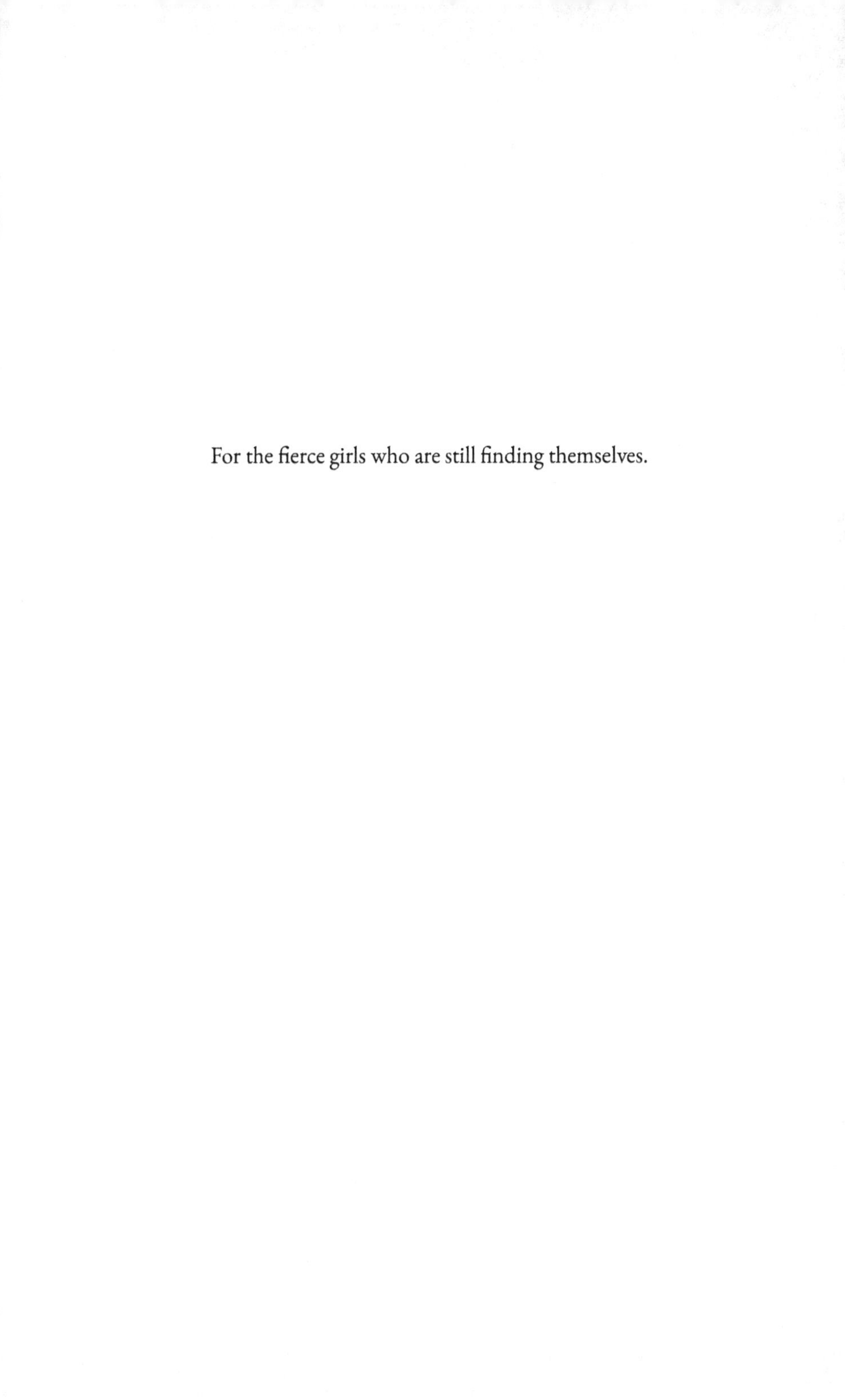

For the fierce girls who are still finding themselves.

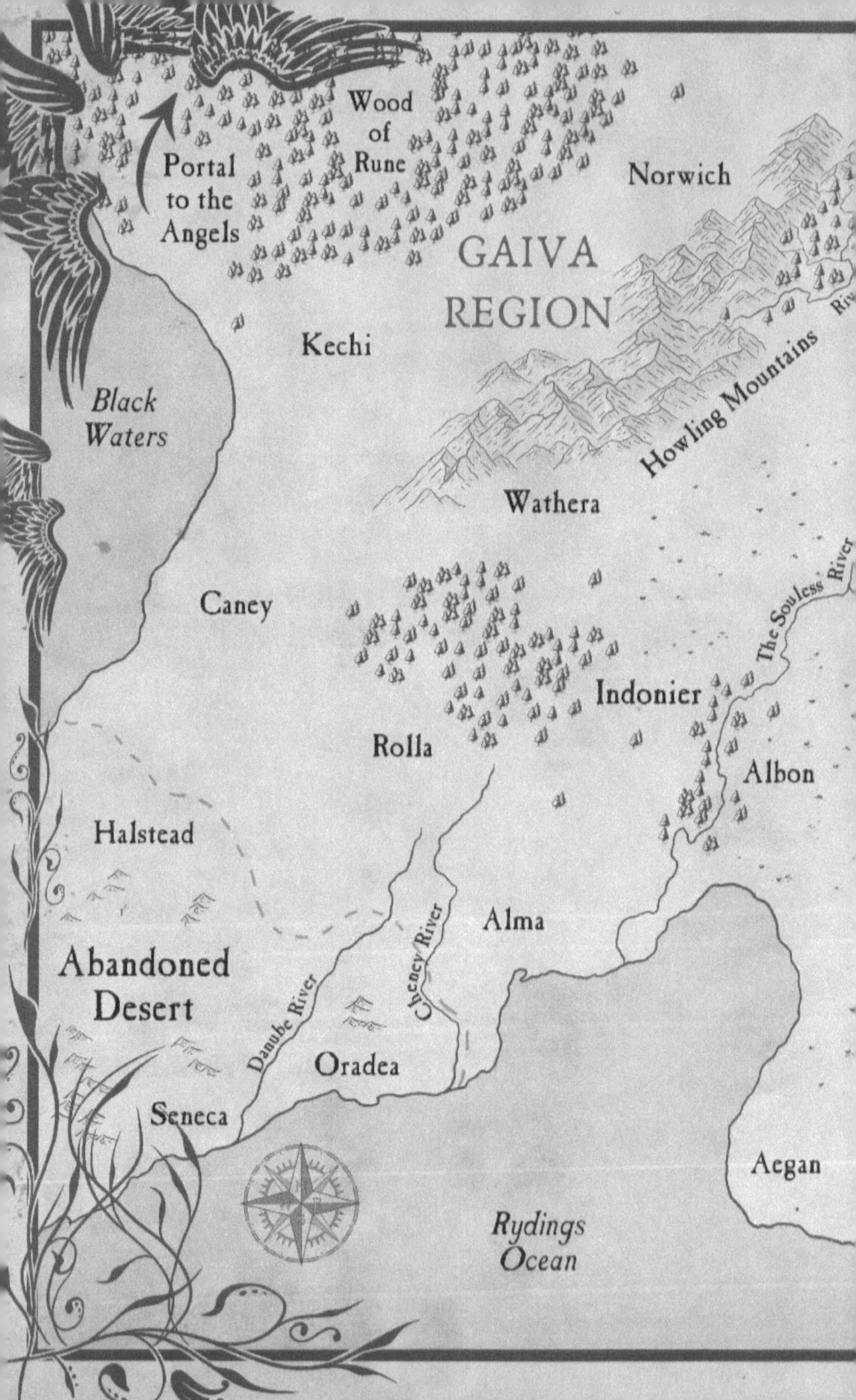

Wood of Rune
Portal to the Angels
Norwich
GAIVA REGION
Kechi
Black Waters
Howling Mountains
Wathera
Caney
The Souless River
Indonier
Rolla
Albon
Halstead
Alma
Abandoned Desert
Cheney River
Danube River
Oradea
Seneca
Aegan
Rydings Ocean

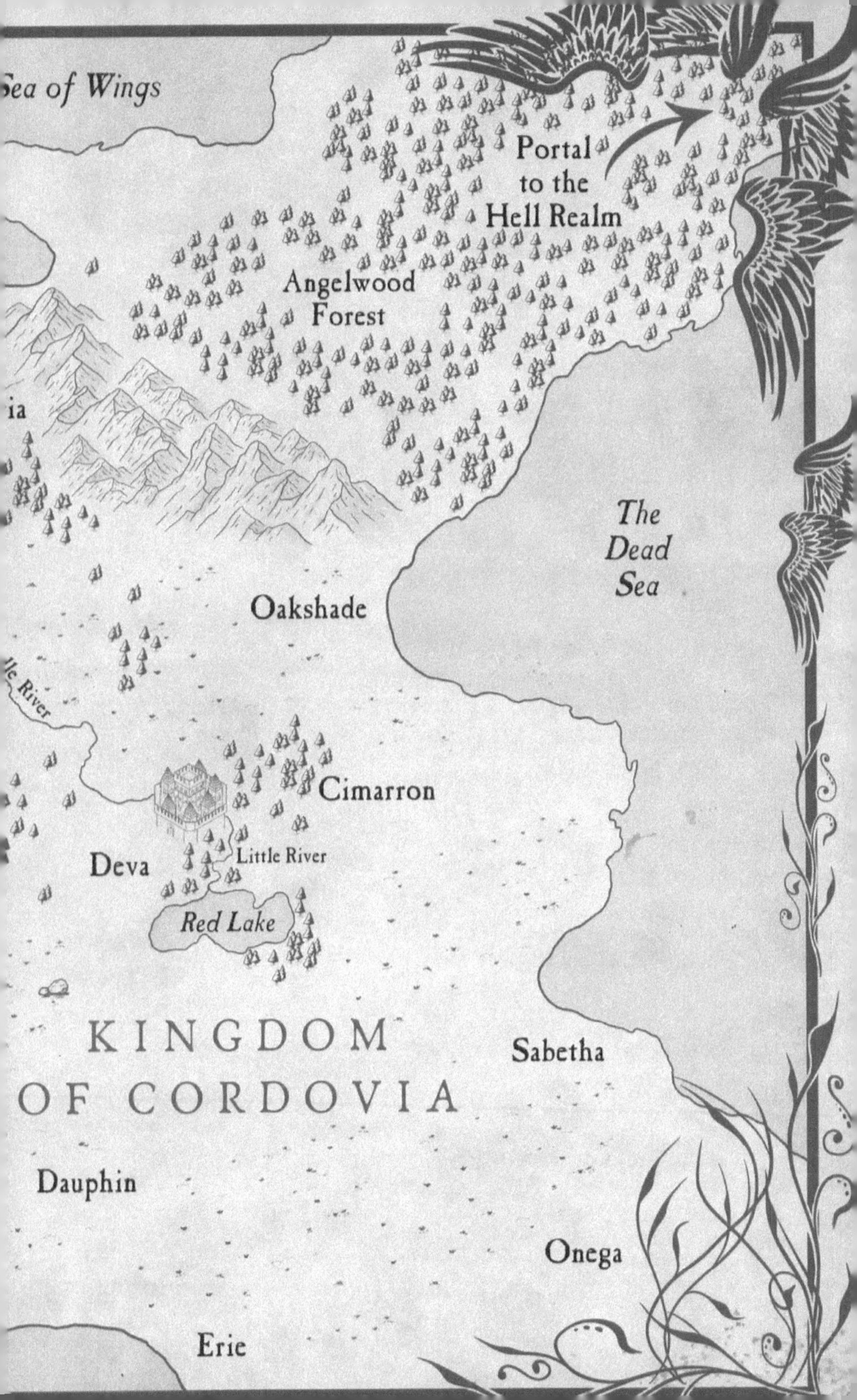

Sea of Wings
Portal to the Hell Realm
Angelwood Forest
The Dead Sea
Oakshade
Little River
Cimarron
Deva
Little River
Red Lake
KINGDOM OF CORDOVIA
Sabetha
Dauphin
Onega
Erie

ONE

Even though I hadn't moved in over an hour, I could still feel the stabbing pain of the shackles cutting into the torn flesh at my ankles.

The drunken revelers appeared completely oblivious to my presence though I sat chained to the throne on full display. Music and dancing continued shamelessly in the crowded ballroom. High lords and ladies from all over Cordovia had come to celebrate the prince's engagement to Lady Violette of Onega. The lady in question sat studiously nearby in a golden gown that hugged her slim figure. A woman I guessed was her guardian hovered over her shoulder sending guarded looks my way.

Not everyone enjoyed the sight of a young girl chained to the throne. Most of Cordovia enjoyed the company of wanderers, as we mostly kept to ourselves and often provided cheap entertainment. Even those who practically worshiped King Elroy as if he were one of their beloved angels, often enjoyed our performances. We'd been called many names in our wide history—scum, witches, even thieves. Yet the king's most loyal companions hardly hesitated to hire a performing family for one of their many festivities.

I rubbed at the tender skin beneath my chains. My wrists were bound together making it hard to tend to my ankles. My once-vibrant golden skin now appeared dull and blotched with bruises and scabs. Even my generous curves have diminished in the four months the king has held me captive.

I winced as I settled my hands into my lap once again. The guard standing over me jabbed his boot into my back—a signal to keep still. My mouth clamped shut against the cry of pain that tried to break free from my throat. I shifted slightly to allow more slack against my chains, relieving some of the pain they caused and putting some distance between the guard's boot and my back.

My leash was always kept close to the throne—a place the king thought would provide him with a sense of power. The scene was meant to show his subjects that he was the one in charge. To make them believe he was more than capable of catching the culprit responsible for tainting his kingdom and creating a rift between the classes.

My hands curled into fists in my lap, the soft burgundy fabric of my gaudy gown crinkling in my knuckles. The king could blame me for whatever he wanted and get away with it. Those of us who lived on the road knew the true devastation of Cordovia came from King Elroy's greed for wealth and power.

The music changed, and a tune suitable to a slow waltz echoed through the room. Couples broke apart as men sought out new partners, and women giggled and curtsied as men approached. Their gowns were made of pastel-colored tulle and lace designed to hug their waists and pool at their feet. A much more reasonable alternative compared to this ridiculous outfit the king forced me to wear when on display.

This dress was only one of the two that had been made for me. Today, I was in the dark red gown that hung to my ankles. A sheer veil of burgundy and gold threading wove its way over the fabric and hugged my curves in various designs. My sleeves were made of the sheer veil alone. An irritatingly itchy design that I loathed, yet didn't dare complain about for fear of the king's wrath.

My thick obsidian curls hung down my back and landed in a tangled mess at my waist. I had never let my hair get this long. It was too thick and too curly to keep tame. Living with my family in constant travel, it was easier to keep my hair cropped at my shoulders. Now, having been a prisoner for four months with no access or availability to tend to my wild curls, it had grown beyond reason. Yet it was the easiest way to tell how much time had passed since I had been taken from my family.

"You look like you could use a dance, milady," came a slurred voice over my shoulder.

I glanced up to see a man standing between where I sat on the dais steps and the dance floor beyond. His coat and shirt were untucked and nearly unbuttoned down his chest, and his black curly hair appeared far more disheveled than usual.

"She's not permitted to leave her chains, Your Highness," the nearby guard replied stiffly.

The prince sighed loudly; the smell of wine was strong on his breath. His dark skin gleamed with sweat from the aftermath of taking a woman to bed. In my four months at the castle there was hardly a night—on the rare occasions I was let out of my room—where I noticed the prince spending the night alone.

"Well, she's hardly made for a decent-looking decoration." I bristled at the prince's remark but held my tongue. "Surely she can be used for something decent."

My guard stiffened further as he cast a glance at Lady Violette's guardian who stood by, scowling at our interaction. While her guardian may not miss a thing, poor Lady Violette didn't seem to have a single thought behind those round brown eyes of hers.

"Perhaps you should spend time with your betrothed as opposed to sneaking under another girl's skirt, Your Highness," I said with false innocence.

Prince Elias flashed a crooked smile, his full lips widening over bright white teeth. "Shall I visit your room tonight then, Miss Loutari? Since you seem so concerned about my ventures into others' beds, perhaps you merely wish I was there to warm yours."

I snorted but it was cut off by the guard's sharp kick to my ribs. I doubled over in pain as breathing became temporarily painful. When I looked up, the prince moved away and slumped into his chair near Lady Violette. Her hands twined through her golden hair as she giggled at whatever absurdities the prince whispered in her ear.

"No talking, *witch*." The guard spat at the floor near my feet, causing me to flinch away and wince at the pain the movement caused from my steel shackles.

Disgusted, I hugged my knees against my chest. My back ached from sitting on the stone steps, but I didn't dare shift position as my ribs were still screaming from the aftermath of the guard's boot.

A sudden burst of gasps and cheers erupted from the far end of the ballroom, drawing my attention. I squinted through the crowded dance floor to see what had caught everyone's attention. The performers had arrived for Prince Elias and Lady Violette.

My heart raced as I scanned the entertainers. I hadn't seen my family in four months. The memory of being dragged from our caravan still burned bright behind my eyelids as I desperately searched the room for them. I needed to know they'd survived.

The families hired to perform wore matching clothes of brilliant colors, ranging from greens and blues to yellows and pinks. The young children moved through the room with bells on their ankles and hips swaying enthusiastically to the beat of the music they created. Skirts of greens and blues spread through the ballroom as the orchestra on the mezzanine finally acquiesced the spotlight.

Men and women appeared in the doorway to follow the path the children created through the crowd. The women wore similar bells on their wrists and ankles, creating their own tune to match that of the children. Others carried ribbons in their hands to twirl through the air with their dance.

Bright smiles were plastered on all of their faces as they entered. It was considered a great honor among performing wanderers to be asked to entertain the king. My family had been lucky enough to perform once many years ago when my older brother Mousa was only a babe.

I loosened my grip on my knees as the entertainers moved closer to the dais. Behind me, I could hear the king and Queen Isolde return to their thrones. Hiding behind my veil of hair, I turned slightly to glance in their direction.

Queen Isolde sat between her husband and son in an elegant black gown, silver beading lining its seams. She reached for her husband's hand, a cheerful smile on her face as she watched the performers below, just as enthralled as the rest of the room. Jewels decorated her fingers and dangled from her neck, giving the illusion of wealth amidst a kingdom drained of luxuries.

The king, however, seemed more concerned with his son's drunken state. He sent a scowl toward Prince Elias, who now sat slumped over the arm of his chair, his head resting on Lady Violette's shoulder. I bit the inside of my cheek to hide my smile as the lady appeared overjoyed to be sitting so close to her betrothed.

"Girl, eyes forward," King Elroy snapped just as the guard shoved me down another step. The movement caused my shackles to tear through the nearly closed wounds at my ankles as the chain drew taut.

I sucked in a breath through my teeth as I righted myself with shaking hands. Gently tucking my feet, I used the skirts of my gown to hide the blood now dripping from the freshly opened wounds.

I forced my attention back to the performers as I fought the stinging in my eyes. Their voices echoed beautifully throughout the hall. Their instruments and cheerful words brought smiles to so many faces. My own heart fought to burst out of my chest as memories burned behind my eyes.

Blue skirts and yellow shirts wove theatrically through the crowd. Together they painted the dull room with a vibrant burst of color. The family in shades of green and gold each had freckled skin and fire red hair, making them stand out as they sung and spun through the crowd.

Each family wore their own colors for performances, making it easier for towns to pass on the news of which family they preferred or when they would be seen next.

My family, the Loutari clan, wore deep reds and purples with gold stars decorating our caravan.

The king's guests shifted out of the way in a rush as the family in blue, with hair as dark as night, swarmed the ballroom. They drew their knives and loaded their bows with arrows lit with fire to awe in their daring performances.

With another eruption of cheers, my gaze returned to the others. They'd truly begun their performance now. A woman stood near the far wall as her partner threw his knives in her direction. She moved in an elegant dance as he managed to hit the wall behind her. Not a single knife brushed her skin, though they were close enough to make the crowd gasp in unison.

The longing I felt for my family grew as I watched these wanderers perform. While the king was quick to blame me for his kingdom's suffering, he had yet to speak on the fate of my family. The only thing that kept me from trying to escape this imprisonment was the hope that they were still out there somewhere, safe and far away from the king's brutality.

I quickly wiped a stray tear from my cheek as I forced my attention back to the present.

The white, blue, and gold banners of Cordovia hung from the ceiling and decorated the walls while the performers continued in their vibrant shades and patterns. The cold display of Cordovia's control contrasted with the warmth radiating from the wanderers as they overwhelmed the room.

Slowly, I shifted to hide in the shadows of the banners above. The performers held the focus of the entire crowd with their talents, giving me the freedom to hide from questioning gazes. The story-telling children had dispersed and now offered palm reading or fortune telling to anyone brave enough to accept. I smiled as I watched their brows furrow at others' palms. This was a talent very few could truly master, most just offered vague guesses at someone's future before taking their money. The pity was people were quick to believe these simple claims. Despite never living their prophesized futures, many people were still eager for ambiguous answers. I knew this irrevocably, as it had been my duty among my family to perform these readings for those who sought them.

The strange essence that lived near my heart pulled against my control in an effort to join the others. I never understood what this part of me was, but I guessed it was what allowed me to read the glimpses of a person's soul more clearly. The manacles at my wrists jingled as I placed my palms over my chest, hoping the movement would keep the urge to practice my gift at bay.

"Will you read me, please?"

Startled, I turned to see a young girl no older than ten standing before me. Brown curls hung around her round face which was flushed with color and bright with a smile.

I stared at her outstretched hand, palm up. A quick glance past her shoulder told me the other children remained huddled together, laughing at the glimpses of their futures.

With shaking hands, I reached for hers and held on tightly. The paleness of her hand clashed with the dark bruises covering my own golden skin. I could feel her eyes studying the manacles at my wrists, but I looked deeper into her palm, ignoring her questioning look.

The dark essence living near my heart erupted to life, encompassing my mind. It was a dangerous gift that allowed me to be one of the very few who could do this properly. I never understood what this gift meant, but my mother was always quick to assure me that it was a blessing and was to be honored as such.

Pushing that thought aside, I returned to this young girl's palm. The shadows of the banners kept us out of the king's direct line of sight—a fact I relished as I was sure this would end in another beating if he spotted us now.

The darkness in my chest bled down my arms, leaving a heated trace through my veins. Only I could see it work as it settled in the palm of this girl's hand. To anyone watching, it would just appear that I was truly enthralled with the lines of her palm.

"What do you see?" she asked excitedly, practically bouncing on the balls of her feet.

I smiled. "I see many things," I said, returning my gaze to her palm, "but I shall tell you three."

She gasped as I gently ran a finger over the lines of her palm. Whatever my gift was, it moved easily in the path of my finger drawing the truth from her soul. There was no art or science to what I did. Many healers throughout the kingdom attempted to call us witches, claiming what we did was vile. Many of us were imprisoned because of it. All I knew was that whatever this darkness living near my heart was, it allowed me to recognize the truly wicked. I could identify the souls so black and tainted with blood that they'd earned a special place among the vilest of demons, destined to suffer at the hands of Death himself. At least that was what Nonna said.

But the soul of this young girl was not scarred or tainted. It appeared like the sun reflecting off the sea. Bright and peaceful. I let myself drown in the warmth of her soul as it formed along her small frame, answering the call of my gift. When I looked into it, I could see a lifetime of opportunity and peace, but also the choices that would stain her soul with darkness.

The futures of others were never set in stone, and with a single choice everything could change. It was because of this knowledge that I refused to reveal the entire truth of one's soul and the secrets it possessed. When given only half-truths, many would still carve their own path through their futures. Without the possibility of destruction haunting their every decision, many went on to live full and joyous lives.

I opened my mouth to begin to tell half-truths to this young girl when my gift shifted.

My power surged out of me now, moving past the girl to a man standing a few feet away. His face was half-hidden in shadow, but his eyes darted from the performers to the girl before me. I knew then, from the hungry look in his eye when he looked at this girl, that he was one with a soul so dark, it appeared as its own shadow.

I gritted my teeth against the burn of the horrible things hidden in his soul. The heavily pregnant wife at his side surely had no clue what went on in this man's private moments. The secrets that troubled his heart remained branded across his soul. My strange gift fought to surge deeper into his secrets. The tugging sensation within my chest tore the breath from me.

"First," I said, forcing my gift to return to the girl's palm, "do you see this line here?" Slowly, I drew my finger across a line along her palm. Her eyes widened in wonder as she nodded excitedly. "Continue your studies and great things will come of it."

Her face fell. "Continue my studies? You mean go to school? But father says I am to marry when I come of age."

I nodded slowly, keeping my eyes on her palm. "Marry if you must, but know good things will come if you continue your studies. You are far brighter than you give yourself credit for."

She puckered her lips as I continued. "And this line here?" I said, pointing to another, "This tells me many things about your heart."

"My heart?" Her voice kicked up an octave, desperate not to be drowned out by the cheering and music roaring through the hall behind her.

I smiled at her widened eyes. "Yes. You have a big heart. There are many things I see in your soul regarding your heart."

"My soul? My soul is in my hand?"

My throat tightened with the burn of tears as I forced a laugh. It had been so long since I'd used my gift it felt like a relief to unleash the tether I kept it on. "No. I can see into your soul though. That's what I'm reading now. Your palm just helps me understand what I'm seeing."

The girl's mouth popped open into a small O. "What does it say?"

Again, my gift leaped to latch onto the man half hidden in shadow. I struggled against it and smiled at the girl again. "You see that man behind you?" I quieted my voice so she had to lean in to hear me.

She cast a glance over her shoulder and caught sight of the man in question. He smiled warmly at her before his wife demanded his attention at a dancer's approach.

"Yes, who is he?" she asked, returning her wide eyes to me.

I shrugged. "I don't know. But your soul is telling me you need to stay with your mother for the rest of the night. Don't wander alone without her."

She nodded vigorously, taking my words to heart.

I dropped her hand then, the heaviness of my chains settling deep into the weakened muscles of my arms as my gift retracted into itself. Trying to hide my wince as the pain shot through me with the movement, I settled further against the wall and stretched my feet before me. Small beads of blood remained beside me from the pinch of the chains.

"Why are you chained?" the girl asked, seeming to just notice my shackles.

I forced a gentle smile; her eyes had gone wide at the sight of my bloodied and bruised skin. "Because some people are scared of what I can do," I said, thinking of the king's own fear.

"Is that why you aren't dancing with the others?"

"It is." My gaze flicked back to the performers in question. The crowd continued to cheer for their performances, though from the way they shifted I knew the true talent was about to begin.

"Do you want to dance with them?" She glanced down at her palm with a furrowed brow before her gaze returned to mine.

My chest ached with the notion. Even when traveling with my family, I was never one to perform in the open with them. I was always forced to assist Nonna in the caravan when she did her readings before she taught me how to perform my own. Most of the readings she had me perform involved her crystal ball, which I used to think of as a cheap decoration.

"I do," I whispered in reply to the girl's question.

A young man, probably not yet thirty, stood on a raised platform in the far corner of the room. The royal family watched him curiously, apart from Prince Elias who remained slumped over and snoring softly.

The hairs on my arms rose as the atmosphere changed. The entire room fell silent as the storyteller took his place before the crowd. I watched his gaze sweep over the room, drawing everyone in for the story he was about to weave. When he opened his mouth to begin his tale, my shoulders slumped, my emotions overcome with the familiar magic one can release through a tale. I tried to focus on his words, but my mind grew distant. His easy baritone voice echoed through the deafening silence of the hall. Everyone became entirely enthralled with his lyrical tale.

"What is he doing?" the girl beside me whispered.

I opened my eyes to find her staring at the man with wide eyes. I smiled. "He's telling them a story. A magical story with wraiths, demons, angels, and heroes. You should find your mother and listen to his tale. You might just enjoy it."

A bright smile lit up her face before she turned back to me. "But you promised to tell me three things and you only told me two and you never told me what you saw in my heart." She held her palm out to me again, waiting for her last bit of half-truth.

Blinking back tears that gathered through the magic in the storyteller's tale, I reached for her hand again, my gift opening at her touch.

"What do you think you are doing?" A voice roared over the subtle baritone of the storyteller's words.

The girl jolted away from me as if stung. Her expression turned to one of horror and I knew then who stood over my shoulder.

I offered her a comforting smile. "Go find your mother and don't leave her side for the rest of the night."

She turned on her heel and sprinted into the crowd, most of whom had turned to study the commotion the king was causing. Even the storyteller and the other performers watched in horror as the king jerked my chains harshly.

I bit down on my tongue, drawing blood but refusing to cry out against the pain. The gesture of being dragged by my feet caused my skirts to rise up to my knees, revealing my bruised and bloodied ankles for all to see. The collective gasp and murmurs of disgust echoed through me as the king finally stopped dragging me to the throne.

Panting, I lay curled on my side, nervously awaiting the public punishment the king was sure to execute.

"You are not permitted to speak to those of superior birth to your tainted blood," he spat as he towered over me. The king was a large man, both wide and tall though his body was soft with age. His dark skin reddened with rage as he tightly gripped the manacles binding my wrists together.

I gasped as he yanked me to my knees. Sweat trickled down my back beneath my thick veil of tangled hair as I forced my eyes away from the king's glare.

"I will not allow you to spread your witchcraft to others in my kingdom," he bellowed. Queen Isolde sat silently on her throne, appearing bored as she watched her beloved husband once again direct his temper toward me.

"Father," Prince Elias cautioned. His gaze was trained on the blood staining the chains at my ankles. I watched his eyes widen in horror before diminishing to their usual cool exterior.

"You will learn your place, Esme Loutari-Ayres." King Elroy's voice echoed throughout the deathly quiet of the room. Out of the corner of my eye, I could just make out the other wanderers staring in frozen anger before the king's fist collided with my cheek.

The sudden pain sent a shockwave through my body and the king released my wrists so suddenly, I fell crashing to the dais steps.

As my vision darkened, I could hear the faint tone of the storyteller's words. I forced my eyes open, ignoring the stares of everyone gazing at my prone figure and instead meeting the gaze of the storyteller himself. The other wanderers moved to join him, each of them placing a fist over their heart, eyes narrowed at the king. This time when the storyteller spoke, he told the tale of a family tied to the god of Death. And to the sound of this haunting tale, I succumbed to the darkness.

TWO

TWO DAYS HAVE PASSED since the king punished me in front of his court. Though I avoided glancing in the tiny mirror hanging on my wall, I knew from the constant ache in my cheek that my face remained purple with bruising.

The warmth of my bed tempted me, but as I shifted on the small cot I caught sight of the blood staining my pillow. Tentatively, I reached up to brush the tips of my fingers along the tender skin at my brow and sighed as they came away wet with blood. The cuts must have opened again overnight.

Stiff with the soreness that came from being chained every day, I slipped out of bed. The rattle of my chains echoed through the small, pathetic room I was kept in. With only a small cot, a barred window, the wash tub in the corner, and a fireplace that appeared to never have been lit, my room felt far from welcoming.

The chain that kept me tied to the center of the room dragged across the cold stone as I stumbled to the small pail of fresh water beneath the mirror. A servant filled the water each morning and cleaned my other pail every night. Apart from the guard who constantly stood watch outside my locked door, that servant was the only person I saw daily.

Gently, I dipped my hands into the tepid water that filled the clean bucket. My skin, damp with sweat, cooled at the feel of it. Careful of the tenderness I knew lived in my bruises, I washed away the blood dripping down my cheek. Nearly hidden in the dark bruises covering the side of my face was a cut just above my brow from the king's many rings that would certainly leave another scar.

As I watched the blood mix with the water dripping down my cheek, I noticed a hollowness to my face that wasn't there before. As the blood slowly cleared away, I stared at my reflection in the dim mirror coated with grime. My hair, which once used to hang flatteringly around my face in thick dark curls, now hung limp to my waist. A layer of dirt and sweat covered my skin and a thick slab of grease had grown in my hair.

Father used to say how much I resembled my mother. Round face, large dark eyes that took in everything, and a full mouth that he said could craft enough sass to make any man tremble to his knees.

I didn't see that girl he had spoken about now. What remained of my mother's appearance lay in the golden shade of my skin which now appeared dull and grey with fatigue. My cheeks were hollow, my mouth chapped and dry.

I sat back on my heels and pressed my fists against my eyes. I would not cry. My early days being locked in this room had washed away with tears that still burned my throat. No matter how battered I appeared now, I had to believe that I would make it out of here again. There must be a way to find my family.

A sharp knock at my door startled me out of my reverie. The tender skin beneath my chains screamed in protest as I stumbled to my feet. My breath caught at the sting of pain that lanced up my legs as I moved against the manacles. If I wasn't allowed to bathe soon, infection would set in, again.

The door opened immediately. "His Majesty King Elroy requests your presence within the hour." The servant who tended to my room stood awkwardly in the doorway as she studied where I stood, hunched over the bucket of clean water.

"What does he want to see me for?" I asked, knowing I probably wouldn't get an answer.

Her thin mouth tightened into a hard line as she scowled at the grubby knapsack I was forced to wear. The faded and stained brown slip hung to my knees and provided little warmth on the cool nights during early spring. This late in the summer it did little other than collect the sweat off my skin.

Without a word she moved further into the room, a guard on her heels as he closed the door behind them and leaned against it, scowling.

I returned his scowl as the servant moved to fill my tub with the pails of water she carried in from the hall. Of course, they'd want me to appear clean and presentable before the king. Though I was sure he knew of my usual condition in this room locked so far away from the rest of the castle.

The guard continued to scowl in my direction as I tracked the servant's stiff steps into my room. His pale skin and hair matched the coldness coming off of him in waves. Even his pale blue eyes held little warmth as they stared at me in obvious revulsion.

Once, the thought of being naked and bathing before the strange man would make my cheeks heat with humiliation. Now, I couldn't find it in myself to care for my lack of privacy.

The servant gingerly touched my arm, guiding me toward the tub. She stayed silent as I pulled the tunic over my head and dropped it to the floor before carefully stepping into the shallow tub.

My skin stung against the sudden submersion but I bit my tongue hard enough to draw the pain away and relax slightly. The water was cool, but I welcomed it as it washed away my layers of grime and blood.

The servant, whose name I had never learned, gently massaged the soap into my hair while I scrubbed my body. Normally, I was left to my own devices to bathe, but today it seemed I had a time limit.

"Am I to wear the tunic or shall I don one of the ridiculous gowns the king prefers I wear for public affairs?" I asked no one in particular. I kept my back to the guard who remained against the door, but I could feel his dislike of my casual disdain. Neither dress resembled anything close to what a self-respecting wanderer might wear.

"Neither," the servant said quietly.

I glanced at her again, studying her a little closer while she rinsed out my hair. She was small, not much taller than me, and I was only tall enough to see no higher than a man's chest. Her figure was slim and gaunt, like she didn't do much other than tend to me. Her plain ash-colored hair was kept back in a tight knot at the nape of her neck, making her face stand out harshly against her frame.

"Then what? Does he expect me to run through the castle naked?" As soon as the words left my mouth, I feared they may be true. King Elroy loved humiliating me before his court. He claimed I was to be made an example for everyone he blamed for the draining of his kingdom's wealth. And to do that, he stripped away a little of my dignity every chance he got.

Her mouth hardened. "No. He has graciously provided you with a new set of clothes to wear for this moment."

My face throbbed from the bruises as I splashed water over the dried blood on my cheek. "How generous of him indeed."

She remained silent as she helped me from the tub. The warm air kissed my damp skin, causing a shiver to crawl down my spine and rattle my chains. The guard kept his eyes downcast to provide a false sense of privacy while the servant handed me a towel. I hugged it tightly around my middle as she dug around in the bag she tossed onto my cot.

My mind began to wander the way it usually did when I was forced to stand for the servant to dress me. Only today, the guard moved to unlock my chains to allow my feet to slip through the tights. That brief moment of relief was enough to make tears spring into my eyes before the chains locked around my ankles once again.

My hair dripped down the plain tunic until the servant quickly yanked a brush through the tangles and braided it down my back. I pulled at the sleeves of my tunic, hiding the bruises at my wrists, while she tied off the end of my braid.

The guard, seeming impatient with watching the servant girl help me into slippers, yanked the chain free of its tie in the middle of the floor and pulled me forward. The servant disappeared down the hall, leaving me alone with the serious face of my guard.

This corner of the castle remained silent as we passed through the halls. The only sounds were the slow din of the chains as they rattled off the stone walls and the pounding of my heart as I followed the guard. My room only held a single small window which provided little view of the outside world, but from the large windows we passed I knew it to be near midday as the sun offered a blinding light across the pale sky.

My new clothes bristled against my sensitive skin as we took turn after turn through the silent halls. Dust clouded the air and settled along the faded paintings that haunted this far corner of the castle. Each step taking us farther from the safety of my room and closer to the threat of the king.

I hugged my arms around my middle as I heard the whisper of voices ahead. The cool stone beneath my bare feet provided some unexpected comfort as I forced my eyes downcast as the familiar, deep tones of the prince filled the halls. From the responding squeal of a young lady, I knew he wasn't alone.

My guard nearly faltered as he caught sight of the prince, whose face was buried against the woman's neck, his back to us as he kept her pressed against the wall. I could hear whispers leaving his mouth as he taunted her with his tongue, hands moving slyly down her waist before gripping the thick fabric of her pale dress. The woman, her hands equally hungry to touch the prince as they tightened on his shoulders, blushed a deep crimson before her eyes found mine, effectively erasing any trace of amusement. The gasp that left her forced me to swallow back a snort of laughter at her distraught expression.

"Sorry, Your Highness," my guard said uncomfortably. "Your father requested the girl."

Prince Elias didn't turn to look at us before speaking. "Then I suggest you take her to him."

The guard mumbled an apology and dragged me along. The force of his grip on my chains causing me to trip and fall onto my back with a grunt. The girl giggled as she watched me struggle to my feet.

"What a poor pity of a girl," the stupid young woman whispered dramatically to the prince. Her bright eyes scrutinized the blood dripping down my feet.

I snorted and limped after my guard who frowned at me.

"You have something you dare say to me?" she retorted, pulling herself away from the prince.

I heard him sigh before he leaned back against the wall to cast a frown in my direction. The girl he was nearly entangled with crossed her arms over her chest and glared down her very steep nose at my hunched stature.

A smile nearly threatened to show on my face, but I ignored her as I dared to look at the prince directly. "Don't you think your time could be better spent learning the ways of your kingdom with your father? Or perhaps learning of the true cause behind your kingdom's financial decline and how you can go about helping the people who are dying under your father's rule?" At my question he stiffened considerably. "Or perhaps with your betrothed who is much more visually appealing than this one."

The young woman gasped in shocked rage that caused Prince Elias to tuck his chin, hiding his amused grin. Her cheeks reddened in anger as she dropped her hands to her sides, fingers curling into fists.

"You have no right to speak to me in such a way," she snapped furiously.

The guard tugged harder on my chains, causing me to crash down to the floor once again. I grunted as my elbows smacked against the stones.

"You stupid witch. You cannot speak to those with cleaner blood in such a way." The girl stepped closer so she could watch me struggle to my feet.

I laughed coldly. "I am no witch, you moron."

The corner of my vision barely registered the rise of her fist before it came crashing toward me. I grunted in pain as her hand collided with the bruises already marring the side of my face.

Gingerly, I reached up with shaking hands to cup my bruised cheek. The girl's eyes darkened with cruel delight as she raised her hand again. Shame filled me, heating my cheeks and burning my tear-filled eyes, as I knew I could not stop her. Not if I wanted to live to find my family.

"I think her face is bruised enough, don't you?" the prince asked calmly. The sharp lines of his body remained taut as he stepped to the girl's side and gently lowered her hand.

She cast me one long, hateful look before the guard tugged me back through the corridors and away from the girl whose gasps and giggles echoed through the hallway now that their interruption was out of sight.

My knees and elbows burned from the fall, but I ignored them as the guard silently led me through the halls. The farther we walked from my room, the brighter the castle seemed to feel. Sunlight filtered through the stained-glass windows, casting the widened hallways in a colorful glow. Vases of flowers sat at every corner in an attempt to overshadow the dark memories of our kingdom's war with the demons. Memories which haunted the walls in every dark painting. Each painting served not only as proof that our king's ancestors remained loyal to the angels, but also as a reminder that the demons could return at any moment.

Guards were stationed at corners, and servants moved about silently while members of the court walked cheerily through the corridors. My presence became an unwelcome beacon for curious stares as I made my way to the king's chambers.

My heart beat furiously in my chest and my cheeks heated with embarrassment as I caught bits of whispers and accusations sent my way.

Most called me a witch and cursed my existence. I knew of the rumors the king had spread upon my arrival as he told his court of the deeds I did for the demons of Hell. None of which were true. Most wanderers didn't believe the same superstitions that the townspeople did. We knew of the war between the angels and demons that wreaked havoc on our lands so many centuries ago, but we didn't worship the angels the way the king and his people did. We feared the demons of course, but only the truly dark witches would dare summon them. Wanderers were peaceful folk. We wouldn't lower ourselves to associate with the creatures of Hell.

Yet, far too many of us had been arrested and accused of witchcraft. With the amount of cruelty in Cordovia--thanks to the king's harsh laws and financial greed--it was too easy to blame wanderers and performers for any oddities of the kingdom.

I didn't know why they thought such absurd things about my people, and I didn't really care. My heart simply ached for my family.

"Lady Loutari-Ayres," a soft-spoken female voice said, catching my attention. My shoulders tightened with nervous tension as those surrounding my guard and I fell silent. In all the months I'd been captive, no one had dared to address me in public—not even the king unless his purpose was to humiliate and punish.

I caught sight of Lady Violette walking toward me. Her stern-faced guardian at her back looked on the lady's greeting with strong disapproval.

I bowed my head though the guard continued to drag me along. "Lady Violette," I greeted politely.

Her smile brightened her young face. She couldn't have been much older than me and I was only two months away from my eighteenth year.

"Have you by chance seen Prince Elias? I was hoping to ask him to show me through the gardens this evening. I hear the flowers glow in the moonlight."

Members of the court stood by and watched in muted horror as Lady Violette spoke with me. The anger at the prince and his newest conquest's remarks rose to combat the confusion I felt as others whispered and scowled in my direction. "His Highness probably has his pants around his ankles and his hand up another girl's skirt at the moment. He should still be up in the corridor just past the stairs though." I let the false cheer ring through my voice loudly. Those watching nearby fell silent at my words. Lady Violette's face flushed scarlet as a pair of court ladies giggled to each other nearby, only silencing when Lady Violette's stern guardian cast a scowl their way.

"Good to see you, milady," I said with a bow. I turned and followed after my guard. My anger dimmed further as whispers followed me through the hall.

"You will be punished for that," my guard whispered as he stopped me just outside a large set of unfamiliar doors.

I swallowed; perhaps he was right.

The doors opened a moment later and the guard dragged me through unceremoniously. I stumbled again but managed to catch myself on the edge of the broad table that took up most of the room.

I glanced around nervously. King Elroy sat just in front of me, his wife at his shoulder. On his other side sat the Royal Adviser and other members of his court who scowled at me distrustfully.

"Esme Loutari-Ayres," Queen Isolde said in her scornful voice. I bowed my head in silent greeting as I felt her eyes narrow on the blood still drying at my feet.

"It seems," the king began over the unnervingly hushed room, "that the monstrosities you caused while free have spread to something more." I dared a look at his face before casting my eyes to my feet again.

"More people than usual have been reported to be causing mayhem and destruction throughout villages all over Cordovia," the king continued in his deep tones. "Many families have found themselves slaughtered in their sleep, businesses and homes destroyed and burned, pets disappearing only to reappear in pieces. There are even rumors of a rebellious group seeking destruction in the North. You see why this is a concern of mine?"

I swallowed my fear and gave a stiff nod. My eyes found his reluctantly. His face, so similar to his son's, yet different in many ways. Prince Elias may be crude, but there was a warmth to his face that the king's did not have. The sheer coolness in his stare alone was enough to start my knees trembling.

"You were brought here those weeks ago to be made an example. A promise of power owed to my place on the throne," he said slowly. "Yet all you have done is continue the cursed witchcraft forbidden in my kingdom. Should you continue to disrupt the novelty of my kingdom, I will have your guard remove first your right hand, then your left. Do I make myself clear?"

My mind mulled over his words as I cast confused glances to the others at the table. Though from their furious stares I was the only one not understanding. As his words sank deeper into my mind, I felt my heart rate spike with nervous energy.

"I'm sorry Your Majesty, but I don't think I understand," I croaked nervously.

His face grew cold in anger. "A deal was made with your blood. Because of the power that deal wields, you were arrested for witchcraft and sorcery. Yet you continue to defy your king and your imprisonment by using your cursed tricks to soil the people of my kingdom."

I shook my head, his words causing a panicked tightening of my lungs as confusion battled for dominance. "I haven't done anything. I'm not even a witch."

"Preposterous," the Royal Adviser cursed loudly, making me jump. "You are a witch. And you are continuing to defy your king by speaking out of turn and poisoning his kingdom. You should be executed with the others."

My blood grew cold. The air left my lungs in a rush as I studied the men at the table before me, each of them appearing as cold hearted and cruel as the king. When my gaze finally met his, I understood why. The small teasing smile lifting the corners of his mouth sent my heart into a frenzy.

"As we speak," the king said, answering my unspoken question, "people with tainted blood, witch blood such as yours, are being captured and brought to the castle. From villages as far as Wathera and Caney to those near Deva. Anyone observed to be a witch or associating with demons will be imprisoned and tried for treason and witchcraft."

I swallowed back the bile that threatened to rise in my throat. The pain of my bruised and battered body forgotten as my pulse roared in my ears.

Mother and Father. Nonna. Mousa, my adventurous older brother. Cordelia, my fierce younger sister. Or Alfie and Amara, the youngest siblings of us all who were still so curious about the world. Their names circled through my mind as I stared, dumbfounded at the king. If they still lived, I hoped they'd run far away.

Far past the mountains bordering Gaiva, and remain safe where the king could not find them.

"Then," he continued before I could calm my panic, "they shall be executed. One by one. Until only you remain. Then you shall burn like the witch you are."

THREE

The next day, the manacles attacking the skin at my ankles barely registered in my mind. It seemed no matter how much they dug into my sensitive flesh, I could only think of the men and women before me tied to pyres, awaiting their burning.

The midday sky remained covered with dark clouds, giving the once pristine and green yards an eerie feeling that left little hope for a joyous afternoon. The subtle murmurs of the gathered crowd sounded like a dim humming as my eyes remained focused on those before me. Pyres built overnight now held men and women of all ages, as they were tied down with rope too thick to struggle against. My heart remained lodged in my throat as the guards sneered at them.

The king had ordered his guards to bring a crowd to serve as witnesses to this crude trial. A trial where the accused were already sentenced in the king's mind. The crowd shuffled with an excited air about them as they studied the scene. I scowled at their fine clothing that gave the illusion of attending a ball rather than a mass execution. Children smiled and toyed with their tulle skirts or clean, pressed trousers while their parents gossiped among themselves. Every one of them seemed far too happy to be here.

I shot a glare over my shoulder at the royal family who stood on the castle steps. My chains remained in the hands of my guard who stood nearby and scowled at the growing crowd with a tangible hatred.

King Elroy and Prince Elias stood shoulder to shoulder as they studied the crowd before them. People from the surrounding towns had come to witness the first mass execution Cordovia has held in decades. We hadn't needed one since the war that ended the Old World.

Both men stood on the steps in regal wear of Cordovia's colors. The king wore a suit of blue and gold that appeared to reflect the light of the faint sun against the harsh lines of his aging face. Next to him, Prince Elias kept his eyes fixed on a point straight ahead and looked equally regal for once, wearing his golden crown that seemed to mirror the gold flecks in his eyes—eyes I had never dared look into directly before.

My face heated as his gaze easily found mine. I quickly turned away, letting my veil of hair fall forward to hide my flaming face. My stomach tightened as I felt the prince's eyes continuing to burn a spot between my shoulder blades.

"It is unfortunate that we should all come together for a time as sad as this," the king began in his deep tones, effectively silencing the stirring crowd. "Our world hasn't seen a time this wicked since the angels and demons of beyond brought war onto our realm. Since their retreat to separate realms, we have known peace, comfort, and joy.

"We all know the history of the battle between the Angel of Life and the god of Death," he continued stoically. "Death's jealousy for the power the angel could wield caused him to break through the barrier which kept his demons out of our realm, therein forcing the angels to act for our protection. War ravaged our lands for decades before a deal was struck with the angels. What you may not know, however, is that a deal was struck with the demons, too."

The crowd gasped as one, sending horrified looks at those accused.

"Yes, yes," the king said with a raised hand, silencing their worry. "There are people who have allowed the demons to capture the souls and minds of others, making today's deaths a mercy for some and an adequate end for those to blame."

I fought the urge to groan as I stood on the hard packed earth below the steps. All around the castle yard, townspeople looked toward the king with such trust and pride in their faces, soaking in every word he breathed like it was their lifeline. How foolish they all were.

"Cordovia was the birthplace of our salvation after the war between those godly beings. Today," the king continued, "we are brought together once again to rid our kingdom of treason against our gods. These betrayers," he jabbed a stubby finger at the people struggling against their binds, their cheeks reddened and tear stained. "These abhorrent *things*," he spat the word like dirt, "have been brought here today to be executed for witchcraft and trading secrets with demons. For too long our towns and villages have been overrun with those who call themselves healers, wanderers, or entertainers. But we all know the truth."

My back began to ache from the tension I held in my shoulders. Those in the crowd shot hate filled glances my way and toward those sprawled along the pyres.

I glanced wearily over my shoulder and spotted the prince, once again watching me curiously. Something akin to pity was barely hidden in his gaze.

I wanted to scream at him for his lack of empathy for those about to meet their end based on his father's baseless fears.

My knees trembled as the king continued. "It was my ancestor, you see," he said proudly, puffing his chest, "that struck a deal with the angels in our favor. Demons would not again walk our lands so long as our kingdom thrived under my family's rule. However, it took one wish granted by a member of Death's realm, for that deal to be threatened. Now, I will do whatever necessary to keep our kingdom safe from the hands of demons."

The crowd answered his promise with a roar of applause. I felt sickened as I watched them jeer and curse at those about to die. Tears blurred my vision as I turned toward the wrongly accused, and what I saw there nearly sent me to my knees.

A girl no older than thirteen lay crying closest to me. Her long red hair hung around her in waves like the flames that would soon envelope her small frame. Even over the pounding in my ears I could hear the hoarseness of her voice as she cried for her mother. The girl's body shook with sobs as she strained against the ropes. I watched her struggle cause the harsh ropes to break through her skin and let her blood flow freely as she cried out.

Beside her lay a man so aged he appeared no more than skin and bones with hair as white as the dawn in midsummer. Though tears streamed down his cheeks, he remained silent, already accepting his fate. My vision blurred as dropped my gaze. The memory of their cries would be enough to brand my soul with guilt. I wasn't sure I could stomach seeing their faces contorted in pain too.

Seven people were tied to makeshift pyres as a guard stood by, lit torch held in perfect view. I held my fist over my heart as tears streamed down my face—the only sign of peace and solidarity I could offer before their cries of anguish would turn to those of pain.

I blinked back tears as the guard carrying the torch stepped closer. But what I saw next robbed the breath from my lungs. Next to the old man, with a familiar tussle of brown hair that hung in his eyes, lay Kesson. The first boy I ever loved and the first boy to hold my heart in his hands and shatter it.

Like me, his eyes filled with tears as he waited for his death. There was no hope left in the dark of his eyes, but the pain contorting his face told me he didn't want to die this way. Not by fire. Not accused of something as ridiculous as associating with the demons that hadn't roamed these lands in centuries.

My silent tears burned paths down my cheeks as I stared at him. He was innocent. They all were. I knew they were, for as I forced myself to study their faces, I knew them. Every face I knew from years performing side by side at festivals, or meeting them in village markets while traveling, or camping far in the mountains outside of the Angelwood Forest. I knew them all, and every one of them was innocent of these crimes.

As if he could feel my gaze, Kesson turned to me. The strange essence in my chest opened wide as our gazes locked. My lip trembled as he gave me the barest hint of a nod, accepting his fate. My body shook with silent sobs as I stared into his familiar brown eyes.

Whatever thing lived in the center of my chest burst wide open now, my emotions weakening the control I usually held. My knees threatened to collapse beneath my weight as I breathed through the strength of my gift, whatever it was. I stared into the souls of those bound before me. Every one of them gleamed with life and kindness. Hardly any of them were tainted with scars of cruelty on their souls.

I choked back a sob as my gift sprung back into itself, hidden away, as a small form stepped out from the crowd. Kesson and I shared a look of mirrored horror as his little brother stood before the king now. The familiar pout of his mouth seemed more prominent as he glowered at the king on the steps behind me. His round eyes seemed to fill his face as tears created paths through the dirt along his cheeks.

"Give me back my brother!" Zaven's voice broke with the force of his tears as he spoke to the king.

The others began to stir uncomfortably as they watched this child, no older than seven, approach the king on shaking feet. My heart threatened to burst from my chest as I waited with bated breath for the king to tie him beside his brother.

"He is a good man," he pleaded desperately.

"Zav," Kesson spoke gently, "It's okay. Go back to mother. Don't interfere."

"No," Zaven screamed at his brother, voice breaking from his pain. Tears spilled out in a ruthless stream down his face. "I can't leave you. Please, Kes. Please don't go. Don't leave me."

My throat tightened as more tears stormed down my cheeks as I stood nearby, knees shaking. I felt the prince's eyes on me again, but I didn't dare turn to look. This was for me. This torment of executions was to make me hurt. I wouldn't give the king or his family the satisfaction of seeing my tears.

"Bring him forward." The sound of the king's command echoed through the deathly quiet of the yards.

I turned to glance at him then. The king had a dark, hungry look in his eye as he glanced from Zaven to me. Zaven followed the king's gaze to where I stood at the bottom of the steps, dressed like a show pet. His eyes widened in fear as he was brought to his knees only mere steps from my feet. A knowing smile crossed the king's face at the same time my guard moved to grip onto my arms tightly, keeping me in place.

"Esme, please," Zaven's cries came to me in a haze. I felt surrounded by a thick fog as I watched the king speak to him. Words I couldn't hear sent the surrounding crowd murmuring their quiet agreements with whatever he demanded.

Prince Elias watched my face closely before turning his gaze to his father. Disinterested, yet again.

"Zaven, run!" Kesson screamed over the growing chaos.

"He can't," I croaked breathlessly. The truth of my words broke something deep in my chest. Kesson realized this as well as he too collapsed against his ropes, chest shuddering with his silent sobs.

My knees went weak with agony as I watched others I knew break through the crowd to go to Zaven. Their faces were as familiar as my own. Kesson's brothers and cousins were all there, only his mother was missing. I suspected she was bedridden again. The pain she would suffer every day after this would be unbearable.

One by one I watched in frozen horror as his family members were forced to their knees before the king; Zaven only mere feet away from where I remained stuck in the guard's firm grip. They cursed and struggled against the guards, but it was no use. I could see the moment they began to realize their doom. Their eyes turned hollow and lost what little light they contained.

"You have all proven your connections to the accused," King Elroy announced to the now silent crowd. "Each of you will pay for your crimes."

I struggled harder, my mind whirling with the pain I knew would come. My body protested against my struggles as my ankles bled and my arms remained held behind me.

I knew what was coming. And there wasn't a thing I could do to stop it.

"Execute them."

The king's order rang through the castle yard. As one, the guards pulled knives free from their waists and pulled them across the necks of all of Kesson's family members. I gaped in horror as they tossed their bleeding bodies to the dirt.

A cry erupted from me as I placed a hand to my own throat. The small scar there burned with a frigid cold as the sensation of a knife pulling through my tender flesh yanked itself from my memories. Flashes of a cold gaze, pale hair, dark horns, and grey wings reflected in the scene before me before I could bury them deep in my memory.

The gathered crowd grew more uncertain as they shifted uncomfortably and watched the bodies fall to the earth in growing puddles of blood. More screams erupted then as the pyres became lit.

"Esme!" Kesson yelled, pulling my attention from Zaven's crumpled body at my feet. "Esme, you have to run."

I pressed my fists against my mouth to silence my cries as I watched the flames lick at the hem of his pants, growing with every breath. My body felt hollow as I glanced at the small, crumpled body of Zaven who once told me he hoped I would marry him instead of his brother. The memory made my heart nearly burst with pain as Kesson's cries grew.

As smoke filled the yard, my eyes burned with the resulting tears. The guard holding me took an unsteady inhale as the screams grew with the flames.

When I finally tore my gaze away from Zaven, I hated what I saw. Every person tied to the pyres writhed against their bindings as their bodies became engulfed in flame. The sight of them struggling, and the sounds they made as they burned, would forever remain ingrained in my mind. Their screams grew shrill as the fires grew to new heights. The old man writhed on his pyre, seeming incapable of crying out though his mouth hung open in a silent scream.

The girl closest to me, with hair the color of the flames, did not scream like the others. I watched as her mouth moved on near silent words as the flames tore apart her clothes and burned her skin.

Movement in the corner of my vision drew my attention away from the flames. The prince turned away from the chaos at hand, disgust and shame prominent in every line of his body. The flames seemed to taunt him as smoke blew in his direction, and he took a deep breath through his mouth.

Only then did he notice me watching. My body tensed once again as he held my gaze in his. The same sort of hollowness filled his eyes as he watched me. Only when his gaze dropped to where my hand remained over the scar along the side of my neck did I finally turn away.

As the flames grew, the cries slowly fell silent. With each one, the essence that thrummed in tune with my heart beat harder against my ribs, begging to be unleashed. Screams turned to whimpers and whimpers turned to stillness as the flames took over, leaving only a haunting echo in the still gardens beyond. It was only when Kesson finally fell silent that I unleashed my gift and let the pain fill me completely.

Time meant nothing as the sun moved across the sky and my friends burned before me. Their bodies had long melted away and turned to ash and scorched bone.

The crowd didn't dare leave until dismissed by the king. They held onto their loved ones and watched with something akin to fear in their eyes; I knew they were questioning this method of punishment. Only a few true believers remained gathered at the front of the crowd as they watched, wide eyed and eager while the pyres continued to burn.

Smoke filled my lungs and blood coated the grass at my feet, but I didn't dare take my eyes away from the bones of those who died merely so the king could spite me.

The dark essence that lived near my heart thrummed as the souls of the dead parted with their mortal forms and sought peace with the stars. The feeling of it beating out of rhythm with my own heart sent my feet staggering as a cool brush of air blew against my cheek in a caress.

My guard, who'd remained holding tightly onto my shoulders, released me at once, sending me crashing onto my knees into the blood-soaked earth.

I gasped at the warmth that remained in Zaven's blood as it soaked through my skirts and coated the skin of my legs. I struggled to my feet only to slip again and crash onto my hands. More tears filled my vision as the soft sounds of the king's cold amusement echoed through my head. No one dared help me to my feet as I remained a crumpled form in the puddle of blood.

The shackles at my ankles felt tighter as I remained on my hands and knees in the blood of those who hadn't deserved to die.

"Someone, do get her out of that blood," the king drawled, no longer finding entertainment in my pain.

The shuffle of feet sounded before the king said, "Not you Elias. Do not lower yourself to such a task."

As my guard yanked me to my feet, I caught a glimpse of the prince. He stood halfway between where I stood in the puddle of blood and where his father remained on the steps of the castle. His face hid what little emotion I could see in his eyes, but his shame became palpable as his eyes settled on the blood now soaking through my skirts.

Without a word he turned on his heel and followed his father inside. Many of the guards followed but others stayed to usher the crowd beyond the castle gates and begin clearing away the ashes of the dead.

My body felt light as a feather and heavy as iron all at once. I barely registered the manacles cutting through the broken flesh at my ankles as I was dragged back inside. My mind echoed with the screams of the burned while my vision filled with that of Kesson burning—writhing in pain—and Zaven with his throat slit.

But when I turned back to study the scene I left behind, my eyes only caught on the pyre where the girl with the hair of flame once lay. Her bones lay charred beneath the smoking remains of her bindings. What was once her bright red hair, now a burned mess. She did not scream when she burned. She prayed. She prayed the god of Death would provide her an opportunity of vengeance in her afterlife. And as I watched her soul depart this realm, I hoped she would get it.

FOUR

My body protested as I lurched upright with a gasp. I blinked through the memory of the knife across my throat. My hands shook as I reached up to touch the scar that would remain with me until the end of my mortal days. The small scar burned with the memory of that night only a year earlier, nearly to the day. That must be the reason why I dreamed of it for the first time since my capture.

My moth-eaten blanket did little to provide comfort for the tenderness in my joints as I swung my feet over the edge of my cot. The bruises across my knees and elbows forced yesterday's burnings to the front of my mind. I swallowed back bile as I tried to shove away the memory of their screams, and the smell of burnt flesh. But I didn't think I'd ever rid myself of the memory of seeing little Zaven with his throat split open.

A sharp knock sounded at the door. My heart began beating harder in my chest as I rose unsteadily to my feet.

No one came to visit my room.

The knock sounded again, impatient this time.

I took a step slowly, stiffly, hesitant to answer my visitor. The guard outside my room wouldn't let just anyone venture this far in the abandoned wing of the castle. And if it were the servant assigned to keep me watered and fed, she would've entered my room of her own accord.

The knock came harder this time.

The rattle of the chains keeping me tied to the center of the room echoed with my movement as I made my way to the door on trembling knees. I hadn't been able to eat after yesterday's events and my daily meal wouldn't be arriving for a while longer. According to the grey light in the window, dawn was just approaching.

As the knock sounded again, I swung open the door. What I saw before me sent my heart into a nervous frenzy.

"Did I wake you?" Prince Elias asked with a half-smile framing his full mouth. I stared at the prince in shock, and awe. He was fully dressed in his royal finery from the day before. His tight curls seemed clean pressed and oddly formal compared to their usual disheveled state.

"What?" I asked, unconsciously running a hand through the wild tangles of my hair in a weak attempt to tame them. My mind raced to find the reasoning behind this visit. In the four months I'd been held in this room, not once had the prince bothered to visit, let alone speak to me without an ounce of liquor clogging his thoughts. I looked to the guard's usual post and found his chair empty.

His crooked smile grew as he scanned my face. "I said, did I wake you?"

"You come to my room at dawn and ask if you woke me?" I asked, my mind not wanting to catch up with his words.

"Yes," he said slowly, nearly amused. "I suppose it is quite early for a visit, isn't it?"

He watched me expectantly, waiting for some sort of reaction. Yet I couldn't do more than push my energy toward keeping yesterday's losses far from the forefront of my mind. Forcing them deep in my memory where they wouldn't haunt me every time I closed my eyes.

"I'm sorry," he said suddenly. He took an uncertain step back. I noticed the dark bruises under his eyes then. He didn't seem to have slept at all. I assumed the only time the prince would be awake before dawn was when he was still too busy with his nightly tumbling to have gone to bed at all. Yet from the haunted look in his eyes, that didn't seem to be the case. "I shouldn't have come."

"Why did you?" I asked, unable to contain my curiosity.

He gave a half shrug and rubbed his hands over his face. The action barely hid the brief flash of pain in his eyes. "I wanted to see how you were doing. After yesterday."

The memory of falling to my knees in Zaven's blood sent a phantom pain through my body again. I rubbed a hand over my bruised skin tentatively, trying and failing to rub the pain away as my mind flashed with the tragedy. For a moment, all I could hear were their screams, and all I could smell was the smoke clogging my lungs.

"Why wouldn't I be okay?" I asked quietly.

"Well for one, it wasn't exactly a quick death," the prince said, pulling me back to the present. The misery in his eyes mirrored my own.

"No, I suppose it didn't feel that way to them either," I replied stiffly.

His eyes darkened and turned distant as he appeared to swallow back whatever memory he was reliving before he dropped his gaze. "I don't know why he's doing this." His voice came out in such a mumbled whisper I could hardly hear him.

I leaned closer to decipher his words. "Who? Your father?"

He nodded, still not meeting my gaze. In this moment he didn't look like the promiscuous prince I knew him to be, he resembled a horrified boy. Eyes wide and haunted by death, mouth tight with the tension I guessed now beat through his heart. "He won't tell me why. He just tells me to focus on marrying Violette and solidifying our throne."

I sighed. "He told me it was my fault," I said hesitantly. I didn't want to voice the words aloud for fear of hearing the truth in them, but he seemed too miserable to ignore. "He believes I am causing the destruction of Cordovia, and because of that I am to be punished."

The prince's dark eyes appeared to fill with more horror as he ran a hand nervously through his curls, giving them their usual disheveled appearance. The ghost of a smile threatened to pull at my mouth before yesterday's deaths pulled the emotion from my body, turning me hollow once again.

"How can you possibly be smiling about this right now?" he asked, a little disturbed.

I shrugged and immediately regretted the movement as it sent a wave of pain through my sore muscles.

"I just didn't realize your hair always looked the way it did because you were the one running your hands through it," I said without fear.

He looked taken aback before a smile lit up his face, chasing away the lingering darkness. "You thought others were running their hands through my hair?" He barked a sharp laugh before he turned back to me; something like curious amusement lived in his face. "I suppose I can't say that wasn't part of it."

I felt my face fall as I took in the wild gleam in the prince's eye. Seeing the prince like this reminded me too much of Mousa. My brother thrilled at the attention of women nearly as much as the prince did, and he certainly wasn't shy when it came to bragging about his lovers.

"You judge me for this," he said without accusation. "Why?"

I shoved away the memory of my brother at the first threat of tears. Wherever he was, I hoped he was with my family, and they'd stay hidden somewhere safe. I couldn't bear to watch them burn too.

"You are the Prince of Cordovia, and its sole heir," I said seriously. "I am a prisoner in your castle accused of witchcraft. I am in no position to judge your bedroom habits."

He flashed a quicksilver smile, crossing his hands over his broad chest. "You didn't seem to have a concern for your *position* when you told the entire castle I had my hand up another lady's skirt the other day."

My face burned hotter, this time with shame. "I apologize, Your Highness. I spoke brazenly and it was uncalled for." I kept my chin tucked and my eyes down as I awaited his threat to report my outburst to his father and the inevitable punishment that would follow. My heart began to race in my chest as my nerves chased away the lingering despair.

The tips of his fingers grazed my bruised cheek. His touch was gentle, like a whisper of air. When I looked up questioningly, his hand was already at his side, as if the touch never happened. But his eyes remained focused on the bruises his father's fist had left behind, now beginning to yellow in their delayed healing.

"My father fears what he doesn't understand. And because of that he often turns to greater forces in moments of desperation," he said quietly. He remained focused on my bruise for a moment longer before returning to my gaze, his eyes filled with a tender understanding. "I know the feel of my father's fists against my own skin. I could never sentence someone to such punishment simply for stating a fact. No matter how that fact may make me appear in the eyes of my court."

Surprise flashed through me as I scrutinized the prince. "You're not going to report my outburst to your father?"

He shook his head, a gentle smile tugging at his mouth. "No, Miss Loutari-Ayres. I couldn't live with myself if I was the cause behind my father bruising you further."

I fought the urge to glare at the shackles digging into my scabbed skin. "Esme," I said instead.

"Esme," he repeated. The sound of my family name rolling off the prince's tongue tugged further at my heart as I ached for the feel of my mother's hug.

My hands balled into fists nervously at my sides, a fresh glean of damp sweat making them slick.

"I will say this though," he said, leaning against the corridor walls. "Violette's governess didn't waste the opportunity to nearly bite my head off when she found out I was otherwise occupied."

"You deserved it," I said, allowing annoyance to replace my grief.

The prince laughed—the sound warm and musical. "Yes, I suppose I did. Though Lady Violette didn't seem to think much of it."

"I don't think Lady Violette has many thoughts regarding much of anything."

He laughed further, the sound nearly enough to fill the emptiness I felt. "You insult my betrothed so coldly, Miss Esme."

This time I let myself scoff. "I think if you truly cared for your betrothed, you would honor your engagement and refrain from bedding other women."

He stepped closer, the heat of his presence stirring the darkness that lived too close to my heart. I shuddered as I felt it flutter uncomfortably. "Why are you so concerned with my sleeping arrangements?"

"I don't think you do much sleeping Your Highness," I said, stepping back into my room. I gripped the door for support as the dark thing in my chest tugged harder against my rib cage. "I just think a man should respect his vows to his beloved. And she, him."

"You speak like a true romantic," he said, studying me with a smile. The sight of my stained brown tunic didn't seem to disgust him as he surveyed me.

"I liked to read," I said with a shrug. Alfie, my younger brother, came to mind as I thought over all the stories I'd read to him before he learned to read for himself. It was his love of books that kept our caravan filled with pages of dramatic stories of heroes and monsters. Yet somehow, I truly was living among the monsters now.

He tipped his head to the side as he continued to study me. "I wasn't aware you read."

"Because I belong to the wanderer people you think I can't remain literate enough to pick up a book?"

He shook his head, hands up in surrender. "No, that's not what I meant. I just didn't peg you for someone who fantasized their romance from the tales in books."

I snorted. "I think it's quite obvious that there is no prince coming to save me from this wicked castle. Don't you think?"

The prince considered my words a moment before he nodded. "I suppose a romantic notion of that accord wouldn't exist in your story at the moment."

"I don't mind," I said stiffly. The essence in my chest filtered down my arm a little as I stood there, leaning heavily on the door, my body exhausted from lack of steady sleep. "I'll find a way to rescue myself."

He smiled warmly. "I truly believe that you will, Esme."

The sound of approaching steps and muted conversation filtered through the halls, announcing the arrival of two guards. My usual guard appeared along with another I didn't recognize at his side. Both men studied the prince and I together before I noticed the tray the strange guard carried.

Prince Elias narrowed his eyes at the pitiful tray of food. "That is her meal?"

The guard gave a shallow bow of his head. "Yes, Your Highness. His Royal Majesty has ordered her to be fed the scraps left over from the guard's first meal each day."

I studied the guard silently while the prince looked at my tray with a horrified expression.

"That's absurd," the prince said under his breath. The guard bowed and moved to place my tray on the floor just inside my door. I stepped aside to allow him access and winced at the pain that lanced through my ankles at the movement.

The darkness that lived near my heart nearly lurched out of my skin as the guard stepped close. I held my breath as I leaned away from his presence. Only when he disappeared down the corridor did I relax again.

"I'll have someone bring you a proper meal at midday supper," the prince said as he continued to scowl at my tray. My guard had taken up his post on the worn chair against the wall behind the prince.

"That's not necessary, Your Highness," I said with a polite dip of my chin. The guard watched our interaction curiously.

"Please," the prince said, placing a hand over his heart. The smile he gave me was warm and privately tender, "call me Elias. And the meal isn't up for debate. You look horrible. You could use a fresh meal."

His smile widened as he watched my face go slack with surprise at his bluntness. Elias turned and left without another word, leaving me to stand in my doorway and watch his retreating figure.

"Return to your room." My guard slammed the door in my face before I could reply.

As I carried the tray to the edge of my small cot in the middle of my room, I finally felt the mysterious pull in my chest lessen and settle into a calm stir. Only when it relaxed in my solitude was I able to lie back on my thin blanket and return to a fitful sleep.

FIVE

My knees ached as I remained kneeling by the king's makeshift throne. The sun burned against the back of my neck as I kept my hair pulled over one shoulder. An attempt to allow the sweat forming down my spine to dry in the faint breeze. This late in the summer, the sun was always brutal near the castle. My family liked to travel north near the Gaiva Region when it grew too warm this far south. Unfortunately, as I knelt there, chained to the throne of King Elroy, I was forced to burn in the sun.

The king sat relaxed in his throne, chin resting in his hand, slouching as if he were merely bored with the scene before him. The pyres, full of new innocents tied down to suffer another fake trial and burning did little to disturb him. Today, he wore a suit of bright gold with white accents at the hem. He looked like a star plucked directly from the night sky. Made of bright light and sent to save our mortal lives. Instead, he sat there on his throne and doomed those he didn't understand—those he feared—to brutal deaths. A star unworthy of belonging in the night sky.

Beside him sat the prince, Elias. It was only this morning that the prince had visited my room, and the warm lunch he promised had been sent to me two hours ago. My belly still remained full from the heavy meal. Though the prince seemed to be content in pretending our conversation hadn't occurred as he studiously ignored my presence altogether now.

Even Queen Isolde and Lady Violette, who sat just behind the men, seemed unbothered by the events about to occur as they whispered quietly to each other with pleased smiles on their faces.

The cries and cheers of the crowd gathered at the castle gates rattled my bones as they waited for the trial to end. After the interruption at yesterday's burning, the king only permitted a select few members of his court to enter his castle grounds and observe the burning up close. Now, the rest of those who wished to bear witness to his brutality had to watch from the gates several yards away.

Their presence answered my unvoiced question regarding the king's temporary dais placed so far from the castle steps. This far from the castle, we were nearly surrounded by trees just off the stone path leading to the town beyond the castle walls. I could even smell the flowers in the queen's garden nearby.

I forced my eyes to focus on those tied to the pyres before me. The king kept me farther back this time so those who watched could see me crouched beside his throne. I was merely a pawn on display for his wicked games. My only relief was found in the simple pants and tunic I was allowed to wear instead of my usual gaudy gown.

Another new accommodation the king provided for this trial were witness accounts. The four people dragged forward by guards, wearing dirty rags or trousers with mud stains on the knees, were today's witnesses. I guessed they were some of the farmers or even wanderers brought from nearby villages or campgrounds based on the lightweight material of their clothes.

"You claim witness to these accused of witchcraft?" the king's royal adviser said in his stuffy voice. I glanced at the man who rarely left the king's side. His dark blue robes and greying dark hair put his appearance at odds with the bright gold of the king's garb.

The witnesses nodded, making the crowd outside the gates cheer louder. Those the king allowed onto the castle grounds remained silent, statuesque. Yet their eyes told the story of their excitement and anticipation as they stood straight-backed and ready for violence.

"Give your witness accounts if you will," the Royal Adviser said with little patience.

The young woman closest to me was shoved forward and landed harshly on her knees. My chest tightened at the swell of loyalty and respect she held in her gaze as she looked to the king before her.

I cast a sidelong glance at the prince. He looked on as if bored, his dark hair styled into neat curls once again. Though he looked freshly washed, the dark bruises beneath his eyes remained. He looked as tired and ragged as I felt.

As if he could feel my gaze, he turned and studied me as the woman began to speak. For a brief moment, I could see indecision over his duty to his father before his wall of indifference returned, effectively removing any trace of the hidden pain he may have felt.

He looked away before I could think of it too deeply.

"Audric was seen conversing with a winged female two nights ago, Your Majesty." Her voice held firm as she spoke directly to the king.

"Winged female?" the Royal Adviser asked, trying and failing to gain her attention.

The woman nodded, her face coated in a sheen of soot and sweat though she didn't seem perturbed. "Wings as dark as the night and horns that curled back over her skull. Never seen anything like it, but I knew it wasn't human."

"How did you know it wasn't someone in costume?" Prince Elias asked, speaking for the first time.

The king's face turned down in a frown, but he didn't look away from the kneeling woman before him.

She lifted her chin higher, gently tossing back her golden-brown curls, and stared at the prince. "Because I know what a demon looks like. We farm folk know what to look for, what it feels like to have a demon nearby. There was no mistaking this woman for a demon belonging to the god of Death himself."

I shivered. Nonna used to tell us stories growing up, describing demons in great detail. I knew what she saw existed. I'd heard of them, even saw one for myself once, when he tried to slice a poisoned knife through my neck.

"She lies," the man, Audric, cried from his pyre. "Demons cannot enter this realm if Cordovia still thrives under King Elroy's bloodline. She couldn't have seen me speaking with a demon here." His voice ended in a grunt as a guard brought his fist into the man's gut.

I winced as he struggled for breath. I tightened my hands around my middle as the woman finally caught sight of me kneeling at the foot of the king's throne.

Her gaze, full of disgust, hit me like a sword to the gut. The anger in her eyes as she slid her gaze to the chains keeping me tied to the throne only strengthened as the next witness moved forward to speak. I assumed, like most of the king's devoted followers, she truly believed the lies he spread about my involvement with witchcraft.

"Never seen anything like it," the next witness spoke, tearing my focus away from the woman. His voice shook with age as he remained hunched over a cane, balding hair half hidden behind a worn hat. "He was fine the day before, but he came back from watching the performers and didn't behave like himself. Began talking all kinds of crazy and even beat a stray dog near death. Poor thing had to be put out of its misery."

"What does this have to do with the woman you claim to have used witchcraft?" The Royal Adviser's voice was tight with impatience, his round face reddening with anger at the old man.

He shrugged. "He was friends with the accused. But it also has to do with the rest of the happenings in Cordovia."

"What else is happening?" the prince asked before his father could stop him.

"It seems there is a particular tainted group of people traveling and using some sort of witchcraft to make people lose their minds." He looked up the high dais at the prince before him. "It's like their minds are being torn apart and they've lost part of their good souls after those people come through town. They go mad and lose all reasoning."

I quickly filtered through the king's words when he first spoke of these burnings days before. Whatever was happening to these people, the king believed I was somehow causing it with the witchcraft he believed flowed through my veins.

My gaze turned to focus on the king as the witness's words settled. The king's dark eyes captured mine as a haunting smile spread over his mouth. My breath came in short gasps as my heart beat frantically against my ribs. I had no idea what was happening to the people of Cordovia, but from the way the king's eyes gleamed at the sight of my fear, I knew he still believed I was involved. And he was ready to make me pay for it. Even though I guessed these oddities had more to do with his greed draining Cordovia and forcing people to desperate measures.

"It's true," the next witness said as she stepped forward. She didn't look much older than me. "My dad went to one of the campgrounds a few weeks ago and came back different. He started beating on my momma and me before he left into the night. Haven't seen him since."

"Your father's drinking habits are no concern of ours." The king dismissed her words with a wave of his hand.

"He doesn't drink, Your Majesty," she said softly now, cheeks reddening in embarrassment. "He never laid a hand to my momma or me before that night."

I tried to wrack my brain for any explanation. Wanderers were a close community. There wasn't a single family of performers that I hadn't met at least once. Yet, as I knelt there by the throne, I couldn't think of a single family who may know the cause behind this absurdity. None of us actually knew how to use witchcraft. That was a completely different sort of craft compared to the shows we put on for entertainment. There was a certain bloodline that could perform smaller magics in healing but nothing quite like what these witnesses described.

Another bead of sweat dripped down my neck as I swayed on my aching knees. I silently hoped my family didn't become the next victims to this mystery.

"None of these reports pertain to those accused I presume?" the Royal Adviser drawled as he scowled at the gathered witnesses. Everyone remained silent for a beat as the world paused, awaiting the inevitable.

"Start the fires." The king's command echoed without question.

The atmosphere shifted as tension rose in the air. The crowd surrounding the dais stiffened as the guard brought forth the torch to light the pyres. Cries of protest came from those accused, yet there was nothing I could do to stop what I knew would happen.

Those who claimed witness to these crimes shifted away, merging with the gathered noblemen and women, while the innocent remained tied down, their voices growing hoarse with screams.

All at once the world seemed to fall silent. The crowds, both around the garden and at the gates, fell silent with it. The birds stopped chirping, the trees stopped bristling, and the world held its breath as a cold darkness settled over the gardens. The breeze on the air shifted, the strange essence living in my chest moving with it and tightening around my heart.

Suddenly, a vicious scream erupted outside the castle gates, causing me to cringe against the tug from the darkness in my chest. Silence followed as the scream cut off as abruptly as it had started. For a moment, the only sounds I could hear were my ragged breathing and the pounding of my pulse in my ears. Then another scream sounded, louder this time. Then another and another, creating a chorus of shrill agony and fear. Chaos ensued. Those gathered at the gate began to run frantically.

"What is this?" The king barked his question to no one in particular.

The thing by my heart pulled tighter against my hold as I shifted uncomfortably, the movement enough to force the manacles deeper into my skin.

The screams grew louder and more panicked outside the grounds until all at once, it was silent again. Those of us in the gardens froze, waiting to understand the cause behind the chaos.

"Dear," Queen Isolde said as she leaned over her husband's throne. Violette stood slowly, her gaze unusually sharp as she scanned the garden around us. "I think we should return to the castle and let the guards handle today's burning."

He waved her away and turned to glower at where I knelt by his feet. "This is your doing."

I started. "No...no, Your Majesty."

"She hasn't done a thing Father," Elias protested with false patience. He remained slouched in his makeshift throne; though I could see the way his body appeared strained with tension.

"She has," the king argued as he bent to glare into my eyes directly. "What is it you're doing?"

When I didn't immediately answer, his hands gripped tightly to the collar of my shirt, pulling me closer so I couldn't avoid his gaze.

"Answer your king, witch," he yelled.

I didn't get a chance to answer before the screams sounded again. This time, those gathered within the castle grounds began to scream and run in panic. And now, we could see why.

Three people, dripping in fresh blood, stumbled through the crowd. A man, nearly as large as a tree, began picking people up off the ground and nearly ripping their limbs apart with his bare hands. He was human at a glance, until I looked into his eyes and only saw a black void, empty of emotion.

I stared in horror as the other two with him, another young man and a gray-haired woman, joined him in the violence.

I swallowed back a scream as I watched the smaller man bite into a woman's neck and rip it apart with his blunt human teeth.

"Elroy," the queen whispered over the screams of the panicked court. "We must go. It is not safe."

Without a word, he scowled at me once more before turning to lead his family inside, the guards quickly surrounding their king.

The remaining guards shifted to escort others to safety outside the gates while blood spilled freely into the grass, turning the once-green garden into a red pond.

Screams echoed off the dark stone of the castle, clear through the trees behind me, but I couldn't seem to draw my eyes away from the horror. Not even as the young man began hacking away at one of those tied to a pyre with a knife already soaked in blood. The man screamed loud enough to shake the dais beneath me.

The larger man had continued to break people apart as they attempted to escape. I shuddered at the crack of bone as he slammed a man onto the stone path, effectively crushing his skull and silencing his screams.

But it was the woman who quickly stole my attention as I caught sight of the torch she held now. The torch for the pyres, forgotten by the guards in the growing panic. She knelt to light the hem of a child's dress and laughed as she burned. The girl's tears did nothing to stop the flames from climbing her skirts and engulfing her completely as she attempted to flee the crowd.

Tears tugged at my eyes as the darkness in my chest nearly pulled me to my feet in search of whatever wickedness lived in their souls. My hands hit the floor before me as I gasped against tears and struggled to keep my lunch while she lit three more people on fire. Her laughter was nearly loud enough to drown out the screams filling the garden. The sound caused the darkness in my chest to fill me completely as it reached for the dying. I shuddered against its silent demand as I remained crouched by the throne.

Guards moved in to strike down these strangers, but their fight lasted mere seconds. Each guard who approached the chaos went down, whether torn apart, impaled, or burned. Those that didn't flee didn't survive, though it seemed the entire royal army had come to settle the destruction.

Only when the woman caught sight of me did I realize the danger I was in, too. I watched as her eyes tracked the chains at my ankles keeping me bound to the throne. I couldn't run, and from the twisted gleam in her eye I could tell she knew it.

A tauntingly slow smile spread across her face, displaying her blood-stained teeth. As she slowly crept toward the dais I fell back onto my heels, desperately pulling against the chains. My tender skin protested but it became easy to ignore as her croaked laughter rang in my ears.

I yanked harder against the chains, praying to the stars they would eventually come loose as she took her time ambling toward the dais. My palms grew sweaty and slipped, tossing me onto my back. The screams and cries continued around me as the few remaining guards slowly lost their fight against the crazed onslaught. Others escaped to the safety of the castle, a blood trail in their wake.

Wiping my hands along my trousers, I grasped the chains again with shaking hands. Fear threatened to turn my body to a useless heap as my chest tightened with it. The woman drew closer still, torch held high above her head as she now stood only a few yards away.

I wasn't going to make it. She would light this dais aflame, leaving me to burn with it. Tears blurred my vision as I tugged harder, not willing to accept this fate.

"Here!" Elias' voice sounded in an urgent whisper as he appeared beside me.

I nearly wept at the key in his hands as he knelt before me, his back to the woman heading our way, to unlock my chains. My body began to shake as she continued her unhurried pace, seemingly thrilled by my growing terror. Our eyes locked and the empty darkness I saw there called to the darkness that lived in me. The sensation sent a chill down my spine as I cringed against it.

Elias' hands shook as he fumbled once again with the lock and cursed.

"Hurry," I begged as she grew closer, torch held high as she readied to throw it onto the wooden dais and watch us both burn.

"Go," I said as Elias finally managed to release one of my shackles. The key remained lodged in the other, keeping me attached to the throne. "You need to go. She'll kill you if you stay."

He cursed loudly. "I can't just leave you here like this."

Before I could respond, a dark shadow crashed onto the dais beside us. The wood beneath my hands shook with the sudden motion. Elias and I froze. Slowly, I dared to look up at what stood before me.

I was unable to see the face buried beneath the dark hood before he leapt down and slaughtered the deranged woman with a single blow of his sword. Black feathered wings grew from this man's back as he stood upright over the woman's body which lay scattered in pieces.

I froze at the strange familiarity of this man. Though I knew for certain he was not the demon who tried to cut my throat as the essence in my chest seemed to still and soothe at his arrival. This man was built for war—shoulders broad and tense with limbs corded with muscle. There wasn't a soft edge to the demon that stood with his back to me.

Soon others joined him, though they didn't carry wings like his. There was a woman carrying two short swords, one in each hand, with long red hair styled in messy twists that fell down to her waist. Her body appeared soft like mine, though she twisted and turned through the disruption around her, offering a quick death to those writhing on the ground in lingering agony.

Two men moved like soldiers as they fought the large man in tandem, each providing a swift hit of their own before dodging his return attack. The larger of the two, a man with dark copper skin and black hair that hung down his back in a single braid, carried a large sword which he drew from the scabbard he wore across his back, his face intent on the kill. The younger boy with blond curls leapt back to shoot arrows into the man's gut. His arrows flew fast enough to be nearly imperceptible apart from the whisper of air they left behind.

The second manacle finally opened with a loud click as I turned my gaze back to the winged man nearby. Even with his back to me I could see him shift at the sound, turning in my direction. My breath caught in my throat as I felt his gaze meet mine beneath the shadow of his hood.

"Let's go," Elias shouted over the screams as he yanked me to my feet. I stared toward the castle gates and allowed myself just a moment to dream of running to freedom. As tempting as the thought was, I knew I wouldn't be fast enough to escape the demon and his warriors before me.

I let Elias drag us through the trees and to the castle where his mother waited just inside the open doors, screaming his name. The king stood in a barely controlled rage nearby as he continued to glower in my direction.

A sheen of sweat broke out along my back as I hustled up the steps, Elias' grip on my arm tight enough to leave a lasting bruise.

Only when my bare feet hit the cool stone of the castle corridor did I turn back to glimpse the destruction we left behind. Screams still sounded on the air as people raced through the castle yard to the gates and to safety.

But it was what I didn't see that made my steps falter slightly. For no matter where I cast my gaze, I didn't see any of the warriors in the trees, the winged demon gone with them. As if I'd conjured their existence in my imagination.

Before I could understand their disappearance, the castle doors slammed shut in finality.

SIX

ALL AROUND ME CHAOS continued to erupt as guards tried to keep the king safely huddled between them. The few witnesses who managed to make it inside the castle before the doors were firmly shut flooded the halls in an uproar. Their panicked cries seemed muted compared to the agonized screams still audible through the thick doors.

My knees shook as the faint smell of charred flesh crept through the room, clinging to the clothes of everyone seeking safety in the castle. The strange darkness living inside me continued to stir uneasily as it sought a way out of my body. A new sheen of sweat broke out along my brow as I fought against it, while the souls of the recently deceased found their way to the stars.

Queen Isolde's voice, thick with tears, carried over the others as she scolded Elias for returning to help me. I could feel his gaze as he tried to catch my eye, but I ignored him as I hid in the corner of the room, contemplating my chances of escape.

"What were you thinking?" the queen cried as she pulled her son into an awkward embrace. "You could've gotten yourself killed! And for what? Some wicked girl? You would've left Violette all alone without a husband. What would've become of her after your death? You foolish child."

Elias gritted his teeth as he finally turned to look at his mother. His brown skin was stained with soot and ash as he wiped the sweat from his brow. "You couldn't honestly expect me to just leave her out there chained like that. They would've killed her."

"You stupid boy," the king roared as he turned on his son, dark eyes blazing with anger. "She is a prisoner. You need not risk your life for someone so low."

My knees began to quake as the adrenaline of the past hour suddenly began to subside. All eyes turned to me as the king stepped closer, glowering just within arm's reach.

"This is your doing," he said in quiet anger. The king's round face darkened.

Without warning, his hand fisted in my hair as he pushed me back against the cold stone wall. I collided with a resounding smack, the jolt of his anger knocking the breath from my lungs. As I struggled to regain my breath, he yanked my head back so he could look directly into my eyes. The guards all shifted to surround me, weapons pointed at my throat as they waited patiently for the king's order to kill.

"What witchery did you perform?" he spat in my face. I felt his hand shake as it held tight to the back of my neck. Almost like he couldn't stand to be so close to me but couldn't deny himself the chance to provide punishment in front of a crowd. He wanted to break me, by any means necessary. But I couldn't let him.

"Father, stop," Elias yelled as he tried to get between us.

"Darling, perhaps this isn't the place for such a scene." Queen Isolde spoke softly as Elias tried to fight his way through his father's guard. Even Lady Violette appeared concerned as she huddled, wide-eyed, with her guardian.

"She did this," the king roared in my face. His cheeks turned purple in rage as he stared at me in disgust.

King Elroy struck me then and I tasted blood. My face ached from his fist as he pulled tighter against my hair, nearly ripping it from my scalp.

"You are the only one who caused those people harm." I spat my blood in his face. He released his hold on my hair causing me to fall back against the wall. "I did nothing to them."

Elias stared on in horror and worry, his gaze flicking between his father and me as he awaited the king's next attack.

"You stupid—" But the king's words were cut off by an unexpected arrival.

The wall at my back shook with the force of the slamming doors. For a moment, the hall fell quiet as the sun framed the bloodied warrior standing there in a haunting silhouette. With calculated movements, we watched as this newest arrival stepped out of the shadow of the doorway and into the light. My breath caught in my throat as recognition steadied my shaking knees.

This newest arrival wasn't just anyone, it was Aiden. I had hardly spoken to him in the many years I'd known him. He usually only stopped by our caravan at the wanderer campgrounds to speak privately with Nonna, but here he was. His red-brown hair hung to his shoulders, plastered to his cheeks with blood, and his clothes hugged his muscular frame, saturated with sweat. I took note of the blood that stained nearly every inch of his clothes and dripped from the weapons he held at his sides.

Just as I remembered, there was the cold familiarity of his stiff jaw, hard mouth, and furrowed brow. His face looked young, no more than twenty, though his eyes held a darkness to them one could only gain during years of battle. He glanced through the room, taking careful note of everyone in the hall before he found where I stood in the corner, pressed against the wall, and surrounded by the king's men.

Aiden narrowed his eyes on the swords pointed at my throat before he took another careful step closer. His suntanned skin gleamed with sweat as his muscles rippled with the promise of violence. Yet the darkness inside me settled at his approach, completely oblivious to the threat in his storm-grey eyes.

Behind him, four others slowly moved into view as they too held their weapons raised in warning. My breath caught as the guards moved simultaneously toward the newcomers. I was left clinging to the wall, desperate to become a hidden shadow as I scanned them for any sign of the winged demon I saw earlier.

"What is this?" Queen Isolde called at the same time the king said, "Who do you think you are?"

Aiden turned his head toward the tall woman standing proudly at his shoulder. With dark, blood-splattered skin and hair cut short across her scalp, she looked as fierce as he did. She kept her twin axes strapped to her hips whereas Aiden kept a tight grip on his knives, clearly ready for an attack at any moment. Aiden's eyes never left my face, noting the blood dripping down my cheek, as the tall woman strode toward me, the crowd moving apart around her. She stopped at my side, her eyes trained on the king and his closest guards, as she gently gripped my arm.

King Elroy appeared just as confused as I was when the woman gently pulled me from the crowd. I took a step toward the door, enraptured with the scene slowly playing out before me until Elias voiced his protest.

"You can't just take her," he barked, storming through the wall of guardsmen to glare at Aiden.

As Aiden opened his mouth to speak, I felt Elias' hand grip onto my other arm, pulling me back against his chest and out of the woman's grasp. My throat tightened as Aiden's eyes narrowed on Elias' hand.

"She is my prisoner, boy," King Elroy said, finally speaking up as he moved to step between where Elias held me and where Aiden and his comrades stood in the doorway.

"That is where you are tragically mistaken," Aiden replied slowly. I'd forgotten the musical, deep tones of his voice as it sent vibrations through my body.

He moved closer now. Mere steps separated where I stood with Elias and where Aiden remained.

"You may not know who I am just yet," he said to the king without taking his gaze off of me. "But you will. I don't let people get away with touching what is mine."

Though he spoke softly, there was an underlying threat to his tone. Behind me, I felt Elias' grip tighten, causing me to wince.

The king scoffed. "This filth does not belong to you!" His voice rang loudly in anger. "She is a mere traveler girl caught in cohorts with demons. She deserves the death coming to her."

"I told you," I said through gritted teeth, my anger focusing on him, "I would never associate with demons. I'm not guilty of what you accuse me of."

King Elroy turned quickly, and his face filled with rage as he glared down at me. "You do not speak to your king out of turn."

I watched silently as his hand pulled back, preparing to land another blow along my bruised face. My body shuddered back against Elias. But the blow never came.

When I opened my eyes, I understood why. The king stood there, Aiden gripping his wrist in midair. Fury lined every angle of Aiden's posture as he squeezed the king's wrist hard enough to break it, though the king did not cry out.

"Touch her again," he said in a soft voice that promised violence, "and your kingdom will find itself without a king."

Queen Isolde whimpered miserably as she clung to Lady Violette's thin form. The king swallowed his retort as he yanked his arm free and stepped away from me. Yet Elias didn't move. The prince tightened his grip on my arm yet again as he pulled me away from Aiden and further behind the shield of guards.

"That goes for you too, princeling," Aiden warned without taking his eyes off the king.

The tall woman, her form corded with the lean muscles of a warrior, moved then to grip my hand and pull me from Elias's grasp. Her hand, gentle yet firm, on mine as she shielded me with her body until the light of the sun blinded me.

I squinted up at her face. Her scowl remained in place as she led me down the castle steps; the others close behind keeping their focus on the guards spilling from the doorway.

"Stop," Elias protested as he shoved his way through to the front of the emerging crowd. "You can't take her. Stop!"

"Elias, get back here!" Queen Isolde's voice rang out in a panic as I watched Elias storm down the steps after us.

The woman dropped my hand and moved ahead to lead this strange group of bloodied warriors down the stone path. I scanned the trees around me for any sight of the demon I saw earlier. But no matter where I looked, I couldn't see any trace of him. The redheaded woman brushed her knuckles against mine, in what I guessed was an attempt at comfort, before stepping away to take up the rear.

With every step I took away from the castle, my confusion grew and my heart beat erratically. There was no promise of safety if I left with these warriors, but there was even less if I stayed. My only knowledge of these strange people was the little I knew of Aiden from our brief interactions over the years.

"Esme," Elias yelled as he continued to chase after us, guards quick to follow along with his parents who protested his outburst, "you can't go with them. It's not safe."

I turned to look at him but froze when I caught sight of the yard where all of the chaos had erupted such a short time prior. The path Aiden was leading me down ran parallel to it. Only it was nearly unrecognizable now, coated in ash and blood. Pieces of the dead lay scattered throughout the small clearing, blood covering every blade of grass and every tree. A disfigured set of wings were painted in blood on the throne, causing my stomach to twist with uncertainty.

Was that the sign of the demon? As my feet rooted themselves on the stone pathway, I considered how much danger I truly might be in. If Aiden was in cahoots with a demon that would be an immediate death sentence on not only me, but my family, should they be found.

The redheaded woman looked at me curiously. Her cheeks were streaked with blood from those she'd slain though her brown eyes only showed welcome warmth. Her hair, its messy twists hanging down to her hips, seemed to drip with the blood she'd spilt.

I glanced at the rest of this odd band of warriors. Each of them turned to watch me with mixtures of curiosity and impatience.

While my mind flashed with the fresh memories of seeing them slaughter so easily, I could see that their eyes were filled with none of the bloodlust I saw earlier. Though their stiff postures told me they remained prepared for violence.

"Esme," Elias called again as he grew closer. His voice cut off in a shallow gasp as he too spied the wreckage in the yard.

My heart began to beat faster as fear finally set in. Fear I probably should have felt as soon as Aiden appeared.

I turned to stare in horror at Elias, his expression mirroring mine. My mouth went dry as the carnage before us violently churned my stomach. A tug in my chest forced my eyes to turn back to the bloody display in the once serene gardens. The bright sun reflected from the pools of blood but did little to diminish the faint trace of lingering shadows shifting through the air. The essence in my chest filled me down to my toes as it stretched for the remaining souls of the lost. For whatever reason, this strangeness inside of me wanted to reach for them, to pull them in.

I gasped as the strangeness tugged harder, stealing my breath and tightening its hold around my heart. My hands held onto my knees as I remained bent over, gasping against the strange sensation. It felt deprived of something, but I didn't know what that meant.

"Esme?" Elias' voice rang through the debilitating quiet of the garden. He began to approach, but the sound of his steps stopped suddenly as I felt strong hands gently grip onto my shoulders and pull me upright. The darkness within me settled at the touch.

When I turned, I saw Elias staring with wide eyes as he remained surrounded by his father's guards and Aiden standing over me, his eyes filled with mild concern and irritation.

"Take her and be done with it then," the king barked as he ordered his men inside. Every one of them stared wild eyed at the massacre in their yard. Even the king looked mildly terrified as he eyed the bloody wings painted on his throne.

"What?" Elias snapped as he glared furiously at his father. "You can't let them take her. You saw what they did." He pointed to the destruction before us, but it didn't matter. For whatever reason, the king was done with me.

Aiden had already begun gently pulling me back toward his comrades. Panic spread like a wildfire through my veins as the castle completely disappeared from view, taking the sounds of Elias' protests with it. I planted my feet into the ground and fought against his hold. The sharp edges of the rocks cut into the skin of my bare feet making me wince, but I ignored the pain in protest.

"Stop," I said through gritted teeth. He continued to drag me along effortlessly. "I said, stop!" My voice rung with a determination he couldn't ignore.

"I thought you would want to see your family again," Aiden noted a little impatiently. His full mouth pressed into a hard line as he scowled.

My hands dropped from their place on my hips. "My family? They're alive?" Aiden's gaze lost some of its harshness as he noted the disbelief on my face.

The girl with the red hair stepped forward, her eyes filled with sorrow. "Did you not know? This whole time you thought them dead?"

I blinked away tears. I'd hoped they were safe, but I could never be certain.

"Would you like to return to them, or shall I leave you here with the king and his son?" Aiden asked, ignoring the girl's questions.

I swallowed the burn of tears and returned his scowl. "Are you going to hurt me?" I knew it was a stupid question to voice. Especially when the youngest of the group, a boy with pale blond hair which hung in curls around his pale blue eyes, smiled under his hood.

"Not today," Aiden said stiffly. I watched as his eyes, blue enough to appear almost grey in the bright midday sun, cataloged the bruises along my face.

I crossed my arms over my chest. "I demand to know where my family is."

The tall thin woman behind him appeared to lose her patience as she rubbed a bloodied hand over her face in exasperation. The blond boy smiled wider as he glanced up at Aiden to watch his reaction.

"You demand it?" Aiden asked, voice tight with impatience.

I nodded. "If you wish to drag me away from here, and claim you are returning me to my family, then I think I have a right to demand the knowledge of where they're staying."

"You want me to tell you where they are so you can travel on your own, is that is?" he asked. Anger looked good on him, much like it did when he would argue quietly with Nonna in the shadows at our performances. I hated that he appeared so violently beautiful.

I shoved the observation down to the far corners of my mind and instead nodded again. "I have a right to know."

He watched me for a moment, his body deathly still. I narrowed my eyes at his large form, forced to squint against the bright sun behind him. The light made the red in his hair stand out against the brown.

"Hakan," he barked. The other man, whom I'd nearly forgotten, moved then. His hands gripped onto my shoulders tightly, though not in a way that caused me pain.

"What are you doing?" I snapped as I watched him begin to lift me off the ground. "Stop it." The muscles in his cheek tightened against a retort as I struggled in his grasp.

Only when I was completely lifted off the ground did I strike. I flung my elbow back and felt myself swell a little with pride at the grunt Hakan gave as it collided with his stomach. I pulled free from his grip and turned to glare at Aiden while Hakan rubbed a hand over his now-tender side. The others watched me with amusement.

"You cannot treat me like a prisoner," I said through gritted teeth.

Aiden crossed his arms over his chest. "You are under my protection. If this is the only way to protect you until I can return you to your family then you'll just have to deal with it."

I snorted and mirrored his stance. "I hardly know you and you just expect me to take your word for everything? How do I even know you're going to take me to my family and not that filthy demon I saw you with earlier?"

They all stiffened at my words, but it was the blond boy who spoke first.

"I thought you knew her?" he asked, looking to Aiden. He stood not much taller than my small frame, his face still rounded with youth, but he appeared just as deadly in his dark armor as the others.

"I do know her," Aiden replied stiffly. His gaze never left mine as we continued to glower at each other.

"Hardly," I scoffed. "You bring me your balls and I give you mine. That hardly counts for friendship."

"Wait," the blond said with his palms raised in surrender and an amused grin on his face. "Did she just say you bring her your balls?"

"I have so many questions," the redheaded girl said with a smile as she eyed Aiden and me.

"Crystal balls," Aiden articulated clearly. "The siphons." My spine stiffened at the unfamiliar term, my confusion only growing and adding to my frustration.

"Okay," the blond said with a nod, though a smile remained on his playful mouth. "That makes more sense than what I was picturing."

"We all know what you were picturing Killian," Hakan groaned. He eyed me briefly before turning to stand closer to the tall woman. She hadn't spoken a single word and instead just watched us with impatience set in her jaw.

"Just tell me what this is about," I snapped. "I've been here for months and you're just now coming for me? Why come at all? What could my family possibly offer you to come get me?"

He dropped his arms to his sides and studied me for a moment longer. I nearly bristled under his steady gaze, but I forced myself to hold firm.

"There is a debt," he said slowly. "What do you know of it?"

I shrugged. "Nothing."

Killian sighed. "Can we at least find a place to get a meal and sleep before you begin the hours-long lecture of the Loutari family debt?"

"What Loutari family debt?" I asked, refusing to be distracted by the promise of food.

"He's right," Aiden finally said before turning away. "Now is not the time for this discussion."

I groaned. "I think now is as good a time as any if you truly want me to come willingly."

He turned then, so quickly I nearly ran into his chest before stepping back. "Will you stop being difficult and keep your questions to yourself for a while longer?"

"Only when you stop being such an ass."

The redheaded girl smiled. "Perhaps you can tell her at least some of the truth while we travel," she suggested calmly. "She does have a right to know what she must do."

"I think that sounds more than fair," I added with a bit of arrogance.

Aiden, sensing the emotion in my tone, grit his teeth before bending to wrap his arms around my knees. As he threw me over his shoulder, I screamed in protest which seemed to only bring another amused smile to Killian's face.

"Put me down. This is absurd," I yelled, slamming my fists against his back. He didn't even seem to notice as I hit him over and over again.

"We have a long way to travel if we plan to find somewhere safe to rest by nightfall," Aiden said to me, though his voice sounded concernedly close to my ass. "I suggest you keep quiet unless you want something to become attracted to your screams and come looking for trouble, princess."

I bit my tongue to silence my retort, settling for slamming my fists into his back once more before succumbing to the truth that my life was now entirely in the hands of this near-stranger.

Behind us, the castle gates slammed shut with a final clang that resonated within my bones. I was officially free from the king's wicked captivity, but what sort of imprisonment would I now enter as I left with these strange warriors?

SEVEN

"Please put me down now." My voice croaked as I spoke into his back once again. My voice had grown hoarse from complaining over the past hour as he refused to acknowledge my request.

Killian, the young boy with pale blond hair, smiled as he walked behind us, his eyes always scanning our surroundings for any sign of danger. Though, as I glanced around our group, I couldn't think of a reason anyone would want to pick a fight with Aiden and his comrades. They were all still covered in ash and blood, weapons still poised at the ready.

"Aiden," the redheaded girl said slowly, "perhaps it wouldn't hurt to let her walk awhile. There's no harm in it at least."

I liked her already. When she sent me a small wink I smiled and tapped a hand on Aiden's shoulder. "She's not wrong," I added. "I am capable of walking on my own."

Beneath my stomach, his shoulder sagged in a sigh. "Fine," he finally snapped.

He set me down, muscles shifting my weight effortlessly. With little grace I stumbled a few steps before a hand at my elbow steadied me.

I leaned into the warmth it provided momentarily before the blood rushed back to my feet. When I nodded my thanks, Aiden wordlessly released his grip on my arm, taking the faint scent of cedar with him as he stepped away.

He continued down the dirt path we'd been following without a backward glance, his two silent warriors at his sides. I allowed myself a moment to study him from behind before I caught sight of the others watching me.

"We'd better keep moving if you don't want him to carry you again," Killian said with a knowing gleam in his eye.

I ignored it, moving past him and the girl with fiery twists in her hair. The tenderness in my feet surprised me. As I glanced down, I realized why. I was still barefoot. Dried blood and small scrapes covered my feet while the skin at my ankles remained raw from the abuse of four months in chains.

"Would you prefer I carry you instead?" the girl asked as she too studied my bare feet.

I shook my head. "I haven't worn proper shoes in months. I'll be fine."

"He didn't even let you wear shoes?" Killian asked, astonished. The innocent roundness of his bright eyes appeared to grow as he too glanced at my feet, and quickly away.

I snorted. "Do the sight of my feet truly look that abhorrent?"

Killian's pale cheeks flushed with color. "Not at all. I just didn't think you'd want me staring."

The redhead smiled. Her brown eyes appeared the shade of honey in the light. "Don't make him feel too terribly," she said warmly, catching sight of my scowl. "He is about as young as he looks."

My gaze returned to Killian. "How old are you?" I asked as I studied the pureness of his expressions. He seemed wholly unaware of how easy it was to read his emotions.

He shot me a look. "I'm nearly ninety-three."

The redhead laughed at the startled look that crossed my face. Ahead of us, the others paid us no mind though our pace was certainly slower than the treacherous one they set.

"Did you say ninety-three?" I asked, still not entirely believing.

"We serve the god of Death," the redhead stated casually. "Our mortal lives ended when we took our positions with him which also ended our aging. I was twenty-seven when my mortality ended, but I haven't aged in over three hundred years."

My mouth hung open as I studied her closer. Her lush curves and pale, freckled skin didn't show any signs of wrinkles that might signal the truth to her words. And yet, as I stared into the honey-brown of her eyes, I could see the knowledge there that only someone who has seen too much for too long might have.

She smiled warmly at me as I continued to digest her words. My gaze returned to those walking ahead. Hakan, the man with the long black hair tied back in a braid, appeared younger than Aiden, if only by a couple of years, but could I trust what I saw? The tall, slender woman on Aiden's other side appeared even younger than him, though her permanent scowl seemed all-knowing as she cast a glance over her shoulder in my direction.

Immediately I dropped my eyes to my feet as I continued down the dirt path, warm from the day's sun. I wiped my damp palms against my tights, all too aware of her glare as it lingered on me.

"Ignore her," the redhead whispered at my side. When I looked up the woman had turned her back on me once again. "She doesn't socialize well."

Killian snorted though he spoke just as quietly. "I doubt Tarsa has anything against Esme. She's probably just still mad you're dating her sister."

The redhead smiled longingly as her thoughts turned inward. "Fen." Her voice came out gently, only a kiss of air leaving her mouth. "It's been decades; she'll get over it." She shrugged casually, glancing in Tarsa's direction. Her eyes hardened for only a heartbeat before returning to smile at me warmly.

"Seraphine here is our optimistic queen," Killian said as he leaned in with a false whisper, light eyes dancing playfully as he eyed the redhead on my other side.

Seraphine rolled her eyes but smiled with him. "There's no point in not thinking happily about the world now is there?"

"Is that how you ended up losing your mortality to work for the god of Death?" I asked before I could stop myself. Ahead, I could've sword Aiden's steps faltered ever so slightly at the sourness of my tone, but Seraphine ignored it and laughed musically.

"Not exactly," she said.

My mind reflected back to the winged demon. As I remembered the feeling of his eyes meeting mine beneath the shadow of his hood, a shiver shot down my spine. "Who was the demon with the wings? Was that the god of Death?"

"No," Seraphine said slowly. The others began to slow their pace to allow us to catch up as we spoke. "That was his son."

"The Prince of Death," Killian added with a slight smile.

Hakan turned to shout over his shoulder. "It's kind of a pretentious title if you ask me."

"Well, his father is the King of Demons who calls himself a god, so what did you expect?" Killian replied with a laugh. Aiden sent the two of them a stern look though he shook his head in subtle amusement.

"And why was he here?" I asked before they could continue.

"To free you from the king," Tarsa said shortly. She sent a glare in Aiden's direction before she moved ahead of the group, Hakan just a step behind.

"What?" I asked. My chest tightened, knowing there must be some underlying reason for the demon prince to have felt the urge to help me escape the king.

"Our loyalties are to the prince," Aiden said, surprising me.

"Though we traded our mortality to the god of Death, we serve in the prince's court and provide protection as his guards," Seraphine explained. I nodded, still not understanding how I fit into this puzzle.

"Or we just piss him off," Killian teased with a wink.

"It really depends on the day," Hakan added over his shoulder, causing Killian's smile to widen.

My palms began to sweat with added nerves as I trailed after these immortal warriors. "Will he come back?"

"No," Aiden said quickly. "Not so long as you remain under our watch." I scowled as he sent me a pointed look. There truly would be no escaping them until I could return to my family, maybe not even then. That thought made my heart quicken its pace.

"We just needed his leverage to get you away from King Elroy." Seraphine placed a gentle hand on my shoulder, most likely sensing my rising nerves.

"But why?" I asked. "Did he have something to do with my capture?"

"No." Tarsa's voice rung with finality as she turned to scowl at each of us.

"We don't know why you were taken," Killian said softly.

The temptation to question further was on the tip of my tongue but disappeared as pain shot up my leg. I winced and collapsed to my knees in a gasp. The warriors stopped immediately, concern etched across each of their faces.

"Are you all right?" Seraphine asked as she helped me back to my feet.

I shrugged out of her grip politely and gave a stiff nod. "I'm fine. It's nothing," I said firmly as I caught Aiden's eye. His gaze racked over my body briefly before he nodded and turned to continue down the path.

When the others began to follow, I quickly glanced down at my foot. There, sticking out of my left heel, was a broken piece of metal – possibly something that had broken off of someone's carriage. It was hard to tell as my blood dripped over it and onto the dirt below.

"Esme, are you okay?" Killian asked, voice laced with concern. His eyes widened at the sight of metal protruding from my flesh.

Without bothering to answer his question I grit my teeth and yanked it free. The pain forced my stomach into knots, but I refused to be sick in front of these strangers. I dropped the bloodied fragment into the dirt and gingerly placed my foot on the ground. Already, my battered and bloodied feet seemed more tender than I expected after only being allowed to walk for a short time.

"You shouldn't walk on that," Seraphine cautioned as she watched me take a few delicate steps after the group, whose pace hadn't slowed in my favor.

"I'm fine," I said again through gritted teeth. My palms broke out in a fresh sweat as I limped after Aiden.

"She's right," Killian said as he moved to cover the blood trail I was beginning to leave behind.

"Aiden," Seraphine yelled up ahead. She ignored the glare I sent her way as he turned back slowly. "She can't walk anymore."

"This nearly went through her entire foot," Killian added as he tossed Aiden the treacherous piece of steel.

Aiden frowned at the bloodied thing for a moment longer than I would've thought necessary as I continued to limp down the path. I kept my gaze on the winding road ahead as it disappeared into a cluster of trees blocking out the red sun on the horizon.

Killian and Seraphine stopped at Aiden's side as they continued to study the uninteresting object. My body ached and longed for rest. But I knew if I stopped now, I wasn't sure I would be able to start again. And I refused to be carried simply because I was too weak to keep up with the group.

I thought briefly of my chances of getting away from them and finding my way to my family on my own even though Aiden said my protection only lasted if I remained with them. Traveling with people who worked for the god of Death wouldn't bode well for me or my family if anyone found out. Demons were nothing more than crude, destructive creatures that cared little for mortal life in our realm. Though Aiden claimed to only want to return me to my family, I couldn't help the suspicion I felt regarding his motives. He was only here because their demon prince ordered it, and that knowledge alone made me uneasy enough.

As I limped past the group, a hand shot out to grip onto my upper arm, firm but gentle.

"Where do you think you're going?" Aiden asked. He didn't look in my direction until after he handed the object to Hakan who studied it further.

I tried to yank my arm free to no avail. The movement shot pain up my leg, forcing me to lean further into his grip.

His thick brows pressed together as he glanced down at my feet. My cheeks warmed though I refused to acknowledge the feel of embarrassment that shot through me.

"I'm going to my family," I said hotly. "Isn't that the whole point of you storming the castle and stealing me away?"

His eyes returned to mine and the brief emotion I saw there nearly threatened to knock me off my feet before his cold detachment returned. No matter how deep I looked into the blue-grey of his eyes, all I could find there was the immortal warrior as he kept his emotions behind a mask.

Behind him, someone cleared their throat. I blinked out of my reverie and forced my face into a scowl. "I can walk just fine," I said before he could throw me over his shoulder again. "I don't need you to carry me like a child." I refused to look up at Aiden as he continued to tower over me. His grip on my arm held me in place as the rest of our band continued down the road.

"If you continue with those injuries it could lead to infection," he said seriously.

I snorted. "Which would only slow you down further, would it?" My voice came out cold as tears I refused to show burned the backs of my eyes. "I assure you; nothing will slow me down or stop me from seeing my family again."

The grip on my arm softened ever so slightly as his thumb shifted to brush over my bare skin for a moment. The seemingly unconscious gesture sent the flutter of darkness in my chest into an excited flutter as it longed for his contact.

"You will not be able to fulfill your duty if you are lying in bed with infection." His tone left little room for argument.

"And what duty is that?" I snapped, returning my gaze to his. "I do nothing but sit in the caravan until Nonna brings people for readings. I assure you that my duties to my family will be of no concern to you once you return me to them."

Aiden's jaw tightened briefly as his eyes roamed over my face, looking everywhere but meeting my gaze. My face heated under his glower, but I refused to back down.

Suddenly, without a word, he scooped my small frame into his arms again. My face slammed into his broad back as he settled me over his shoulder.

"Bastard," I growled under my breath.

His shoulder sagged with another sigh, but he refused to respond to my insult.

We traveled like this for hours. Seraphine and Killian occasionally attempted to coax me into casual conversation, but I mostly ignored them. The humiliation of being tossed over Aiden's shoulder again rang through me as I hung there like a limp child's doll, his arm wrapped around the backs of my thighs.

Only when the sun settled over the horizon did we finally stop. Hakan and Tarsa disappeared into the small village we'd come across, so small I was certain only wanderers knew of its existence from our travels. The cool night air settled across my skin as Aiden finally set me on my own feet.

I took a comforting breath as the blood rushed back through my legs. All around us, the village seemed quiet with the night. Only a single street created access through the town, allowing us to see the few buildings that occupied the area. A pub nearby offered the only noise apart from the small forest beyond. The few houses scattered about were silent though lights shone through the open windows.

"Surely they have an inn or space in a barn available," Killian mused quietly.

"If not I'm sure Esme wouldn't mind camping in the trees," Seraphine said with a teasing smile.

I groaned. "I'd rather not." The thought alone made my body grow stiff and throb with an ache not dissimilar to what I felt from spending months chained to the throne.

Aiden's mouth twitched at my sour tone though he continued to scowl into the near-silent village. The light of the moon above cast shadows across the lines of his face making him appear every bit as dangerous as the weapons at his waist.

"There," Killian said at last. Hakan and Tarsa reappeared on the street as they exited the small building just beyond the pub.

Aiden shifted to pick me up again, but I quickly stepped out of reach. "Don't you dare," I snapped, ignoring the agony shooting up my legs from the pain in my feet.

Seraphine looped her arm through mine and nodded to Aiden as he stepped aside.

"I'll walk with her," she suggested kindly.

Without waiting for a response, she began to lead me down the path to where the others waited patiently. The pain in my feet seemed harsher now as my exhaustion grew and my anger dissipated. Seraphine sent me a sympathetic look as she escorted me into the building, her arm gentle on mine as she lent me her strength.

As we entered the small inn I relaxed into the warmth from the fire in the corner as it filled the room casting it in a comforting glow. An aged man stood behind the counter to my left. His clothes appeared thoroughly worn as they held patches at the elbows and had torn seams near the collar of his tunic. He smiled cheerily at us all, completely oblivious to the many weapons that were hidden beneath tunics and cloaks or the blood dripping down my ankles.

"Enjoy your stay," he said as we began to disappear down a narrow hall. "Breakfast at dawn."

I sent a thankful smile over my shoulder which he returned fervently. Tarsa led us to a set of rooms near the back door. The hallway was shrouded in darkness, lit only by the reaching light of the fire in the front room. I squinted, trying desperately not to trip on anything in the presence of these immortals, who had little issue with the lack of light.

Tarsa nodded to the doors at the end. "These two."

Aiden nodded and gestured to me. Seraphine released me at once as he pulled me into one of the rooms and shut the door. The others could be heard disappearing into the rooms across the hall.

"What do you think you are doing?" I crossed my arms around my middle and stepped toward the door.

Aiden ignored me as he studied the entirety of the small room in a brief, sweeping glance before turning to the small bathing room behind the other door. Only then did I realize where we were.

The single bed took up the majority of the room. A ragged dresser was tucked into the far corner, and a mirror leaned against the wall at its side.

"I'm not sleeping in here with you." My voice came out slightly panicked as I turned away from the bed.

Aiden shot me a look that said otherwise before he disappeared into the bathing room. A moment later I could hear the water churning as he presumably filled the tub it contained.

When he returned, the sleeves of his tunic were rolled up to reveal the sun-tanned skin clear up to his elbows. His gaze swept over me once again as he stood there, filling the entire doorway.

"What?" I finally snapped when he didn't say anything.

His eyes shot to mine again, surprised by the anger in my tone. "You need to bathe, and your wounds need tending to," he said seriously.

I rolled my eyes. "What I need are answers. Why am I here? Where is my family? Why are *you* taking me to them? And for the love of angels, why are you working with demons?"

His steely eyes hardened as I spat the last word in disgust. A muscle ticked in his jaw but still he did not speak.

When I was about to demand answers, a knock sounded at the door making me jump. Silently, Aiden moved past to let them in.

Seraphine stepped into our small room, arms full of a bundle of clothes and boots and what appeared to me medical supplies. "This was all I could find on short notice," she said with a shrug. Her brown eyes scanned the tight space of our room before turning her gaze back to Aiden, a question in her eyes which he ignored.

"Get her bathed and her wounds treated. I'll send food in shortly." And with that he disappeared through the door, not offering me a single answer to any of my questions.

EIGHT

I STARED AT THE door as my frustration grew, hands balling into fists at my sides while Seraphine shifted to dump the bundle onto the bed.

"Let's get you cleaned up, okay?" Her voice was strangely tender as she studied the bruises and cuts that marred my body.

Silently, I let her pull me into the attached bathing room. My body barely registered the sting of pain as she removed my bloodstained and torn clothing, the movement jarring the cuts and bruises along my limbs. The only thing I registered completely was my reflection in the large mirror. The mirror I'd had while imprisoned had been so small and dim that it hardly provided for a decent reflection. But as I stood there and watched while more scars and bruises were revealed with each piece of clothing hitting the floor, I felt a crack growing wider through my fragile dignity.

My face, once full and round, now appeared sunken and sallow as the months with a single poor meal a day took their toll. Bruises in varying stages of healing marred my eyes, chin, and mouth. I watched my lip tremble in the reflection as I studied the result of my imprisonment.

As tears burned the back of my throat, I dropped my gaze to step out of my tights, marveling at the exhaustion in my bones. My fingers grazed over the bruises lining my ribs and hip bones. Even down my thighs from the many hours I'd spent crouched on the stone dais at the foot of the king's throne.

Seraphine turned off the water from the small faucet over the drain and helped me into the tub. Once, I would've blushed at being seen naked before someone else. Now, after months without a moment of privacy, I felt nothing remotely close to embarrassment or shame.

I winced as the warm water stung the open wounds along my feet. The tender and marred flesh at my ankles protested the adjustment as well. Muscles ached and tightened as I settled myself into the tub. The mirror remained in sight as I watched Seraphine clean the blood from my skin and the dirt from my hair.

My reflection no longer showed me the girl I once was, full of life and joy. Now it only displayed a broken heart; a girl who didn't appear whole. Part of me was lost when I was taken captive, I just didn't know how to get it back.

"Is the water okay?" Seraphine asked as she began to scrub soap into my hair.

I nodded. "It's fine."

My knees pressed tightly into my chest as I wrapped my arms around myself, examining the skin at my wrists. I didn't have to wear the manacles there too often, but the skin was still tender and reddened from their brutality.

As she rinsed the soap from my hair, I pulled a foot free from the water and settled it along the edge of the tub. My fingers moved slowly over the raw, bleeding skin there. My ankles looked ravaged, and my stomach dropped knowing I would wear those scars for the rest of my days.

"Do you want to talk about it?" Her voice soothed the growing agitation I felt as I studied my body.

With tears threatening to fill my eyes I shook my head. "I'm fine."

Finished with my hair, she moved into view, careful to keep her back to me, allowing me a small amount of privacy. "I get it you know," she said gently. "It'll take a while before you start to feel like yourself again."

The truth to her words made my throat tighten as I blinked away tears. "I'm fine," I repeated.

"If you ever need to talk," she said, glancing over her shoulder, "I'm here. We all are."

I nodded, not trusting my voice.

When she turned back to watch the door, I let myself relax into the tub, silent tears blending with the water I splashed on my face.

"King Elroy spoke like he had a specific reason behind my arrest," I said slowly, filling the silence as my body began to ache as I relaxed further. "He wouldn't tell me what it was other than blaming me for destroying the peace in Cordovia and threatening to burn me on a pyre."

When Seraphine didn't immediately respond I opened my eyes to find her staring at me thoughtfully.

The door to the bedroom opened. Soft footsteps sounded through the small room before stopping altogether in the doorway.

"What?" Seraphine snapped when Aiden didn't speak.

"I assumed you'd be done," he said stiffly.

I fought the urge to cover myself as I turned. His gaze moved between the marred flesh of my ankles and wrists to the bruises along my neck and face. A flash of emotion showed in his eyes before he hid it again behind a cool mask of disinterest, though his back remained rigid and his fists were clenched at his sides.

His eyes lingered a moment, then shot to the floor, the wall, the ceiling. Careful to keep his eyes anywhere but focused on me, he said, "Her food is on the bed."

"I'll make sure she eats," Seraphine said slowly, voice full of impatience as he continued to linger.

Aiden appeared to catch himself as his cheeks displayed the barest hint of color before he spun on his heel and left in a rush without another word.

As soon as he disappeared Seraphine gently helped me from the tub, wrapping a worn towel across my middle. My steps remained stiff and tender, cuts still screaming from the bath, as I followed her into the other room. Seraphine ushered me to the edge of the bed, pushing the food Aiden brought closer to my lap.

The sight and smell of the warm beef stew sent my stomach thundering with hunger. Seraphine pulled a brush from the pack she brought with her and began to work on my tangled hair while I shoveled food unceremoniously into my mouth.

"When was the last time they fed you?" Her voice had gone stiff as she studiously ignored my lack of manners.

I shrugged. "I got fed once a day. Today the prince had another meal sent to my room, but that was hours before the burning."

Seraphine considered my words, her hands working through the tangles in my hair. Only when it was tied into a long damp braid did she move to sit beside me. She looked to be on the verge of saying more before she caught site of the wound at my foot. Her eyes narrowed as she studied it. The hole slicing through my left heel raged as she began to pull the medicine from her bundle.

"What is that?" I asked, eying it suspiciously. Nonna and my mother always preferred to use herbs from local healers during our travels when one of us fell ill or became wounded. We had our usual herbal healers at nearly every village as it was common for one of my siblings or myself to grow ill or injured when we were younger. This strange ointment carried a strong and unfamiliar scent as she opened the small tin.

Aiden entered the room before she could respond. His eyes briefly noted me sitting on the bed wrapped in a towel before he registered the ointment in his friend's hands.

"You haven't treated her wounds yet?" he asked, voice tight with tension. I narrowed my gaze at him as he scowled at Seraphine.

She didn't seem perturbed by his rudeness as she handed him the ointment and stood. "Perhaps you can treat her injuries since you seem so keen on keeping them clean."

He mumbled something unintelligible which made her grin. She sent me another friendly smile before disappearing into the hall.

Aiden remained frozen for a beat, looking everywhere but in my direction, before he moved to kneel on the floor before me. I was suddenly very aware of the towel being the only coverage I had, causing my cheeks to burn even more.

Without looking directly into my face, he took my foot in his hands. With a gentler touch than I assumed he was capable of, his fingers traced the lines at my ankles. A burning trail of tension remained in their wake as I struggled to keep my breath quiet. Seeing this boy, one I'd known for half my life and yet knew nothing about, kneeling before me sent my heart into strange flutters. Even the thing that lived in my chest seemed to stretch, relaxed at his contact.

"This is going to sting," he said quietly as he began to apply the ointment to my torn flesh.

I bit my lip to keep my gasp of pain to myself. The hole in my heel screamed against the strange medicine for all of three breaths before settling into a soothing tingle of relief. As soon as the pain dimmed, the exhaustion I'd held at bay pulled at my consciousness, causing my shoulders to sag and my eyes to droop.

His hands moved deftly, confidently, as he applied the medicine to every cut and scrape along my skin, taking extra care with the ruined flesh at my ankles. The calloused feel of his fingertips as he drew his left hand over my skin seemed to draw the dark essence in my chest toward his touch. I could feel it pulling against my restraint now as it sought him out. For whatever reason, this part of me was lured to the immortal warrior, and that was a question I wasn't sure I was ready to have answered.

When he finished with my ankles, he took my hands in his and studied the skin at my wrists.

"Are you ever going to answer my questions?" I asked, hoping to distract myself from the tingle of the medicine as it settled into my skin, allowing exhaustion to grow more demanding.

"What questions?" he asked distractedly.

"Why am I here?" I said, quickly losing patience, ignoring the way the warmth of his touch embraced my hands in comfort.

His eyes shot to my face momentarily before he returned to his work along my injuries. "I was ordered to return you to your family. We are here because this is where we decided to stop for the night while we travel."

"Where is my family?" The thought of seeing them again made my throat burn with tears I wouldn't let myself shed in front of this immortal.

He shrugged. "Somewhere near Indonier on the other side of the Soulless River."

I shivered. The last time I had crossed that river with my family we nearly lost our mules. The river's reputation was formidable. Even if the larger trading bridges were taken, they flooded often, and many lost their lives in their attempts to cross it.

"Why were you ordered to return me to my family?" I asked, forcing myself to stay focused. He'd begun to wrap my wrists, ankles, and bloodied feet in bandages now. The cool feeling of the medicine soaking further into my skin left a tingling sensation in its wake.

"That's a rather long story and probably best answered by your family," he said.

I grit my teeth. "It's not like I have anywhere to go, and they're not here to tell me."

Aiden sighed. "Your family owes a debt to the god of Death, and they need you in order to repay it."

I nearly barked a laugh, but only a small choking sound managed to escape my dry throat. "My family wouldn't dare make a deal with demons like the god of Death. We are not so wicked."

A muscle tightened in his jaw as he took a steadying breath. His gaze remained on his hands as they worked to finish the bandages. "As I said, I think your questions would be best answered by your family."

My body flooded with anger as he stood and took a step away from me. His eyes remained downcast, careful to not look in my direction as I sat there in my towel.

"Get dressed and get some sleep. You're going to need it," he said stiffly.

I lurched to my feet, ignoring the pain and my body's exhaustion. "I'm not sleeping here until you tell me the truth."

He glared at me then, eyes hard and cold. "Get dressed," he said slowly, carefully controlled anger lacing his words, "and get into bed."

I crossed my arms over my chest as I returned his glare. "I'm not sleeping with you." A brief flush covered his cheeks though his glare didn't diminish.

"Don't worry, princess," he said, voice darkening. "That is not my plan this night."

And without another word he disappeared into the bathing room where I heard the turn of the faucet as he filled the tub once again.

I dressed quickly. The tender ache in my muscles more pronounced now as exhaustion settled over me, battling for dominance with my growing annoyance with Aiden's reluctance to answer my questions. Questions which I figured were very reasonable considering I just traveled for an entire day with him. My long, braided hair dripped water down the back of the clean tunic Seraphine fetched for me as I yanked loose fitting pants over my bandaged feet.

A soft splash of water told me Aiden had settled into the tub. I fought the urge to interrupt his bath and demand answers while he wasn't in any position to run from me. But the mere thought of taking more than a single step filled my mind with a sleepy fog as exhaustion threatened to drag me under at that moment.

I collapsed onto the bed, not bothering with the blankets as I settled onto the pillow. The faint scent of dust filled my nose as my eyes drifted closed of their own accord. As the darkness of sleep filled me, my mind continued to whirl with questions about my family. Surely Aiden was wrong; they wouldn't make a bargain with a demon, and certainly not one as powerful as the god of Death.

I hadn't realized I'd dozed off until the faint scent of mint and cedar filled my nose again. My eyes remained closed as a blanket drifted over me, falling still at my shoulders and instantly providing comforting warmth. I waited for the shift of weight on the bed to signal Aiden lying beside me, but it never came.

My eyes opened a fraction, just enough to adjust to the small amount of light casting through the crack beneath the door. Beside me, perched on the floor with his back leaning against the side of the bed, sat Aiden. His hair damp from his bath, and chest bare to the night. His eyes remained open as he watched the door.

I fell back into unconsciousness while the immortal remained guarding the room.

NINE

I shifted comfortably beneath the warmth of the blankets. The unfamiliar bed seemed to will me back to sleep as I pulled the blankets tighter around my shoulders. I took a steadying breath, the memories of yesterday coming back in a rush. But I refused to dwell on them. Instead, I focused on what lay ahead. Though I kept my eyes closed, I knew it was not yet dawn as the room remained shrouded in darkness.

My body ached far less than it had in weeks. I suspected the warm meal the night before and the fresh bath and bandages on my torn skin contributed to that as well.

The scents of dust and mold filled my nose as I inhaled deeply. It was only as I breathed deeply that I caught the other scent on the air. This one oddly comforting, settling the fluttering near my heart.

I opened my eyes then, searching for the warm fragrance of cedar and mint. The room beyond remained mostly in darkness, letting the shadows stretch across the floor. From the small window in the bathing room, I could see the greying of the sky as dawn slowly approached. It was far too early to be awake.

A shift in the darkness drew my attention. Aiden sat relaxed on the floor, in the same spot where he'd positioned himself the night before. I couldn't see his face, but from the small amount of light in the room I knew he was awake. His shoulders were rigid, muscles clenched in tension as he remained focused on the door.

My thoughts whirled further as I watched him slowly stand. Every slight shift in weight seemed calculated, the way a warrior might gracefully move through battle. As he stepped through the open doorway into the bathing room, I felt my breath catch in my throat. He wasn't wearing a shirt.

In the dim light I could see the lines of his body plainly. Trousers hanging low on his hips, abdomen rippling with muscle as he reached for his tunic out of sight. My gaze trailed over his warrior's build as he turned. For as long as I'd known him, I'd always found him handsome, but seeing him half naked assured me that my imagination never did him justice.

My heart hammered away in my chest as I watched him glance out the small window, the faint trace of dawn allowing me to see his face, and for once he seemed relaxed, content. I tried to pull my eyes away and focus on anything else, but I couldn't seem to take my eyes away from this strange man as he slipped into his shirt. It was only then that I noticed the scars covering his body. Scars only a warrior who had spent far too much time in battle could carry.

Aiden must have realized I was awake then. His already stiff posture went uncomfortably rigid as he turned to face me.

My throat tightened as his dark gaze locked onto mine. For a moment he remained the relaxed man I'd just witnessed, a slight flush dusting his cheeks as he caught me watching him. Then the humanity disappeared as his cool mask returned, erasing any trace of emotion.

"Hi," I whispered foolishly. My hands tightened on the blanket as I pulled it tighter against my chest.

Aiden merely gave a slight dip of his chin in acknowledgment before moving to sit on the foot of my bed, his back to me. "I suggest you dress quickly," he said stoically. "We have a lot of traveling to accomplish today if we hope to make it to your family by the end of the week."

I sat up slowly, the blankets falling to my hips. "Where are we going?" I moved to join him at the edge of the bed. I'd slept in the clothes Seraphine brought for me the night before so there was little I had to do to prepare for travel. As soon as I settled at his side he stood and moved to lean against the far wall, eyes still not focusing on my face.

"We will travel north. When I checked this morning, your family was headed toward Gaiva."

I started; Gaiva was much farther away than Indonier. "How do you know where my family is all the time?"

Aiden gave a shrug of his shoulders. "It was once my job to know where you were at all times. Now, until I return you to them, I keep track of your family's whereabouts."

I repressed a shiver as I glanced down at my feet. Only my toes poked out through the bandages.

The socks and boots Seraphine brought for me lay on the floor a few steps away. Tenderly, I stood to retrieve them. I stumbled from the pain that shot through my foot and reached out to steady myself against the wall.

A hand at my elbow tightened, helping to settle me back on to the edge of the bed. When I looked up, I was embarrassed to find it wasn't the wall I caught myself on, it was Aiden. I could feel the warm muscles of his chest beneath my hand, his heart picking up its pace ever so slightly as we both realized I was gripping the front of his shirt.

Cheeks flaming, I yanked my hand away and stumbled to my shoes stubbornly. Only when I returned to the bed, boots in hand, did Aiden move to lean against the wall again.

"There are reports of a festival taking place outside Albon this evening," Aiden said casually. I pulled the stockings over my bound feet, refusing to acknowledge the pain they caused as the bandages tugged against my tender skin. "We'll head in that direction as soon as you're ready and you can begin to complete your duties there until we find your family."

I sighed. "It's going to be hard to do anything useful at a festival where my family won't be present. And I don't even know what my duties are."

"Your family is not required for you to perform your duties owed to the god of Death," Aiden countered. I could feel his eyes watching my every movement as I began to slide on the other stocking. "Did Adine ever explain what occurs during your readings with the siphon?"

"What is the siphon?" I asked.

Aiden ran a hand over his face in barely contained frustration before scowling at me. "The soul siphon is what you refer to as your crystal ball."

I could feel the annoyance growing to match my confusion. "What? Why do you call it a soul siphon?"

"So, your grandmother never told you your purpose then?" he asked, ignoring my question.

I shook my head as I reached for my boots. "Just that it was my duty to do the readings at every performance because her gift for it had aged."

He seemed to consider this before speaking. "That's partially true. You are what the god of Death calls his Soul Collector. When you complete those readings, you are essentially removing someone's soul and locking it away in the siphon. It is then my duty to retrieve them and return them to my realm."

My heart felt as if it stopped altogether; even the fluttering of the darkness in my chest paused at his words. "That can't be. Why would my family let me steal people's souls? How is that even possible?"

"I think that is a question you should ask them when you return to them."

"But why me?" I asked, starting to panic. "Why does it have to be me? Is there some rule that I don't know that says I have to kill these people?"

"You're not killing them," Aiden said slowly like he was speaking to a petulant child. "Their mortal bodies live on. Their souls are just removed."

"What does that mean?" I said, quickly losing my temper. The boot pulled against my bandages and I hissed a wince in response but otherwise ignored the pain as I shoved on the almost-too-small boot.

"It means many things," Aiden said, refusing to elaborate.

I snorted. "That's a fantastic and detailed answer," I said, voice dripping with sarcasm. "I thank you for your glorious response."

The corner of his mouth twitched slightly. "There is more that perhaps is best told to you by your family. I'm not privy to the entirety of your family's history."

Ignoring his tone, I shoved my foot into the other boot and stopped abruptly as pain shot through my heel at the contact. My fingers fumbled around the boot as it dropped to the floor. I grunted as I gently ran a shaking hand over my heel, fresh blood began soaking through the bandages turning it a sickening red.

"Here," Aiden said softly. I watched silently as he knelt before me yet again. With surprisingly gentle hands he removed the bandage and replaced it with a new one from his medical supplies. I sighed as the ointment soothed the pain into a dull ache.

Aiden moved carefully as he pulled the boot over my foot. The bandages made the leather squeeze tighter along my ankle as he laced it up my calf.

Aiden glanced toward my face, but his eyes paused along my neck. Unconsciously, I reached up to feel the familiar raised skin of my scar. I went still as a thought occurred to me.

"That's why that demon showed up last year, isn't it?" I asked in a voice barely above a whisper. Aiden looked contemplative. "He attacked me because of what I've been doing?"

He shifted then, leaning back on his heels as he looked up at me from beneath the ragged cut of his hair. "Yes," he said carefully. "His name is Ephraim and he was under specific orders. Your life should not have been threatened as it was, but he has always gone to the extreme to make his point known."

I brushed my finger over the raised scar again, remembering the feel of his knife pressed to my throat as he threatened my family.

"And what was his point exactly?" I said now, temper rising. "Was Ephraim told to come cut me for a specific reason? Or was he the god of Death himself?"

Aiden snorted, amused. "Ephraim is certainly not Death. He's no more than a messenger."

"Is that what you are, too?" I asked before I could stop myself.

Aiden's eyes dropped to the scar at my neck for a breath before he responded. "No," he finally said. "I'm nothing more than an errand mule."

I wasn't sure whether to believe him or not. Something about the way he said the words told me there was more he wasn't saying. His body remained rigid as he threw a pack over his shoulder and strapped his knives and sword at his belt.

"Why did you sell your mortality then if you were just going to be used to run errands for him?" I asked quietly. My heart began to race as I considered my connection to the god of Death. He'd been unknowingly involved in my family's lives for too long.

Aiden kept silent for so long that I wasn't sure he was going to respond. Even as he opened the door to the hall and beckoned for me to follow, I thought perhaps he hadn't heard me.

"Your family's attempts to fulfill the duty bestowed upon you has caused some trouble that even Death cannot fix without involving himself further. And that is something no one in the mortal realm needs."

I bristled at his words; the insult against my family stung. "They can't have possibly done anything worse than me," I said under my breath. "I'm the one stealing people's souls apparently." A sheen of sweat broke out along my palms as I fisted them at my sides.

Ahead, I could hear the voices of the others as they gathered near the door to the inn. They seemed surprisingly solemn for a group of immortal warriors. We couldn't have gotten more than a few hours of sleep, assuming no one stayed up to keep watch overnight.

"You are the chosen Soul Collector," Aiden continued as we approached the group. "It is your duty and yours alone to collect these souls. Any attempts made by anyone else borders too closely on the black arts of witchcraft. They rip the souls apart instead of coaxing the essence from their mortal bodies. This causes far more attention to be thrust upon your family than they need."

"What attention are they getting?" I persisted. "Is the king after them now because I left?" That thought sent my stomach spiraling as I pictured my younger siblings, Alfie and Amara, chained to the king's throne the way I had been.

"The king is no longer relevant. As for your family," he looked at me sidelong before turning away, "that's another matter. For now, we need to find some place for you to continue your duty."

"You mean steal souls. I won't do it."

He spun around to face me. "This is not up for discussion."

Crossing my arms over my chest I returned his scowl with one of my own. "I'm not going to damn innocent people for something that you claim is true. For all I know, these stories of my family owing a debt and needing me to steal souls for the god of Death is a ruse to gain you more favor in his eyes." I scrutinized every miniscule emotion flickering behind his closed expression as I added, "How can I trust you?"

Aiden considered my words for a moment, eyes burning into mine as I impatiently awaited his response. "You don't have a choice," he finally said.

"Well, I'm not stealing anyone's souls," I argued. "I need to hear the truth from my family."

He sighed deeply, running a hand through his hair as he continued to scowl. "Are you always this tiresome?"

"Are you always this inconsiderate?" I snapped. "You are asking me to steal someone's soul. Though I suppose for someone who willingly sold their own soul to Death, your lack of sympathy isn't surprising."

Aiden stepped closer, towering over me as his anger rolled off of him in waves. "You should consider minding your tongue or you may just lose it."

I calculated his threat with the little I knew of his character. "You wouldn't dare."

"The silence might be nice," he mused, stepping away. "Don't tempt me."

"You're despicable," I growled, fists clenching at my sides.

"Morning," Killian said cheerily, pointedly ignoring the mirroring scowls Aiden and I wore. "How are your feet feeling, Miss Loutari?"

I nodded stiffly, forcing myself to rein in my temper. "I'm well, thank you."

His playful smile widened until he caught sight of Aiden's stern face. There were no lines of laughter that I could see on the warrior, only his ever-present scowl and cold mask.

"Clothes fit okay?" Seraphine asked as she looped her arm through mine again.

Aiden and Tarsa took the lead, while Hakan took up the rear a few steps behind Seraphine and me.

"They fit fine."

She smiled. "I have an extra pair in my pack for when you need them."

I nodded my thanks and followed as Aiden led us out of this small village made of crooked wooden buildings and dust covered houses. From windows and doors, I could see curious sets of eyes as they peered out at the well-armed strangers moving through their village.

"I hope he didn't keep you up all night with his snores," Killian called over his shoulder from where he walked beside Aiden a few steps ahead. The curls of his pale hair bounced with his steps. "Traveling with him is hard work when you have to lie awake listening to his snoring every night."

I bit my lip to hide my amusement as Aiden shot him a look of reproach. Seraphine laughed beside me, but it was Hakan who spoke next.

"His snoring is much preferred to your constant chatter," he said with a smile in his voice. The usually quiet man stepped closer to walk just behind my shoulder as he winked teasingly at Killian whose face turned a shade of red.

"I don't mind you talking," I said to chase away the flush in his cheeks. He seemed far younger than anyone here no matter that he remained several decades older than my nearly eighteen years.

He smiled then, a full face-splitting grin. "I like her," he said to Aiden, who merely grunted nonchalantly.

"Sir," Tarsa said, running gracefully into view. I started as I scanned our group again. I hadn't noticed her disappear.

"What is it?" Aiden said. The darkness in his gaze returned as he glanced to me before giving his attention fully to the lean warrior.

"The king, sir," she said as she stopped before him. "He's issued a warrant for her arrest."

My stomach fell, hands clenching and unclenching at my sides. We'd only just lost view of the village, yet I could now hear shouts and the rumble of boots as the townsfolk followed us into the trees.

"There's a bounty for her," Tarsa was saying as I turned back to stare at her in horror. Sweat glistened along her dark skin, making her appear to glow in the early morning sun. "The king is welcoming anyone to capture her and return her to the castle. He says she has something he wants, but he refuses to say what that is. Just that his prisoner was taken, and he intends to get her back."

"They're coming for her," Hakan said a few steps behind. His head was tilted slightly as if listening to the village people slowly growing closer.

"How many?" Aiden asked, voice tight with tension as his eyes shot in my direction and locked me in his gaze.

Hakan shifted, listening intently to the growing crowd. "All of them."

TEN

My feet screamed in protest as I raced after the others. I knew they kept their pace slow for my benefit, but the grueling pace Aiden kept at the front of our group left little time for rest as I struggled to keep up. Tarsa disappeared into the shadows of the trees often as she monitored the villagers' steady approach, and every time she returned, I knew from the scowl she sent my way that they'd gained ground.

Seraphine remained within arm's reach as we traveled. The sun was steadily rising in the distance, forcing the previously cool dawn air into a balmy heat. My neck dripped with sweat as we traveled west.

"We need to lose them, Aiden," Hakan repeated as one of the villagers finally came into view. My heart thudded unevenly in my chest as the young boy studied us, his eyes widening at the sight of my armed companions.

Tarsa appeared then, dropping from the trees to slam the hilt of one of her axes into the boy's head. My mouth fell open on a gasp as he collapsed in the dirt.

Aiden scowled as he studied the boy on the ground. "We can't risk killing them all."

"You'd kill them?" My hand clamped over my mouth in horror as I looked to the others. Only Killian seemed bothered by that idea as a muscle flickered in his cheek, eyes downcast.

Hakan nodded, face displaying little emotion. "We cannot risk them capturing you or spreading word of your location."

"If they follow us for much longer it could lead them directly to your family," Seraphine added gently. Her brown eyes softened as she studied whatever emotion remained on my face.

"You can't kill them," I repeated stubbornly.

Aiden seemed ready to throw me over his shoulder again, but he spoke calmly. "Do you propose another solution then?"

I ignored the bite to his tone and forced my breathing to even out. His gray-blue eyes scrutinized every minute expression on my face as I stood there, panting from our hours-long race through the trees, feet aching painfully.

Turning my back, I studied the trees around us. My shirt clung to my sweat clad skin as I shoved back the strands of my hair that had come loose from its braid. It was near midday now, if the rising sun was any indication, so we needed to stop for rest and food soon. I wasn't sure what the immortals ate, but my stomach felt empty with the unexpected excursion.

I spun around again, scanning the trees as the sounds of those preparing to take me back to the king grew louder. My heart skipped at the familiar sounds of rushing water just out of sight.

I smiled as I turned back to Aiden, his scowl still present. "The river," I said as I forced myself to step closer to him. "If my family is still near Indonier, as you say, then we need to cross the Soulless River at some point, but it might be faster if we cross the Ruelle River just to the south. Then we can head west from there."

Killian turned his back, keeping his bow trained in the direction of the villagers as they grew closer. With every step they took my body shook in response, heart beating in time to their rhythm.

"It could help us lose them," Seraphine added calmly. "We could head straight to Albon and rest there for the night before continuing across the Soulless River tomorrow."

Aiden seemed to consider this. Though my skin already felt heated from our travels, something about his pondering gaze made my cheeks heat further. No doubt he was weighing the risks of crossing the river now when we were already so tired and famished.

"Aiden," Hakan said in warning. His head remained tilted slightly as he listened to our followers' approach. Beside him Killian and Tarsa remained armed and ready.

"Fine," Aiden finally muttered, eyes never leaving mine, "but we make it quick and we don't go searching for a bridge. If we want to lose them, we have to cross here."

My heart stuttered slightly as Seraphine grabbed my arm and pulled me along. Hakan led us through the small path in the trees as Tarsa and Killian remained a few steps behind, weapons poised for attack.

"I hope you can swim," Seraphine said. The pace she set made my tender feet ache in an unforgiving protest. I bit down on my lip to keep from whimpering as we wove through the thin trees towering overhead.

The river only lay a few yards away, but through it all I could feel Aiden's eyes watching my every movement. No doubt calculating the shallow steps I took to hide my limp or the shaking in my hands as we neared the water.

As the Ruelle River finally came into view my body fought to rebel as I collapsed to my knees. Tears streamed down my face of their own accord as the pain in my feet became unbearable.

"We'll cross here," Hakan announced as he began tightening the straps of his weapons.

I remained kneeling as I watched the others. Tarsa had disappeared yet again, presumably to scout the path ahead. Though how she managed to cross this river so quickly and unseen was a mystery to me.

The sounds of the crashing river raced by in a torment of waves as I knelt beside it. My heart pounded against my ribs as I watched the water writhe, thoughts churning with the strong possibility of being dragged to the earth below where air was nonexistent.

"Let's move." Aiden's voice left little room for argument as one by one, the others finally leapt into the water.

Hakan disappeared beneath the surface first as he swiftly moved through the waves. Killian remained just behind me on shore as he scanned the tree line for any sign of our pursuers.

A warm hand gripped my elbow as Aiden gently pulled me to my aching feet. I had little doubt my bandages were now stained with blood as my wounds reopened and the marred flesh at my ankles pulled against the bandages inside my boots.

"I need you to swim," he said coolly. There was no hint of fear in his eyes as he watched Seraphine join Hakan in the raging waters. How had I forgotten how fierce this river was? The Soulless River earned its name for being the largest and harshest waterway in the kingdom, yet this river somehow seemed just as daunting.

"Can you do that?" Aiden's voice cut through my panic as I watched the river with wide eyes.

I nodded once, forcing my nerves to hide beneath the dark essence that thrummed beside my heart. "I can do that."

His hand tightened on my elbow once before he followed the others into the river. My breath came in shallow gasps as I stared after him. I should've mentioned that I had never learned how to swim. But if we wanted to lose the bounty hunters, this was our only chance.

"Esme," Killian said as he stepped up beside me. "You need to go. Go now before they get too far ahead in the water. I'll be right behind you."

I forced my eyes closed, only for a moment, to send a prayer to the stars, before I jumped into the water.

The sudden frigid temperature expelled the air from my lungs as my head sunk below the surface. Arms flailing, I struggled to get above water again. The shockingly cold river seemed to seep into my bones as I struggled against the current. There was no light, no sound other than the pounding in my ears as my lungs burned for air. Even the darkness in my chest seemed to dull as it curled around my heart.

An arrow pierced the water mere inches from my face as I struggled against the current. Whatever air remained in my lungs left as I gasped, trying to get out of range of the archer.

A hand gripped my ankle then, pulling harshly. I tried to scream, tried to fight, but without air I only swallowed water. The hand tightened as I struggled feebly. My lungs burned now, burned with a white-hot agony as they echoed the pain in my ankles under the hands that had turned to constricting vices, pulling me back toward the shore.

I continued to kick out against the grip threatening to pull me under before my head finally broke through the water. I gulped down air, coughing against the harsh waters filling my lungs.

"Esme," Killian's voice called from shore. "Don't move."

I watched again as he shot an arrow into the water, this time landing it in the back of the man who still held onto my feet. The river turned a dark shade of red as the man cried out in pain. His hands released their grip at once as he disappeared underwater, never to rise again.

With my head above water, I could see the chaos ensuing around me. Our pursuers had gained ground, a lot of it. Some were jumping into the river after us while Killian fought off more on the riverbank. His bow armed and gripped tightly in one hand as he pulled a knife free from his boot to cut down another opponent. Seraphine and Hakan fought others in the river that'd gotten too close, the water turning red around them as well.

The river's current twisted, pulling at my limbs again as I was forced back under. The air left my lungs in a rush as the freezing temperature seized my body. I flung my arms out in an attempt to reach the surface. I spun in a tumble as the current pushed and pulled at me, tossing me into the bodies of the dead.

As soon as my lungs began to burn, familiar hands wrapped around my waist, pulling me up and out of the water. I coughed harshly as I breathed in the warm air. The burning in my chest eased as the darkness there calmed, soothing itself at the prospect of being safe.

"Swim, Esme," Aiden ordered as he held onto me.

I struggled in the wild rage of the water, my movements clumsy and too slow as he kept me pressed tightly to his side.

I blinked against the harsh light of the sun, now directly overhead, as the sounds of fighting continued around us. My stomach threatened to empty as I took note of the bodies being carried down the river's harsh current.

Tarsa appeared just at the water's edge. Her hand outstretched as Aiden pulled us closer. Knee deep in the blood-soaked water, she gripped onto the collar my shirt and hauled me onto the grassy shore. I collapsed there, hands and knees sinking into the mud as I expelled the water from my lungs. The feel of the cold water burned my nose and throat, making my eyes fill with unwanted tears.

"Killian?" Tarsa asked, ignoring me altogether.

Aiden stood beside her, scouring the crowd that had braved the water's treachery. "There," he said, pointing to the very center of the struggle.

I turned my head slightly and spotted Killian's pale head bobbing in the water as he swam through the crashing of the current.

Aiden stepped away from me as the rest of the immortals joined us on the shoreline, all of us panting from the unexpected attack in the water and dripping in the blood of the slain. Seraphine caught my eye and winked as she got to her feet and grabbed onto Killian. The youngest immortal had managed to swim his way out of the strongest pulls of the current and close to the bank of the river.

"It seems the king wasn't as willing to let her go as we thought," Killian groaned as Seraphine helped him to his feet.

"So it would seem," Aiden muttered under his breath. "Only question is *why*."

No one answered as we all turned to the raging waters that now ran red.

ELEVEN

By the time we reached the outskirts of Indonier, my feet throbbed with each step. Passing the Soulless River was much easier than expected. The immortals had managed to intimidate our way onto the trading bridge, which towered far above the raging waters.

"We're nearly there," Seraphine whispered encouragingly. Since crossing the river, she'd stayed by my side and often let me lean my weight against her strong build when the pain grew too much. Aiden's medicines certainly helped seal my wounds faster than they would have on their own, but the pain still lingered.

Tarsa dropped from one of the towering trees lining the main road into town. The traders and villagers moving past us paid her no mind as if they hadn't noticed her sudden appearance. My breath caught in my throat as she walked toward Aiden a few paces ahead. I waited to hear if she'd seen any sign of my family near Indonier's campground to the north—the thought alone enough to erase the pain from my mind as I limped toward them.

"Well?" I asked impatiently. We'd been traveling at nearly all hours, only stopping long enough so I could rest and replace my bandages.

Tarsa gave Aiden a barely perceptible shake of her head. If I wasn't looking for it, I wouldn't have seen it.

My stomach dropped to my feet as Aiden turned to face me, his cold mask in place so there wasn't even a trace of warmth in his eyes.

"How long ago did they leave?" Killian asked from my other side.

Tarsa shrugged. "Days at least."

My eyes burned with unshed tears. I'd dared let myself hope that I could be returned to them so soon. A dream that remained just out of reach.

"There's something else," Tarsa added as she handed a folded sheet of paper to Aiden.

I watched his brow furrow as he stared down at the paper, a flicker of emotion crossing his face for only a breath before his mask returned. I tried to get a glimpse of the paper he held but Hakan snatched it before I could see what it said.

"What is it?" Killian asked as he moved to look over Hakan's shoulder. The two of them studied it for a moment before their eyes slid to me, a newfound concern upon their faces.

"What?" I snapped when they moved to study the travelers around us. The road we took was busy this time of day. Horses and mules pulling caravans and wagons filled the wide path and many families travelled on foot around us. I couldn't help but notice the way more people began to look our way as we stood still on the side of the road. The immortals dressed head-to-toe in battle garb catching more attention than I would've liked.

"It's the bounty," Tarsa explained with little patience. "It seems the king has posted your face throughout every village labeling you as a witch for capture."

The injuries along my wrists and ankles burned with the memory of being in the king's care. Careful to avoid the bandages, I pulled my sleeves over my wrists and clutched the seams in my hands to keep them hidden as my heartrate spiked. If these announcements truly were posted everywhere then the entire kingdom and all its poverty-stricken and desperate inhabitants would know my face and what the king would pay to have me returned.

Aiden's eyes registered the gesture as I kept my bandages hidden. "We should find somewhere to sleep for the rest of the day. We can travel at night."

"There are some performers at the campground," Tarsa added as she moved to lead us down the road. "She can siphon there."

Seraphine placed a plain cloak over my shoulders, pulling the hood up to cast my face in shadow as Aiden took his spot at my side.

"No," I said firmly. Tarsa ignored me as she led us through the surrounding trees and away from the crowded road. "I told you I'm not going to do any of this until I see my family."

"It is your duty," Aiden replied stiffly.

"I refuse to believe that."

Aiden grabbed my arm, spinning me around to face him while the others continued through the trees. "The consequences of ignoring the debt your family owes are grave. Are you willing to let your family pay them, should you refuse?"

My stomach spiraled, forcing my breath to grow shallow. "I think my family would agree that it is not right to steal someone's soul so a demon can gain strength."

I watched a muscle tighten in his jaw as he took a steadying breath. I expected him to snap at me the way he usually did when I refused to submit to his orders.

"I can't destroy someone that way," I said quietly, trying a different tactic to get him to understand. "I know I've collected souls for him before, even if I didn't know that's what I was doing. But it's different now. I can't knowingly tear someone away from their families and their loved ones. I will not be responsible for that kind of pain."

As his hand dropped from my arm I turned away, ignoring the display of emotion and understanding breaking through his carefully placed mask. Seraphine waited for me ahead and looped her arm through mine as I limped after the group.

A few hours later, deep in the trees north of the crowded campground, we set up camp for the night. Dusk was close on the horizon, but Hakan and Aiden agreed to let us rest an entire day before traveling the following night. I knew their only hope was that I would join the revelry currently filling the campground and siphon souls for them.

Killian and Seraphine had disappeared into the crowd a while ago. Both claiming for a night of entertainment, but I knew they only wanted to see if there was a large enough crowd for me to join the performers.

I could hear Hakan pacing outside, keeping watch over the two tents hidden in the trees while Tarsa disappeared to check our deeper surroundings. The two of them remained quiet and distant with me but at least Hakan wasn't as cold.

Aiden shifted beside me, his hands carefully replacing my bandages once again. "They look better," he noted quietly, voice oddly gentle.

My gaze returned to the raw skin kept hidden beneath layers of bandages and clothing. If my family saw these marks, they would never look at me the same. I would no longer be me, but simply something to keep under constant guard.

As soon as he finished tying off the last bandage, I pulled my pant leg down to hide both of my ankles, my wrists already hidden beneath the long sleeves of the thin tunic. Aiden shifted, giving me room to lie back on the cot they somehow managed to fit into the small tent.

"Your scars are not something to be ashamed of." He spoke gently, like a hunter trying to coax its prey. "They're proof of your strength and your ability to survive. Do not feel like you need to hide them to retain your family's love."

I turned my back toward him, refusing to let him see the way his words brought tears to my eyes. The fact he could read me so clearly felt unnerving – nearly comforting.

"You may have sold your soul," I said into the following silence, "but you do not know what it means to carry scars such as this."

Fabric shifted behind me, revealing Aiden's presence as he took his usual place on the ground beside my bed. "I have gained many scars in my long life."

I wiped the tears from my cheeks. "Scars from battle are different. They're proof of strength. These," I look to the bandages covering my wrists, "they were not earned in battle fighting for a noble cause. These are the marks of imprisonment."

"I think you felt imprisoned long before the king took you," he said slowly, voice carefully void of emotion.

Pulling the blanket tighter over my shoulders, I refused to respond to his comment. Outside, Hakan continued to pace, and the sounds of the revelry filtered through the trees. My heart beat in time with the familiar music but my mind couldn't find joy in it the way it once did. I forced the music from my mind and the memories it harbored with it.

As the sun disappeared along the horizon and the music gradually faded, sleep still evaded me. Though my body ached and throbbed with the invisible chains still pulling at my ankles, my mind wouldn't sleep. I tossed and turned well after Killian and Seraphine returned to change watch with Hakan and Tarsa.

Faces passed through my mind. A constant stream of the souls I'd taken over the years burned into my memory stealing my sleep. I could feel tears trailing down my cheeks, but I didn't dare shift and risk awakening Aiden who remained slumped nearby, his faint cedar scent coating the tent in comfort.

I wanted to hate my family for keeping me from the truth and making me steal those souls, but I couldn't find it in myself. Guilt threatened to replace my shame as the invisible chains shackled to my ankles seemed to change, now tying me to the souls I'd damned to the god of Death's mercy.

"It's not as cruel as you think," Aiden whispered, startling me. I heard him shift so he now sat on the edge of my cot, keeping a careful distance between us though I felt his presence like a fire along my skin. "It's almost peaceful. When you take the essence of their souls a part of them remains behind, lingering just enough to keep them human. Without that little bit remaining they'd become savages."

"From what I saw at the castle they seemed like savages already," I said with a sniffle. I wiped my cheeks on the edge of my sleeve, careful to keep my back to the immortal.

Aiden sighed. "I fear there is more to those victims than we know. Usually, after you collect a soul and I retrieve the siphon, I hunt down your clients," he said, putting careful emphasis on the word Nonna would use. "And I kill them before they can cause their loved ones too much damage, whether emotionally or physically."

"That doesn't sound very peaceful."

Aiden huffed a breath, the sound nearly like a soft laugh. "It is. When the remaining part of the soul is released in death it seeks out its missing counterpart.

When they find their way back to each other, the soul only knows happiness and peace in the afterlife."

The image filled my mind so clearly. What I knew of Death's realm was sorely lacking, but I chose to picture these souls coming together and finding peace no matter how their mortal lives may have ended.

Aiden continued to speak, telling me of the souls that found their loved ones as well. Together, those souls would remain in peace and content in whatever incorporeal form they existed in. I pictured the bright light that would fill the siphon, only a thousand times brighter as the souls filled the night sky in the form of stars. Stars that would light our path during our travels and cast an ethereal glow on the world.

It was to those words, his deep voice recounting his many stories of souls coming together in peace, that I found myself finally relaxing into a deep sleep.

TWELVE

I DON'T KNOW HOW long we traveled under the cover of night. It felt far too long. Several more days than I first expected as we continued to pass through village after village, dodging the dozens of posters displaying my face to the kingdom.

With the growing poverty in Cordovia, its people grew more desperate for coin and therein we had far too many people hunting me, desperate for the large reward the king offered for my return. I was once no one of consequence, simply a wanderer girl who watched her family perform most nights from the hidden shadows of the caravan. Now, everyone knew my face and sought me out whether for their own financial greed or because of the accusation of my witch blood.

Our constant need to remain hidden from the public and travel at night had kept Aiden and his friends on alert at all hours. While Tarsa and Hakan continued to keep their distance, Seraphine and Killian remained open and friendly toward me. If I didn't already know better, I wouldn't think them immortals at all. Let alone immortals who served the god of Death, the cruelest demon in existence.

Now, after traveling the entire night before and clear into the following day, my feet ached painfully. Killian offered to carry me when the pain became near unbearable, but between the cold expression Aiden always put on display and my shriveling pride, I always declined. We were already so close to our next resting place, Caney. I was determined to make it there before collapsing.

"It's not far up ahead," Tarsa said as she came back into view. I'd gotten so used to seeing her disappear and reappear suddenly that I never bothered to pay attention to her whereabouts, though her sudden reappearances did often make me nearly jump out of my skin.

"What of those bounty hunters?" Hakan asked as he marched along at Aiden's shoulder. He stayed close to him during our travel. Close enough that it was clear he felt protective over the young immortal.

Tarsa shook her head, her short, cropped hair shifting over her forehead. "None that I noticed, but her face is on a few posters in the square."

I shuddered. Part of me wondered if my family saw the posters and knew I'd gotten away. I had to stop myself from thinking about them too often lately. The knowledge that I would get to see them again, and soon, always made my eyes burn with tears that I refused to shed in front of Aiden. As he rarely left my side, this became harder to do.

"We'll settle there for the night," Aiden said with a slight glance in my direction though he didn't meet my eyes. "We could all use a chance to clean up and rest."

Tarsa nodded her agreement and disappeared again. We were close enough to the edge of the Abandoned Desert in the west that there were hardly any trees nearby. The land here was hard-packed and hot from the late summer sun. Even now as the sun disappeared on the horizon, the sand and dirt still radiated heat it had absorbed throughout the day.

"Here," Seraphine said, reappearing at my shoulder with a small canteen of water in her hand.

I took it and drank heavily before passing it back, a smile of thanks on my lips. My skin had grown tight and dry in the last several days as we traveled closer to the dry desert corner of the kingdom. My chapped lips would begin to bleed if I didn't take care to drink more.

"We'll find them soon," she stated encouragingly. She seemed to sense when I began to lose hope or trust in Aiden's promise to return me to my family. Even now, as exhaustion curled its way around my body in a tight embrace, I could see the knowing in her eyes as she studied me.

I offered a slight nod. "I know," I returned, voice lacking conviction.

When I looked up, Aiden was watching me closely. His eyes always appeared to take in and assess every detail of my appearance. Every slight limp in my step, every wince as I touched a tender bruise still healing on my skin, even the hollow look I knew I carried in my eyes which remained over dark bruises from the little sleep I'd managed to snag. I hated to admit that the only reason sleep found me at all these days was because of Aiden's continuous tales of souls finding peace after I tore them from their mortal bodies. As comforting as those tales were, they did little to lessen my guilt.

I lowered my eyes as my cheeks warmed under his gaze. I hated admitting that I found his words comforting. I shouldn't find anything about him comforting. He was an immortal; he sold his soul to the god of Death for unknown reasons and now served him for an eternity. I couldn't fathom the kind of cruelty he had likely caused in his time serving that demon.

"I've reserved rooms at the inn near the northern edge of town," Tarsa said, returning to the group. Today, her axes gleamed shiny and polished in the evening sun. Anyone would catch one look of those hanging off her hips and turn in the other direction. Part of me admired her for her ability to appear so deadly within a single glance, but most of me was just terrified of her skill to kill.

"Please tell me there's a pub nearby," Killian drawled as he shoved the last of his dried jerky into his mouth. We were on our last day's supply of food. If we didn't restock soon the warriors would have to take to stealing a pig from a farm to slaughter for our meals.

Tarsa's mouth thinned as she looked toward the young immortal.

"I don't know if they'll let you drink, kid," Hakan noted with little humor. His voice always sounded in the same droll tone, though only a glint in his eye would reveal what he was feeling. "You look far too young to be allowed a drink."

Killian scowled at his jerky. "I wasn't thinking about drinking," he mumbled under his breath. I felt myself nearly smile at his expression as he stuck out his lower lip in a slight pout.

"Probably just looking for females to tumble," Tarsa snorted. Though her back was to me I could feel her cool disinterest settle on my skin. A chill ran down my spine as I stepped closer to Seraphine, hoping her warmth would chase away the hidden threat that came with being the center of Tarsa's attention.

"I doubt there is a female desperate enough to settle for him, but who knows, maybe after a few glasses of liquor one might find him tolerable enough," Aiden said sarcastically.

As the thing that lived in my chest shifted at his voice, I felt myself stunned by what he said.

Seraphine and Hakan laughed while Killian continued to pout. Their musical tones of laughter echoed in the silence of the road around us.

"Did you just make a joke?" I asked. I hadn't spoken a single word to Aiden in nearly a week, both of us ignoring the offer of comfort he provided with his tales. From the way his brows rose as he finally looked down to where I walked at his shoulder, I knew he found my sudden question equally shocking.

The corner of his lips quirked up slightly before returning to their normal frown. "It has been known to happen," he said rigidly.

Seraphine snorted. "I think in the two and a half centuries I've known you, you've made exactly three jokes, including that one."

Aiden's spine seemed to stiffen as he kept his eyes on the empty road ahead. I studied him in the faint sun, highlighting the red tones of his whiskey-colored hair which remained tied back from his face. There was no way for me to ignore the obvious beauty this man possessed. But what I could do was pretend I didn't notice the way his tunic hugged the muscles along his shoulders and arms, and more importantly that it made my heart warm like I was still the young girl I had been when I first met him.

"There is little in my life that could be considered humorous," Aiden replied stiffly. My eyes caught the way his hands briefly turned to fists at his sides.

The others fell quiet as he spoke. As I glanced over my shoulder, I caught their mixed expressions of pity and sorrow. Only a slight shake of Killian's head had me holding my tongue as the urge to question his words grew.

The cracked stone buildings of Caney came into view quickly after that. The group remained silent as we followed Aiden and Tarsa through the winding cobbled roads to the inn at the far edge of town. Each of us careful to keep our faces down and hidden in shadow as the locals went about their daily lives. We'd barely taken time to settle into our rooms before Seraphine entered the room Aiden and I shared yet again and dragged me across the road to the pub. Thankfully I didn't see a single poster displaying my face, which gave me the encouragement I needed to drag my feet into the crowded pub.

The sounds of laughter and drunken conversations filled the air as we stepped into the heated building. A bar lined the far wall, filled with drunken men and women in low cut bodices who perched on stools nearby watching with hungry eyes. The tables and chairs filling the rest of the small space were mostly filled as well. Only a single table in the back corner remained mostly empty. Once I noted its current inhabitant I realized why.

"I'm glad you were able to get us a large table," Seraphine said cheerily as she perched in the chair beside Tarsa who scowled at the passing men.

"Men can be easily persuaded when you mock their ability to handle liquor," she said with a casual shrug.

"What did you do?" I asked curiously, sitting across from them.

Tarsa shrugged a shoulder, eyes barely glancing in my direction. "I merely challenged a group of men to chug an entire mug of beer. If they could all finish theirs before me then they'd keep the table."

"And that worked?"

Her eyes sparkled slightly at the admiration in my tone, but her expression remained frozen in its scowl. "Men have fragile egos. Try and convince them you are better than them at any small thing and they will do just about anything to prove themselves the stronger opponent."

Seraphine chuckled. "You should try that with Hakan."

Tarsa nearly smiled, just a quick twitch of her thin mouth. "He would spend the next century trying to regain his pride."

A barmaid appeared then, her corset tight around her middle making her chest nearly burst from her too-small shirt. I fought the urge to wrap my arms around myself. I'd always been blessed with proud curves, but I preferred to wear well-fitting clothes that I could hide beneath. I'd grown used to living my life in the shadows of the caravan; I felt no need to draw more attention to myself with gaudy clothing.

I sipped from the water she placed before me as Seraphine ordered enough food to feed a small village, and the barmaid disappeared with an expression that said she was equally as shocked as I felt.

"Why so much food?" I asked once she was gone.

Seraphine smiled, her flushed cheeks blending in with the freckles that lined her cheekbones. "The boys will join us shortly and I know they'll need their food as soon as they get here. Otherwise they'll get cranky."

I smiled against the rim of my glass. "What is it they're doing now?"

Tarsa glanced in my direction before glaring at someone just over my shoulder. Seraphine didn't seem to pay her any attention as she spoke. "Aiden is searching for your family again and I suspect the others are looking for a family of performers nearby should you decide to continue your duty."

I fought the urge to roll my eyes as I leaned back against the stiff chair. That knowledge simmered along my skin like the growing heat from this overcrowded room causing my frustration to match its urgency.

"He's not so bad you know," she said as she studied me over the table. "Aiden really is trying to return you to your family."

This time I did snort. "He's been saying that for days. We've traveled through three towns now where he said my family would be and there hasn't been any sign of them once."

Tarsa kept her eyes on whatever she saw over my shoulder but spoke seriously. "Then why not leave and search for them yourself?"

Seraphine shot her a look. "With the entire kingdom eager for the bounty placed on her head, you really think it's a good idea for her to wander alone?"

I shrugged in casual agreement, not wanting to admit the truth of my reluctance to leave this small group of companions.

"You feel safe here," Seraphine said gently, warm brown eyes full of understanding as our gazes met.

The strange flitting in my chest heated at her words. I had to admit, something about Aiden and his comrades made me feel something close to safe, even if I had seen them all fight off soulless monsters and hungry villagers desperate for spare coin. But I couldn't find it in myself to keep denying the way Aiden seemed to calm the darkness living near my heart.

Before I could find a way to deny her claim, a man sauntered up to our table. I cringed away from the foul odor of liquor on his damp clothes as he leaned down to look us in the eyes. With a chipped tooth filling the front of his mouth he smiled drunkenly, letting his gaze brush over Tarsa and I before settling on Seraphine.

"Well hello there," he crooned in a raspy voice. The faint balding of his pale hair made the sweat along his scalp appear more noticeable as he wiped a stained cloth over his brow.

Seraphine, looking elegant in her white tunic and dark hip-hugging trousers, smiled warmly at him. Her bright red hair, still in its usual long twisted braids down her back, fell over a shoulder as she leaned back in her chair to look at him. I watched as her brown eyes tracked over his hunched figure.

"And who are you?" he asked when she didn't reply.

I watched in mild admiration as she tilted her head slightly to expose the column of her neck. The man swallowed audibly at the sight. Tarsa kept her eyes steadily on the man, but I couldn't help the smile that lit up my face as I watched Seraphine.

"Sera," she said in a sultry voice.

A smile lit up the man's face. "Sera. Beautiful name for a beautiful woman."

Her smile widened. "And you are?"

"Karter Tenthlon, at your service." He bowed unsteadily as the liquor filling his body appeared to impair his balance.

I took another drink from my glass to hide my smile though Seraphine caught sight of it and gave me a wink.

"What do you want?" Tarsa asked impatiently.

Karter righted himself and squinted at Tarsa as if just noticing her. "Jus' came to make acquaintances with Miss Sera here." His voice began to slur as he leaned heavily on the table.

"She's not interested," Tarsa said slowly, enunciating each word. Beside her Seraphine continued to smile at the man with false interest.

"I am actually already spoken for," Seraphine admitted with a shrug, a guilty smile teasing her mouth.

The man glanced around at the empty seats of our table before turning back to her. "I don't see him here."

My stomach knotted as more men at the bar began to turn and watch as he leaned closer in Seraphine's direction. Though Tarsa said this town was relatively empty of my wanted posters, that didn't mean someone here hadn't already seen my face posted somewhere else. It only took one person recognizing me to force us to keep running.

"It wouldn't be a man that you would be looking for actually." Her voice was more clipped now.

Karter straightened immediately as his eyes darted between Tarsa and Seraphine. I could almost see the moment he made the connection. I had to swallow back my laughter as he nodded feverishly.

"Pardon, miss," he said with a bow. "Can't blame a man for trying."

He cast a glance in my direction then. His gaze sobered as he studied my face with suddenly clear eyes. The force of his attention as his eyes tracked over me sent the marks at my wrists and ankles burning in remembrance. I hastily tugged at my sleeves, careful to keep the bandages covered from view as he watched me. A crooked smile lit up his face as he nodded to me before turning to rejoin his friends at the bar.

"Why'd you have to ruin the fun?" Seraphine asked.

Tarsa rolled her eyes and took a drink from her water as her eyes continued to scan the room around us. "And what exactly was I supposed to tell my sister when we return to her? That I watched by idly as you flirted with a drunk stranger in a pub?"

Seraphine sighed. "It was harmless fun."

I chuckled under my breath as the barmaid returned with our large meal. Bowls of soup and stew and plates of steaming meat settled on the table between us making my mouth water at the inviting smells.

My throat burned as I swallowed spoonfuls of the stew but I ignored the pain. My stomach ached with hunger from our long travels.

"Careful, Esme," Seraphine teased as she slowly ate her stew with a grace I could never possess. "You'll burn yourself."

I shrugged, not caring. "Already did. But it's so good."

She smiled. "We're not feeding you enough, are we?"

"You're doing fine," I said before shoveling more stew into my waiting mouth.

"We're not used to having a mortal with us this long," she admitted quietly.

When I looked up, I noticed her staring at her bowl with something akin to shame in her eyes. And Tarsa was gone again; I hadn't even heard her leave.

"What do you mean?"

She sighed. "Well, it's different for us. A single meal can sustain us for far longer than it can for a mortal whose body changes and grows at a much faster pace. Our bodies are frozen in time the moment our mortality ends."

"Really?" I asked, shocked. "You don't need to eat every day?"

She shrugged. "We do eat every day, sure, but mostly our bodies just need that constant sustenance to keep us healthy and strong. Our bodies heal quickly and are much stronger than a mortal's so we just require different things than a mortal might."

I considered this as we ate in silence. I could feel glances in our direction though I refused to look up to see who studied us now. Someone as obviously beautiful as Seraphine was surely going to draw a lot of attention.

"Is that why Aiden hardly sleeps?" I asked finally. I'd wondered if immortals didn't require some of the basic mortal needs. But I never truly thought of what might be different for them until I watched Aiden sit by each night and hardly rest.

Seraphine stilled for a moment before setting her spoon down to study me. "He's not sleeping?"

I shook my head. "Not that I've noticed." She leaned back in her chair as her gaze turned far away, thoughtful. "Is that bad? It might be my fault. He usually talks to me while I fall asleep but he's always awake before me too."

Her face softened as she studied me. "I didn't realize you were having trouble sleeping either."

My spine straightened as I shoveled more food into my mouth. "I'm not," I said quickly.

"He really doesn't intend to trick you," she said carefully. "I know you doubt him, doubt all of us. I've seen it in your eyes every time we reach a town where your family was expected to be, but he truly does intend to return you to them."

I fought the urge to roll my eyes. "Only because he gets something out of it, doesn't he?" I asked a little harshly.

"What makes you think that?"

"Because," I said, defensive now, "he works for the god of Death. You all do. If what I do only strengthens him, and therein all of you as well, then of course you'd want to return me to my family if that were your only way to get me to steal souls."

As she opened her mouth to respond, the dark essence in my chest fluttered excitedly making my breath catch in my throat.

A wall of warmth and scented of cedar and mint appeared behind me. I kept my eyes downcast as I noted Killian and Hakan finding seats across the table, leaving the one at my side for Aiden.

I stuffed my mouth with more stew as he took his place at the table, each of the males greeting us warmly. Seraphine seemed to find something in my face amusing though she luckily didn't press the issue as she turned to greet them.

"I see you ladies got started without us," Killian teased as he pulled a plate full of warm rolls his way.

Seraphine chuckled. "If you boys didn't take so long to bathe then perhaps we wouldn't have needed to start without you."

"Don't blame us," Hakan said with a pointed look in Aiden's direction. "We would've been here sooner had the little prince over there not taken so long in his rooms."

"Prince?" I asked, nervous that their winged prince returned for me again. Aiden shot Hakan a look from behind the mug he held against his lips, but the others fell silent for a beat.

"It's a nickname," Killian joked.

"Only because he tends to act like a pompous prick on occasion," Hakan added quickly.

"Pompous prick?" Aiden asked in a deathly quiet voice. There was a slight upturn to his mouth, but his eyes remained guarded.

Hakan shrugged as Seraphine spoke. "He said *on occasion*. Not all the time."

Killian glanced at me from across the table then. "Being a prick comes in handy when we've got the Soul Collector under our protection anyway."

I stiffened. I hated that title. Nothing good could come from it. Especially not since I was still expected to steal souls away from innocents and damn them to Hell just to fulfill a debt I knew nothing about.

Aiden shot Killian a look that sent the young warrior apologizing and quickly returning to his meal.

As my stomach filled with rich, warm foods I felt my exhaustion growing. I could hardly bare to listen to their conversations, not even noticing when Tarsa finally returned. I leaned back in my chair and wrapped my arms around myself as my head grew heavy. It had been a long time since I felt this tired or my mind stayed this quiet.

"Do you need to return to the room?" Aiden asked quietly. I'd forgotten he'd become so accustomed to tracking my every subtle movement.

I shook my head and stood ungracefully. His hand shot out to steady me at my elbow. I stepped away as the warmth of his skin against mine sent a strange sensation through me and settled comfortably with the movement in my chest.

"I just need a moment. I'll be back," I said as I hurried to the bathing room down the hall hidden behind the bar. My cheeks blazed as I felt his eyes tracking my fleeting form.

"Are you okay?" Seraphine asked as she caught up to me easily, stepping into my path and forcing me to stop.

"Sure," I said casually. "Just tired I think."

"Are you feeling feverish?" My cheeks warmed further as her gaze narrowed on my flushed skin.

I shook my head. "I'm fine."

Her gaze flicked back to Aiden over my shoulder before returning to me. I knew he still watched us; I could feel his gaze on my back. What I didn't expect was that look in her eye as she returned her gaze to me.

"I'll be back. I promise I'm fine," I said hurriedly as I ducked into the bathing room and out of view.

As soon as the door closed behind me, I bent over the faucet to splash cool water on my face. What was happening? I spent a week's worth of nights with a stranger I hardly knew and suddenly his very touch made me blush? Cordelia would scold me for behaving this way.

The thought of my younger sister made my heart ache, quickly replacing the strange flush I felt at Aiden's touch. I'd seen Aiden with my family after every performance for years. I'd always thought him handsome, but now that I was forced to be near him at all hours of the day it felt different somehow, weighted.

When I was certain the color of my cheeks had returned to normal, I stepped back into the darkened hall. Seraphine was nowhere in sight. The large crowd in the main part of the pub still echoed loudly so I guessed she went to rejoin the others. Though knowing how closely Aiden kept me under his watch, I was surprised he didn't make her wait outside the door for me.

I made it one step before an arm wrapped around my waist, pulling me back against a warm chest. Another hand clamped down on my mouth as I prepared to scream.

"Do not make a sound, Esme Loutari," the familiar raspy voice said into my ear. My throat burned from my muffled scream as I was pulled through the back door of the pub and into the night.

THIRTEEN

As the sounds of the pub faded with the slam of the door, my heart beat frantically against my ribs as panic stole the last of my breath and the hand clamped over my mouth tightened.

As soon as the latch on the door sounded with a final click, the hands holding me slackened their grip, dropping me into the dirt. The wind left my lungs as I lay gasping for air. The sun had set long ago, leaving us cast in darkness, the only light a faint glow of candles from the kitchen window overhead.

"This the girl?" a man asked nearby.

The man standing above me grunted in response. I scanned the clearing and noted five men watching me from the shadows, all staring at me with greed lighting their eyes.

The nerves wracking my body caused my knees to grow weak, but I clambered to my feet clumsily. I opened my mouth, preparing for a scream, only to have the strange man tie a piece of fabric over my mouth. I struggled in his grasp but it was no use. He was easily twice my size, and I knew nothing of combat.

"Now, now, sweetheart," he mocked. "We won't go having you draw your friends out here, now will we?"

I choked on a sob as he tightened the gag, effectively silencing my protests. Tears blurred my vision as I struggled harder in his grasp, but he held firm. My blood pounded loudly in my ears like a war drum as I frantically searched the surrounding darkness for an escape. Maybe I could outrun them and find my way back to Aiden and the others.

A man came into view, blocking what would have been my only chance at an escape route. I froze as soon as I recognized him. Karter. Bastard.

"I thought you looked familiar," he said, voice clear and sober though his clothes still reeked of liquor. He held up a crumpled paper. My face was painted across it with the bounty listed below my name at the bottom. My heart stuttered nervously in response.

"Think of what we can get with money like that, boys." He turned his head slightly to direct his words toward his friends, but his eyes remained on me. I looked into his eyes—his very clear and sober eyes.

I winced as another man grabbed my arm roughly. There was little I could do as I was dragged from the small clearing and into an alley a few streets away where a small carriage waited. This far from the pub it was quiet, dark with abandon.

Karter watched with a smile as his friend tossed me to the ground, the cobblestones cutting into my knees as I collapsed.

"When we return you to the king we'll be richly rewarded." The man that spoke was plump, nearly as round as he was tall, with a beard that hung to his belt. I took a tentative step back, deeper into the dark alley as the men slowly crept closer. My breath grew shallow as I studied the ropes they carried as they tried herding me toward the waiting carriage.

The man who dragged me to the alley gripped my hair tightly and yanked my head back, forcing me to look up at his face. He would've been handsome had he not been covered in grime and what smelled like a recent visit to a brothel. The strangeness in my chest twisted painfully, urging me to seek his soul in a way I hadn't felt since the king's men took me all those months ago.

"I wonder what a simple girl like you did to earn such a large bounty on your head," he mused. His finger trailed down my cheek, cutting through the tracks made by my tears.

"Who cares," one called from the end of the alley. He cast a nervous glance in the direction of the pub before turning back to glare at me.

"Let's just be glad the bounty says nothing about returning her unused," Karter mocked as he scratched a hand at his chin.

Fear overwhelmed my lungs, making it harder to breathe through the fabric tied across my mouth. Even the strange thing in my chest seemed to shudder at the hungry look in his eye.

Before I could devise a way out of this situation, he lunged. His grip on my shirt was strong enough to tear it right down the middle as a shrill scream erupted from my mouth, the fabric tied there dimming the sound. I struggled away from his grasp though the others laughed as they moved to block my exit. The *only* exit I realized with horror.

I silently begged – pleaded – for them to let me go, words failing me through the gag at my mouth. As the man reached for me again, I kicked him hard in the groin, letting a sliver of pride fill my chest as he crumpled to the ground.

Karter laughed cruelly, his chipped tooth glinting in the faint light. "I love it when they try to fake pureness."

Bile rose in my throat at his intentions. I had to get out of here. I didn't want to think about what they would do if I stayed, but I knew I wasn't skilled enough to fight my way out of their clutches.

I turned then and ran right into a wall of hard muscle. I stumbled back, but warm hands gently wrapped around my waist to steady me.

As the darkness in my chest finally settled, I nearly collapsed with relief.

Aiden scanned my face momentarily before turning to the men who stood around us. His mouth was set in a hard line, chiseled jaw tight with the anger he barely kept restrained, yet filled every hard edge of his body. The ruthless light in his eye only a hint at the danger he possessed. We'd be lucky if he left the world standing once he unleashed the anger stirring in him.

With a promise of death on his face, Aiden gently shifted so he stood between me and the men. My hands gripped tightly to the end of his shirt as I hovered in his shadow.

The shadows cast over the alleyway began to move. Subtly at first so no one else seemed to notice, but as they began to take shape I knew what they were. Twin axes gleamed in the faint light and a flicker of fiery red hair slipped from the shadows. Each one took their place behind the men hoping to take me for their chance at the bounty.

"Who the hell are you?" Karter asked as he glowered in Aiden's direction. They had yet to notice the others nearby, weapons at the ready.

Aiden offered a cold smile. "She is not yours to take."

Karter bristled at his tone. "We got her first. The bounty is ours, mate." His friends echoed their agreement.

I felt Aiden shift slightly, his muscles preparing for battle though his posture appeared casual. My heart continued to race in my chest though the familiar essence tucked beside it smothered it as if trying to calm me.

"She is not yours to take," Aiden repeated with little patience. I felt his hand wrap around my own, gently prying it from his shirt. His hand squeezed mine once in silent comfort before releasing me, taking the heat that had begun to grow beneath his touch with it.

"Don't be an idiot," one of the men snapped impatiently.

"She's just a wanderer whore," the plump man said. His eyes slid down to my toes and back to my face in a revolting promise.

I shuddered. A low growl sounded deep in Aiden's chest, rumbling against my side.

"What could you possibly want with a girl like her other than getting under her skirt? She can't be good for anything else," Karter said with a cold laugh.

Aiden snarled, loud enough to echo through the cobblestoned alley and rattle the darkness slowly filtering through my limbs. In answer, his friends shifted, moving closer now.

The men began to take notice of Aiden's comrades, but Karter didn't take his eyes off of me. He either didn't notice or didn't care that he was surrounded by deadly warriors poised for a fight. His gaze promised filthy threats as he blew a kiss in my direction.

Aiden couldn't seem to stop himself then. He was a force to be reckoned with as he lunged for Karter. The sound of the man's skull cracking against Aiden's knuckles sent my stomach churning but the dark essence inside me seemed to sing in response.

Everyone moved at once. While some raced toward the exit in the alley, others began to turn in my direction, the promise of a kingly reward enough to bring logic to its knees.

Tarsa threw her axes with precision, both finding homes in the bodies of men racing for safety. Killian and Hakan sliced through opponents, leaving Seraphine to battle another. Aiden shook with fury as he pummeled Karter, who had surely expired after the first blow.

A new set of hands gripped onto me in tight binds, nearly pulling my feet out from under me as I was dragged from the alley. I kicked and hit him as hard as I could but he seemed entirely unperturbed. Tears blurred my vision as my heart raced in panic, contradicting the calming pulse of the essence in my chest as it reached for every greedy man left alive in the alley.

"Stop it," someone growled into my ear as he dragged me further away from my protectors.

Aiden turned then, his eyes finding mine instantly. Pure rage lived in his face as he stood over Karter's body. The man holding me kept me pressed against his chest, like a shield between him and the immortal.

I saw the knowledge of this register in Aiden's eyes as he continued in my direction. The man holding me took a breath, whether to beg or bark a retort I couldn't be sure, but I moved before he could have the chance. I swung my elbow back as hard as I could and jumped away as he bent over in a gasp. Aiden moved then and ran him through the heart with his dagger.

My breath came in pants as I stood there and stared at the bloody destruction painting the alley. Aiden left no witnesses behind.

Aiden took my face gently in his hands as he cut the fabric away with a small knife.

When he dropped it to the ground, I covered my mouth with shaking hands, begging the sobs to wait until I could be alone to release them. My eyes found Aiden's. He watched me with an expression I couldn't read, as he took in every spatter of blood along my skin, every cut, every mark that would surely result in a bruise. With each wound his mouth grew tighter. This man, the one who took me from the king and killed to keep me from being kidnapped again, studied me with concern.

I started laughing. Hysterics beyond control rolled through my body as I clamped my hands tighter over my mouth, my eyes studying the bloody scene before me.

Aiden's brow furrowed as he watched me laugh uncontrollably. I'd been kidnapped twice now in the span of four months, and nearly again today. When would this end?

My laugher sent me buckling over my knees as I struggled for breath. The absurdity and tragedy of everything I lived through these past weeks felt unreal.

"Perhaps she hit her head?" Seraphine suggested as she too watched me from across the alley.

Killian snorted, sending my laughter into another round of hysterics. "She's always been weird."

"We shouldn't stay here," Hakan said, ignoring my outburst. "There could be others."

Tarsa spoke then, stepping into the light with both axes dripping blood at her sides. "Get her to take their souls," she said coldly. "If she can walk and laugh, surely she can still do her duty and collect the needed souls while we return her to her family."

My laughter stopped abruptly. The thing in my chest did pull me toward the bodies lying in puddles of blood. I could feel their souls now, shifting through the air like they didn't know where to go. But I couldn't bring myself to unleash what lived in my chest.

I looked to Aiden as he watched me with guarded curiosity. His dark hair clung to his neck with sweat and blood though he didn't seem to notice. My body grew heavy with sadness as I felt the last of the souls leave this realm. I wouldn't steal another soul until I saw my family. Maybe not even then.

Without a word, Aiden bent to pick me up, cradling me against his chest. I didn't even bother to protest as he carried me out of the alley.

"Get this mess cleaned up," he ordered the others.

I didn't look to see if they obeyed. Instead, I buried my face in his bloody shirt, hoping this had all been a terrible nightmare and I would wake in the morning with my family.

Only when we returned to the safety of the room we would once again share did he finally place me on my own feet. My eyes had grown heavy, but I refused to sleep now, not until the blood was washed away.

"Are you hurt?" Aiden asked as he set his weapons on the bed. I wanted to tell him that the blood would soak the blankets, but I couldn't find it in myself. Instead, I offered a weak shake of my head.

I remained still as his hands gently searched for injuries. They were careful, tender along my body as he studied me. I tried not to lean into his touch as he cradled my head in his hands, searching among the bruises on my face.

My skin heated with his touch as he grazed his fingers over my cheeks, wiping away the blood and tears that remained there, and moved to my neck. The calloused tips of his left hand halted suddenly.

His eyes narrowed at something there, but I knew what he saw. Aiden reached for a rag draped over the back of the chair. I kept silent as he washed away the blood and grime until only my jagged scar remained.

Aiden stilled, his eyes growing wide for the briefest moment as he recognized the scar that could've killed me a year ago if it weren't for him fighting off the pale-haired demon. My fascination with him had only grown stronger after that night and I suspect it had led to the demise of my relationship with Kesson.

My heart ached at that memory. I wondered silently what happened to Zaven's little body and Kesson's ashes. Probably gone on the wind or buried in a shallow, unmarked grave.

Tears blurred my vision again as the roughness of his skin gently brushed over my scar. Seeming to catch himself, he blinked, and his disinterested mask returned.

His hands moved further down my body, probing my arms and back for wounds. I didn't feel any pain until he poked rather harshly at my ribs.

Aiden noticed my wince. I didn't stop him as he reached for the hem of my torn shirt and pulled it up. He could have just opened the large tear down the front, but as I held it wrapped tightly around myself, I knew he wouldn't leave me that exposed. And I silently thanked him for it.

I gasped and leaned away from his touch as he prodded my ribs again. "Ouch," I ground out between gritted teeth.

His mouth twitched with a slight smile. "I was wondering when you were going to snap at me." The muscles in his cheeks tightened once again as he studied my ribs. "There's nothing broken, but it was close. You'll be sore and bruised for a while."

I sighed. "Why would he want me back?" Giving voice to the question that had haunted my thoughts since we crossed the Ruelle River last week made the answer feel more distant somehow.

Aiden shrugged. "He could have many reasons for wanting you back."

"But he kept me alone," I said, voice tightening with emotion. "I was locked in a room alone for four months. He didn't even bother to protest all that much when you came for me, so why would he decide to get me back now?"

Aiden considered this as he lowered my shirt and stepped out of reach. I watched as he ran a hand through his hair, eyes lowered to the scar at my neck.

"Whatever reasons he may have for ordering your return, I suggest you don't give anyone an opportunity for you to find out."

I rolled my eyes. "I was just using the bathing room."

"Then I suggest you don't do so alone."

"That is not a solution," I retorted. "Do you think this has anything to do with me being your god's soul collector?"

Aiden sighed, bending to pick up his weapons. "Again," he said slowly, "I think this is a conversation that would be—"

"I swear to the stars," I snapped, quick to anger. "If you tell me that this is a conversation I need to have with my family one more time I am going to stab you with one of your stupid daggers."

The twitch of his lips made me want to smack him. He clearly didn't find me intimidating as I stood trembling before him.

"Why won't you just tell me the truth?" I begged, voice tightening again.

I watched as he ran a hand over his face, frustration practically coming off of him in waves. My hands turned to fists at my side as I glared at him, only the slight sagging of his shoulders giving me reason to hold my tongue.

"Get cleaned up," he said at last. "Your family is in the next village over. I'm returning you to them tomorrow. I suggest you try not to look like you visited a slaughter house recently."

Tears filled my eyes then and I didn't care that they spilled over and burned the bruised skin at my cheeks.

"They're really there?" I asked in a whisper.

The taut skin around his eyes softened ever so slightly as he looked down at me. "They are," he said with equal quiet.

My family, they were close. Finally, I could see them again.

Without a word, I retreated to the bathing chamber, refusing to admit that I wanted to hide my tears from Aiden as I stripped out of my torn clothes and stepped into the tub. I let the warm water fill the tub around me, chasing away the last of my worry and settling into a hopeful joy. Joy for seeing my family again after so many months apart, but also a timid joy at whatever change was budding between Aiden and me.

FOURTEEN

I HARDLY SLEPT THAT night. My heart refused to settle after learning I'd see my family in just a few hours. Aiden was still dozing against the side of the bed by the time I had my boots laced up my calf, ready to go.

We traveled the entire day, nerves and excitement battling for dominance keeping my heart at an inconsistent stutter. The wounds at my ankles and feet were still healing but I didn't let that slow my pace. Seraphine constantly shoved food into my hands, forcing me to eat and stay hydrated, but even the thought of stopping seemed unbearable as my family waited so close.

Now, as the sun had long since set beyond the horizon, the faint sounds of the campground could be heard in the distance. Laughter and cheers echoed along the empty dirt road, accompanied by a steady flow of music as the many families offering entertainment continued their performances.

My heart threatened to stop altogether as we reached the hilltop and finally caught sight of the campground. People all around us were moving excitedly, going from caravan to caravan, tent to tent, paying the families there whatever coin they could afford for vague answers about an unknown future. Some choosing instead to purchase a piece of jewelry or some memorabilia from one of the families filling the grounds.

"Are you sure they're here?" I heard Hakan whisper to Aiden a few steps behind me. The others had taken to letting me lead our group as I refused to slow my pace in my excitement. Even the steady throb of pain with each step couldn't deter my motivation.

Aiden spoke with equal softness. "I hope so."

My chest tightened slightly at the hint of doubt in his voice. I'd held the hope of seeing my family here again today too close to my heart. If we reached yet another village where my family was obviously not present, I couldn't be sure that was a heartache I could hide any longer.

"Do you see their caravan?" Seraphine asked gently. Her hand came to rest on my shoulder where she offered a reassuring squeeze.

I shook my head as I studied the caravans before me. Dozens of them led by large horses and mules were parked throughout the space. Colors ranging from blue painted with silver flames, yellow lined with braided greens, and simple stripes of red and black covered each of the nearest caravans. Tents remained pitched and scattered as well, some lit with a fire inside to illuminate the offerings of entertainment or riveting talent of the performer they concealed. The familiar sights and sounds were enough to make my vision blur with tears, but no matter where I looked, I couldn't see my family's familiar colors of red and purple flecked with gold stars.

"Tarsa." Aiden's voice came out as a command, and I knew he was sending her to search the grounds. The slender, lethal woman disappeared without a word.

I dared a few more steps toward the campground, rubbing my sweaty palms against the sides of my pants, hoping to wipe away my nerves. The scent of the food, the sounds of the music and cheers, all engulfed my senses as I forced a deep breath into my lungs.

"They could still be here," Aiden said gently, shifting closer so his presence provided an offer of comfort. His sudden closeness sent my pulse racing in time with the flutter of darkness in my chest.

I offered a weak nod. "They have to be."

Slowly, I walked toward the crowded campground. Children ran about at top speed, laughing and chasing each other with colorful beads and patterned fabric to match that of the family they purchased it from. I dodged out of the way as two children tossed wooden practice knives painted in a bright gold as they raced by. Tarsa and Hakan disappeared into the throng of people while Seraphine and

Killian remained close to Aiden's side as they watched me weave through the crowd.

I ducked and leapt out of the way as knives were tossed in the air, archers wooed the crowd with death defying tricks, and dancers paraded through the maze of tents, bringing the crowd along with them.

Colors blurred together as I blinked away tears and pushed on. I had no way of knowing how close Aiden remained to my side as I quickly became surrounded by the drunken revelry. A pulling in my chest kept my feet under me as I rushed past caravan after caravan in a desperate search for my family. The pain in my feet became a dull ache compared to the thrumming in my chest and the loud strum of instruments which overwhelmed my senses as I slowly lost hope. For everywhere I looked, I couldn't find my family's caravan.

A familiar voice shouted over the crowd; a deep tenor that threatened to buckle my knees and cause my weak body to crumple in relief. The music seemed to fade now, taking the sounds of the crowd with it. All I could hear, all I could seem to focus on, was the sound of my father's voice. Leander Ayres shouted over the crowd as he began his performance with my mother on the far side of the grounds.

Tears streamed down my face in earnest as I forced my way through the crowd. My heart raced so fast it shook my ribs, forcing my breath to come in shallow gasps. All that mattered was getting to my family. They were here. My family was here.

"Father!" I yelled over the noise. It swallowed me whole as I tried to follow his voice. I could hear the ooh's and aah's of his audience as they grew enraptured with my parents' performance.

I ran past caravans and tents so fast the colors became a blur before finally coming into view of my family's corner of the campground. The familiar gold stars sewn into the purple and red fabrics of my family's caravan seemed to glisten in the faint firelight: a beacon home.

My knees nearly gave out as I looked to the makeshift stage built nearby. A woman with obsidian curls stood at one end while a slender man with tawny hair and a knife in each hand stood with his back to me. I clamped a hand over my mouth as a choked sob escaped my throat. Tears blurred my vision with a new force as I stood there, not really believing what I was seeing, for the people on the stage, so close to where I stood now, were my parents.

I took off again, unapologetically shoving people out of my path. Tears burned down my cheeks with an overwhelming sense of relief as I raced through the crowd.

"Father!" I yelled over the noise. Some turned to look at me in confusion or concern, but many hadn't noticed me yet as they remained focused on my parents' performance.

"Mother!" I called louder now. Pain shot up my ankle as the freshly healed skin there split open beneath my bandages. I shoved the pain deep down, ignoring it until I could bury myself in my parent's embrace.

"I'm here!" My voice cracked with tears as I screamed over the momentary silence of the crowd.

My father's hand paused midair as he prepared to throw another knife at the apple settled atop my mother's head. He turned, large hazel eyes searching the crowd with a frantic need.

I waved my hands over my head hysterically, still racing toward their stage. "I'm here," I called again, voice breaking.

My mother paled at the sight of me. Her face, so similar to my own, seemed to have lost its usual glow as her skin appeared ashen from our months apart. My heart ached to hug her again.

"I'm here," I croaked quieter now, pace slowing with the strength of my erratic emotions. Tears robbed me of my voice as the crowd finally parted slightly to allow me a path to the stage.

"Esme?" My father's voice broke on my name as he staggered back a step, not really believing what his eyes were trying to tell him.

He moved with the speed of one of his deadly knives, racing to me with the same unbelieving look on his face that I could feel on mine. My mother followed closely behind him, the crowd keeping back as we closed in on each other, arms outstretched, each of our faces shining with tears.

The wind rushed from my lungs as I barreled into my father. A harsh sob broke free from my throat as his arms wrapped around me in steel binds, and in that moment I'd never felt safer. The familiar smell of the cleaning oils he used on his knives mixed with the scent that was just him, made my body shake with more sobs as I clutched the front of his shirt, refusing to let go. I felt his chest tremble in silent sobs as he held me like he still couldn't believe I was there.

"Esme?" My mother's soft voice sounded oddly loud over the deafening silence of the watchful crowd. I opened my eyes enough to see her stepping closer, her pace slow and eyes wide as she stared at me in wonder and relief.

My father shifted to pull her close, wrapping the two of us tightly in his grasp. As her arms wrapped around me, I felt all control leave my body. My knees buckled, my voice cracked with uncontrollable sobs, and my heart slowly patched itself together as I held my parents close.

The crowd around us cheered excitedly, unsure of the events unfolding before them but enraptured by the emotions nonetheless. Tears flowed unceremoniously down my cheeks as my father tightened his hold around me and pressed a warm kiss to the top of my head. Beside me, mother continued to sob into my shoulder, arms shaking with the force of her emotions as she held me close.

"Esme?" Mousa. My older brother's voice sounded uncertain as he came to stand beside our huddled forms. I saw him standing a few feet away, staring at us with wide, tear-filled eyes.

Without a word, my father opened his arm again and pulled Mousa in. His body pressed against my side as he too wrapped his arms around our mother and me.

"You're back?" His voice trembled when he spoke. His hands shook as they tightened around me.

I tried to speak but my throat remained closed with tears. My hands gripped tightly onto the back of his shirt in answer.

The crowd continued to cheer around us, their sound overwhelming compared to the distant music from nearby performances. Yet somehow, I still knew when Aiden grew near. He made no sound as he moved closer, but I could feel the pull toward him as he came to stand behind us.

"You," my father snapped as he caught sight of Aiden. "What did you do with her?"

"Leander," my mother spoke in calm warning, casting her eyes over the watchful crowd. "Not here."

Father seemed to catch himself, though his eyes remained filled with distrustful anger at the immortal before him. He gave my mother a stiff nod in answer.

"Mousa," my mother said calmly, "why don't you take the stage early for us?"

My brother's arms tightened again before he pulled back. I stared up at him as he pulled away, blinking viciously through the tears that wouldn't stop. He stood taller than when I'd last seen him, posture rigid and formal as opposed to the open warmth he used to portray. His light golden skin, so much like our fathers, glistened in the late summer heat as he studied my face. He was always too good at reading what I tried to keep hidden from others. I was almost certain he could see the level of shame I tried to keep hidden from our parents now as I pulled my sleeves farther down my wrists to hide the bandages. I gave him a reassuring smile, hoping he wouldn't look too closely.

When he turned back to the crowd with a warm smile, I felt my mother's arm wrap around my shoulder and gently pull me away from the stage. I wanted to give in to the sense of comfort she provided, but I couldn't allow myself that luxury yet.

As the crowd quickly became enraptured with my brother's appearance, my mother led me into the nearby caravan, Father and Aiden on our heels. My limbs remained numb with residual pain as I settled on the familiar, worn cot, mother at my side. A sense of rightness filled me as I breathed in the familiar floral smells that filtered through the caravan. One of Alfie's notebooks sat on the small table near a dark crystal ball – or soul siphon as Aiden claimed they were called – and a single candle lit the space, casting us all in long shadows.

Across from the small space, my father sat glaring at Aiden who watched me intimately. My heart dropped slightly when I tried to catch his eye only for him to drop his gaze, his usual cold mask firmly in place.

My mother wiped my tears, regaining my attention. "We've missed you," she whispered into the quiet.

I offered her a small smile. "I've missed you, too."

"Where have you been all this time?"

The memory of the castle caused more tears to burn my eyes, but I forced them away. "King Elroy took me. He held me in the castle," I said slowly. My father's shoulders grew rigid as I spoke, though his eyes never left the immortal. "He accused me of witchcraft and blamed me for the destruction of Cordovia."

"That's absurd," my mother said with a nervous glance at my father. "We're not witches."

I shook my head. "No, but he's rounding up all the wanderers he can find, and anyone accused of witchcraft, and he's having them burned."

My mother's hand grew cold in mine. Father looked away from Aiden and turned toward us. I watched as his eyes found my mother's, their silent conversation enough to confirm that they knew the truth of what I did.

"Why didn't you tell me what it is I really do here?" I asked in a choked whisper. Aiden's gaze crashed into mine. He tried to remain disinterested but his fists remained stiff in his lap, a weak effort to hide the sympathy in his blue-grey eyes.

"What do you mean, sweetheart?" my mother crooned as she leaned against me, her warmth enough to relax some of the nervous tension in my muscles.

"I think the more important question," my father began before I could answer, "is why do *you* have possession of my daughter?"

Aiden barely spared him more than a cool glance before his eyes flickered in my direction again. "I was ordered to remove her from the king's grasp and return her to you. It seems you have fallen behind on the debt your family owes, and we both know what the cost will be if it is not kept on schedule."

A chill whispered down my spine. There were still many questions I need-ed answered, but from the careful expressions my parents wore, I knew they weren't inclined to tell me.

"What's this?" my mother asked instead. Her hand brushed over the bandages hidden beneath my sleeves.

I tried to shake her away, but her grip tightened. "It's nothing," I tried to say, shame coloring my cheeks. Her hands quickly unwound the bandages, putting my bruised and marred flesh on display. The sight of the scars that would remain there until my death filled my parents' eyes with horror.

"What happened to you?" my father asked as he knelt before me, forgetting the immortal's presence altogether. His hands gently traced the marred skin. I cringed away from his touch as the memory of the chains filtered through my mind.

"I was a prisoner," I said as casually as I could manage. My voice sounded cold and distant even to my own ears. Aiden stilled significantly though I didn't look to him. "I wore manacles on my wrists whenever the king brought me before the court."

My mother clamped a hand over her mouth as fresh tears emerged. I silently vowed to hide the marks on my ankles for as long as I could if it kept that look of horror out of her eyes.

Father cursed as he settled back onto his stool. I watched as he ran a hand worriedly through his hair in his familiar nervous gesture.

"I'm okay," I said as my mother continued to stare at my wrists. "Aiden did a good job patching up my wounds."

She didn't seem to hear me, though my father cast an unbelieving glance in Aiden's direction. The warrior shifted slightly, his steely gaze uncertain of the praise I cast toward him. Instead, mother caught sight of the other bruises I carried. Her hands brushed lightly over my jaw where a faded yellow bruise still colored my skin. Had I not been so caught up in the excitement to return to them, I would've taken the time to cover my bruises with powders if only to keep my mother's hands from trembling as she cataloged every minor injury she could find.

"So, you just happen to disappear yourself as soon as my daughter is taken?" Father's voice dripped with disdain as he studied Aiden.

The warrior didn't even bristle as he returned my father's glower. The sharp lines of his face appeared harsher in the faded candlelight. His high cheekbones, stiff jaw, and full mouth cast shadows over his face in a tasteful way.

"The god of Death ordered me to retrieve her. I did so as soon as I was able to locate her and find a way into the castle," Aiden said with equal frankness.

At the mention of the demon, both of my parents stiffened. I fought the urge to roll my eyes as they cast each other nervous glances.

"I know about the debt we owe him," I said into the uneasy silence.

My father's eyes widened as he turned them on me. "You what?"

"I know," I said slowly. "Why didn't you tell me that's what I was doing?" My heart seemed to crack again as all the nights I was forced to spend alone in the caravan came back to my memory in full swing.

"Sweety," my mother started, but she was cut off by the sudden arrival of Nonna with Cordelia, Alfie, and Amara in tow.

My three younger siblings came to a sudden stop as soon as they caught sight of me. All four of them carried mixed expressions filled with disbelief and utter shock as they scanned me from head to toe.

"Hi," I offered weakly as they continued to stare.

Amara recovered first, jumping into my arms. Her sobs burned into the side of my neck as she clung to me. Alfie and Cordelia quickly joined.

"I missed you, Essie," Amara sobbed into my shoulder. The sound of my youngest sibling's silly nickname sent my heart into an uneven rhythm.

I hugged her tighter, pulling her into my lap. "I missed you, too."

"When did you get back?" Cordelia asked as she looped her arm through mine. At only fifteen, Cordelia somehow looked older than me with her painted lips and kohl-lined eyes.

I smiled weakly. "Aiden brought me back just now."

"Who's Aiden?" Alfie asked on my other side.

I nodded in Aiden's direction. The immortal's posture remained stiff as all eyes turned on him. I felt Amara still in my lap as she studied him, her gaze uncertain and cautious while Cordelia's cheeks heated as she studied the warrior. It amazed me how easily he managed to remain unseen in such a small space.

Alfie reached for his notebook, clutching it tightly in his hands as he studied the many weapons Aiden kept strapped across his back and at his belt. I smiled at the curiosity in his gaze as he fought to hold in his many questions.

"Come, children," Nonna said as she attempted to usher my siblings back out into the crowd. "Let's give your parents some time with Esme." She sent a troubled glance in Aiden's direction before turning her back on him altogether.

"Actually, Adine," my father said as he got to his feet, "I think you are best fit to answer the questions I'm sure Esme now has. I'll take the kids outside." He pressed a kiss to the top of my head before following my brother and sisters outside. My throat tightened as I watched my family disappear into the crowd.

"Mother," my mother started.

"No, Emira," Nonna said quickly. "She needs to know nothing of this."

Anger filled me then, a heated force that pushed me to my feet. "I already know, Nonna," I said before my mother could respond. "I know what it is you've had me doing to those people."

Her plump figure seemed to curve inward as she cast a brief glare in Aiden's direction. Her dark eyes and aged face appeared to accept my words, though the stubborn pout of her mouth, so much like my mother's, told me she really didn't want to have this conversation.

"If I'm damning people to Death's mercy," I began slowly, "if I'm stealing souls for him, I deserve to know why."

Aiden shifted, carefully placing himself between Nonna and me. "She's right," he said to her. "Esme has had endless questions these past several days that I cannot answer for her."

"Because you would spin her lies to suit your tricks," Nonna spat.

The immortal continued, unbothered, "Because it is not my place to tell her the truth of her fate. That is knowledge she deserved to have long before this night. It is time she learns the truth, Adine. If you continue to hide it from her any longer then it will be her downfall. Her soul will belong to Him for eternity, and with it, He can control every mortal soul in your realm."

His gaze returned to mine. Almost imperceptibly, his eyes softened, causing my heart to flutter in time with the darkness lingering near it. Without a word, he turned and disappeared into the night. I wanted to reach out and ask if he was leaving or when he'd return, but I held my tongue as I caught my mother glancing between the two of us, a certain light in her eyes I couldn't put a name to.

My cheeks heated but I turned my back on her to face Nonna.

"Please," I said quietly, "I want to know the truth."

She studied me for a moment. Her mouth pressed into a tight line as her eyes narrowed on the bruises my skin still displayed and the marks exposed at my wrists.

Finally, I could see the decision in her eyes.

"All right," she said definitively. "I think it's time you learned the curse of the Loutari bloodline."

FIFTEEN

Hours later I found myself surrounded by family. Uncle Malik and Aunt Kiva stayed at the campground to continue performing while Nonna dragged the rest of us a few miles away so she could tell us the secrets buried in our family's history.

Amara curled up in my lap, head cradled against my chest as she toyed with a strand of her dark hair. Dawn was a few short hours away and I could see the exhaustion weighing on her small frame as her eyes gradually drooped closed.

Cordelia and Alfie took up their spots on either side of me, eagerly waiting for Nonna's story to begin, while Mousa paced uneasily nearby. His eyes continued to shoot to the immortals who remained in the shadows, keeping watch. I could feel Aiden's gaze focused on me, but I shoved down the urge to look toward him and instead forced myself to focus on Nonna who slowly settled onto the caravan steps.

Mother and Father stood at her shoulders though their gazes rarely left me for more than a few moments a time. They seemed to need constant reassurance that I had finally returned.

Cordelia leaned closer. "He keeps watching you," she whispered into my hair.

My cheeks heated. "He's just making sure we're safe." My sister snorted in response, not believing my excuse.

Finally, Nonna took a steadying breath before straightening and asked, "What do you know of your ancestors?" Beside me, Alfie pulled out a charcoal stick and his notebook as he began scribbling words in a rush.

I shrugged. "Little. No one ever speaks of them."

She nodded slowly, eyes far away. "Many generations ago, the first Loutari performer set about joining the wanderer's way of living. He fell in love with the intensity and thrill of performing, especially those deadly tricks. Knife throwing was his preferred talent," she added with a sly smile. "He became so skilled that no matter where he traveled in Cordovia, hundreds gathered to watch him. He was flirtatious and dangerous; women loved him and men envied him.

"When he finally took a wife," she continued, "they would perform and travel together, thus marking the start of the Loutari caravan. Together, their paired performance and many captivating talents would draw in large crowds every night. They were far wealthier than we could hope to be at this time, but they enjoyed the atmosphere so much they swore the money didn't matter. They had everything they needed packed into their caravan."

She paused then, mouth thinning a little more as she took a steadying breath. Her graying hair remained tied back in its knot at the nape of her neck, but a few strands fell loose now, blowing around her face in the light breeze. I could feel the pull of magic that came with her storytelling. It was why so many lingered after my parents' performances, seeking out the old woman whose gift for storytelling was dazzling enough to enrapture an entire village and sway them to her will.

"One unfortunate night," she said quietly, "there was an accident during the performance. Word spread quickly of what had happened, but so did false rumors, and eventually everyone stopped coming to see your ancestors perform. Fear is a vicious thing. Some even tried to burn down their caravan one night when they settled to rest in a small village.

"It was around that time that they welcomed their first child," she continued. "Their money gone, performance faltering, they grew desperate. They traveled to the north, to the Wood of Rune, and begged the angels for help."

"Why the angels?" Cordelia asked as Nonna paused. I hadn't noticed how frail she'd become in my absence, but now it seemed to slap me in the face.

"Because they are pure of heart," she said, as if the answer were obvious. Nearby, I heard the grass crunch beneath a shift in weight as the immortals moved closer. "Your ancestor begged the Angel of Life for assistance. His wife had grown ill after childbirth and their infant was thin with their growing poverty. When no help came, he grew even more desperate."

"He went to the god of Death," I said into the silence that followed.

"He did," she answered. "They spent weeks traveling across the kingdom to the Angelwood Forest where they knew the demons could travel in and out of the hell realm."

Alfie looked up suddenly, notebook clutched tightly in his hands. "Why is it called the Angelwood Forest if it leads to the demons?"

Nonna offered a sly smile. "That is a trick of the demons: to lure those seeking to pray to the angels within their reach and then drag them to their realm for pain. Many have lost their lives on such a journey." Alfie began to scribble erratically in his notebook as she spoke.

Out of the corner of my eye, I could see Hakan studying Nonna through narrowed eyes. At his side, the rest of the immortals appeared bewildered by her tale as they listened. It was only Aiden who kept his usual mask in place.

"They camped there for days," Nonna continued, "and every night as the sun set, he would leave his dying wife and child to travel far into the forest where the white tree grew in deep darkness. He prayed and promised his life away for any help the demon could provide his family."

"The white tree?" Cordelia glanced to the immortals before turning back to Nonna. "What's the white tree?"

"It's a sacred tree for the dead," Seraphine answered calmly. "For centuries mortals and immortals alike would seek the comfort of the tree in life and in death. It is said to have once housed the souls of those who found utmost peace in the afterlife. Now, it is a beacon for prayer among immortals like us, whereas it has become a symbol of Death for mortals."

"It remains very sacred to us," Killian added. Cordelia's cheeks flushed under his gaze. "The tree in your realm is at the border to our own, so it is the holding place of many ceremonies for soul bindings, marriages, and where many deals are settled."

"Which is why he begged at the white tree for three weeks," Nonna continued with a scowl toward the immortals. My heart grew cold as I listened to the rasp of her words. "Only then did the god of Death send one of his messengers in his stead. This messenger nearly slit your ancestor's throat for daring to disturb the peace of the demon but he would not be deterred. He continued to beg and plead for help of any kind. He swore he'd pay anything the demon asked of him if it kept his family healthy and alive."

"Did it work?" Amara asked in a shaky voice. The strangeness inside me warmed my chest in answer.

Nonna offered a small nod. "The messenger returned at dusk the next evening and granted his newborn daughter with a gift from the god of Death. A gift that would be passed down to one daughter at a time.

"You see," she continued. "Death would never admit this, but the Angel of Life had been taking more souls for herself since the dark war ended and ravaged our lands. The god of Death's power waned with the minimal number of souls that traveled to his realm. Mortals were no longer tainted with darkness from war. We lived in peace and filled our lives with happiness and love. So, when we passed on to join the stars, we would go to the angels. Their power would grow with the abundance of our souls whereas the demon realm weakened with every soul that wasn't taken for their own."

My gaze slid to Aiden and his friends nearby. They all wore mixed expressions of disbelief or outright anger.

"So, what souls go to the god of Death?" Amara asked as she tightened her arms around her small frame in my lap.

"The wicked," Nonna said with a slow nod of her head. "Only those who are truly cruel in their mortal lives go to him, or those whose souls have been bound to him in some way." Mother and Father shared a look as she spoke, causing a shiver to whisper down my spine.

I swallowed. "So, he made their daughter the first Soul Collector?" I asked, refusing to acknowledge the truth of where my soul may end up if I couldn't repay this debt.

Nonna nodded. "He did. Now, only one can serve at a time. And once that Soul Collector truly understands the power living inside her the other moves on. It's why I'm still here." She offered a smile that didn't touch her eyes.

"You're a Soul Collector, too?" I asked.

"Of course," she said, matter-of-factly. "Why else do you think I've been hovering so close to you all these years?"

"But why?" Mousa asked as he continued to pace slowly around our small space. "Why, after all this time, do we still have to steal souls for him?"

Nonna's face turned sad as I watched her eyes glance toward the immortals nearby. "Because our family was tasked with acquiring a certain number of souls before our debt could be considered paid."

"How many do we still have to collect?" I asked, bewildered. "It's been generations since he begged Death for help. How many more could we possibly steal for him?"

"He never asked," she said sadly. "He was so excited to see his wife's drastic improvements with her health, and with their ability to return to performing, he didn't bother to ask some rather important questions."

A gentle breeze blew through my loose hair causing a chill to tickle my skin. Alfie leaned closer, nose still bent over his notebook as he hurried to write down every word spoken.

"He became a storyteller after that," Nonna continued. "He told the story of his meeting with the messenger and his promise. But he spun it like a tale, so when less fortunate fools stepped into their caravan to meet with his daughter for a brief telling at their fortune, they were completely unsuspecting as their souls were ripped from their mortal bodies."

I shivered. "So now it's up to me." My voice was laced with sadness as I dared look to Aiden, seeking a sense of comfort I knew I would find in his steely gaze.

"Yes," Nonna said gently. "We'd tried to continue without you, but it seems my power has grown far too weak in the years you've gained your strength."

"I know," I said quietly. "I've seen what happens to those whose souls you've tried to take."

Nonna started at that. "You have? When?"

"At the castle," I said, turning back to look at her directly. "The king would make me watch as his guards brought in those who travel like us and people accused of witchcraft. I had to watch as he burned them for crimes they didn't commit. Only the last time, the burning went wrong."

Memories of the first burning flashed through my mind. My lungs clenched, refusing to give me a full breath as tears burned the back of my eyes. Cordelia's arm tightened around my shoulders in comfort.

"The burning went wrong," I continued quietly. "These people showed up, with eyes so black they seemed to swallow the light, and they destroyed everything. Without thought."

The others fell silent as they stared at me in utter horror, eyes wide, jaws slack.

"Kesson was burned," I whispered, voice aching with the memory. Mousa froze as soon as the words left my mouth. I watched his face fill with the horror and pain I had felt at our friend's death. "I watched as Zaven ran forward and begged for him to be freed." He came to kneel beside me, face pale with anguish as he gripped my hand tightly in his. For if anyone would understand my pain at losing Kesson, it would be Mousa, his best friend.

"They killed them all," I whispered. "Zaven, Kesson, their cousins. The only one left now is their mother. I wonder if she knows," I wondered absentmindedly.

"I'm so sorry," Nonna whispered as she placed a hand over her heart, gazing toward the stars as if she could see his soul mingling with them. "I know you loved him."

"I did," I said, briefly catching sight of familiar blue-grey eyes. "Once, I did. Now it doesn't matter. They're gone. They're all gone."

Nonna nodded sadly. "I will send word to his mother."

"No," I said with a shake of my head. "I should tell her. I was there. It should be me."

Comfortable silence fell between us then. I could hear my uncle singing in the distance as the rest of our family traveled from the campground to join us where we planned to camp for the night.

"I know why Ephraim threatened to kill me last year," I said into the silence.

"You do?" Nonna asked with a stern expression in Aiden's direction. Beside her, my mother's face paled with the memory as her own hand came up to cup her neck.

"Yes," I said. "Aiden thought I had a right to know why my life was threatened last year, and I agreed with him."

"Of course you do," she muttered under her breath.

"Why didn't you tell me?" I asked, my chest still hurt with the knowledge they kept such a secret. Mousa turned to study our grandmother as well. Amara grew slack in my lap as sleep drew near, and Alfie continued to write at an astounding pace while Cordelia watched it all in silence.

"You were so young, so innocent," she said. "We hoped to wait until you were older before we told you the truth about what you can do."

"Do you think this is why the king wants me back?"

She started. "What do you mean?"

"There's a bounty for me," I answered simply as my entire family shifted closer. I pulled at the sleeves of my shirt, careful to make sure they covered the marks I carried. "Aiden's been keeping me safe, but there are posters with my face everywhere."

Mother sighed. "With the growing desperation of those affected by the king's overwhelming greed, I can imagine people all over the kingdom will keep looking for you," she agreed solemnly.

"What are we going to do?" Cordelia asked as she glanced toward the warriors who remained silent and stoic.

Nonna's gaze turned inward, thoughtful. My stomach dropped slightly as I saw the confusion in her face and realized she couldn't understand why the king would want me back either. I feared he'd learned the truth somehow.

I glanced around at my family. My uncle and cousins could still be heard in the distance, growing nearer, but it was silent as a graveyard where we sat. Each of my siblings had grown pale with nerves and my parents shared worried glances when they thought I wasn't looking. And in that moment, as I sat there surrounded by my family, that I realized I would do whatever I could to keep them safe. Even if that meant stealing souls for Death himself and damning my own in the process.

"We must keep Esme hidden," Nonna said suddenly, regaining my attention.

Aiden stepped forward. "There are posters of her face labeling her as a witch in every village we've passed through. Keeping her hidden while also doing her duty will be difficult on your own."

"What do you suggest?" my father asked, face weary with strain.

Seraphine and Killian stepped forward to flank Aiden. The other two kept their distance though their eyes seemed to slice the air between us. "We'll stay with you," Aiden said simply. "My friends and I will offer our protection from the greed of your king and any who may come searching for her."

"Who else would come looking for Esme?" Amara asked, startling awake at his words.

Seraphine moved closer to kneel beside us, offering my sister a kind smile. "Your sister has a great power within her. If she ends up in the wrong hands it could be very dangerous."

Alfie leaned toward her, eyes widening at the weapons she carried along her waist as he reached a tentative hand toward them. Seraphine caught his hand and gently placed it on his notebook. A sheepish grin lit up my brother's face as he began to draw a replica of it in his notebook.

"Esme's gift can be wielded against her," Aiden stated coolly, receiving a glower from Nonna. "If someone wished to capture her and bend her gift and power to their will, then there are endless outcomes that may befall your realm."

"Is there a way to end the curse without stealing souls?" Mousa asked suddenly.

Nonna shook her head. "Not that any of your ancestors could find."

"Why wasn't mother a Soul Collector too?" Cordelia asked, getting to her feet to stand beside our mother who remained on the caravan steps, face pale in the exposure of our family's hidden secrets. "If one daughter at a time was supposed to have this gift then why didn't it go to her before Esme?"

"As it is the god of Death's debt, only he can answer that," Nonna replied harshly, once again shooting a glare in the immortals' direction.

Amara moved from my lap only to be pulled into our father's arms. "So, Aiden has to stay with us now?"

Seraphine smiled, glancing to Aiden before responding. "We all will. We'll look out for all of you."

As my father carried Amara away toward a nearby tent, I heard her say, "Good. Esme always thought he was cute."

Cordelia choked on a laugh as she moved to follow our youngest sister, leaving me sitting alone with flaming cheeks. I dared to glance in Aiden's direction only to see his eyes remained downcast, a light dusting of color along his cheeks.

As our cousins joined us, the others slowly dispersed into their tents. Quiet laughter filled our group as Cordelia sat with Seraphine and Killian outside the tent she would share with Amara. I smiled as I caught sight of Alfie, notebook clutched tightly in his hands, as he stood a safe distance away from Tarsa and Hakan. I could see the curiosity battling for dominance over his uncertainty while he studied their many weapons, questions forming in his eyes.

"Esme, dear," Nonna said, regaining my attention. When I turned, she patted the spot beside her on the caravan steps. "Join me a moment."

I turned away from my family, letting the sounds of their voices fill me with quiet joy. How long had I prayed to the stars to return me to them and now I was here, surrounded by family old and new. Because I knew the immortals had somehow become a new sense of comfort and safety these weeks I'd traveled with them.

As I sat beside Nonna, I leaned into her warmth, amazed at how her bones seemed to protrude from her small form hidden beneath her colorful clothes.

Even within this warm embrace, I couldn't chase away the fear that had found its way into my life.

"Do you think they'll be safe?" I whispered as we watched our family settle down for the night.

Nonna sighed, her frail hand seeking mine. "This debt, it is a curse upon you and I. Your parents and siblings will do what they can to assist you, but it is something that only you can pay now. It is your duty to serve Death and protect your family."

Tears burned my throat as I looked upon those I loved. Amara, who only turned twelve a month ago, was so young to be put at risk. Or Alfie who would rather keep his nose in a book than carry a sword or perform with our family. The simple joy he could find in words was enough to carry his future far from the duties of our family. Mousa and Cordelia were different. Already, they were strong and brave and wicked with blades as they often trained together to take over our parents' performances. They could survive this if they needed to, but could I put such a burden on them if only to make it easier on myself?

"I wish things could be different," I whispered. I could feel Aiden's gaze like a brand along my skin though I didn't dare look to him now. "I don't want to be a Soul Collector anymore."

"I know, dear," Nonna said as she wrapped a frail arm over my shoulders. "If there were a way out of this, I would have found it for you."

Blinking away the tears I wouldn't dare shed in front of my family, I took a steadying breath. "There must be a way to end this," I mused quietly.

In answer Nonna leaned closer, squeezing my hand in hers in a silent offer of comfort. We sat there, watching our family laugh and mingle with Seraphine and Killian who each took to Alfie's endless questions with smiles. I could feel my parents' attention slide my way with nearly every breath and each time it reminded me of what I'd been returned to.

My gaze returned to the darkness around our small camp. I found Aiden there. As I remained trapped in his gaze, I felt the darkness inside me settle, almost calm under his watchful eye. I sat there, staring into the storm of emotions hidden behind his eyes, and I knew while he would spend his days keeping me safe, I would do whatever necessary to protect my family. Even if it put my own life at risk.

SIXTEEN

I SLEPT SOUNDLY THAT night, curled up between all four of my siblings on the floor of a cramped tent. Though my body begged for rest, I couldn't deny the urge to listen to everything my siblings and cousins wished to tell me of their lives these past few months.

My cheeks ached from smiling as I listened to Mousa flaunt his many flings with various girls over the summer. Or Amara blushing over the young girl she met a few weeks ago. My heart swelled with the way she talked about marrying that young girl one day.

Even Alfie, rambling on about his favorite storybooks, kept me awake and eager to listen though this topic of conversation would have once put me to sleep. I marveled at the way my little brother dreamed of owning his own bookstore. I knew he loved being a part of our performances, but the way his eyes lit up when he talked about some of his favorite books was a love I knew our parents wouldn't dare deny him.

Cordelia, on the other hand, had found her love in storytelling. Nonna taught her how to draw in a crowd with her voice each night while I was gone so Nonna could attempt to collect the needed souls in my absence. Now, she was hooked. There was even talk of Alfie recording her stories to put into his books someday.

Even as I sat in the warm caravan the next day lining my eyes with kohl, I could hear Alfie and Cordelia outside discussing which story she should tell tonight. We'd traveled to the next town over, barely half a day's ride away. Aiden and his warrior troupe joined us, of course.

"How are you feeling?" Seraphine asked from her perch on the stool. I caught sight of her reflection in the mirror and watched as she took in every detail of the caravan. Nonna sat nearby, eyeing her warily.

I shrugged. "I think I'm okay."

Seraphine shot me a look that told me she knew otherwise but refrained from saying so. I could hear Aiden sigh outside like he'd heard me and didn't believe me either.

Nonna narrowed her eyes in his direction as though she could see him through the fabric walls. "Must he remain so close to you at all hours? It's suspicious," she said, not bothering to keep her voice low.

"We're just here to keep Esme safe," Seraphine said gently.

"You immortal demons do not provide safety to anyone," Nonna spat rather harshly. She remained reluctant to allow the immortals so close though the rest of my family welcomed them warmly. "Demons are good for only cruelty and damage to one's soul. You wouldn't be here if there wasn't some way for Esme to benefit you."

"Nonna," I cautioned quietly. My mind whirled with the knowledge that I would return to collecting souls tonight. My stomach was twirling uncomfortably enough without their added conflict.

"I speak only truth, child," she said, turning to face me. Some strands of her long grey hair had come loose and now curled around her face. "You cannot trust them."

"They've kept me safe and alive to bring me back to you."

"Again, they must have a reason that you know nothing of that they could pretend to care in such a way."

"Is it so hard to believe that perhaps we actually like Esme?" Seraphine interjected calmly. Her spine straightened as she crossed her arms over her chest. Tonight, she left her battle armor behind to don simpler clothes—a cream tunic that brought out the rosiness of her cheeks and the freckles on her nose, and tan riding pants that hugged her plump curves. Though I knew her to be a formidable opponent in battle, she could pass for a young maiden out to enjoy the performances.

"Yes," Nonna said without question. I tried to keep the sting of her quick response off of my face as I finished lining my eyes with kohl. My lips, already painted in the bright red tones I wore these nights, turned down in a frown.

"Esme is kind and very brave," Seraphine said before Nonna could continue. She tossed a lock of her long, twisted braids over her shoulder so it hung down her back. "I think those attributes have earned her respect and kindness, no matter what you think of people like me."

"Esme is many things that deserve respect and kindness," Nonna said warmly. I tried not to shudder at the possessive hand she placed on my shoulder as I turned away from the mirror. "But no matter what may make her admirable, you could never deserve her trust."

Aiden began his fevered pacing again outside. I could feel his agitation at our conversation. This connection to him should've unsettled me more, but Nonna assured me last night the connection only existed because he was our contact for the siphons.

"Nonna," I said gently. "Whether you trust them or not, I have to. They've returned me to you, to Mother and Father. That is a kindness I cannot thank them enough for."

I watched as the tension around her eyes softened. The light of the candles brought a flush to her cheeks and reflected in her eyes. Her dark golden skin warmed with emotion as she cupped my face in her withered hands.

"You cannot know how happy we are to have you returned to us," she said softly.

I offered her a small smile and leaned into her gentle touch. My heart throbbed painfully as the sudden onslaught of emotions threatened to bring tears to my eyes.

"Come now," she said, stepping toward the door. "I will search for your first client while your siblings finish setting up for their performances."

She left without a backward glance, only offering Aiden a snort of disapproval as she passed by.

Seraphine huffed rather hotly. "She seems like a lot of work, but I think I like her."

I laughed. "Nonna has always been protective of her family."

She turned to me, face suddenly soft. "We do only mean to keep you safe, Esme," she said quietly. Outside, Aiden's pacing slowed noticeably.

I moved to sit on the stool beside her. "I know," I said, letting her take my hand in a reassuring squeeze. "She's tried to keep me in the dark for so long; I think we're all adjusting to the truth of our family's history." Nerves wrapped around my lungs in a steel bind as I stared toward the caravan door where Nonna would soon arrive with my first soul.

"You're afraid," Seraphine noted softly. Her hand squeezed mine comfortingly.

I dipped my chin to hide my face, dark curls falling forward. I felt torn. Torn between fulfilling this duty to protect my family or putting all my effort into finding a way to end the debt. I just couldn't be sure that I could find a solution before the god of Death sought me out to claim my soul. I shivered at the thought of being in his care for eternity.

Seraphine's expression turned gentle as she pulled me close, leaning her head against my shoulder. We sat silently for a moment, emotions keeping my voice distant as I pulled at the sleeves of my shirt. With thoughts swirling of the danger of the present, and the future remaining clouded in darkness, I found myself unable to even feel more than a moment's relief knowing I was surrounded by family again.

"Esme," Seraphine said slowly, sensing the direction of my thoughts, "the fact that you care this much tells me that you are a much better person than He could ever be." Her voice came out hushed yet warm and utterly confident in her words. Aiden's steps outside had completely stopped as he listened intently.

I sighed. "If you want to be completely technical, he's not even a person."

Seraphine laughed and the sound warmed my entire body, chasing away the lingering tendril of fear. "Demon or not," she said, "you could never be as wicked as He."

The strangeness in my chest stirred, signaling Aiden's presence. I could feel him now, shifting closer as he made his way to the caravan door. My heart picked up its pace as it beat against my ribs and my breathing stuttered. Beside me, Seraphine turned her face away as the hint of a smile turned up her mouth.

Aiden appeared in the doorway a moment later. His shoulder-length brown hair, appearing with a tint of red in the candle-light, framed his face handsomely as he looked between Seraphine and me.

"Adine will be arriving shortly with your first soul," he said by way of greeting. I refused to shy away from the indifference in his voice as he took up a position on the edge of the cot in the far corner of the small caravan. His dark clothes did little to help him blend into the bright fabrics hanging throughout the room. The warm, ethereal presence of the golds, reds and purples of the fabrics contrasted with the darkness that surrounded him.

"I'll check in with Killian," Seraphine muttered under her breath. "Make sure he's not getting distracted with your brother and his antics."

I smiled as she left. Mousa and Killian were becoming fast friends. Seeing the two of them bonding over their skills with knives or Mousa's talk of women warmed something deep inside me even if it annoyed Nonna to no end.

The creak of the cot forced my mind to the present. I wrung my hands together as my nerves steadily grew. His presence pressed down on me as we sat in uncomfortable silence. My cheeks began to burn as I stared at the door, fighting the urge to say anything just to break the deafening silence between us. After Amara's declaration of my secret attraction to him the air felt thicker between us now, near suffocating.

"Are you sure you're ready for this?" he asked when I finally cast a weary look in his direction. His stance remained stiff, uncomfortable, as he glared at the door behind me, refusing to meet my gaze entirely.

I nodded. "I have to be."

The tautness around his eyes relaxed as he finally looked at me. His eyes, usually cold, appeared warmer in the candlelight. I swallowed hard as a muscle tightened across his chiseled jaw.

"What is it?" His voice dropped an octave as his eyes scanned every small detail of my face, looking for some clue as to what I might be thinking.

I wasn't sure I could do this. "It's nothing."

The caravan door swung open with Nonna's sudden arrival, a warm smile in place as she ushered in a young woman. My spine straightened as she caught sight of Aiden behind me, but her smile stayed stiffly in place.

"This is Esme," Nonna said, nodding in my direction. The woman sent me a pleasant smile as she sat in the seat across from me at the small round table. My hands fisted nervously in my purple skirts as I glanced between this stranger I was about to damn to demons, and the soul siphon disguised as a crystal ball.

Revulsion settled heavily in my chest as I cast a glance in Nonna's direction. Her face told me very little as she took up her spot near the door.

"You look a little young to be doing this," the woman noted. I offered her a warm smile as I studied her. Her face was slender, probably in her mid-twenties, far too young to have her soul taken from her mortal body, but just young enough to be corrupted by the superstitions of most wanderers.

I reached a hand across the table, thankful it didn't shake though my bones seemed to rattle under my skin. "I've been doing this my entire life," I said in a steady voice. Aiden shifted nearby. No one acknowledged his presence though I felt his every breath go through me.

"Your grandmother said you could do a reading for me." She sounded uncertain as she glanced briefly toward Nonna.

My nod felt stiff as I took her hand in both of mine. I ran a finger through her palm as I studied it. The darkness in my chest stirred excitedly as it dared move up my shoulders and start down my arms the way it once did when I stole souls. With every slight shift in its movement, I felt my stomach twirl with growing exhaustion.

"It would be easiest if we used this," I said, moving the siphon to the middle of the table.

Her eyes lit up in recognition. This contraption was a typical stereotype others told of my people. It was almost laughable that this was the one truly powerful thing my family could do.

Gently, I placed her hands on either side of the siphon; her eyes alight in the candle's glow. Aiden stiffened slightly behind me.

The dark essence inside me shifted, drifting farther through my arms as it welcomed the familiarity of this task. As soon as it reached my fingers, the world darkened, going quiet. The candles went out in a whiff of smoke.

The woman's breath caught. "Does this usually happen?" she whispered into the following stillness.

I could feel the air grow cold as the darkness shifted through me, begging to be released. Aiden moved then, the warmth of his presence breezing over my skin as he made his way toward the caravan door.

"What's going on?" the woman asked, voice laced with concern.

The world had gone quiet outside. I couldn't find it in myself to lessen the woman's fear as a familiar chill seeped into my bones. My breathing grew shallow as memories filled my vision and burned along the scar at my neck. Because the last time I felt this chill, my family, and my life, had been threatened.

"Aiden," I whispered.

He caught my gaze, barely visible in the dark of the caravan. "I know." His voice remained carefully emotionless.

I watched as he disappeared into the darkness beyond the caravan. The sounds of the crowd had grown silent, the only noise coming from the faint howl in the cold wind.

Before Nonna could stop me, I moved to follow Aiden, eager to see if my suspicions were correct.

"Absolutely not," he said as he tried to block the doorway from me. I studied the campground as I peered out from behind his shoulder. Every light and candle in every caravan and tent gathered here had gone out.

"I have a right to know what's going on," I spat in a harsh whisper.

"No," he said with equal frankness. "Stay inside where it's safe."

He pulled the caravan door closed in my face before I could offer a retort. Nonna's hand gently gripped my wrist as she pulled me back to the stool.

"Your husband seems a bit protective of you, doesn't he," the woman said in false cheer. I could hear the fear in her voice though her smile attempted to convince me otherwise.

Nonna shot the woman a look though she refrained from correcting her. I could do little else than offer the woman a halfhearted smile, refusing to acknowledge the heat in my cheeks at her observation.

A chill ran down my spine in a taunting caress. The familiar presence made the scar at my neck burn painfully. I ran a hand over the raised flesh there as I forced myself to breathe through the nausea that dared to unsettle me.

"Esme?" Nonna asked, brows drawn together in concern.

I shook my head and moved past her, mind racing with the growing panic that tightened my chest. No one stopped me this time as I slowly stepped through the door and paused on the steps. I could feel Nonna and the woman move to stare out into the darkness behind me.

A sharp breeze swept through the campground as I studied those gathered here. I could see Mousa, his arm wrapped around the shoulder of a petite blonde girl I recognized from one of the other families that he'd often tangled with during our travels. Mother and Father remained on their stage, and all three of my younger siblings huddled nervously nearby.

My fear only grew as I considered the risks to their safety now that the entire kingdom sought to capture me.

Tarsa and Hakan stood on the far side of the campground, closest to my parents though they kept nearly hidden in the shadows. From their overly stiff postures I knew they recognized the familiar chill as well. Even Killian and Seraphine, both of whom were generally warm and relaxed, looked like statues as they stared off into the darkness toward the east.

My heart beat frantically, a mixture of the darkness there that begged to seek a soul for its taking and outright terror as my hair rose in the chill.

I dared to step closer to Aiden. His familiar warmth settled over me as I tried to force my eyes to adjust to the darkness. Behind me, I could hear my family moving through the nervous crowd.

"What is it?" I whispered to Aiden in the deadly silence.

His hand clamped over my mouth, barely letting me get the words out. I glared at him and debated biting his hand but the look in his eye kept me still. He knew who was coming, and he was nervous.

I held my tongue as he released me slowly, stepping away to put himself between me and the growing darkness approaching at a tauntingly slow pace.

As the distance between Aiden and I grew, so did my fear. Though my family now stood at my side, I somehow felt less safe with them there. I knew without a doubt, that the demon coming now would do whatever he needed to force me to fulfill the debt my family owed. Even if that meant hurting those I loved.

The woman disappeared into the crowd as they began their slow retreat from the campground. Nonna didn't bother stopping her as she moved to join where my family had gathered nearby.

Tarsa and Hakan moved through the night like shadows themselves, their presence comforting as I knew they'd keep my family safe if something were to happen. I could just make out Killian and Seraphine in the darkness as they shifted to flank Aiden on either side.

As the figure in the distance came into view, my heart threatened to stop. Blood pounded frantically in my ears as my breath came in short gasps, fogging on the air in front of me. The chill seeped into my bones. There would be no running from the winged figure as the darkness shifted around him, revealing his enormity.

The demon was just as I remembered. Shoulder-length, pale hair that appeared nearly silver in the faint light, caressed by dark horns that erupted from his hairline and curved backward ending at the nape of his neck. His large dove-grey feathered wings protruded from his back delicately, spreading wide for just a moment in a display of power as he stalked toward us.

Whispers from those who remained began to rise on the air as they shuddered at the winged demon approaching. A cold smile played with the corners of his mouth as he watched their retreat grow more frantic.

Unable to stay still, I took a few steps toward Aiden, hoping to find comfort in his familiar nearness. Without looking in my direction, he held a hand out to stop me just as Killian wrapped an arm around my middle.

"Stay back," he whispered into my hair. "He needs to focus on Ephraim, and trust me, if this gets ugly, you do not want to get between those two."

As he gently pushed me behind him, I felt my mother grab hold of my hand, pulling me back to stand between her and my father. Even the others stayed silent, no one daring to breathe too loudly. My heart pounded loud enough to rattle my ribs as I reached out to grasp Amara's hand. Alfie held tightly to her other hand as silent, fearful tears ran down their round cheeks.

Ephraim came to a stop several yards in front of Aiden who did a fine job of blocking the demon's path to me. I watched with bated breath as his gaze shifted over Aiden dismissively, seemingly disgusted with the immortal daring to block his path. But when his gaze met mine, I lost the ability to breathe. My throat closed up with terror as he smiled coldly, his eyes frozen in a quiet rage that didn't match the upturn of his mouth.

"What do you want Ephraim?" Aiden spat. The anger in his voice soothed the uncomfortable stirring in my chest.

In answer, Ephraim slowly lifted the knife from its sheath at his back, hidden between his wings, and pointed it at me tauntingly. The scar at my throat burned with the memory of the poison it was coated in.

"It seems," he drawled with a secret, knowing gleam in his eye, "that the Loutari family hasn't been paying their dues."

"The Soul Collector has been returned," Aiden retorted. "Their debt will be repaid."

Ephraim shrugged, uncaring. "The god of Death has requested her return to his court nonetheless."

SEVENTEEN

THE GROUND SEEMED TO turn to sea around me. My legs struggled to hold me upright as I leaned heavily on my mother who appeared equally disbelieving. Behind me, my father's breath came in short gasps matching my own frantic tempo. I reached for his hand—a sense of calm in the center of my maelstrom.

Aiden snarled at the demon. "You will not take her." His shoulders had gone rigid with Ephraim's words, muscles taut in preparation for whatever fight may ensue.

The demon just smiled, his eyes flashing to me before returning to Aiden. "That is not your decision," he said with a cold gleam in his eye. "I'm a little surprised you don't want her to return to your realm. Imagine how powerful someone could become with her under their control."

I shivered, leaning back into my father's warmth for comfort. Out of the corner of my eye I could see the others shift uneasily on the balls of their feet as they too kept their eyes on Ephraim. Seraphine dared a glance in my direction which told me enough—if Ephraim tried to take me, I was supposed to run, even if that meant leaving the immortals behind.

"Have you even thought to consider what this could do for the Prince of Death should the Soul Collector be returned?" Ephraim said casually as he took a gradual step in my direction. Aiden shifted, keeping himself between us. Confusion flashed through me at his words.

Hands balled into fists at his sides, Aiden took another step toward Ephraim. "Yes, I've considered it," he said between clenched teeth, as if the words had been ripped from him.

The demon's eyes returned to me. My stomach tightened at the cold emptiness I saw in his pale gaze. A smile turned up his mouth.

"But you won't return her, will you?" he said to Aiden, though his eyes remained focused on mine. "No matter how powerful she could make immortals like us, you would have her remain here among mortals, defenseless and weak."

"She is not without defense, Ephraim," Aiden retorted harshly. As if in answer, Tarsa and Hakan shifted in the dark, appearing only steps away from Ephraim's wings. "And I assure you, she is far from weak."

I watched as the demon cast his eyes to the others, barely scanning the axes gripped in Tarsa's hands, or the sword Hakan held at his side. I could see the taunt on his lips even from where I stood huddled with my family.

"Why does he want me in your realm?" I asked before the demon could taunt them further.

Aiden stiffened, probably wishing I'd stayed quiet. My mother's hand tightened in mine with her own silent plea to hold my tongue.

Around us, the campground had gone silent. Whatever families were once here to enjoy the performances had since run to the safety of their homes. Even the blonde girl currently burrowing into Mousa's side appeared to be alone as her family had undoubtedly returned to the safety of their caravan.

The demon's icy blue gaze studied me in the following quiet.

"You know nothing of your true talent if you dare ask such a foolish thing," he said with a sneer. "Tell me, young Soul Collector, what lies has dear Aiden spun for you?"

"Leave her be," Aiden snarled.

Ephraim smiled knowingly. "Oh dear," he said with a shake of his head. "Don't tell me this weak human has corrupted you into feeling like a mortal, too."

Aiden's answering silence sent my head spinning with questions. The shuffling of feet beside me caught my attention but I didn't dare look away from Aiden as he and Ephraim grew closer with agonizingly slow steps.

The door to the caravan opened behind me, casting a faint glow of light from the freshly lit candles as my siblings moved inside. Amara whispered my name urgently, but I couldn't bring myself to turn to her, not as I watched the demon grow closer to Aiden and my friends.

"She is a mortal, Aiden," Ephraim spat with disgust. "Her lifetime is a mere blink to our own. She serves no purpose other than gaining power for our king. Surely you can see that."

"No one deserves to be damned to his service against their will." Aiden's hands shook with barely controlled rage, as if he were on the brink of ripping the realm apart.

Ephraim straightened, his smile turning into a mocking snort. "She doesn't really know you, does she?"

Aiden snarled.

"I suggest you leave now, Ephraim," Hakan warned. His knuckles turned white over the grip on his sword. My heart threatened to burst from my chest as the atmosphere continued to burn with the threat of violence. The stirring in my chest nearly overwhelmed me as more of my family moved to the caravan.

"I cannot do that, Hakan," Ephraim said, eyes returning to me. A tendril of fear brushed along my spine causing me to shiver beneath his gaze. "I can't return empty handed from such an easy task."

Aiden moved so fast I couldn't track him with my eyes, but suddenly, he was standing nose to nose with Ephraim. "You will not take her. I will not allow it. If you touch her, I will kill you."

Ephraim smiled, the sight sending my stomach hurtling as I knew what would immediately follow the taunt in his grin. The demon leaned forward, putting his weight on the balls of his feet as his eyes came alight with the potential for bloodshed. "I was hoping you'd say that."

I cried out a warning as he struck. Aiden dodged his blow effortlessly and the two quickly became a blur of muted color as they fought.

"Esme," my mother said into my ear as she tried to pull me away.

I turned wild eyes to her. "We can't just leave him."

"We have to," she whispered. Her eyes held a silver gleam from tears I knew she fought to keep hidden.

"Go," Killian said suddenly at our side. "We'll hold him off for as long as we can."

"Run and don't stop," Seraphine said, surprising me with a quick kiss to my brow.

I turned to watch them join the others in what quickly became a bloody battle. My throat burned with tears I hadn't realize I needed to shed as I watched the immortals I could now call friends fight to keep me safe once again.

Warm hands wrapped around my waist, pulling me backward toward the caravan.

"Stop," I cried out to anyone who would hear. The demon didn't listen, nor did my father as he dragged me into the back of the caravan.

Aiden's gaze shot to mine, his eyes lit with urgency as Ephraim raised his sword to strike him down. The caravan door slammed shut, blocking the fight from view.

"Go!" Father shouted to my uncle up ahead. The caravan jolted as the mules pulled us forward at a harsh pace.

"No, we have to help them," I said as I reached for the door.

Father's hand came down on mine as he dragged me toward the center of the caravan. "You can't help them, Esme. They're immortals."

"They'll kill you." The girl at Mousa's side had tears running down her face. I'd forgotten how pretty she was. Her golden hair hung loose around her face making her appear wild; her lips held a stubborn pout.

"No," I said stubbornly. "Aiden won't. None of them will let Ephraim hurt me. I can't leave them behind." The thought made tears burn my eyes, but I forced them away.

Nonna gripped my face in her hands. "You listen to me, child. There is nothing he can bring you but pain. It's best we leave them all now while we still can."

I shook myself free from her grip and stood uneasily as the caravan jerked with the mules' quick strides. "We need him to fulfill the debt—a debt that I have to pay and none of you can help me with. I don't know how to do this alone, and if I don't have Aiden to help me, then who knows what will happen to this family?"

"She's right," Mousa said begrudgingly as he stood at my shoulder. "They're good people, Nonna. Even if we leave now, who knows what will happen to the families who couldn't get away?"

"My family is still there," the girl at his side said quietly. "Our mule is lame, and we cannot travel again until he is healed."

I felt her words wash over my family. This girl, whose name I couldn't even remember, had a family who traveled with us often. They drew in as much of a crowd as my parents with their performances.

"Do not be so foolish," Nonna spat. "Your family will be fine. Your mother is a very smart woman. I have no doubt they have already left for safety."

"Nonna," Cordelia said from the cot where she cradled our younger siblings at her sides. Nadira and Jac, my younger cousins, huddled nearby with their mother though they all remained silent, red-rimmed eyes wide with fear. "If the demon gets through then there will be nothing stopping him from getting to Esme."

"Mother," the sound of my mother's calm voice settled over me. She reached out a hand and gently squeezed Nonna's as she smiled at her. Beside me, Mousa shifted so he was nearly glued to my side. I felt the cool press of metal slide into my waistband.

"Go," he whispered. "I'll make sure they get out of here."

I glanced at him only briefly. But in that moment, I no longer saw the wild boy he once was. Now, he was grown—a man like our father who knew to care for his family and loved with his entire soul.

His hand squeezed mine, then let go before I was ready.

I launched myself at the door and hurled it open, not bothering to stop my momentum as I jumped to the hard ground and rolled through the impact.

Behind me, I could hear Mother and Nonna screaming my name. Even Father called out as he tried to reach me, but I knew Mousa would help them see reason.

I raced through the night. The chill of the early autumn air cooled the sweat that formed along my neck, making the loose strands of my dark hair stick to my heated skin.

The sounds of battle were up ahead—grunts of pain and cries of anguish all searing into my heart. The depth of my concern for these warriors rocked through me, but I quickly pushed it away as I forced myself to think only of the protection they could offer my family. Because their safety was what mattered, not whatever this darkness in my chest pulled me toward.

Silently, I begged my legs to move faster, ignoring the pain from my healing wounds. We hadn't traveled too far from the campground, but no matter the distance it felt too far from Aiden.

Only a single caravan remained surrounded by abandoned tents as I ran out onto the campground. The faces of two small children poked out between the swaths of fabric keeping them hidden, eyes wide and mouths hanging open with tangible fear. The other performers and wanderers who planned to camp here for the night had left at the first appearance of the winged demon, leaving this family stranded here with their injured mule.

I raced past their caravan and toward the fight. The air left my lungs in a panicked gust of breath as I finally caught sight of the battle before me. Ephraim moved like a god. His wings tucked in tight against his back but shot out to provide cover when needed. His arms and blades moved so fast they were merely a blur.

Aiden moved too—fast and sure, each strike purposeful and strong. Dual knives glistened in his grasp as he struck Ephraim across the leg severing the tendons near his knee.

Ephraim grunted and went down momentarily. As he slowly regained his balance, I caught sight of the wound. Already, the skin was closed, no longer bleeding. The only sign that a wound had even been there was the slice through his pants dripping in blood.

"What are you doing here?" Tarsa snapped as she caught sight of me, dark skin spattered with blood. She rushed to my side and shoved me toward the remaining caravan. "Get out of here before he sees."

I yanked free from her grip and moved closer to Aiden. "I'm not leaving him."

Tarsa snorted, the sound catching Killian's gaze. The usually cheerful immortal sent me a subtle shake of his head as he watched me stride past Tarsa before turning back to the fight before us.

A pained cry sounded through the air, drawing my attention. I spun toward the fight in time to see Ephraim standing over Aiden's crumpled form. Aiden shot me an agonizing look and I remained trapped in his gaze, unable to look away as the silent plea to run lit his eyes with new determination. The thrumming in my chest grew, filling me as it begged to be released.

Blood dripped from a cut above his brow, and even more stained the front of his shirt as Ephraim thrust his poisoned knife into Aiden's chest.

A scream lodged in my throat as I raced toward him, shoving my way past the others. The scar at my neck burned with the painful memory of that very knife cutting into my skin only a year ago. The flutter in my chest stirred, begging to be released as it surged toward the foul void living inside Ephraim.

"Ahh, Esme. I was wondering if you'd return for him," Ephraim said as he turned to smile at me. I ignored him, falling to my knees at Aiden's side.

My hands clutched the wound at his chest, willing the blood to stop flowing though I knew it would do little. The knife Mousa had tucked into my waistband dug into my hip, cooling the growing panic as my fingers ran red with Aiden's blood. He seemed to sense my fear as he placed one hand over mine, holding it against his chest, blood smearing over our grip.

"Well, this is interesting," Ephraim hissed as he studied Aiden and me on the ground. The others shifted suddenly, their backs turning to the three of us as the ruckus of a gathering crowd reached the campground.

I pulled my hand from Aiden's grip, reaching for the knife my brother had given me. My hand was slick with blood as it settled over the hilt just as the crowd came into view.

Torches lit, knives and swords on display, men and woman with fierce gazes marched our way. There had to be nearly a hundred altogether as they studied first Aiden, then me, then settled on the demon standing over us. I saw a few faces light up with recognition, and my stomach dropped as gazes flickered between the demon and me. One woman held a crumpled paper in her hand. A new kind of fear settled along my skin as they moved closer, aiming for not only Ephraim, but me as well.

"Go," Aiden whispered, as he too realized what these people wanted.

I shook my head, grip tightening on my knife. "Not while you or my family is still in danger."

"That's her," one of the large men shouted. His beefy hand pointed a knife in my direction. "She's the girl from the poster; I'm certain of it. There's a bounty for her head."

"Oh my," Ephraim said with a soft chuckle. "This is interesting indeed."

As the crowd moved, barreling through the campground in my direction, Killian, Hakan, Seraphine, and Tarsa moved against them, their weapons a blood-soaked blur of movement in the night.

I moved too. Faster than I thought I could manage, I buried my knife deep in Ephraim's gut.

The demon staggered back, eyes blazing with fury as he yanked the knife free and tossed it to the ground. My heart sank a little further as I watched his wound close.

Though the fury remained in his gaze, a smile curled his mouth. "I'm going to love showing you just what your power can do."

His hand reached for me then, only to be cut off by Aiden's sword. The demon cried in agony; the sound so loud it shook the ground as I got slowly to my feet. Aiden shoved me behind him as he held his sword toward the demon.

Ephraim gripped his bloodied wrist in his remaining hand. Blood, such a dark shade of red it appeared nearly black, ran free down his arm.

He attacked with a new urgency, bleeding and crying out in a furious agony. Aiden, though injured and bleeding himself, moved as swiftly as if he were fully healed.

Behind me, the chaos continued. I could hear blades crashing together, along with many of the villagers racing back toward safety as they quickly realized the challenges my capture possessed.

A large hand grasped my arm, twisting it behind my back as I was pulled from my feet.

"Gotcha, girly," the raspy voice crooned in my ear. I tried to shift to see who held me, but he kept me braced as he dragged me farther away from the chaos at the campground. Panic tightened my chest as I struggled in his firm grasp. Unlike my friends before me, I was not a warrior.

I kicked out with my feet, landing a solid strike in the man's knee as he grunted with pain and released his grip enough for me to get free.

He cursed me, face reddening with anger as he launched in my direction again, forcing a scream from my throat.

I jumped away quickly, tripping over my own feet as I landed on my back in the dirt. Cursing myself, I rolled and struggled to my feet again. I felt his hands wrap tightly around my bandaged ankles. I cried out again, struggling harder as I fought to get free, hating my inability to fight back as my panic continued to grow.

His grip slackened as a pained grunt escaped his throat. When I turned back, a familiar knife protruded out of his chest. I watched as his face went slack just before he collapsed to the ground, still and unbreathing.

Quick footsteps sounded behind me, and when I turned my heart nearly burst through my chest. My mother ran through the campground, knives held at the ready as she launched another through the air. The resounding thwack settled over me as it found its home in another bounty hunter nearby. Her face held a barely contained fury as she raced after the crowd who came to take me away again.

Beside her, my father and Mousa ran toward the crowd, each with weapons of their own held aloft as they prepared to engage in the bloody battle. Though I had vowed to keep my family safe, here they were protecting me. Tears pricked my eyes as I staggered to my aching feet.

My body numbed with disbelief as I watched my family return from the road and hurl themselves into battle. My mother and father fought side by side, their knives flying through the air to find their marks in anyone who dared get too close to me.

Mousa fought next to Hakan, the duo wielding swords and knives with such strength and precision I almost couldn't recognize my brother in the thick of bloodshed. He had never been a fighter, always enjoying the pleasures of life as opposed to picking his way through the darkness. That boy wasn't here now; a warrior stood in his place.

Killian shot arrow after arrow into the oncoming crowd, chasing them away before they could get too close. Even Tarsa wielded her axes with menacing skill though she too didn't seek out the kill, rather choosing to scare the crowd away with the threat of her movements.

I spun around, catching sight of Aiden and Ephraim again. The two remained locked in their deadly dual. How anyone could continue such a bloody battle for so long and not collapse from exhaustion astounded me.

Their bodies dripped in blood and sweat but their faces contained all the fury they needed to keep going.

I took a step in their direction and stopped, my toe settling on the knife Ephraim pulled out of his gut.

Ahead, Ephraim disarmed Aiden, twisting his arm behind his back and pinning him to his chest. As soon as his uninjured hand pressed the poisoned knife against Aiden's throat, my blood froze in my veins. The world fell silent as I watched the demon smile coldly, letting me watch as he dug the knife in deeper, nearly breaking through his skin.

I watched Aiden's eyes go wide, silently begging me to run yet again. But I couldn't. The dark essence in my chest swirled around my heart in a deadly caress.

As Ephraim shifted to slice the knife across Aiden's throat, I scooped up the knife at my feet and launched it through the air.

My breath froze in my lungs as I watched it sink into Ephraim's neck with satisfying ease.

He released Aiden immediately, stumbling back. The now-empty campground only echoed the sounds of our ragged breathing as my defenders drew nearer.

Ephraim yanked my knife from his throat and cursed as blood dripped down the collar of his shirt. My mouth went dry as I watched his wound heal between one breath and the next. Sensing my gaze, he turned his glare on me again, the pure hatred in his face filling me with dread, while the darkness in my chest threatened to burst with agitation.

Aiden stepped closer. His presence changed me entirely, giving me back my courage under the weight of Ephraim's gaze.

The demon looked between the two of us, registering something I couldn't see. A smile tugged at a corner of his mouth as he dropped my knife to the ground.

"Fine," he spat. "Keep her tonight. But know there is nothing, and no one, that will stand to keep me from getting to her. I'll kill whoever I have to, even if that means you, Aiden." My blood chilled as I watched his gaze slide to my family. "Or perhaps it'll be them."

My stomach tightened as I felt my family appear at my back, the immortals flanking each of them. My parents stood shoulder to shoulder with me, Aiden a warm beacon at my back and Mousa standing proudly at his side. Each of us was bruised and bloody, but not an ounce of fear was to be found as we collectively glowered at the demon before us. Ephraim considered them with nothing more than annoyance before returning his gaze to me. A shiver raced down my spine at the frigid longing in his stare.

My mother's voice rang into the silent campground in a cold threat so unlike any I'd heard from her before as she said, "Come near my daughter again, and I will kill you myself."

Ephraim snorted as he wiped the blood away from his neck, the wound now no more than a pink scar. His quick recovery was so unlike Aiden's who continued to bleed openly at my side.

It was then, in that brief moment before he turned and disappeared into the night, that I realized the truth with which he spoke.

If I wanted to keep my family safe, I had no choice but to steal the souls needed to fulfill this debt. Or, I had to find a way to break this curse on my family. Because I knew they wouldn't let me endure this threat alone. Only together would we be able to fight, to have any hope of finding the secret to freeing our family from Death's grasp. Only together could we hope to survive. Even if being together ended up being the thing that killed us all.

EIGHTEEN

Laughter now filled the blood-stained campground. Killian and Mousa had taken it upon themselves to build a large fire between the Loutari caravan and the caravan that belonged to Mousa's blonde friend. The two boys sat there now, laughing at each other as they cleaned blood from their weapons, seeming totally at ease after such a bloody hour. The blonde girl—Leesa was her name—sat on Mousa's other side, watching him with her heart in her eyes.

Nearby, Father and Uncle Malik moved through the campground cleaning up whatever destruction remained after the bounty hunters and demon disappeared. Nonna was careful to keep Amara and Jac, the youngest of our family, in the caravan with her so they couldn't see the gore left behind while Cordelia and Nadira were stuck helping our fathers. Only Alfie seemed to be free to roam as he sat across from the boys at the fire. His hands worked tirelessly to scribble in his notebook while Seraphine patiently answered any question he threw her way. Whatever answers he sought from her, I couldn't be sure, but the light in his eyes could compete with the stars.

I shifted uncomfortably as the sting of Mother's ointment regained my attention. "Sit still," she cautioned as she dabbed a little more on my scraped chin.

Luckily, I'd sustained few injuries tonight; nothing more than a few cuts and scrapes and what would most likely be bruises by tomorrow. My feet ached from the old wounds which never seemed to have a chance to recover, but I didn't dare show the injuries they carried to my mother. The sight of the marred skin at my ankles would only add to the worry that weighed down her heart. That thought made me pull tighter at my sleeves, making sure my wrists were hidden from view.

"Ouch," I hissed again as she dabbed at my tender chin.

The look she gave me made me hold my tongue from further complaints. "You're lucky this is the worst of what you received."

"Aiden's far worse than I am," I whined. "Why aren't you hovering over him to clean his wounds?"

Mother cast a glance over her shoulder to the tent pitched near the tree line. "I'm sure he could use some assistance with his wounds, but that's not my place."

I studied her a moment longer before Tarsa came back into view. Her dark skin glistened with water from the nearby well as she returned from washing off the blood of battle. Her axes gleamed at her hips. I followed her movements as she joined Hakan on the far side of the campground, directly where Ephraim had disappeared earlier. The two kept a sharp lookout in case he dared to return so soon.

"Here," Mother said, shoving bottles of ointment and herbs into my hands along with a roll of bandages. "Take these to Aiden and tend to his wounds."

I started, cheeks heating slightly. "What? Why me?"

The corners of her full mouth tilted upward just slightly. "You said yourself; he's far worse off than you and might need help bandaging his wounds."

My heart burst into a nervous race against my ribs. "You just said it wasn't our place to care for him."

"No," she said, brushing away a loose strand of my hair, still damp from a bath. "I said it wasn't *my* place."

She turned to disappear into the caravan, but I gripped tightly onto her sleeve. My heart was racing nervously now. I had no way of knowing what Aiden would do if I showed up to clean his wounds, let alone if he even wanted anyone near him now. He'd disappeared into the tent Tarsa pitched an hour ago and hadn't so much as glanced outside since.

Mother caught sight of my face, seeing the panic there. She sighed, cupped her hands gently on my cheeks and smiled.

"Go to him, Esme," she said quietly. The laughter of the others by the fire nearly drowned out her voice. "He needs it."

Nonna appeared in the doorway behind her, casting a long shadow over us. A frown formed more creases along her face as she glanced between the two of us.

"You will do no such thing," she commanded as she tenderly descended the steps and turned her glower on my mother. "You wouldn't dare send her to the tent of the immortal with that hope in her eyes."

"He will not harm her," Mother said patiently. "I think that much is clear after what he did for her tonight."

Nonna snorted. "You cannot be so foolish." She turned her gaze on me and frowned. "You do not know this immortal. You know nothing of who he is or what he's done. Do not go near him."

"He returned me to you, Nonna," I said gently. My heart fluttered with a mixture of nerves and excitement as I thought of Aiden. I didn't understand it, or even dare to consider what it might mean. I hardly knew him; about that Nonna was right. But I couldn't ignore the memory of the look in his eye as he'd watched me disappear in the caravan when Ephraim attacked. There was no mistaking the utter joy and relief at seeing me escape unharmed. That I didn't understand, but I wanted to. I needed too.

"And he would just as well take you to Death himself if it would better benefit him," she added coldly.

"Mother," Aunt Kiva appeared from the caravan; Amara stood at her hip watching curiously. My aunt's cornsilk hair hung down to her waist in loose waves, and the pale blue of her eyes glowed in the light of the fire as she smiled at me.

"No," Nonna said before she could continue. "This is not up for discussion. Esme will stay in the caravan until we have rested and cleaned enough for travel. Then we must continue to pay the debt. Souls will not collect themselves."

My chest tightened at her words. Though we had no way of knowing how to end the debt, the thought of stealing souls still sent my stomach spiraling with guilt. If it meant keeping my family safe, then I would do whatever was required of me. But the thought of putting them in danger this way only added to my guilt.

I remained frozen on the ground, unable to speak as I watched Nonna disappear after Aunt Kiva into the caravan. Mother stayed at my side, studying the conflict in my eyes.

"Don't you dare," she said in a voice that left little room for argument. Her hands gripped onto my shoulders as she forced me to meet her gaze. "None of this is your fault, Esme. None of what may or may not happen to our family is on your shoulders."

"It will be if he comes back to kill you all," I whispered. My mind whirled with the horror of seeing my family slaughtered if I couldn't repay this debt to keep them safe; or worse, if we were never able to have it expunged from our bloodline.

Mother sighed and pressed her brow to mine. "No one will take you from me again, my dear," she noted quietly. "I can see in your eyes the fear you carry. Do not worry for us, Esme. For we will never leave you to fight this alone. No matter what."

I felt tears threaten, but I blinked them away. Without a word, I watched as my mother joined the others in the caravan, only a small encouraging smile over her shoulder before closing the door.

My heart beat nervously in my chest as I slowly made my way across the campground to Aiden's tent. I had no way of knowing if he even wanted someone intruding in his space, but I knew what the poison of that knife felt like. The knowledge that I didn't carry the antidote made me pause just outside the tent. What use would my ointments and herbs be if I couldn't remove the poison from his blood?

Uncertain, I forced myself to step into the tent. What I saw stopped me in my tracks.

Aiden stood there, his back to me as he hissed at whatever he poured into the wound at his chest.

But it was the sight of his back that made my blood freeze. Scars covered nearly every inch of his skin. Burns, knife wounds, cuts from swords and lashes from a whip, marred his skin. Some even curved around his ribs to disappear along his chest. He was still beautiful, there was no denying that. Only now I could see the warrior beneath. The beautiful man covered in monstrous scars.

He went rigid, shoulders tight as he heard my sharp intake of breath. Slowly, he shifted so he faced me. The single candle lighting the large tent provided enough illumination to add shadows to his damaged skin.

Sweat clung to his body though the blood was already cleaned away. I stood there marveling at the absolute perfection of his form before catching sight of the wound caused by Ephraim's poisoned knife.

Slowly, still waiting for him to order me away, I took a step closer. I clutched the herbs and ointments to my chest, willing the racing of my heart to slow, afraid it could be overheard in the deafening silence of the tent.

Aiden didn't seem to breathe as he watched my every movement with predatory focus. A mask of careful detachment settled over his expression as I came to a stop before him. I stood there, marveling at the wickedness of his scars. Though his posture remained stiff, uncomfortable, I couldn't find any hint of embarrassment as he allowed me to study him. The wounds I hid behind bandages burned in recognition as I raised a shaking hand to trace the worst of his scars, starting in the middle of his back and curving over his ribs to end in the middle of his chest. I heard the breath catch in his throat as I ran a tentative finger over the marred flesh. I'd no way of knowing what could've caused such a scar. But the tender feel of the raised skin beneath my fingers was enough to make my heart race nervously at the power and strength someone must possess to survive such an injury.

My hand came to a stop in the center of his chest. The stab wound carried purple veins outward as the poison threatened to spread from the mark. Gently,

I placed my palm flat against his heated skin as I studied the wound. The rhythmic pounding of his heart beat against my palm in a hurried pace.

"Do you have the antidote?" I whispered as I traced the veins filled with poison.

His hand came up to grip mine, but he didn't push me away. "It's taken care of," he said quietly.

"Ephraim healed instantly," I noted, ignoring the way my breath threatened to catch in my throat. "Why haven't you healed yet?"

Aiden didn't answer right away, leaving us cast in silence. Eventually, I looked up to see him watching me curiously, uncertainty clouding his eyes. I hadn't realized how close we stood until I felt his breath warm my cheeks. My pulse thrummed in my veins as I dropped my gaze and pulled my hand out from where he still held it against his bare chest.

Not waiting for an answer, I pulled him to the edge of the cot placed in the corner of the massive tent. The candlelight just barely reached this far across the space, but it provided enough light to see the worst of the wound.

Gently, I pushed down on his shoulder, silently asking him to sit. He obliged and kept his eyes on my face. I could feel his gaze burn through me as I forced my heart to slow its frantic beating.

My cheeks burned as his eyes remained fixed on my face while I cleaned the wound. Aiden didn't so much as wince at the sting the ointment surely caused.

"Thank you," I said shyly. At his questioning look I added, "for not letting Ephraim take me."

"It was stupid of you to return," he said seriously. His expression gave nothing away as I dabbed the herbs into his wound.

"Let's not forget that he could've killed you if it weren't for my return."

He snorted, though not unkindly. "How do you figure that?"

"It was my knife in his neck that got him to release you there at the end."

His hand came to grip the end of my shirt along my waist, toying with the thin fabric as I pressed a bandage to his wound. "That wouldn't have been necessary had I not been forced to interfere on your behalf again after you returned."

I couldn't help the smile that pulled at my mouth. "Why did you then?" I breathed. I'd finished with the bandage, but I couldn't seem to remove my hands from his bare chest, my palm pressed flat against his bare skin. Somehow the candle heated the tent to a near punishing temperature as my skin grew tight and my cheeks flushed with it.

His eyes, usually such a cool silver, appeared a warm blue now as he studied me. There was no unkindness in his gaze, only tentative heat as we remained close enough to share breath. The unfamiliar warmth and gentle nature in his gaze so unlike everything I previously thought I knew about him.

"You don't want to know what could've become of you had you been forced into my realm." His breath came out almost a strained whisper. My entire body was aware of his as the hand he held at my waist tightened its hold.

I swallowed nervously as his left hand came up to graze the tips of his fingers along my chin, noting the freshly cleaned scrape I carried there.

Shoving away the curiosity I felt at his touch, I turned my attention to the cut above his brow. It had stopped bleeding but remained open as it slowly healed.

"I never thanked you for returning me to my family," I said slowly.

Aiden lifted a shoulder in a casual shrug. "It was my duty."

"It was everything," I corrected. "You gave me everything." Tears threatened to burn my eyes as my siblings' laughter rang through the air outside in answer. I watched as his eyes warmed even further, allowing me to see deeper into the person beneath the mask.

The tips of his calloused fingers continued to trace the sensitive skin at my chin while I dabbed ointment along the cut at his brow. When they moved to my lower lip I froze.

Aiden's gaze found mine, a question held there that I didn't know how to answer.

I forced my gaze to return to his wound using the method of cleaning it to distract myself from the heat in his gaze. My breath caught in my throat as I realized he'd shifted closer. Very little space remained between us now. The knowledge of that change sent my skin singing beneath his touch.

The essence that lived in my chest shifted, completely content in Aiden's presence. The rough skin of his fingers grazed over my lip again, sending my heart into a frantic gallop.

When his hands came up to cup my cheek, gently brushing my loose hair from my face, I remained silent, not daring to move as he focused on the minor injuries I sustained tonight. I hadn't realized I'd leaned into his touch until I felt his nose graze my own.

I gasped and jerked away, afraid I'd crossed some sort of line. But his eyes matched the same heated temptation I felt across my skin.

Laughter from the fire outside reached us then, breaking the trance of his closeness. I could hear the murmurs of my siblings and cousins carrying over the quiet night to the silence of the tent. My heart finally calmed at the interruption.

I backed away but remained in his grasp.

"Do you think he'll come back?" I finally asked as my heart returned to its normal pace.

Aiden's brow furrowed as he studied me a moment longer before releasing me altogether. A cool chill chased away the lingering warmth of his touch. "He will. Of that I have no doubt."

I groaned. "I hate demons." I ran a hand through my loose curls. "Nonna was right. Nothing good can come from them. Do you think he'll hurt my family?" I turned back to face him and froze. At some point in the last few moments, he'd gone stoic; all the warmth that had existed between us now gone. I bit down on the inside of my cheek as I silently cursed my thoughtless actions, wondering if I'd crossed some sort of line drawn between us.

"The truth that you've been taught to believe is warped," he finally said, voice strained. "You mortals created a truth to comfort yourselves against the reality of the world you live in."

His sudden cool tone sent a shiver down my spine in alarm. I stepped back as he stood, his large frame towering over me. Without another word, he pulled on a clean shirt and left the tent without a backward glance.

NINETEEN

EARLY THE NEXT MORNING, I found myself walking side by side with Seraphine as we traveled in our large group to a nearby village for food—and souls. Uncle Malik remained behind with my cousins as they still hadn't been able to replace their caravan after it was burned during my capture many months ago. And now that Aiden and the others were with us there just wasn't room for all of us in the caravan. Which was how I ended up walking with Seraphine.

"You seem quiet today," she noted gently. Today, her long fiery twists were tied up in a knot on top of her head making the freckles dusting her round cheeks stand out.

I shrugged half-heartedly. "I think I'm just tired." In truth I was tired. After yesterday's mishap with Ephraim showing up and the conversation with Aiden, I just couldn't find it in myself to sleep last night.

Seraphine wrapped her arm around my shoulder, pulling me closer. "Nervous?"

"About what?"

"Collecting souls again." Her arm tightened around me in comfort. "Or maybe that we're headed into a village, knowing your face will be posted around the market for all to see."

I shuddered. A blazing gaze settled along my back, but I refused to acknowledge it. "You don't think the king will have his guards all the way out here, do you?"

"His guards are everywhere," Tarsa stated as she marched past us, axes glinting in the faint morning light at her sides.

"It's true," Killian said as he moved to walk at my other side. "We saw them parading through the village east of here."

"Maybe they're just collecting people for the king's burnings," Mousa suggested. He walked comfortably on Killian's other side, his manor a clear sign of the bond of friendship the two had formed in just a few short days.

"They stopped those," Aiden said as he joined us, gaze still scorching my back.

Surprise rattled my bones, but I refused to acknowledge his remark. Whatever happened, or almost happened, between us last night was a mistake. That much he made clear as he'd stormed out of his tent and left me alone.

Mother leaned over the side of the caravan where she sat with my father as he guided the mule. "What do you mean they stopped the burnings?"

"After we rescued Esme, King Elroy pulled his guards away from capturing other wanderers or healers suspected of witchcraft and put all of his efforts into finding her again." Aiden's voice rang with surety as I glanced toward my mother. Her brows remained furrowed as she shared a glance with my father. Something about the look they shared sent my stomach tightening with nerves.

"When did you learn this information?" Nonna demanded with cold frankness. She poked her face through a slip in the caravan's fabrics where it had been poorly repaired. The gold stars along the dark red and purple fabric reflected the orange morning light around Nonna's face.

"An hour ago," Aiden replied curtly.

"And you waited to tell us until now? When we are on our way to a village where your people say there are guards waiting to take Esme again?"

I sighed internally as I felt Aiden's gaze return to me. Somehow, the flutter of darkness in my chest had grown far more accustomed to his every movement as we spent the past couple of weeks together. Just another reason why I resented this duty a long-dead ancestor placed on my shoulders.

"Esme will be safe," Seraphine assured her gently. Killian nodded along with her words before falling back to walk with Mousa. My mouth inched toward a smile as I caught sight of Cordelia through the slip in the caravan, watching Killian with flushed cheeks and bright eyes.

"And if Ephraim shows up again?" Nonna spat. Ahead, my mother flinched at her words, her gaze quickly finding mine as if she needed the reassurance that I was still here. I offered her a weak smile.

"He won't." Aiden's voice rang with finality. I chanced a peek over my shoulder and caught him already watching me. The ferocity in his gaze sent my heart racing again as I turned back to the dirt road ahead. We were still only a couple of days' travel away from the Abandoned Desert so everything here was dry and flat. And come midday, it would be unbearably hot.

"You can't be sure that the demon won't return," Nonna said stubbornly. In the caravan behind her I could hear Amara and Cordelia whispering to each other as they watched Mousa and Killian laugh together behind us. From Alfie's silence I knew his nose was buried in one of his books.

"He won't." Aiden stated again, his tone leaving little room for argument. Nonna shut her mouth with a snap before she huffed and let the caravan flap fall closed.

"She isn't warming up to you at all is she?" Hakan teased quietly. I hadn't even heard him move to join us. While Tarsa took to disappearing on the road ahead to check for guards, Hakan remained a few paces behind to make sure we weren't being followed.

Aiden sighed but otherwise remained silent. I remained on high alert as we walked along the road in silence, only occasionally passing a farmer or a businessman on their way to work, but Seraphine was always quick to pull me behind her to keep me hidden from view.

Now, nearly an hour later, we finally arrived at the outskirts of Rolla. The small village housed many of Cordovia's farmers and remained surrounded by dry farming land where many of our cattle and pigs were raised for slaughter.

Seraphine remained by my side the entire trip into the village. Her comforting presence and easy conversation were enough to keep me distracted from Aiden's overwhelming shadow cast over my path as he too remained close by.

By now, all the townspeople were up and starting their day. The smell of fresh bread wafted through the busy streets. The flower shop next door to the bakery producing its own aroma, mixing enticingly with the scent of frosted cakes. My mouth watered at the smell as we found a large enough alley to park the caravan.

The long shadows cast from the tall stone buildings provided an odd sense of comfort as I leaned against the cool stone. Sweat had already begun to form along my brow in the heat of early autumn, but I refused to shove my sleeves to my elbows and display the bandages wrapped around my wrists. I still hadn't had time to replace the bandages at my ankles, but I'd managed to keep their existence hidden from my family for now.

"Esme," Mother spoke as she came to stand beside me. Behind her, Father remained with Hakan and the caravan. "Cordelia and I are going to the bakery then the butcher. Why don't you join us?"

I smiled at the offer, finding familiarity in the routine, and I nodded my agreement. Nonna whispered to Mousa nearby, but I couldn't hear their hushed conversation over the sounds of Amara and Cordelia arguing in the caravan. My smile grew as I watched them leap down from the back and send mirroring scowls at each other. Amara's dark curls hung around her young face casually, while Cordelia's hair was done in a pleasant knot at the nape of her neck. A slight hint of rouge painted her lips, and as her eyes darted in Killian's direction I understood why.

"Do they have names?" I heard Alfie ask from behind me. I turned to see his notebook clutched tightly in his hands as he studied Tarsa's axes closely. The immortal scowled at my younger brother in obvious annoyance but refrained from snapping at him.

"No," she answered coldly.

Alfie remained unbothered as he leaned in closer, narrowing his eyes to better study the embellishments on the handles. "Do those symbols mean anything?" His knuckles turned white against his notebook as he fought the urge to write down every answer she would allow him.

"Yes," Tarsa responded stiffly.

"Why don't you tell the lad how you came to own those axes you wear so proudly," Killian said with a smile as he moved to Alfie's side. The warrior had already been subjected to my brother's inquiries about the bow he carried along his back and the few arrows he still held in his quiver.

Alfie turned his quizzical gaze on Tarsa, eyes bright with wonder. Though he stood only to my shoulder – and I was by no means considered tall – he didn't cower under Tarsa's towering stature. She stared down her nose at my brother, irritation plain in her face, but I could also see a hint of pride in her weapons light her eyes.

"Alfie," Nonna called suddenly. She waved him over while Mousa moved toward Killian, face serious for once. "You are to go with your brother and Killian into town."

"What for?" my mother asked as she moved closer. Amara and Cordelia had finally stopped bickering, now standing with Seraphine as the young girls giggled and gossiped with the warrior.

"Don't fret, Emira. I'm just sending them to escort Alfie to the bookstore while you and Cordelia gather food."

"We hardly have room for more books, Adine," my father called from his place near the mule. Hakan leaned against the far building, hidden in its shadow though his presence remained a threat for any who thought to bother those left with the caravan.

"Hush, Leander. One more won't cripple the mule." Nonna gently shoved Alfie toward the opening of the alley with Killian and Mousa on his tail. "You have one hour," she called as they disappeared into the busy street.

I felt a warm presence laced with the scent of cedar envelope me as I watched them leave.

"Your family will be safe," Aiden said quietly, reading the concern on my face. "Killian will not let any harm come to them."

My mouth went dry as I tried to think of something to say. Yet the only words that came to mind were in regards to our conversation the previous night. I didn't want to ask what I did that made him cast that cold mask over his features, and yet that was all I could think about.

"Esme. Ready?" my mother asked, regaining my attention. I nodded, but Nonna cut her off with a wave of her hand.

"No, Esme is to stay with me."

I frowned. "We're just going to get food, Nonna. We won't be gone long."

She shook her head, greying hair tangling around her shoulders. "No. Have you not seen the posters, child? They are everywhere in this town."

Indeed, I had seen them; I'd just chosen to ignore them. Even here, in this darkened alley cast in shadow I could see posters with my face and name plainly written and a large bounty listed beneath. The thought of acknowledging them only made my stomach turn violently.

"You will collect souls here," she said instead. "We will set up a small booth at the front of the alley and you will offer services to any who inquire."

"They'll probably think she's a street girl if you put her at the alley like that," Cordelia said with barely hidden amusement. I sent her a scowl which only made Amara chuckle at her side.

Nonna shook her head. "No. She will wear the Loutari colors, and many will come."

"Isn't that putting her at risk?" Aiden said, stepping closer.

"She will be fine," she said coldly. "Now go, all of you." With a flick of her wrists, she practically shoved my mother and sisters from the alley, Seraphine close on their heels. As I watched them disappear too, I felt a growing sense of trepidation tighten my lungs.

Father and Hakan remained at the other end of the alley, watching for any sign of guards or desperate villagers seeking the king's missing prisoner. I remained silent, not even bothering to answer Nonna's prodding questions as she settled me at a makeshift booth just barely in the shadows at the start of the market street. As I sat there, staring at each passing face, I began to wonder who I would damn next. Would it be the mother with a young child clinging to her legs? Or the man who carried a dozen roses and a freshly baked pie as he strode through the crowd with a smile? Whose life would I sacrifice just to protect myself?

Movement caught my eye nearby. When I turned, I saw Aiden and Tarsa standing on the far side of the street, their scowls displayed as they kept watch for any sign of a threat. Whether my soul remained intact or not, at least my family would remain safe.

"Did you hear her, dear?" Nonna's question demanded my attention. When I blinked, I caught sight of a young woman before me, her teeth brown with rot and her thin body nearly drowned in her ragged clothes. She looked like she could have been beautiful once, possibly from a wealthy family. But I held little doubt her life, like this town, had seen drastic hardships thanks to the king's rotten greed.

"Why don't you read the crystal for her, Esme?" Nonna's hand came down on my shoulder. Though I was sure she meant to comfort me, I only felt powerless as I stared up at the young woman before me.

I forced myself to smile, though it remained weak. "Of course."

The woman smiled drunkenly through it all. From the moment her palms touched the siphon I felt the darkness within me swell excitedly, anxious for the chance to be used. As soon as the siphon glowed its familiar pale blue, my stomach turned, knees weakening enough to force me to sit on the stool Nonna had placed behind the booth.

I watched Nonna gently shoo the woman away after collecting her payment before my shoulders drooped with sudden exhaustion. Tarsa followed after the woman as soon as she disappeared into the crowd, leaving Aiden alone to join us in the alley.

"That was good, dear," Nonna said proudly as she placed the siphon in her bag and practically shoved it into Aiden's hands. The immortal turned away without a word and he too disappeared into the crowd. "We can probably get a few more while we wait for your siblings and mother to return."

I sighed, shaking my head to force the exhaustion from my mind. Father spoke then, saving me from rejecting Nonna's praise.

"Why don't we give Esme a break? She's clearly exhausted." His arm pulled me against his side in comfort as he studied me beneath furrowed brows. "Go find your mother and sisters. We'll return to camp when you get back so you can rest."

Nonna opened her mouth to object, but I left before she could stop me. My head spun as I stumbled through the crowd. Faces blurred together with the floral scent of bouquets and pies and herbal shops that lined this road. Though I could feel the late morning sun barreling down on me, my skin felt cool to the touch as I brushed my hair back from my face.

"Esme?" Amara's calm voice called to me through the crowd.

I caught sight of her nearby, Seraphine at her side as they waited outside the bakery. Offering a weak smile, I began to move in their direction. The crowd had grown since we had arrived earlier that morning. I was jostled and pushed around as I wove through the street filled with merchants and children running through the shops.

A hand gripped tightly onto my arm, spinning me around. I felt a scream catch in my throat as I prepared to shove away from whoever held me, but a hand clamped over my mouth, silencing me.

"What do you think you're doing?" Aiden cursed under his breath as he dropped his hands. "You can't go wandering around alone. Anyone here could recognize you and drag you from the street."

I scowled. "Seraphine is just up ahead with my family. I'm not wandering around."

Aiden stepped to the side, blocking me from a nearby merchant who watched us closely. To most we appeared to be having a lovers' spat in plain view. "You should have asked Hakan to escort you at the very least."

With a scoff, I spun on my heel and nearly walked directly into the florist as he wheeled his cart full of bouquets through the street. Aiden's hand wrapped around my waist and pulled me against him as I regained my balance.

"Flowers for your lady, sir?" the florist asked Aiden with a nod in my direction. My cheeks flushed as I stepped out of Aiden's grip, ignoring the way his own cheeks pinkened.

"There you are," Amara said as she joined us, the others only a step behind her. "I bought you a biscuit, Essie." I took the warm treat with a smile and bit into it, hoping to hide my embarrassment as the florist remained in our path, looking expectantly at Aiden.

"Are you getting flowers, too?" Amara asked as she looked through the pre-pared bouquets with joy in her eyes. My cheeks burned again as my mother and Seraphine took turns glancing between Aiden and me.

"Can I have some?" Cordelia asked our mother. The rouge on her lips had completely wiped off from the many pastries I suspected she tasted during their visit to the bakery.

"Not today. We must get back to the caravan before your father sends out a search party to look for us." Mother smiled at the florist in passing as she led us through the crowd.

Seraphine linked her arm through mine, a smile on her face as she glanced at Aiden's flushed scowl. "How did it go?"

I sighed, watching my sisters run ahead to show our father their purchases and help Nonna take down the booth. "I took one."

Her hand squeezed my arm in silent comfort as our whole group reconvened in the alley. Alfie disappeared into the caravan immediately, two new books clutched tightly in his hands while Mousa and Killian spoke softly with Nonna in the shadows.

My mother's hand brushed a stray hair from my face. "Are you okay? You look a little pale."

Seraphine left us alone, moving to join Hakan and my father near the mule to offer us a small moment of privacy. My stomach twisted again as Tarsa joined us, one axe shining and clean, the other with traces of blood still on display.

Something deep inside me cracked, spreading through my entire being until I felt it threaten to open completely, casting me into oblivion.

Though tears threatened to burn my eyes, I nodded. "I'm just tired."

Arm in arm with my mother, I joined my siblings in the caravan while the immortals and Mousa walked with the mule ahead of us, creating a path through the crowded village streets. I lay on the small cot; Alfie huddled beside me as his nose remained in his book. By the time I fell asleep, the sun had risen fully into the sky, and a small rose had been placed on the cot beside my head with a faint trace of cedar clinging to the stem.

TWENTY

THE DAYS PASSED TOO slowly. Nonna had been anxious for me to collect as many souls as possible in the few days since Ephraim's visit. Just watching her elbow her way through a crowd in search of my next victim sent my stomach rolling every night. Though that could have had something to do with seeing her force my siblings to help her as well. Amara was far too young to be involved so closely in something this cruel, and I knew Alfie would rather bury his nose in one of his books than bring me a soul to steal.

Each night, Mother would hover while I decorated myself in the garb I was growing to hate and Nonna would disappear into the crowd. Seraphine would occasionally sit with me, but I knew she was needed with the others as they kept watch over my family.

"How are you feeling?" Mother asked as she, too, donned her outfit for the evening. We sat alone in the caravan while the rest of the family roamed outside to prepare for the night's performance.

We'd had little luck lately in finding a worthy crowd as word of our last interruption spread faster than we could travel. No one wanted to come see the Loutari clan perform if there was a chance a demon might show.

I sighed. "I'm fine," I lied. The thing that lived in my chest welcomed the opportunity to steal souls for Aiden to take, but it had begun to take its toll. I grew tired far easier now than I ever used to. Not to mention that when I finally did lay my head down to sleep, it evaded me. I'd listen to Aiden's pacing outside the caravan every night and silently wish to speak with him, but I didn't dare.

Each time I looked at him I could only think of the crumpled rose that now remained hidden beneath my pillow and the insinuations it may hold.

"Tonight should be a good night," she said, ignoring my obvious lie. "The duke here married a commoner this afternoon and everyone should be out to celebrate."

As if they'd heard her, the sounds of the entire village arriving at the campground exploded around us. The sun was sure to set soon, the evening overly warm in the autumn heat, but that didn't seem to stop the drunken revelry as the campground grew loud with laughter and music.

Leesa's family, the Montamen wanderers, had come with us. Though Mousa rarely shared a lady's bed for more than a single night, he seemed content to share hers these past few days. Her family set up camp on the far side of the campground, a few others setting up their performances nearby as well.

"Is this really the best place to perform then?" I asked stubbornly. This was a conversation we'd had many times the past couple of days. Aiden, oddly enough, agreed with me, though Nonna refused to listen to our hesitant words. We were only an hour's ride away from the castle in a campground just east of Deva. If the king got word that I was here there would be no stopping the damage his guards would cause just to get to me. Of that I was certain.

"Esme," Mother scolded softly. Her dark curls were pinned up and out of her face as she crouched beside me so we could share the small mirror. "I know how you feel about being this close to the castle. But I promise you, we will not let him take you again."

I sighed, ignoring the trembling of my lip as I painted it red. "It's not me that I'm worried about. Don't you think it would be safer for Amara and Alfie and the rest of the family if I just left with Aiden and the immortals to do this alone?"

"Don't you dare say such a thing," she said, spinning me around to face her directly. Her face, so much like my own, suddenly appeared older as she studied me. The warmth of her hand on my cheek seeped through me as I forced the emotions away. "If you try to leave, I will follow you anywhere."

I forced a smile. "Why do you think I haven't left yet?"

Mother rolled her eyes and dropped my cheek though a soft smile pulled at her mouth. "Get ready, dear. I'm sure Nonna will find many customers for you tonight."

With that she left, leaving me alone in the caravan.

My heart clenched tighter as I listened to Aiden greet her in passing. Aiden was once no more than a stranger who traded our crystal balls after a performance, yet somehow he had become someone gravely important to my family's survival. I'd refused to let myself think further about the slight skip in my pulse when he neared or how my entire body thrummed under his gaze. He was an immortal who served the god of Death. I shouldn't trust him, I shouldn't even like him, and yet I couldn't find it in myself to think of anything other than him.

The music distracted my thoughts then. The familiar beat of the parade song filled the grounds. Even now, as I sat alone in the caravan, I could picture the bride and groom being paraded around the dance floor in a chaotic mixture of dance and cheer.

Nights in the caravan had grown lonely as nobody bothered to sit with me anymore – not even Nonna. She found herself too busy searching for more souls. Seraphine would occasionally join me for a while, but she too had kept her distance since Aiden's cold exterior returned, leaving only the stirring in my chest for company.

My bones shook with the loud music. The crowd's laughter rocked through me as I leaned back against the small table. Surely I wouldn't be missed if I only stepped out for a moment.

Carefully, I made my way out of the caravan and caught myself smiling at the sight. The campground was full of men and women and children as they laughed and cheered at the revelry. Many were already indulging themselves in the many foods and drinks provided by Leesa's family, but others had gathered at my parent's stage where they waited for their jaw dropping performance.

The grass felt brittle beneath my boots, drying into nothing from the day's heat. Colors of tents and caravans blended together as I scanned the crowd, smiling wider as the music filled the crack growing in my soul.

"What are you doing out here?" Mousa asked, pulling me from my reverie.

I turned to see him standing nearby, Killian and Aiden at his sides; the former with his usual warm smile on his mouth. I returned his smile as I moved to join them. Aiden stiffened significantly at my approach though he didn't look in my direction. I didn't let the change affect me as I refused to acknowledge his presence altogether.

"Why must I wait in there alone?" I asked teasingly as I elbowed my brother gently in the ribs. "Besides; someone has to make sure you behave yourself. Leesa is still here after all. We don't want her family coming to grab you in your sleep if they catch you attempting to bed another girl."

Killian choked on a laugh, but Mousa placed a hand over his chest, feigning hurt.

"I wouldn't dare," he said.

I rolled my eyes. "You're despicable, you know that?"

His smile widened. "You've been listening to Alfie's romantic storybooks too much. It pains me that you don't see me as the romantic prince, come to sweep a girl off her feet."

I snorted. "The only sweeping you do is simply to get a girl on her back."

Killian barked a laugh, his young face reddening with the notion. Mousa merely sighed exasperatedly though he wore an equally cheery smile.

All around us the dancing continued. Far too many people filled the dance floor and crowded around the caravan and Aiden's tent nearby. I could just make out the top of Uncle Malik's head as he and our cousins continued to play the music that had everyone in such high spirits. The familiar sounds of the tune sent my heart thrumming.

"Alfie's not making as much progress as we expected," Mousa said suddenly.

My brow furrowed in confusion. "Progress with what?"

This time it was Mousa's turn to appear confused. "Has no one said anything to you?" Beside him, Killian and Aiden shared a look.

"Said anything about what?"

"Nothing," Aiden said quickly, coldly.

I scowled, turning toward the dance floor before us. The music danced across my skin welcomingly, enticing me to join the revelry for once instead of remaining in the shadows.

Sensing my temptation, Mousa grabbed my hand and pulled me into the middle of the crowded dance floor. I felt a smile fill my face, replacing the scowl it previously held, as he pulled me close and spun me around with the others. My brother's face relaxed, the tension I hadn't noticed in his shoulders released as he laughed with me. My skin burned with the force of Aiden's gaze though I didn't dare look to him. As if sensing my distraction, Mousa spun me again, nearly knocking my feet out from under me with a laugh.

I'd so longed to dance just once with my siblings. While they spent their nights in the center of the festivities, I was forced to spend my nights in the caravan with Nonna and possibly one stranger for company.

Now, I felt the cold tension leaving my body as sweat formed along my neck beneath the canopy of my thick curls. Mousa laughed with me as we clumsily made our way across the dance floor. No one paid us any mind as there remained no rhyme or reason to the dance. Some paraded around, dragging the bride and groom in tow; others spun each other around with hoots and hollers.

A familiar trill of laughter caught my attention. Mousa and I turned as one to watch Cordelia and Amara come barreling through the crowd to join us, our cousin Nadira appearing shortly after.

We collided together as our laughter rang loudly over the music and cheer. Nonna sent an undecipherable expression in my direction, but another set of hands grabbed me and spun me back into the crowd. Amara and Cordelia pulled at Mousa's hands as he spun them around chaotically. The sight filled me with laughter, lifting my heart from the dark place it had gone to hide and letting it fill with light.

Killian held me now. His face remained cheerful as he skillfully spun me around the other dancers.

"You dance quite well for an old man," I shouted over the music.

His smile widened as he spun me around delicately again before pulling me closer so as not to shout. "Believe it or not, I was once a nobleman. Learning proper dance technique was a requirement before I could ever court a lady."

I barked a laugh. "Why does that not surprise me?"

His brow furrowed slightly beneath the curls of his pale hair. "That I had to learn to dance?"

I shook my head. "That you were raised a nobleman."

Killian laughed, spinning me away only to release my hand and replace me with Cordelia. My sister flushed at being held so tightly against the immortal, though he appeared oblivious to her attraction as he winked at me.

"You wound me, Esme," he called over her head.

I laughed as I watched them disappear into the crowd. My chest throbbed as I was unable to recall the last time my sister smiled so broadly.

Mousa continued to dance with Amara nearby, but I didn't dare interrupt them. The sight of Nonna frowning from the caravan steps was nearly enough to make me return to the confinement of that cramped space. Nearly.

I turned a little then, scanning the crowd for the familiar set of grey eyes and whiskey colored hair. When I caught sight of him standing in the shadows, my lungs constricted. For the first time in days our eyes met. It was strange that such a small thing stole the breath from my lungs, but he didn't drop his gaze even as I dared to step in his direction.

"Esme," a strangely familiar voice said in my ear just as the familiar hands found mine.

I spun around; shock overruling any other feeling I may have had a moment ago.

"Your Highness?" I asked, forcing my voice to remain quiet. Prince Elias stood before me now, face alight with a smile.

Panic struck me as I glanced around frantically in search of the men I knew would soon follow to take me away.

"They're not here," he said, reading my unspoken question. "While my father has made it his single mission to have you returned, I have had my best spies out on the road tracking your movements. I've been able to lead my father's men astray. They're farther north, searching for you near the Gaiva Region, though I suspect he's growing suspicious of their continuous failure."

I felt myself start at his words. "You lied to your father about where I am?"

He gave a slow nod, almost shy and unwilling. "When I heard you were here in Deva, I knew I had to come see you." I flinched at his words, the memory of Aiden's touch blasted through my mind as the prince pulled me close in a slow dance. "I merely wanted to be certain of your safety," he added as he sent a glare over my head. I could guess where his eyes were focused as I felt Aiden's familiar gaze burning through my back.

"I'm safe," I answered honestly. Though Aiden hadn't spoken to me as of late, I knew he worked tirelessly to keep me and my family safe. That much was evident as he hardly seemed to rest for more than a few minutes at a time.

"And you have no idea how glad I am to see it."

My cheeks heated of their own accord. Though the prince and I had hardly spent any time together, he was never cruel toward me. His brief kindness toward the end of my captivity told me he had a kind heart, if only his father would let him use it.

"Can I ask you something?" My voice was nearly drowned out by the surrounding music.

Elias tilted his head to study me, his playful smile returning. "Anything, Esme."

I hesitated, unsure if I was ready to hear the truth. I'd spent these past weeks searching for any reason behind King Elroy's motives, and yet I found none. My heart beat erratically in my chest as the familiar, cold nerves froze the blood in my veins.

"Why does your father want me back?" I finally asked, my voice shaking slightly. Elias' brow furrowed as he shot his eyes over my head, dropping my gaze. "He let Aiden take me away. So why does he want me back so suddenly?"

The prince studied something over my head a moment longer, eyes growing distant as a muscle ticked in his jaw. Eventually, he sighed, shoulders drooping with the motion as his hand tightened around my waist. "I don't know any details," he said slowly, reluctantly. "All I know is he seems to believe there is something you can give him. It's what he kept going on about those first days he took you."

I started, shoulders tightening as I remembered that night so long ago. "But he hates the wanderers. There isn't anything I could possibly give him," I said, though my lungs tightened at the possibility that the king may know the truth of what I did for my family.

Elias shrugged, unbothered. "He believes otherwise."

My mind began to wander, no longer noting the way his hands tightened around me, or the way his eyes softened as he studied me. Thoughts roared through my mind in a panic. If the king knew the truth—if he even had a suspicion of what I could do—then I had little doubt that he truly would stop at nothing to have me returned to his captivity. What I couldn't figure out was exactly how he would find a way to make my duty to my family benefit him.

We danced in silence for the remainder of the song, only occasionally laughing at a misstep or catching sight of a drunken villager tumble over.

When the song ended, a familiar heat filled the space behind me. I froze, not daring to look as Elias frowned at the presence over my shoulder. I didn't need to look to know who stood there now. The heated flutter in my chest told me all I needed to know.

"Leave." Aiden's voice came out cold enough to bring a chill to my skin.

Elias scowled at the immortal behind me. "Excuse me?"

"If you don't mind, Your Highness," Aiden said coolly, slowly. "I do believe it is time you disappear yet again as your presence has begun to draw attention. And I think we can both agree that any attention coming in Esme's direction wouldn't be good for her or her family."

Prince Elias paled slightly as his eyes scanned the surrounding crowd. Sure enough, a few people had begun to stare at us in wonder. Being this close to the castle, it was possible many of the villagers here had seen the prince many times before.

My chest tightened as I considered the implications of the prince's stay.

"Of course," Elias said with a slight bow. He brushed his lips against the back of my hand, the gesture causing Aiden to still at my shoulder. "It was a pleasure to dance with you and see you in good health, Esme. I do hope I can see you again soon."

I returned his smile. "The pleasure was mine." His mouth twitched in a smile at my words.

Without another glance in Aiden's direction, the prince disappeared into the crowd. I turned to glare at Aiden as soon as he was gone but froze as I realized his intention.

Aiden stood there, hand outstretched slightly, almost as if he was uncertain about this decision. His face warmed a little under the candlelight and the darkened sky.

"Dance with me." His deep voice melted through my bones as he spoke in a hushed tone. The world seemed to disappear around us. Even the music seemed to fade as I gently placed my hand in his.

TWENTY-ONE

My BREATH CAUGHT AS Aiden pulled me close, our bodies pressing together tightly. The tender touch of his hand in mine sent a thrill through my chest that I didn't try to understand. This was the first time we'd stood this close since that night in his tent. I wasn't sure what to think now as his usual cold exterior seemed to melt away as he stared down at me.

His other hand wrapped around my waist, settling at the small of my back, keeping me pressed against him. Without a word, he began to spin us around the dance floor. I couldn't hear the music above the pounding of blood in my ears, and no matter how hard I tried, I couldn't drop his gaze. I remained enraptured in the deep grey-blue of his eyes. For every detail of my face he took in with his gaze, I felt it like a brand against my skin.

"You weren't so melancholy when dancing with the prince," he noted quietly.

I felt myself smile. "Perhaps I'm merely mirroring my partner."

The corner of his lip twitched with the barest hint of a smile. My heart stuttered at the sight of such a small movement. The hand at my back began to shift, tracing agonizingly slow circles with the tips of his fingers.

"I hadn't realized you and the prince grew so close during your months at the castle," he said, refusing to change the subject.

I sighed internally. "Hardly," I admitted. "He was just kind to me."

"He was kind?" Aiden's voice grew colder as he continued to spin us slowly through the crowd, his fingers continuing their tantalizingly slow perusal against my back.

"Yes," I snapped, growing frustrated. "He was kind." I caught Killian's frown as he glanced our way, Cordelia still held firmly in his arms as they spun away from us.

"Tell me, how many times *exactly* did he stop his father from harming you? Because you had far too many bruises covering your skin to have had someone truly interfering with his cruelty."

My spine went rigid at the reminder. "He couldn't interfere," I argued. "His father is the king. He couldn't stop him."

His words came out in a growl as he said, "I would have."

From the steel determination in his gaze, I knew his words to be true. Of that I had no doubt.

"You don't know what you're talking about," I whispered stubbornly, blinking away the tears that threatened to fill my eyes.

Aiden's face turned cold, dark. Shadows filled his eyes as he stared at me. "You didn't see what I saw when we first took you from the castle." My skin grew cold with the memory of pain, now distant and faint thanks to whatever ointment he had used during our earliest travels.

"You were hollow," he said in a strained whisper. "There was no life in your eyes; no joy. Not a single part of your body was not painted in bruises or broken from his chains. That is why I cannot forgive your prince so easily."

I swallowed my retort as he spun me again, further into the crowd and away from the curious faces of my family as they stood nearby.

"Are you so certain the prince is your friend?" Aiden asked coolly, pulling us farther from the crowded dance floor.

His hand at my back tightened ever so slightly as I leaned away to look into his face. "I trust that he means me no harm."

Aiden considered my words, his brows furrowing as he frowned at me. The barely-gone bruises seemed to grow tender beneath his gaze.

His hand moved, slowly at first so I nearly didn't notice as it moved from the small of my back up to my neck. My breath caught as his thumb grazed the scar I carried there. His eyes studied it, turning distant. I didn't dare breathe too harshly though the pounding of my heart against my ribs made me feel on the edge of bursting beneath his touch; both of our eyes haunted by the memory of what caused this particular scar.

"When will he come for me?" I finally asked, my voice coming out far too breathy for my liking.

Aiden caught himself then—one blink and his hand returned to my waist. "Who?"

"Ephraim," I said as I watched his eyes return to the present.

He cast a glance over my head where I knew Tarsa remained hidden in the trees. "We've had no sighting of him in days, but that could mean anything."

"How do you know him so well?" I dared ask. The song changed then, turning slower. A romantic ballad echoed through the campground as couples pulled each other tight and spun onto the dance floor. The cheers of those gathered around distant performances throughout the campground dimmed beneath the blood roaring in my ears as my gaze dipped to Aiden's mouth of its own accord.

Aiden pulled me closer, his hand tightening around my waist. "We grew up together. There was once a time I considered him a brother."

"What changed?" How long had I dreamt of knowing Aiden more intimately than just the stranger who provided my family with our siphons? And now, as I stood here wrapped in his arms, I couldn't imagine going back to not knowing him.

"There are many truths to your mortal lore of the war with angels and demons that your ancestors have changed," he finally said softly. "I lived through those times when angels were seen as cruel, and demons were the ones to provide safety and comfort to your kind. It took only one moment of weakness for the perceptions to change."

"And now we are taught to fear and hate demons while we worship the angels for their kindness," I continued his unspoken thoughts.

He nodded gravely. "There are things you may learn in your days yet to come that will warp the way you will view your world—your family even. If I could take that pain away from you, I would."

I offered a sad smile. "But you won't because you want me to know the truth. Whatever that might be."

Aiden returned my smile a beat too slowly. "Sometimes I think that."

"And your prince?" I dared ask. "The one you serve. Is he kind, or is he like Ephraim?"

"He is nothing like Ephraim," he said quickly. More questions rose on my tongue, but from the sudden coolness touching his eyes I refrained from asking.

We fell silent then, neither one of us daring to speak as the music continued around us. And as we danced, his face, always so cold yet handsome nonetheless, warmed a bit with each beat.

As the song continued, every inch of my skin heated and grew taut under his unyielding gaze. There was nothing fearful about him in this small moment—nothing that made me want to run in fear. I saw none of the warrior I knew him to be. In this moment, he was merely a young man who held me tightly as if afraid I might disappear beneath his grasp.

I leaned forward then, tentatively, watching his eyes widen slightly. I let myself breathe him in; the faint scent of cedar covered his skin and clothes. There was no telling whether he might return to his cold demeanor after this night, and I wanted the moment to savor his touch no matter how brief and selfish that might be.

As I leaned in further, letting my cheek rest on his shoulder, I felt the tension leave his body. Whatever control he might have been fighting for a moment ago disappeared as he pressed his palm flat against my back, pulling me closer as his cheek came to rest atop my head. The touch erased any pain from my body, whether in memory or lingering physical exhaustion. My eyes shuttered closed as I stood there, letting him hold me in a brief moment of comfort.

We didn't move for what could have been hours, or days. Not even when the song changed did we move. My skin grew too tight as I felt his breath warm my cheek. The air left my lungs entirely when I felt his cheek brush mine in a caress.

My heart beat so loudly against my ribs I was almost certain he could hear it though he gave no indication he could. His hand released mine, instead moving to pull at my chin.

Breathing became more difficult as he ever so gently pulled my face up to meet his. Only a fraction of space separated my lips from his. I needed only lean forward slightly for our lips to touch.

His gaze burned along my skin as he scanned my face for any sign of rejection, any hint that I wanted to escape his touch. The mere thought of letting him go now twisted my heart painfully. I'd gladly live out the rest of my days here, wrapped in his warm embrace with my skin afire beneath his touch.

"Esme." Cordelia's familiar voice shouted over the surrounding crowd, startling Aiden and I apart though his eyes remained firmly on my mouth.

"Esme," Cordelia said breathlessly as she approached, oblivious to her abrupt interruption. "Nonna is asking for you to return to the caravan."

I nodded, not looking away from Aiden, waiting for the inevitable return of his cold mask. My heart continued to ache in my chest at the sudden loss of his touch.

When his face remained open and warm, I sighed. Pleasure filled my chest as I felt my cheeks warm beneath his hungry gaze, his eyes a storm of emotions as he refused to look away.

Without a word, I turned to follow Cordelia back through the crowd. All the while, I could feel Aiden's gaze burning into my back with longing. A longing I could no longer deny I felt.

The remainder of the night flew by quicker than I thought possible. In total, Nonna managed to find seven people whose souls were currently being carried away by Aiden in the siphons. Tarsa disappeared shortly after him to dispose of those I'd damned.

All around me, the campground grew quiet as the revelers of tonight's performances lingered, slowly returning to their homes farther into town. My parents were assisting my aunt and uncle as they packed our belongings into the caravan while Mousa and Nadira set up the tents our family shared on nights we didn't travel to an inn. I was careful to note the distant placement of my own tent from Aiden's. The knowledge of my older brother's slight interference made me smile through the heaviness I felt in my chest.

I hadn't taken so many souls in a single night before and now it weighed heavily on me. My body ached with every inch I moved and my muscles remained tight with exhaustion. My stomach rolled slightly as I shifted to better see the campground.

Leesa, my brother's current bed warmer, continuously shot glances his way as she watched him pitch tents in the light of the fire burning nearby. My youngest siblings currently sat there with Leesa's siblings. While Alfie was physically present at the fire, he refused to acknowledge his companions as he took notes furiously from one of his new books.

Father shot worried looks my way as I worked to braid my hair down my back. My skin felt oddly clammy in the night air, though the light breeze offered to cool the sweat clinging to my skin. From where I sat, I could also smell the food my sisters cooked at the fire, but the thought of eating anything sent my stomach rolling again. I closed my eyes, breathing deeply through my teeth to keep the nausea at bay.

"Are you okay?" Killian asked, coming to sit beside me. I hadn't seen him since he'd disappeared on the dance floor with Cordelia hours earlier. But as per usual, as soon as he sat beside me it was as if he'd never left.

I shrugged, the movement stiff and uncomfortable. "Just tired I think."

Killian studied me a moment, the bow slung over his back sticking out over his head to cast a strange shadow over his young face. The blue of his eyes darkened as he cataloged the ashen tone of my skin and the bruises that had begun to form below my eyes upon collecting tonight's souls.

"You can sleep in Aiden's tent until he gets back," he said softly so his voice wouldn't carry. "He wouldn't mind and I'm sure the cot in his tent is much more comfortable than the roll laid out on the ground in yours."

I dipped my chin to hide my blush. "I'm okay for now I think."

"Hey," Seraphine said as she came to join us. Her long, twisted braids hung loose around her shoulders tonight making her appear more fierce than usual, though the smile threatened to reveal her kind nature. "Shouldn't you two be doing something useful with yourselves?"

Killian chuckled, ignoring the sudden flush to my cheeks as my skin heated uncomfortably. "We both know Hakan can watch her entire family at once."

Seraphine gently shoved him aside to sit between us on the narrow steps, our bodies pressed together in close proximity. The heat of their bodies so close to mine sent my head rolling uneasily. Why was I suddenly so feverish?

"Esme?" Seraphine's voice was laced with concern as she caught sight of my slumped stature.

"I'm okay," I said, running a hand over my face, trying to expel my unease. "Just tired."

Killian mumbled something unintelligible under his breath that I chose to ignore but Seraphine scolded him anyway. "Why don't you go check in with Hakan? Tarsa won't be back for a while yet and I'm sure he could use some company."

Killian sighed, reluctant to leave. "If you're so concerned with his wellbeing, why don't you join him instead?" he said as he stood and slowly made his way through the campground.

"Because it's just so fun to watch you walk away, Killian," Seraphine shouted cheerily. The giggles of my sisters echoed through the following silence as Killian shot a wink over his shoulder.

"They'll all be in love with him before the end of the week," I said with mock concern. Cordelia had begun to hover nearby whenever Mousa and Killian were spotted together. I feared she'd grown too attached to the immortal during their brief dance, but I couldn't bring myself to tell her to look elsewhere for romance. Not when her heart was so present in her gaze.

Seraphine chuckled. "Much like you and Aiden I expect."

"I beg your pardon?" I sputtered as I glanced in her direction. Her knowing smile made my cheeks flush further.

"I saw you two, you know," she said quietly so as not to be overheard. Mousa and Nadira had moved to the fire now where the others sat, Mother and Father included, but the campground was still quiet enough for us to be overheard if we weren't careful.

"When you were dancing," she clarified as I forced breath into my lungs. "We all did. Your grandmother was not happy, but your mother seemed to find it sweet."

I snorted. "Nonna would rather I not interact with anyone beyond our immediate family so I can focus on this stupid debt."

"Don't you want to as well? It would keep them safe."

"Of course I want to," I admitted softly. "I'd do anything if it meant keeping them safe." The memory of Ephraim's last visit flashed in my mind making me shudder. Should he return, I'd gladly let him take me if it meant my family could be left unharmed.

Seraphine read my expression as her face turned down in a scowl. "Esme Loutari-Ayres. I swear, if you even consider letting Ephraim take you away, I will lock you in that caravan myself and throw away the key."

I forced a smile though I knew it didn't touch my eyes. "I wasn't going to," I lied smoothly. "I just wish things could be different—that I didn't have to hurt people this way. If I could end the debt, I would."

She studied me a moment more before moving to join those gathered at the fire. Alfie had grown fond of her and moved to allow her to sit beside him. He had endless questions for each of the immortals about their lives and the weapons they carried, particularly for Tarsa's axes. We all found amusement in watching him pester the cold woman with questions she seemed reluctant to answer. Seraphine, however, was kind and gentle with him, answering all of his questions without hesitation. I watched now as he pulled his notebook from his waistband and looked up at her expectantly.

It amazed me how close my entire family had grown to Aiden and his friends. Nonna seemed to be the only one reluctant to welcome them as she sat nearby, frowning in Seraphine's direction.

I thought of Kesson then and my heart ached with the memories. On nights like this, after a performance, his family would join ours, just as my family sat around the fire now, sharing stories and laughter. That's how we'd grown so close; how I grew to love him.

I glanced north, toward the road to Deva. It was only a couple of miles through the trees, but I knew his mother remained there in the care of a healer as her sickness kept her bedridden. I wondered if anyone had told her of her children's murder yet.

Silently, and on unsteady feet, I disappeared into the dark knowing my family would remain distracted for a while longer.

The village was quiet. With dawn so close I knew nearly everyone here slept soundly in their warm beds. The cobblestones of the street kept my footsteps silent as my boots wove a path through the streets. My vision tilted slightly, but I refused to give in to this weakening feeling as I pushed forward. The rolling of my stomach threatened to be my undoing, but this was something I couldn't put off any longer.

The familiar red doors of the healer's office came into view. Each surrounded by large windows lined with different antidotes and ointments permeating the air outside the shop with a strong, medicinal scent.

Carefully, I pulled myself up the vines lining the stone siding of the building to peer into the upstairs window where I knew the healer kept his patients. Slowly, so as not to cause the window to creak, I pushed it open and stepped inside.

There, sprawled like the dead beneath worn sheets, lay Kesson's mother. A woman who was once a force to behold, now reduced to bones and labored breathing. My eyes snagged on the light shadow drifting upward from her broken form: her soul, nearly ready to depart for the stars. I swallowed against the constricting of my heart as I watched her.

Her eyes opened at once, her light sleep interrupted by my sudden appearance.

"Esme?" her voice croaked into the silence, making my skin grate uncomfortably. "Is that you?"

I offered a smile. "It's me."

Her answering smile sent my heart tumbling. "Is Kesson with you?" she asked hoarsely.

I shook my head slowly, sinking to my knees beside her bed. "No ma'am. Kesson is not with me any longer."

Her brow furrowed. "He told your father he was going to help look for you after you were taken. Did he not find you?"

Tears threatened to burn my eyes as the memory of his screams shot through me while I watched him burn. "He did, but he was too late. I was too late."

"What happened?" Her voice came out a whisper as pain flickered across her face. Her hand gripped mine in a surprisingly tight grasp.

I squeezed her hand in comfort. "The king captured him while I was held at the castle," I said slowly. I took a steadying breath before continuing. "He burned Kesson. Zaven and the others died trying to save him, but there was nothing they could do. Nothing I could do."

The heartbreak that shot across her face now made my heart crumble, all thoughts of my own pain and discomfort forgotten as tears trailed down her cheeks.

"No," she croaked in a broken cry. "That can't be."

As she cried in my arms, I told her everything. The truth of my family, the reason I was captured, the reason behind her children's deaths. She, more than anyone, deserved to know why she was the last of her family to live. And I held her through it all as sobs wracked through her frail form.

Tears burned my eyes as I sat with her, refusing to let the dark thoughts of my own family's possible fate drag me into an endless agony. Instead, I began to tell her of the adventures Kesson and I would drag Zaven on. I told her of our mischief through the villages during our travels while she remained bedridden at the healer's shop. The memories tore through me, pulling at the darkness living near my heart as death grew near, too near.

Only when the healer arrived to shoo me away and give her a sedative did I finally release her. Her pale hand shot out to grip mine once more, tears leaving harsh tracks down her cheeks.

"He always loved you," she sobbed. "He'd be glad to see you free again, even if he isn't here to be with you."

My own tears spilled over then. I refused to let myself look back as I quickly crawled through the window, the sounds of her harsh breathing echoing through the night air.

The night remained quiet and cool as I made my way back to the campground. Tears blurred my already tilting vision as the exhaustion from before seemed to return in full force, leaving me stumbling through the streets. The memory of Kesson's pained screams and Zaven's pleas for help rolled through me, tangling with the sight of their mother's tears.

I slipped then, catching myself on something warm and solid.

"Where have you been?" Aiden nearly growled as he pulled me upright. His hands remained on my shoulders as he waited for me to find my footing.

"I had something to do," I said hoarsely. I hated that my voice sounded so broken. Quickly, I tried to brush away any evidence of tears before looking up at him. His face immediately warmed, losing its cool mask as he took in my tears.

"What happened?" His voice was gentle as it spilled over me.

The words nearly split my heart in two again as I forced the memories away.

"Come," he said softly. His arm wrapped around my shoulders as he let me lean heavily against his side. My vision suddenly threatened to shift again as the strange exhaustion caught up with me. "Let's get you home."

Aiden stayed silent as I stained his shirt with my tears. Though the night remained quiet, my ears were filled with noise of the lucid memory of the screams of those who burned as a punishment for my own ignorance. In that moment, I could have sworn their souls lingered nearby if only to haunt me further.

TWENTY-TWO

Exhaustion kept me bedridden for days at a time, only coming out of my tent to perform the duty required of me each night. We'd stayed near Deva the past four days, awaiting the arrival of the end-of-harvest festival that the king hosted each year. Luckily, it was such a huge celebration that all the wanderer families came to perform in the villages surrounding the castle, so I wasn't worried about being caught. Especially since my parents had finally convinced Nonna to let us wear our travel clothes instead of our Loutari colors.

Even though we hardly traveled – only moving from one campground to the next—I found it difficult to perform my duty. I slept through it all. My eyes burned every time I opened them, my limbs felt weighted with lead, and my lungs felt too tight in my chest as I tried to keep my breathing normal and relaxed.

I knew they worried for me, especially when I refused to join my family for meals. Every time I took a soul, it took something from me as well. I grew weaker with every soul that I tore from its body. Nonna pretended to believe the lies I told, but I knew mother—and Aiden—could see past them.

Even now, as the autumn breeze blew through the open flap of my tent, my skin felt feverish. My hair clung to the sweat at my brow and my clothes hugged my sweat-soaked skin, but I couldn't find it in myself to move to the river to wash. I could hear the sounds of the Little River just beyond the tree line, but my legs felt too heavy to move and my soul too fractured to care.

Aiden sat at the opening of my tent; his usual position these days. He only left my side now to kill those whose souls I took before they could do something to draw the king's attention. I'd gotten used to having him so close, especially as Mousa had taken it upon himself to pitch my tent beside Aiden's for the past week.

Soft footsteps nearing the tent forced me to open my eyes. I wasn't worried, not really since Aiden sat so close by, but I recognized the soft, measured footfalls.

"How is she?" Mother asked as she sat beside Aiden. She wouldn't admit it, but I could tell she'd grown fond of the immortal, and though he didn't show it, I knew the feeling was mutual. Where he was once serious and cold, I could see him relaxing more with my family each day. And thankfully they were beginning to see the warmth in him that I had discovered long ago.

"She hasn't moved in two hours," he said quietly. "Her skin is feverish and pale. I've offered her water and food but she won't eat anything."

I found myself surprised at the worry lacing his tone. Even though I couldn't see him from where I lay, I could picture the furrow of his brow and the subtle pout of his lips.

Mother sighed. "I worry for her. She's never been this ill."

"Her duty takes a heavy toll," Aiden said slowly, and I knew he was being cautious so as not to worry her further. "Many souls are due to pay your family's debt. It will be a long while before she will feel like herself again."

"Is there not some way to remove the debt so she doesn't have to be the one to pay it?" my mother asked softly.

Aiden's sigh was nearly inaudible, but my mother continued before he could respond. "Alfie has read nearly every book he could get his hands on and still we have found nothing. There must be some way to end this for her. She can't go on like this."

I could feel their gazes settle on my back as silence fell between them. My chest tightened to know that my family still looked for a way to end this when I couldn't. Tears burned my throat as I lay still in the tent, listening.

"This will kill her," my mother said in a choked whisper. I was certain there were tears growing in her eyes as her gaze bore into my curled frame. "If she continues like this, it will kill her, Aiden."

"I won't let it," he said just as certainly.

"Promise me you'll keep her safe. No matter what, you do whatever it takes to keep my daughter safe."

A moment of silence passed as I felt their gazes settle in my direction yet again. I forced my breathing to remain even, face turned away. Tendrils of the darkness within me reached out, searching for the comfort Aiden's presence often lent.

"She means a great deal to you, doesn't she?" My mother's voice was soft, filled with wonder.

I felt Aiden's gaze like a brand along my skin as the darkness curled around his presence, marveling at the connection it felt toward him. "There are no words for what she means to me," he said with absolute surety. My stomach tightened at the ring of truth to his words, whatever they might mean.

"Promise me she'll be safe with you," my mother repeated, gentler now.

Consciousness slipped from me again, taking the sounds of the world with it and hiding the promise Aiden undoubtedly made to my mother as my hand gripped the wilted rose hidden beneath my pillow.

When I next woke it was to Mother sitting beside me. A cold cloth pressed against my brow. I tried to speak, say anything, but my mouth felt brittle and dry.

"Here," she said, understanding.

I swallowed a few gulps of the tepid water before the nausea returned. Carefully, I propped myself up on my elbows to view the tent around me. Blankets were haphazardly thrown around the small corner of the floor where I slept. My socks and boots lay near my feet as if they'd been taken off in a chaotic rush. My cheeks heated as I considered my family discovering the injuries I had worked so hard to keep secret. Slowly, so she wouldn't notice, I pulled the sleeves of my shirt down to cover the wounds still garnishing my wrists, hoping to keep at least part of the truth of my captivity hidden.

"What day is it?" I croaked as I finally found my voice.

Her hand brushed my sweaty hair from my face. "The festival begins tonight."

I nodded, the movement slow and heavy. "I'll be ready."

My mother's face softened. Her round brown eyes, so much like my own, studied me closely.

I glanced down at myself. My shirt clung to my skin, soaked with sweat, which was now an ashen grey. I couldn't imagine the bruises that lingered beneath my eyes after spending so many days holed away in my tent.

"We worry for you," she said quietly.

I turned to the spot I knew Aiden usually inhabited as he kept watch. Surprise coursed through me when I found it empty.

"He's at the river with Mousa and Killian," she said, reading my mind. A small knowing smile briefly touched her lips. "He worries for you too."

I sighed, the sound raspy and harsh. "It's his duty to keep me alive until I can fulfill this debt our family owes. Of course, he worries. If I fail, who knows what will happen to him —" My mother raised her brows, but I pushed on. "—or to the others Killian, Seraphine, Hakan, Tarsa? I have no way of knowing how my failure will affect them."

"I think he worries for reasons other than his duty, dear," she said carefully. She moved the cloth along my skin again, wiping the dripping sweat from my brow. I could smell its stale, salty tang on the air and knew I needed to bathe soon before the festival started.

"He hardly leaves, you know," she added as she dipped the cloth in the pail of water again. "He refuses to leave your side for even a moment. I had to enlist Killian and Mousa to get him to leave even for this short time."

I snorted. "Again, it's his duty to keep me alive."

"Seraphine agrees with me," she said slyly with a gleam in her eye I'd missed in recent days.

"Is that so?" I replied a little sourly.

My mother's smile widened at the familiar snap in my tone. "He adores you, Esme." I snorted but she continued, choosing to ignore me. "Trust me. No man ever behaves that way for just some woman he is duty-bound to protect."

"Met many men who are duty-bound to protect someone, have you?"

She flashed another brief smile before setting the wet cloth against my forehead. I sighed at the coolness of it. "He's changed; Seraphine even noticed. The longer he spends here, with you, the more human he seems to become. He's not so serious or cold all the time. He's warm—he even assisted Seraphine in helping teach your sisters how to protect themselves yesterday, and they loved it, I might add."

I smiled. The idea of seeing Aiden with my sisters warmed me more than I would have liked to admit. He was so detached and cool those first few days I spent with him, but even I could admit how much he has softened lately. Since our dance, he'd changed drastically toward me. Every time our eyes met, I felt my heart rate spike and pound against my ribs, and I could've sworn his cheeks would flush the slightest bit as if his heart beat in time with mine.

"I wish you would join them, or even leave your tent for a few hours," she said quietly. I watched as her expression turned inward, finding a reason to place blame on her own shoulders for what had become of me.

I squeezed her hand. "I will," I promised. "Once this is done, I'll never leave them alone."

She rolled her eyes, though a smile quirked up the corners of her full mouth. "That's not entirely what I meant. I just wish you weren't so ill."

I offered her a smile, weak as it was. "Perhaps when this is all over, I'll be good as new."

My mother's face turned somber as she studied me. As her gaze turned to my scarred ankles I fought to keep still, to refrain from hiding them beneath the covers. In the few weeks since I'd been returned to my family, I'd never told them the extent of the injuries I sustained.

She hugged me then, though my skin felt too hot for an embrace. It had been so long since I'd been well enough to stay awake and talk to someone, apart from my duty to collect souls. I hadn't realized how much I missed spending time with those I loved, even if it were just listening to my mother attempt to push Aiden and I closer together.

A familiar head of whiskey colored hair appeared just at the tree line. I felt myself smile as he watched me, a beautiful look of wonder on his face. Mousa's tangle of brown hair clung to him, damp with the river water, but he didn't seem to notice Aiden's sudden stillness as he caught sight of where I sat with Mother.

Leesa appeared to drag Mousa away and out of sight from the small opening in my tent. But Killian and Aiden remained, the former smiling in greeting before he too disappeared from view, leaving only Aiden behind.

He smiled then; really smiled. My heart threatened to stop at the beauty of it. I hadn't seen him smile in such a way, so at ease and joyous. Tears burned the back of my eyes but I pushed them away. I could feel the exhaustion threatening to take me under again. I fought against it as I sat there in my mother's arms, focused on the immortal as he made his way toward me, smile still pulling at the corners of his mouth.

The flutter of the darkness in my chest eased a bit at his return and that was enough to confirm my mother's suspicions regarding Aiden's intentions.

Darkness clung to the ground outside, but the light of the lanterns and candles kept the campground lively as villagers and townsfolk slowly arrived to enjoy the performances they had grown to love.

My fever remained, but I forced the mint tonic Seraphine gave me only moments earlier to settle my stomach while I stepped inside the caravan. Nonna expected to steal ten souls tonight, as the first night of the festival was usually the largest. The thought alone made my stomach turn violently.

Aiden was furious with her for asking so much of me. That argument amused Mother to no end, but I found it irritating as they debated what they thought I could or couldn't handle.

My limbs felt heavy and my skin remained slick with sweat as I battled the growing exhaustion. There was a cool breeze on the air tonight and I welcomed it eagerly as I braided my obsidian curls down my back. I even tied on a strip of red cloth at my hairline to keep any loose strands from sticking to my face. It was a nice change to wear a simple black tunic and pants as opposed to the usual garb Nonna preferred I wear.

Aiden stood nearby, as he always did, guarding the caravan where I would do my duty. His eyes roamed over the horizon, forever in search of danger. Though the burnings may have been paused, the king's search for me was never ending. Guards patrolled the traveling roads across the kingdom and more had been sent to surveil each village. It was thanks to Aiden and his friends that we hadn't been found yet.

As I drew closer and stepped up onto the caravan steps, Aiden's hand shot out to assist me. His fingers were cool to the touch against my own heated skin, but I welcomed it with a pleasured sigh as I stepped into the warm caravan.

I didn't turn to watch Aiden close the door behind me as he remained outside. Nonna had refused to let him join in on these collections as she felt certain he was the cause of my weakened state, claiming his presence and our budding "friendship" was an unnecessary distraction.

I'd only just taken my place at the small table, siphon positioned in the center of the bright tablecloth outlined in yellow and orange flowers on a field of green and blue, when Nonna returned. Her smile was full and forced as she ushered in a young man from the nearby town. His pale green gaze rushed over the interior of the caravan excitedly before settling on me.

I knew what he saw on my face to turn his smile hesitant. My usual golden skin had grown pale and even more ashen than it appeared early in the day, bruises grew beneath my eyes, and the scar at my neck had reddened and now appeared as a harsh line across my skin.

"This is my granddaughter Esme," Nonna said as she practically threw the young man into the seat opposite me. "She'll be doing your reading today."

He swallowed audibly and gave me a brief nod before shooting his gaze about the caravan again. I guessed he was looking for a quick escape other than the door that Nonna sat near.

"Hi," I said warmly. "What reading can I do for you today?"

The man hesitated again, eyes roaming over the stack of tarot cards and the crystal ball before me. He nodded at the siphon. "Does that really work?" His voice remained laced with disbelief.

Nonna scoffed, amused. "Of course, it does. Esme is the best at pulling fragments of a future for those with questions."

I ignored her false confidence as I reached for the stranger's hands. "May I?" I asked as I pressed his hands against either side of the siphon. He didn't respond as I moved.

Slowly, the familiar pull in my chest began. The darkness moved outward from its home near my heart, spreading through my shoulders and down my arms to latch onto the man before me.

My fingertips warmed with the darkness as I unleashed it fully. My breath came in harsh gasps as exhaustion filtered in. The siphon before us began to glow such a bright shade of blue it was nearly white as it pulled the soul from the man before me.

He didn't seem to notice the tearing of his soul as he stared, enraptured with the show of it.

The light filled the caravan in its entirety as the darkness within me spread wider, threating to cast me in shadow and swallow me whole. I could even feel it now as it dared to reach toward Nonna who sat by, watching in critical silence. I could feel her frown focused on my face as a bead of sweat dripped down my cheek.

I gasped as the light disappeared altogether, only remaining in the siphon now, giving off a gentle glow. The man blinked, unsure of what just happened.

"That's it?" He turned to glare at me. His hands pulled violently from my own. "I paid for a light show?"

Anger filled every line of his face as he stood to tower over me. It was common for clients to be dazed after collecting their souls, but rarely were they so quick to anger.

"It was more than that," Nonna said as she moved to stand between us.

My body suddenly felt too heavy, my eyes refusing to stay open, though I fought the urge to close them. I stood uneasily as I moved toward the door, the air in the caravan suddenly far too hot on my tight skin.

"Esme?" Nonna called as the man shoved past her to get to me.

The door flung open, Aiden's ferocious stature filling the opening as he took a brief moment to study me before turning to glower dangerously at the man over my shoulder.

"Don't do it," the man said to Aiden as if he were a mere client. "It's a scam."

The man shoved past me, sending me flying to the ground, as he stormed out into the night. Aiden's broad arms wrapped around my middle before I could hit the grass. His skin was marvelously cool against my own as I felt my fever grow.

"Hakan," he barked into the night.

Hakan appeared silently. His long black hair was tied back in a braid, hanging beside the sword he kept between his shoulders. The immortal studied me a moment before nodding to Aiden and disappearing after the stranger.

"I'll find another," Nonna said casually as she stepped out into the night.

"No," Aiden said quickly. I found myself suddenly thankful for his frankness with her as he helped me regain my balance. "Esme needs to rest. She is not well enough for this, and you know it."

Nonna scoffed though she narrowed her eyes in my direction. "Fine. She can have a few minutes to gather herself first."

My body grew heavier with each breath. Only when I couldn't stand any longer did I let myself lean into Aiden's grip. He hugged me against himself willingly.

"No, Adine." His voice was tight with anger now, hands nearly trembling with it. "You know this will not work. Not like this."

"She will be fine," Nonna retorted coldly. "You doubt her strength too much."

"I know precisely how strong Esme is," Aiden said hotly. "She is stronger than you give her credit for. Which is exactly why you need to stop this. If she continues it will only weaken her further, and eventually it could kill her."

"If she is as strong as you believe you know her to be then you know she can handle it."

"No," he said again with a shake of his head. Aiden's hands tightened around my waist as my head fell against his chest, too heavy to hold upright. I could feel the beat of his heart beneath my cheek, smell the cedar and sweat on his skin. "If she were anyone else, she would already be dead. She's alive now because of the strength in her heart."

"Stop," I begged between harsh breaths. My eyes suddenly felt too heavy to keep open. "I just need a moment. I'll be fine."

"There," Nonna said pointedly. "See? She's fine. I'll be back soon."

I didn't hear her disappear. My eyes remained closed as I stood there, leaning heavily on Aiden for support.

His hand came up to cup my cheek, turning my face upward. When I forced my eyes open, I saw him studying me closely. His lips were turned down in a frown that seemed to weigh heavily on him; his shoulders sagged at whatever he saw in my eyes.

"I'm really okay," I croaked. The familiar cheers welcoming my parents' performance sounded in the distance. I sighed as I leaned further into his touch, the coolness of his skin soothing the burn in mine.

"Esme," he said slowly.

His words were cut off as a scream sounded in the distance. The panic it contained pushed the exhaustion from my limbs, replacing it with my own fear.

Aiden hugged me tighter as he turned toward the direction of the shrill cry. All around us, the campground grew quiet as everyone froze in terror, waiting to see what horror would haunt the festival.

The screams sounded again, louder this time, closer. My heart contracted painfully at the sound.

"The village," I breathed. "It's coming from the village."

TWENTY-THREE

"Stay here," Aiden ordered. I didn't protest as he gently pushed me toward the caravan door, exhaustion hovering too closely over my head to allow me to fight the chaotic crowd.

"It's coming from the path to the village," Seraphine said as she appeared in the darkness. Her long red hair was tied up in a knot atop her head tonight, giving her a battle-ready appearance.

"Who is it?" I asked as I searched the campground for the familiar faces of my family. The music had stopped, and performances halted as the crowd shifted about nervously. The screams grew steadily now and grew shriller as if others had joined in. Everyone from the surrounding villages was out celebrating the end of the harvest tonight. It would be all too easy for the chaos to spread.

"Just stay here," Aiden repeated as he moved to close the door of the caravan between us.

I reached out with my hand to stop him. "Aiden, what is it?"

His gaze found mine for only a second. The tender look flashed in his eyes for a moment before the familiar cool exterior returned.

"Esme," Father's voice sounded over the crowd. Aiden turned and followed Seraphine and Tarsa who had appeared in her usual unexpected manner. "Are you all right?"

I nodded as I moved to allow my family entry into the caravan; everyone except Nonna who had surely found some other place to seek refuge. "Did you see what happened?" Panic threatened to fill my chest as I watched the nervous glances my sisters sent my way before curling up together on the edge of the cot, Alfie at their side.

"We couldn't see," Mousa said as he helped Mother into the caravan.

"It sounded like it came from the direction of the river," Mother said as she sat beside her youngest children.

"Where's Aiden?" Father asked as he remained perched in front of the door.

My heart clenched of its own accord. What if Ephraim had returned? My mind conjured up the worst of my fears, all of which involved Aiden's death or that of my family. I forced myself to keep my breathing even and remain calm. The screams had faltered slightly now but the panicked movement of the crowd grew to resemble a stampede rather than a night of revelry.

"I saw him with the others heading toward the village," Mousa said when I didn't answer.

"Where's Leesa?" I forced myself to ask as he too stood near our father and glanced through the crack in the door to keep watch.

His shoulders tensed slightly, the only sign that he cared for the girl more than he dared admit. "With her family. They've made camp closest to the river." The tension in his voice had me reaching for his hand in an offer of silent comfort.

He sent me a thankful smile and squeezed my hand. Before I could blink, the door was ripped from its hinges and Mousa was yanked into the night, torn right out of my grasp.

A scream erupted from behind me as my mother and sisters cried for our brother as he was dragged through the grass. Father yelled in fury as he moved to help his son, but I was faster. I forced away all manner of exhaustion as I jumped from the caravan and into the night. Mother cried my name but I ignored her. I would not lose my brother to whatever mayhem was surely caused by a debt I inherited.

It wasn't hard to find him. Mousa was barely conscious beneath a burly young man who continued to drive his fist against the side of my brother's skull. Blood dripped from the man's hand and poured from a cut at Mousa's brow and even more from his nose.

I cried out in panic and moved as fast as my body would allow to help my brother. My foot caught on a large rock half buried in the grass, bringing me to my knees as I stumbled for balance.

The man crouching over my brother stiffened at the sound. I bent to retrieve the rock and held it aloft with a shaking hand, preparing to slam it into the man's head when he turned around.

His eyes, once a kind pale green, were now empty black pits. A memory of similar eyes flashed in my mind as I recalled the last burning I witnessed at the castle. There was no other emotion on his face apart from fury.

My hand froze, the rock held above my shoulder as recognition swarmed through my bones. I had just stolen this man's soul moments earlier.

I gasped, dropping the rock to the ground again as I stared at this strange man. He appeared to recognize me through his haze of feral rage. Slowly, he stood from my brother's unconscious body and took deliberate, slow steps in my direction. I swallowed back a scream as he wrapped his hand around my throat and glowered down at me.

"You did this," he spat.

My feet left the ground as he threw me several feet through the air, only to slam against the side of the caravan before collapsing to the ground. Inside, I could hear my sisters scream at the sudden jostling of their hiding place.

My back screamed in protest as I forced myself to roll onto my side and onto all fours. My throat burned as I coughed, forcing air into my aching lungs. The darkness that lived near my heart turned so cold it burned as it threatened to release itself on the man before me.

"Esme," Father's voice resounded over the chaotic noises of the campground.

I remained on all fours as my father rushed toward me, Mother moving to help Mousa who remained bleeding and unconscious a few yards away.

Father's hands burned against my feverish skin as he helped me into a seated position. His face was filled with a tender worry as he studied me. Breathing felt difficult as my ribs refused to shift around my lungs to allow air into my body.

My hands shook as I placed them against my side, a painful groan escaping my lips as I bent over against the pain.

"What is it?" Father asked, forcing himself to remain calm though the black-eyed man continued to glare at me as he slowly moved in our direction.

"You have to get them out of here," I croaked as I returned the man's stare.

"We're not leaving you, Esme," he said calmly. His hands prodded the tenderness at the back of my head where I could feel the warm trickle of blood dripping down my neck and into my shirt.

"You have to," I gasped as more pain ruptured through me. "You have to get them out." Tears blurred my vision as I caught sight of my younger siblings moving into the night to help our mother carry Mousa's unconscious form into the caravan. They somehow all appeared so much younger as our brother's blood stained their clothes.

"Esme!" Aiden's voice echoed through the campground. He raced toward me, the worry on his face quickly replaced with deadly rage as he caught sight of the haunted man moving toward me. In each of his hands were knives large enough to cut through bone as they glinted in the faint light of the campground.

Tarsa disappeared then, somehow hiding in the darkness as she raced toward us. Seraphine and the others remained at Aiden's side as they moved like a single being. I saw the sea of terrified people blocking their path, slowing them down and knew they wouldn't get here before this man hurt my family.

As quickly as I could manage through the pain and nausea, I got to my feet. I had no idea what I was going to do, but the flutter of darkness in my chest warmed in understanding.

The darkness shifted, moving outward from my chest until it filled my entire being. I could feel it from my toes to the tips of my fingers, every inch of my skin felt alive with it. The air seemed to still around me. Breathing became easier; the darkness lightened as I dared a step toward the haunted man. A tether stretched between me and the stranger, and on the end of it, oblivion. Where there should have been a soul inside this man, there was only an empty void that felt like ice in my veins.

"Esme," Father warned as he moved to step in front of me. His eyes widened at whatever he saw in my face. "Esme, stop. Whatever you're doing, just stop. Let us help you."

My voice evaded me as I tried to offer some word of reassurance. I knew not what I was going to do, but the thing that lived inside me—the thing that tied me to Death—knew exactly what it would take to send this man to his end.

"Esme, stop!" Aiden cried, nearer now as he surely heard my father's pleas. I didn't turn to look at him as I remained focused on the man. His black eyes studied me, unfeeling. The stranger's body remained taut, like a serpent ready to strike.

I stepped around my father's frozen form, his eyes wide with horror as he begged me to stay. His voice faded the more I let this darkness seep through my bones and fill every corner of my existence.

A gentle pull through the tether connecting me to this man forced my feet to stop as Nonna appeared, eyes alight with fury as she studied the soulless man before us.

"Enough of this," she spat at the man. He stiffened at her words. His form no longer held the promise of violence, but instead bent to her will.

Slowly, she turned away from the stranger to face me, and in her eyes I saw the familiar darkness that lived in me. I often forgot that Nonna was the Soul Collector before I was born. The same power that lived in me lived in her.

Her hand, soft and tender, came up to cup my face as she smiled at me with tears in her eyes. "Do not be afraid, child," she said softly. "For you are far braver and more powerful than you even know. Let your heart lead you, and there you will be safe."

The tears I had pushed away earlier returned, spilling over my cheeks. Familiar hands wrapped around my waist, pulling me back against a warm chest as Nonna stepped away. She cast one brief nod at Aiden as he held me against him, and turned one last lovely smile toward our family, who watched in horror from the caravan.

I could feel the darkness as it surrounded her, emanating around her in a dark halo. Her graying hair hung loose tonight, waves of it cascading down her back and blowing softly in a breeze that only she seemed able to feel.

"Nonna," I whispered through the tears.

My heart cleaved in two as I watched Nonna approach the man. He hadn't moved since the command she issued earlier. His eyes followed her willingly, eagerly awaiting her next order.

I watched through a blur of tears as she lifted a hand and placed it over the man's heart. My mother's sobs could be heard over my shoulder but no matter how much I wanted to, I couldn't take my eyes away from the man before me. Nonna's power, much more potent than my own, demanded my full attention as it trickled into the man's body.

Aiden whispered comforting words against my hair, but I couldn't hear them. With a sharp burst of air, the man crumpled as the last of his soul left his body. I was almost certain I could see the darkness of it lift into the air to return to the stars where it belonged. My heart ached as Nonna turned back slowly, the crumpled body of the stranger forgotten at her feet.

"Be brave, girl," she said kindly. Her eyes were filled with the familiar blackness that I knew lived inside me too. "It's your turn now."

With a slight exhale, she fell to the ground and came to rest near the man's body.

Mother cried out in agony before launching herself through the campground and collapsing beside Nonna's lifeless form. I watched in silent horror as Father moved to kneel beside her, then Uncle Malik as he took Nonna's crumpled body into his lap. The same sorrow that lived in my mother lived in him as he too mourned the loss of his mother.

The darkness inside of me surged momentarily before settling, finding its resting place once again near my heart. As my body slowly stitched itself back together, I stared on in horror.

I was only barely aware of what was happening around me. Aiden continued to support me, my legs having refused to hold me upright. Part of me found solace in his embrace, the rest of me felt numb.

Mousa remained unconscious, but I caught sight of Hakan moving his body into the tent my brother shared with Alfie who remained close on his heels, hands full of medical supplies. Tarsa and Killian had already begun to drag the strange man's body away into the trees. I'd no idea what they planned to do with him, but right now I couldn't find it in myself to care.

"I don't understand," I finally whispered. I forced myself to turn into Aiden's embrace, burrowing my head against his chest, begging his warmth to chase away the chill that lived in my bones.

"Understand what?" Aiden said softly.

"I feel fine," I whispered, not wanting my parents to overhear. "When she died," I continued, "my body healed. I'm not tired, and my ribs are no longer broken though I'm sure they were just a moment ago. I feel fine."

My heart threatened to break in two again, but the darkness living beside it seemed to notice and wrapped itself around my heart in comfort. Tears tracked down my cheeks. I remained there in Aiden's arms while my family continued to weep at the loss of the one person who had kept us together, who had kept us safe, for so many years.

Because now, without knowing how to end this debt, it was up to me and me alone to keep my family from the grasp of Death.

TWENTY-FOUR

It was far out in wanderer territory where we buried Nonna—far from any sign of villages or the curious eyes of the king's men. In the same spot where we once spent our early morning hours after a festival, our grandmother now lay buried beneath the earth, her soul gone to the stars.

I stood there as the sun settled over the horizon, the others long since retreated to their tents where we made camp a couple of miles away. With Nonna's favorite shawl draped over my shoulders, the faint trace of her perfume still lingering on the thick fabric, I could almost feel her with me.

My vision drifted, returning to a time where Nonna and I sat here together to watch the sunrise. I was only seven at the time. It was the first time she allowed me to watch her collect someone's soul, only I didn't know that's what she was doing. I merely thought it a trick of the light for the performance's sake.

"Now there's something you should know about yourself, Esme," she'd said softly, as if not wanting to wake my sleeping siblings who lay curled together nearby.

"What is it?" I'd asked with wide, eager eyes.

She smiled sadly as she turned to stare at the arriving sun. "There is something you have that makes you very strong and very special."

"Stronger than Father?" I remember tucking my knees up to rest my chin atop them as I waited for her to continue. My heart swelled with excitement as I thought of what I might contain that made me stand apart from my gifted family.

Nonna winked at me. "Far stronger than your father. You see," she'd said, "our family holds the key to the ruin of a very powerful demon. When I go to the stars, you will be the only person in our family with that key. You must keep it safe and keep it from the demon's hands."

My nose scrunched in confusion. "Why would I give it to a demon?"

Nonna's arms draped over my shoulders, her shawl wrapped around both of us. "You are powerful, Esme," she'd said. "Stronger than even the god of Death if you only allow love to fill you and the stars to guide you. Someday, this power will rest on your shoulders alone child. And when that time comes you must remember that no matter how dark things may seem, you can always find peace and light in those you surround yourself with."

At the time, I'd felt confused by her words, if not a little happy at being thought of as special compared to my siblings who already displayed such amazing talents for performing.

Now, as I stood in that same spot, alone, I didn't feel special at all. I felt cursed.

The wind shifted behind me, making my loose curls move with it. Seraphine moved to stand at my shoulder, her long twisted red braids hanging over her shoulders down to her waist. Tonight, she wore simple black leggings and a dark tunic that hugged her curves making her look like the deadly warrior I knew her to be.

"How are you?" she asked quietly. Her weapons were not visible for once; probably well-hidden or even left behind in the tent she shared with Tarsa.

I shrugged, my eyes remaining on the far setting sun.

Her arm wrapped around my shoulder, letting me rest my head on hers as she held me comfortingly. "Are you feeling better?"

I knew she didn't refer to Nonna's death. Though I didn't want to admit it, her death somehow healed whatever had caused me to become so ill in recent days. That knowledge was something I wouldn't dare say aloud.

"Tarsa has a theory about that," Seraphine said quietly, somehow following my thoughts. "She thinks since your family was only supposed to have one Soul Collector at a time, and your family had two for so many years, that it took its toll on you. Somehow having two of you together started to drain your own soul." Her arm squeezed tighter as she spoke, comforting. "That's also why those whose souls you took grew to their violent demeanors so quickly."

I pulled away to look at her. "That man, the one who killed Nonna, became that way because we both lived? That doesn't make any sense. Wouldn't all of the people whose souls we took together behave the same way then?"

Her lips pursed as she considered her next words. "They did, eventually," she said slowly.

My chest tightened with the information. "What about Ephraim?" I asked, eager to change the subject.

"There's no news," she said carefully. "Aiden is keeping a close watch though for any sign of him. And King Elroy's men."

I sighed. "After last night, everyone who is currently hunting me must know where we are."

Her hand tightened on my shoulder comfortingly. "He'll make sure you're safe—that you're all safe. We all will."

"We can't run, can we?"

The sorrow in my voice caused a frown to pull at her delicate mouth. I watched the light leave her eyes as she turned her gaze to the horizon, searching for something I couldn't see. She knew as much as I did that my family had little success in finding a way to end the debt. Every time I voiced the question, Nonna shooed me away and told me to only focus on collecting souls. And every time she said that I wanted to scream.

"I think if you ran, you might outrun your king's men," she said slowly, "but I don't think there will be any outrunning Ephraim."

Another shiver wracked through my body as her words settled along my skin. I tightened my arms around my middle as I allowed one last glance toward the setting sun. The second night of the harvest festival was tonight, which meant we had to return to the campground outside Deva and prepare before the crowd gathered.

The presence in my chest shifted excitedly and I knew who joined us then, even before I turned to see him striding in our direction. His movements, always filled with a deadly grace, now seemed more electric as his presence demanded attention.

"Esme," he said quietly by way of greeting. I almost hated the way my heart beat erratically at the sound of my name coming from his lips. A smile teased the corners of his mouth as if he knew exactly how his presence affected me.

"The others?" Seraphine asked, sparing me from finding my voice.

A breeze swept Aiden's dark hair across his brow as he turned to his friend. Part of my mind registered the way he carried himself since Nonna's death; almost like he too felt stronger after her demise.

"Killian has left for the Angelwood Forest to guard the gate to our realm," he spoke slowly, carefully.

"Why?" I asked as confusion and panic swept through me.

It was Seraphine who answered, though seemingly reluctantly. "It's possible Ephraim or even Death felt Adine's demise. The death of a Soul Collector is no small thing. They might come looking to see if you're still alive."

My arms tightened across my middle. "They'll come here?"

A muscle ticked in Aiden's jaw as he caught the wave of fear that chilled my bones. "They won't touch you or your family. Not while I'm here."

When I met his eyes, that familiar thrill surged through me as the darkness in my chest begged me to reach for him. His familiar blue-grey eyes darkened as he studied me. My cheeks flushed in answer.

"Hakan and Tarsa have already moved to keep watch over the others," he said to Seraphine without taking his eyes off of me. "Every member of her family is to be kept under watch."

Seraphine nodded, her warrior exterior returning. Without another word she left, leaving Aiden and me alone as we continued to stare at each other, my cheeks burning under his gaze.

His mouth curved in a crooked smile. "How are you?"

I sighed. "I'm not ready." The admission made my shoulders sag with the harsh truth of it.

My skin tingled beneath his touch as he tipped my chin upward with the tip of his calloused fingers.

"You are ready," he countered gently.

His breath blended with mine as we stood there, the cool autumn air remaining heated in the space surrounding us. The sun fading further on the horizon brought with it the sounds of revelry from nearby and the faint sounds of my family awakening to prepare for the festival ahead of us.

"I should go," I whispered reluctantly as my mother called for me in the distance. They still relied on me, and me alone, to fulfill this debt our ancestors owed.

I didn't wait for a response before stepping out of his grasp and striding past his large frame. The entire trek back to camp, I could feel his eyes on my back watching, as he always did, for danger. Though this time I could almost feel the same need in him that I felt in myself as my skin dared to tingle from the lingering heat of his touch.

The evening passed slowly as I performed reading after reading and managed to collect a few souls in the process. As was becoming usual, Aiden remained close by, only disappearing from sight to allow me the privacy to perform readings in the caravan. Leesa, Mousa's girlfriend as she took to calling herself, remained in his tent where he lay healing. She'd taken to patching up his wounds and keeping them clean as he dozed under the effects of Mother's sleep serum to help with the healing.

Mother and Father were on stage now, which meant for once between readings I was alone in the warm caravan. Tonight, everyone seemed more on edge as we anxiously waited for any sign that Ephraim or one of the other demons may have sensed Nonna's death. We had managed to remain inconspicuous thus far, but with the king only a village away and Killian gone to the forest, we felt far more exposed.

I stared at my reflection in the dusty mirror—the kohl along my eyes making them appear wider, more innocent. Though I'd seen so much death in recent weeks I wasn't sure the word could apply to me any longer.

My eyes caught on the scars covering my wrists. The memory of the chains burned there and at my ankles which were hidden beneath my boots. As the silence of the caravan became overwhelming, the memory of rattling chains and the screams from friends being burned at the stake flashed through my mind. I forced my eyes closed, pushing the horrors from my mind as my thoughts betrayed me and replaced the faces of those burned with my family. A fear I hadn't wanted to admit until now.

The door opened behind me, pulling me back to the present. In the mirror's reflection I watched as Aiden entered the caravan, standing uncomfortably in the middle of the space like he couldn't decide if he should be there or not. His hands balled into fists at his sides, then relaxed. I watched patiently as his eyes darted around, refusing to meet my gaze in the mirror.

I finally spun around to face him when he didn't speak. "Has something happened?" My heart raced in my chest as I considered Killian's possible return with news of a demon's arrival.

He shook his head, eyes refusing to meet mine. I could've sworn a slight flush formed along his cheeks. "Nothing yet."

My brows drew together as I slowly got to my feet to better study him. "Then what is it?"

I felt far steadier than I used to after collecting so many souls at once. It seemed Tarsa's theory regarding Nonna and me was correct. My heart ached a little at the thought. I hadn't let myself wonder yet if Nonna knew this would happen. Whether she knew or not that I'd grow weak and become unable to help our family while she lived remained a mystery I didn't want to solve.

The warrior before me appeared younger now as his hands fisted at his sides before relaxing once more. His once steady and sure presence now felt uncertain, nervous—an emotion I noticed he only felt when we found ourselves alone together.

"Aiden," I prodded again. "What is it?"

Finally, his eyes met mine. The breath went out of him as our gazes connected. The swirl of blue hidden in the grey of his eyes shifted in the faint candlelight, drawing me in.

"How are you?" he finally said. There was a flash of tense muscle in his jaw before he appeared relaxed once more.

I shrugged as I turned my back to adjust the fabrics dangling from the ceiling to give myself some time to collect my emotions. "I'm fine I suppose." When I turned back, he was watching me intently, and I felt my face heat.

"After the festival tonight, I think your family should leave," he said into the following silence. The caravan walls dimmed the sounds of the festival outside though the cheers from my parents' thrilling performance could still be heard.

I nodded slowly. "Okay, where do you suggest we go?"

His head shook to the side slightly. "No," he said. "Just your family. Once Ephraim gets word of your grandmother's death, I have no doubt he will come for you again. I'm surprised he's waited this long. Not to mention, all of King Elroy's men must know you are here now."

I shivered against the thought of the demon's return. The scar at my neck burned slightly at the memory of his knife cutting into my skin. My hand reached up of its own accord to brush against the marred skin.

"Will he kill them?" I wasn't sure I wanted to know the answer.

Aiden considered his words carefully as his mouth pressed into a thin line. "If he sees that as the only way to get to you, I don't doubt that he will."

I sighed, rolling my head back as I forced calm into my body. "I can't lose them," I said quietly.

Aiden didn't respond, filling the caravan with a heated silence. I could feel his eyes on me as I kept mine closed, forcing myself not to picture my family bleeding to their deaths beneath the demon's feet. Or worse, burning alive on one of the king's pyres.

Tears pricked my eyes as I whispered again, "I can't lose them." His expression didn't change as he studied me patiently. "I will do whatever it takes to keep them safe."

Aiden's gaze shifted, turning gentler now, almost empathetic. "I know." He took a hesitant step toward me, eyes dropping to his feet momentarily. "And I will do whatever it takes to keep you safe."

The dark essence in my chest curled toward him at the truth in his words. A shiver of need trickled down my spine as I stared at the man before me. "Has Elias returned?" I asked instead to break the heated silence.

The air cooled considerably at the mention of the prince. The immortal warrior stood before me now, his expression resembling too closely to the man he was when he first took me from the castle all those weeks ago.

"Are you expecting the prince to return?" Even his voice came out as icy daggers.

My hands balled into fists as I spoke. "I was merely wondering if he could help keep my family safe."

His stiff posture relaxed a fraction, but the cold demeanor remained. "Do not fool yourself with the prince's intentions, Esme," he said coolly. "He will sooner betray you for his father's good graces than go behind his back to protect your family."

I fought the urge to roll my eyes. Anger came quickly as the exhaustion of these past weeks caught up to me. "Elias wouldn't hurt them," I spat. "He's human."

Aiden laughed coldly, stepping so close now that I could feel the heat of his body along mine. "You give humans far too much credit," he retorted. "Among the creatures in the world, they are some of the most wicked."

"Says the man who sold his soul to the god of Death," I said harshly. "Tell me Aiden, what could've possibly caused you to do such a thing? Who in their right mind would think that being in his debt for eternity would compare to living your life in peace?"

"Says the mortal who currently serves him as much as I."

My knuckles turned white with the rage that filled my fists. "Not by choice."

"Right," he barked. "And you are so quick to assume so little of my character that you think I had any choice in my debt to him either."

Surprise washed through me, replacing the anger I felt a moment before. My hands relaxed at my sides as I watched his cold mask falter. For I knew then that the warmth I felt from him was truly his. The coldness was his mask placed there by his duty to the demons.

"Tell me, Esme," he continued. "This is your opinion of me? A mere weak human who sold his own soul to the god of Death in order to spend eternity serving his every command? No choice, no life of my own—merely a pawn to be moved at his every whim?"

I suddenly found myself at a loss for words. His gaze continued to wash over me as he searched for any sign of the judgment that had appeared there a moment before.

"Why do you do it then?" I finally asked. "What happened that made you want to serve him in such a way?"

A muscle flexed in his cheek as he studied me. "You still assume I ever had a choice in the matter," he spoke slowly, carefully. "The decision to serve him was made before my birth. My soul has always belonged to him."

Though he fought to hide it, I could see the lingering pain in his eyes as he spoke of his ties to the god of Death. "Is there no way to free you?" My voice shook slightly as emotion tightened my throat. "Can't there be some way to break the tether keeping you bound to him so you can be free?"

Aiden flashed a crooked smile that held little warmth. "There are only two people with enough power to end my tie to him, and I am not one of them."

"What about the Prince of Death?" I dared to ask. Aiden's shoulders tightened slightly at my words. "You serve him, don't you? Couldn't he do something?"

With a sigh he stepped closer, the cool frustration once haunting his features now calming to something akin to acceptance as he gave a slight shake of his head. Sorrow threatened to fill me as the darkness inside strained for him, eager to comfort him in some way.

His gaze changed, growing darker and warmer as he leaned closer, leaving little space between us.

The air grew stifling as his hand reached to tuck a strand of my obsidian curls behind my ear. The hesitant brush of his fingers against my cheek sent a thrill through me, answered by the fluttering of the strange essence. I marveled at how it responded to Aiden's closeness.

I found his eyes, darkening with every breath, focused on my mouth.

"Esme," he whispered. I shivered as his breath brushed across my face. "With the numerous threats to your own life, how do you manage to still have room to worry for me?" He shook his head sadly, wonder filling his eyes.

I swallowed, heart racing against my ribs as nerves took over. "Because I care about you."

His expression changed, turning inward, as he stepped back putting space between us again. I rushed to continue as I saw the start of his mask building in his eyes again.

"I'm sorry," I said hastily. "I just meant that you've been so kind to me and my family."

Aiden nodded, a slight smile at his mouth. "Esme," he began slowly. I watched the emotion in his eyes before he set his jaw and pushed it away. "Whatever happens, do not let him have you."

My brows furrowed. "Who?" I whispered.

He shook his head once, eyes glancing between mine before returning to focus at my mouth. "If he captures you, promise me he won't break you. Please fight him."

Before I could find a response, his mouth met mine. Surprise sent my heart racing as his hands cupped my face, holding me against him. As I began to reach for him, seeking to pull him closer, Aiden pulled away.

In his eyes I saw warmth and devotion before the emotions vanished with a blink.

"I apologize," he said, taking a slow step away. "I shouldn't have done that."

I brushed a finger over my mouth, feeling the lingering warmth of his kiss. Aiden took another step away, cheeks slightly flushed despite the cool mask he forced over his emotions.

As he took another step toward the door, I reached for him. My hands fisted in the front of his tunic, pulling him closer as my mouth found his again. Aiden froze for a breath before relaxing against me, a smile brushing up the sides of his mouth as he returned my kiss.

My knees threatened to buckle as my hands found themselves burrowing in his hair, pulling him closer. I sighed against him, relishing his touch as I felt one hand tangle in the curls at the nape of my neck while the other wrapped around the small of my back, holding me flush against him.

How long had I dreamed of holding this immortal in such a way? My mind couldn't conjure a single coherent thought as he kissed me with equal passion.

The flutter in my chest burned through me, my own heart racing against my ribs in answer. Somehow, in all this chaos, this small moment felt pivotal, and wholly right.

My body heated at every brush of our skin and left a cold longing in the wake of his hands as they moved to cup my face. There was a need to his touch, his kiss; an urgency that stole a faint breath of desire from me.

In answer, his desperation grew as my back collided with the caravan door. Our bodies were pressed together now, from head to toe. My skin grew tighter as my head tilted back to allow his lips to press their gentle kisses along my jaw, my neck.

I might have breathed his name as he pressed a gentle kiss against the scar at my neck.

I felt his lips turn up in a smile at the sound. "Esme." His breath tickled my skin with its heated caress. "I am eternally undone by you." His mouth moved to claim mine again before the words faded into the silence of the caravan. The scent of cedar filled my senses as I breathed him in, finding it entirely out of my control to release him from my grasp. Not that I could even wish such a thing.

Aiden breathed my name along my skin, the pure longing and desperation to his tone bringing tears to my eyes as it mirrored the feeling I had kept hidden for so long. The essence inside me sang in pleasure.

The door Aiden pressed me against opened suddenly.

Aiden stepped back unexpectedly, leaving me to stumble for my footing as my mother stepped into the caravan. I caught her eye and recognized the knowing gleam that lived there as she took in our disheveled state. Aiden's hair hung around his face in a rumpled mess, and I surely looked equally unraveled.

"There's someone here who wishes to glimpse their future in your crystal ball," she said calmly, slowly enunciating each word in careful precision. I watched as her eyes narrowed in Aiden's direction, effectively dismissing him, before returning to me.

"Right," I said breathlessly. My cheeks continued to burn as the two of them watched me with mixed emotions. "I'm ready."

Mother nodded, her gaze brushing over Aiden as she ushered in the client. I hardly registered the arrival of the young woman as mother sat her down at the small table and backed out of the caravan to return to the stage. My eyes lingered on Aiden as he caught my gaze for only a moment before retreating to the darkness outside where I knew he would keep watch.

"Miss?" the stranger seated behind me said, breaking me out of my reverie.

I brushed a hand over my mouth where Aiden's taste still lingered. When I turned back to the client, I forced all thoughts of the immortal away.

The reading went quickly. I marveled at how much easier it became to steal a soul now that I was the only Soul Collector for the Loutari line.

What I did notice though, was the strangeness that accompanied this reading. Even now, as I stood at the foot of the caravan steps to watch the young woman disappear into the large crowd, I couldn't help but feel that something went wrong. Behind me, the siphon held the usual glow it always did when it contained a soul, but somehow it felt wrong, empty.

"What is it?" Aiden said as he moved to stand at my shoulder. His eyes roamed over the crowd in his usual practice.

"I don't know," I answered honestly. "Something about that one felt different."

"Different how?"

I shrugged. "Small?" I offered uncertainly. "Like I didn't take everything or the soul was somehow smaller than the others?"

Aiden appeared to consider my words as he too stared after the disappearing figure of the now-soulless client. I could feel his confusion though he didn't speak of it.

Tarsa appeared, as she usually did, to follow after the client and tear her down before she inevitably grew wild. My mother and Seraphine joined us as she left. From where we stood, I could hear Father continuing his performance with Alfie who'd begun to learn Mousa's routine while our eldest brother healed.

"What is it?" Seraphine asked as her glance bounced between Aiden and me.

"Hope we didn't interrupt you two again." My mother's words, and the reminder of her sudden appearance when Aiden kissed me, made my cheeks burn in the night.

Seraphine raised her brow in question though she didn't press for answers. All around us, people danced and laughed and drank heavily from goblets of wine or ale. Few people glanced in our direction though many let their stares linger on Seraphine.

My gaze snagged on one man, half-hidden in the distant crowd. He wore simple clothes, but a crumpled paper was held out in front of him. My stomach dropped as his brows furrowed and his gaze shot up to my face again.

"Aiden," I warned quietly. Recognition lit the man's face as he shoved the paper listing my bounty into his pocket, eyes eager as he turned fully toward me.

"I see him." Aiden's voice rang with a deadly promise as his gaze caught Hakan's across the campground. The immortal nodded in answer and followed the stranger's retreating figure.

"How did the collecting go?" Seraphine asked. Her eyes brushed over the man as well before turning back to study me.

Only when the man disappeared from view altogether, sending my heart into a panicked race, did I force myself to respond. "Different, I guess." My mind grew with worry as I frantically searched for my siblings in the crowd, seeking confirmation of their safety.

"Perhaps you're not ready yet," Seraphine suggested. "It's only been a day since your grandmother died and you became the sole bearer of this gift. It might take you awhile to adjust to the strength of it."

"She's right," Mother conceded gently. "You've been so ill lately it's possible you need a few days to rest."

Aiden opened his mouth to speak, most likely to agree with them, but I spoke before he could. "I'm fine," I said curtly. "We can't afford for me to rest any longer. Whatever number of souls he needs I will give him. We can't risk Ephraim returning. Not now. Not when we have no way of knowing how to end the debt in the first place."

My mother opened her mouth to speak but a slight shake of Seraphine's head had her holding her tongue.

"Maybe you should take a break from collecting souls for a while," Aiden suggested calmly.

I shot him a look which made his lips twitch toward a smile. "If I stop now Ephraim will just come again. I can't risk that."

"Esme," my mother said with a sad smile. "Stop worrying about us. It is your soul at stake, not ours."

I shrugged out of her grip. "Not if the king catches word that we are here. Not if Ephraim thinks the only way to get to me is to kill you. All of you."

"You carry too much, dear," she said patiently. "Don't carry the burden of our lives on your shoulders as well. We will be fine."

Tears threatened to blur my vision as I stepped away, retreating toward the caravan. "I'm not taking that risk."

I returned to the comfort of the caravan before anyone could respond. Even through the walls I could feel Aiden's attention on me. I pressed my hands against my eyes, forcing the tears to stay away as the weight of my duty pressed down on my shoulders. It seemed no matter how hard I tried to keep my family safe, there was already a risk. Whether it was the king or Ephraim, a threat was always there to harm my family. My soul be damned, but I couldn't lose my family.

TWENTY-FIVE

I HATED THAT I didn't feel drained after such a long night; I felt alive. My limbs felt stronger and my mind felt awakened. My family brought a total of seventeen people whose souls I stole tonight. In the past I wouldn't dream of attempting to drain more than one, maybe three at most, a night. Now, my body felt whole and the darkness inside me sang with the joy of collecting these souls.

"Are you all right, Esme?" Aunt Kiva asked as she shuffled around the caravan. The festival had mostly ended about an hour ago though many villagers remained behind to finish their drinks and dance to whatever drunken songs they could conjure.

I straightened from my slumped position against the small stool. "I'm fine," I said with false confidence.

"Your mind looks preoccupied," she noted with a casual glance toward my mother who worked nearby to pack our decorations into their totes. Aunt Kiva's golden hair was left down to hang in waves to her hips, making her appear ethereal in the dim light.

Mother grunted her agreement. "Spoken to Aiden yet?" she asked too casually.

I rolled my eyes, hating the flush that rose in my cheeks. I hadn't seen Aiden in a few hours, nor had I felt a shadow of him. Most likely, he was out with the others keeping watch over my family, or worse, he was waiting in his tent which happened to be directly next to my own. Though I could still taste him on my lips, I wasn't sure I was ready to see him just yet. No matter how much I may have wanted to continue where we left off.

"Isn't he really old?" Amara asked from the cot where she laid, half asleep. Cordelia sat beside her brushing out the tangles in our youngest sister's hair. My younger sisters had grown closer in my absence over the summer. Now, not only did they resemble each other with their brown hair and sun-kissed skin, but Amara had begun to resemble Cordelia even in the mannerisms she portrayed. It warmed my heart to see them so close.

"Killian is ninety-three," Alfie said as he ran a hand through his hair. He once kept it so short you could see through its dark tendrils to his scalp. Only now he appeared to have become accustomed to letting it grow to hang in his eyes. I smiled at the disheveled appearance it gave as he bent over his notebook, scribbling in a feverish rush.

"Ninety-three?" Cordelia asked in astonishment. I hadn't missed the way she fawned over him since the night he danced with her. Father didn't seem to find it as adorable as I did as he took to keeping her away from the immortal warrior.

Alfie nodded, dark hair falling forward into his eyes. "Seraphine is even older than that, and Tarsa even older than her."

"You spoke to Tarsa?" I asked, surprised.

He nodded again as if it were an everyday occurrence. "She has good stories," he said sheepishly. My brother clutched his notebook to his chest as a slight flush covered his cheeks.

"Alfie, will you go check on your brother, please?" Mother asked then. "He might be ready for a bandage change."

I watched my brother leave without a word, notebook still clutched tightly against his chest. Mother and I smiled after him. We both knew the life of a wanderer wasn't for my younger brother. He'd much prefer to write stories and live in the world of books. I hoped someday he could find a way to accomplish that life he always dreamed of.

My gaze turned toward my sisters, both so young and innocent in life. I needed to find a way to keep them from the darkness that threatened to drag my soul directly into the god of Death's hands.

Prince Elias flashed through my mind then. Perhaps if I could find a way to get word to him, he'd keep my family safe. Maybe he could even help them secure safe passage to the Gaiva Region, or the Abandoned Desert, anywhere that was far enough from the king's grasp or Ephraim's search.

"Esme," Mother said softly, regaining my attention. From the darkness lingering in her gaze, I knew she was following my train of thought. "Whatever you're thinking, don't do it."

"Even if it could keep you all safe?"

The caravan grew still. Aunt Kiva paused in her folding of the fabrics and scarves to sit beside my sisters on the cot. Nadira, my older cousin whom I nearly forgot was here in her silence, shifted to join her mother.

"Nonna told me a story once about how to kill the god of Death," Nadira admitted quietly. Her voice barely carried over the noise echoing from the campground outside. Father and Uncle Malik remained out there tending to the grounds and making sure everything was ready for the following night of the festival.

"That sounds too dangerous," Mother noted.

Nadira shrugged. "She also told me a possible way out of the debt, but I don't know if it's any easier than killing the god of Death."

Surprise shot through me. "There's a way out of the debt? When did she tell you this?" Mother scowled at the excitement in my voice.

"About a week ago." At the frown on my face, she quickly continued. "We didn't want you to worry about it—you already had so much to do—but she said one way is to have the god of Death dismiss it." I snorted and she offered a weak smile. "Yeah, she said that wasn't very likely either."

"What's the other way?" Amara asked, eager eyes wide.

"No," Mother said before Nadira could continue. "It's too dangerous. Whatever it is, if it involves the god of Death, it's too dangerous."

"As opposed to what?" I countered. "Who knows how long it could take for me to pay this debt. Wouldn't it be better to find a way out of it so our family won't have to live under the constant fear of Ephraim showing up to kill you all?"

Mother shuddered at the recollection of the demon.

"What did Nonna say?" Cordelia asked, oblivious to our mother's discomfort.

Nadira sent a weary look toward my mother before turning back to face me. "She said the only other way to be free of the debt is to kill the demon who offered it; that is, if the god of Death refuses to dismiss the debt himself."

I scowled, gaze turning inward. "I don't remember if Nonna ever told me who offered the debt to our ancestors." My mind struggled to recall the story Nonna told me of our family's debt only a few weeks ago, but already it seemed faded like a distant memory.

Amara shook her head, eyes heavy with sleep. "I don't remember her telling me anything about it. Maybe Alfie knows."

Nadira pursed her lips as she glanced toward her mother. "There's one more thing."

"What is it?" my mother asked as she moved to tuck Amara into the blankets.

Nadira took a steadying breath as she glanced around at our family. "She said only the Soul Collector has the power to end the god of Death's reign."

My family froze. The air in the caravan felt tight with tension as all eyes slowly turned toward me. I swallowed audibly, heart racing against my ribs.

"So, either Esme has to find a way to get the god of Death to dismiss the debt," Cordelia said, ticking off her thoughts onto her fingers. "Or, she could end his reign, or kill the person who offered the debt. Well, those all sound incredibly easy." Sarcasm dripped from her tone with the end of her remarks. I fought the urge to murmur agreement.

"It's too dangerous," Mother said again as she brushed Amara's hair back from her eyes.

"It may be the only way, Emira," Aunt Kiva said softly, voice calm.

Mother sent her a look before turning back to me. I'd gone silent and she knew better than anyone what that might mean. She knew I considered the possible ways to achieve these tasks, even if it meant leaving my family.

"Esme," she cautioned.

The look on her face sent my stomach to my feet. "Did you know?"

My mother's face turned sad, apologetic. "We didn't want you to carry anymore on your shoulders. You already carry too much."

I stepped back as she reached for me. "How long have you known?" When she didn't answer I looked to the others, none of whom could meet my gaze. "You've all known. This entire time you've known how to end this debt and you didn't tell me? You made me continue collecting souls when there was a way out?"

"You were so sick, Esme," Cordelia added gently. "We could hardly get you out of bed for nearly a week."

My mother stepped closer, hand slightly outstretched. "We don't even know who offered your ancestor this debt. And the immortals have been tight lipped about it any time we asked. It was an unnecessary stress you didn't need."

"Aiden knows too?" I felt my throat begin to burn with tears. "Everyone knew what needed to be done and none of you thought I should know this?"

"He's been helping us find answers," my mother noted cautiously. "They've all been trying to help us figure out how to keep you safe."

I snorted, running a hand through my tangled hair. "I should have been told this. I had a right to know."

"We didn't want to tell you until we had a solution." Cordelia shifted closer, hands knitting in front of her nervously. "We wanted to find out how to accomplish what Nonna told us before we told you."

I forced a lungful of air into my body as I drove my frustration under my control. "I need some air," I said on a sharp exhale.

I left the caravan before anyone could stop me, ignoring Aiden's lingering tent that cast a shadow over my smaller one at its side. As I passed through our small cluster of tents, I half expected him to appear in his usual way and linger nearby to watch, but he never did. I suspected my mother stopped him and warned him to give me some space until I could better control my frustration and this nagging sense of betrayal.

My feet carried me well past the campground and into the trees, hidden from the view of those who lingered to finish the night's celebrations. When I finally stopped walking, I found myself at a small stream I guessed led to the Little River. I knelt in the damp grass at the stream's edge and bowed my head over the water. The essence in my chest fluttered comfortingly against my heart, working to settle the panic as my mind raged with this feeling of betrayal. They'd known. For days they'd all known how to end this, and no one thought to tell me.

I wasn't strong enough to kill an immortal; that much I knew. I wasn't even sure how to go about finding the demon who offered the debt in the first place. I was certain if Aiden knew then he would've told my family, but it seemed we were all in the dark now. Not to mention, I had no way of ending the god of Death's reign, whatever that meant. I already knew I wasn't powerful enough to kill him. My heart sank further with that acknowledgment.

The air turned cold from one breath and the next. The darkness in my chest swelled and beat against my heart erratically as it reached for my limbs. My breath clouded on the air before me, blocking out any scent of the water or the damp grass that had frozen beneath me.

Breath caught in my lungs as my mind slowly awakened in recognition. Hands shaking at my sides, I rose on unsteady feet to turn and face the demon.

Ephraim tilted his head to the side, the way a cat might eye a mouse caught in its trap. A cold smile played with the corners of his mouth as he studied me. "Well hello, Soul Collector."

A shiver ran down my spine. "What do you want?" Though I meant to sound sharp, my voice came out nervous and breathy. My hands turned to fists at my sides to hide the shaking.

Ephraim took a slow step closer, hands outstretched as if bewildered I would ask. Both of his hands. "I'm hurt that you've forgotten our last encounter so soon, Esme."

I swallowed nervously. "You can't take me," I begged. "Not yet."

"Ahh, I see," he said tauntingly. "So, your mind has been filled with stories and false hope."

As he stepped closer, I was surprised to see his wings were missing. The shadows they once cast over his features no longer existed, allowing the moon to display his face fully. Not even his rounded horns remained. He appeared as if a normal man. My heart beat erratically as I thought of how he might've come directly from the campground where my family remained. But that couldn't be, not with Aiden and the others keeping watch over them. Then again, no one seemed to have noticed that I disappeared.

"What happened to your wings?" I asked as I studied him nervously. Weapons glistened at his sides, and the familiar knife seemed to taunt me as it reflected the light of the moon. The black handle curved slightly and held a pair of wings embellished along the hilt. My heartbeat stuttered as I studied it.

His smiled widened slightly, bright eyes registering every breath that left my lungs in nervous gasps. "It's called magic, darling," he whispered, though his voice carried over the sound of the water just fine. "Some of us contain enough power to hide them and appear human should we wish it."

"I suppose that's how you got your hand back?"

Ephraim's eyes glistened as he tracked my racing pulse in my neck. "It's good to see you're learning to be more perceptive."

I shuddered. How many times had I walked past a demon as cruel as Ephraim and not known it? The thought made my stomach roll.

"It amazes me how you've been kept so blind to the truth," he noted curiously. His head remained tilted to the side, brows furrowed, as if he couldn't believe the confusion sweeping through me.

"I know the truth," I protested stubbornly.

He chuckled and it sent another cold shiver through me. "No, I don't think you do. You see, if you did in fact know the truth as you claim to, then I know you wouldn't place your trust in someone like your dear Aiden."

My spine straightened at the mention of his name. "Aiden is far more trust-worthy than you," I retorted coldly. I was glad my voice had stopped shaking.

"If that makes you feel better about kissing him..." His smiled broadened at the look of horror I felt spread across my face.

He laughed darkly. "You are such a naive girl," he said, taking another step closer. "I see there is much that you are ignorant of, and I can't wait to see the look on your face when you realize the truth."

"And what is the truth, exactly?" I spat.

"Oh, there is so much you don't yet know," he said softly. He stood close enough now to run a cold finger across my jaw. My skin froze over with the brief contact. I swallowed nervously.

"Are you here to take me then?"

"Not yet," he said with a furrowed brow. His head turned slightly as if hearing something far away, though his eyes never left mine. "It seems there are more interesting things in your future that I hope to witness before retrieving you."

"You won't be able to take me," I said coldly. His hand dropped from my face as he took a step back and out of arm's reach. My lungs sucked in air at the growing space between us though the darkness in my chest continued to shift around in a panic, rattling against my ribs like a caged animal.

"You have put far too much faith in your guardians, Esme," he noted quietly. "You see, it is not your family we are interested in," he said, "just you. We care not for the wellbeing of your family. In fact, it would be easier if they were all slaughtered."

My skin went cold. "If you harm them, I will surely let myself drown in the river before letting you take me."

He smiled—a cold and heartless smile that would've made me shake in my boots had I been able to feel my toes through the cold that surrounded him. "Your soul is tied to the god of Death. You are too important to simply forget. He's already thought of many ways to use the power that lives in you, and he doesn't intend to let just anyone control it; especially the angels as they too continue their search for you."

"I won't let him take me," I snapped, ignoring the mention of the angels. The thought of being in Death's grasp made my stomach clench painfully.

Sounds erupted from the campground, but Ephraim blocked the path that led back to my family.

"If the king gets you," he said suddenly, "just know that the fate of remaining in his clutches is far worse than what I have planned for you."

Confusion filled me. "What do you know?"

"Oh, he's never stopped looking for you," he crooned tauntingly. "And he intends to return you to his chains."

The memory of the manacles singed across the mangled flesh at my ankles and wrists. The marks remained, but I swore I'd never let them grow. I would not return to the king.

"Aiden won't let that happen."

Ephraim snorted harshly. "Your innocence is astounding. I cannot wait to see how you handle the truth when it becomes known. For that, I will be there if only to witness the shattering of your heart."

As the sounds of rushed footsteps grew, heading directly toward our little clearing by the stream, Ephraim retreated to the shadowed darkness. My heart raced as the racing footsteps neared: Aiden had come after all. Relief replaced my fear as I stepped away from the demon. But it soon became clear that the footsteps did not belong to Aiden after all. They were too loud; too uncoordinated.

Ephraim smiled as realization dawned on my face. "You should be careful with the secrets in your heart, Esme," he said quietly. "Just know, had you come with me, your fate would have been different."

"Go to hell," I spat.

His wings and horns returned with a pop of air. "I will see you again, Esme," he said, slowly disappearing into shadow. "You are an important tool and I look forward to making use of you."

He disappeared just as Mousa came running into view. I stared in horror at the bloody bandages that covered his bare torso. His face remained bruised and bloody from the attack the night before, and he still seemed unsteady on his feet as he gripped my hand tightly and began to drag me away from the stream.

"Hurry," he said as he pulled me along. "We have to hurry."

"Mousa, what's wrong?" I asked as panic quickly replaced anger.

His breathing sounded ragged and forced as he stumbled through the trees. "They're here," he croaked. "They've come for you, and they've got everyone."

Horror filled me as I forced my feet to move faster. "Aiden?" I dared ask.

Mousa shook his head, sweaty hair stuck to his forehead. "We don't know. The other immortals are missing too."

My heart clenched. Thoughts of Aiden lying bleeding and half dead somewhere filled my mind in a rush. I didn't know how I would be able to keep my family safe if Aiden was gone too. He was the only person I had who might be able to help me rid my bloodline of this debt.

Mousa's long strides propelled us forward as I dared a glance over my shoulder to where Ephraim once stood. The demon was gone, as if he had never been there. Had Ephraim kept me occupied at the stream as a distraction so he could have my friends killed?

"Who is at the campground?" I dared ask as fear threatened to weaken my knees. "Mousa, who came for us?"

He shot me a look of pity before turning back to drag us forward. Now, as the campground grew nearer, I could hear the sounds of the horses and the horrible sound of swords connecting with bone and flesh.

His voice came out in a broken rasp, thick with fear. "The king."

I opened my mouth to speak but a hand clamped over it before I could voice my question.

Mousa might've cried out for me, but the sound of his voice was cut off by the blood pounding in my ears. Strong arms wrapped around my middle as my feet were lifted off the ground. I watched in muted horror as another guard appeared to pin my brother to the ground and bind his hands with familiar chains.

I tried to cry out, to scream, or beg, but no sound came out of my mouth. The guard carrying me dragged me away from my brother as he lay on the ground screaming at me to run away. Tears blurred my vision as his voice bled into the shouts all around us.

My entire family lay on the muddy ground. Father bled from a cut on his face, and Mother lay unconscious at his side, a bruise already forming on her brow.

"Essie," Amara cried when she saw me.

Tears ran in tracks down my youngest sister's face as she struggled against the manacles at her wrists. My entire family lay bound together. The king's guards surrounded the entire camp. Tents were torn down, caravans burned, families screaming and running for safety.

If the king's greed for luxury wasn't destroying our kingdom before, his desperation for power certainly was now.

My foot collided with something warm and soft on the ground as the guard set me roughly back on my feet. When I glanced down, my stomach turned violently.

Leesa. Her corpse lay at my feet, staring up at the sky, unseeing. Blonde hair clung to the dark red blood leaking from the hole in her skull, the sight of it horrible enough to burn behind my closed eyes.

I struggled harder against the guard's hold, screaming unintelligible nonsense.

"Esme, stop." Father's voice sounded over the chaos. Cordelia knelt beside him while leaning into Amara's side, letting our youngest sister soak her shirt with tears.

I stared at my father, and my mind was filled with horror as I noted the bodies that lay scattered across the campground. His face was slightly reddened with forming bruises, but his eyes were firm, hiding the fear I was sure he felt.

"I know," he said gently. "It's going to be okay."

Tears burned tracks down my cheeks as the guard holding me tossed me unceremoniously onto a horse. I felt him mount behind me and tie my hands to the horn at the front of the saddle.

Guards shouted at one another as they tore through the campground. The large fire remained, though no one alive sat near it now. The cheery smells of spices and liquor faded into nothing as the rusty, metallic smell of blood and death replaced them. My stomach threatened to turn again.

"Esme," Mousa's voice called frantically.

I turned to see him being shoved to his knees beside the rest of our family. All of them remained on their knees, wrists chained together and already bleeding from the harsh metal.

"I'm sorry," I cried, begging them to forgive what I couldn't accomplish. All I ever wanted was for them to be safe, and I had already failed to do even that.

"It's going to be okay, Esme," Father repeated calmly. His pale skin glowed orange from the fire that remained lit behind him, casting my family with an ethereal glow. My chest ached at seeing them this way.

Before I could cast my eyes around the campground in search of a familiar set of silver eyes and whiskey-colored hair, the guard sitting behind me kicked the horse and we lurched forward.

Tears continued to slide unbidden down my cheeks as I forced the sound of my family's cries into nothing more than a whisper on the wind. I only hoped Aiden's body wasn't among the dead strewn out about the campground. If he couldn't survive a fight against the king's guards, then there truly was no hope for my family.

Yet again, I'd failed them.

TWENTY-SIX

I WAS LEFT IN a dark cell far below ground. My heart remained in my throat as I sat silently in the dungeons. Only a single torch in the hallway provided a faint gleam of light into my cell. The floor was damp and cold, already chasing away the heat from my body as I waited for any sign of my family.

Forcing the fear behind a wall of anger, I wiped my tears away on my sleeves. The shackles at my wrists jostled with the movement, pulling at my skin.

The door to the dungeon burst open, shaking the bars of my cell. Guards shuffled in with my family in tow and they proceeded to shove them into a small cell across the aisle from mine. The smell of blood rose on the air as manacles pulled at tender wrists. Amara cried out as her knees hit the bars of the cell with the guard's forceful push. I winced as she collapsed.

With one last look in my direction, the guards left without a word.

I stood there on shaking knees as my family found their bearings, ragged breathing and quiet sobs echoing through the abandoned dungeons. These cells were wide enough to allow one man to lay comfortably, but certainly not for an entire family.

"Are you all right?" Father asked as he stepped to the edge of their cell. I reached through the bars toward his outstretched hand, silently cursing when he remained just out of my grasp.

"I'm fine," I said, forcing my voice to remain firm. "Are you okay?"

Mousa wrapped Amara in his arms, wincing slightly as his broken and bruised body tightened with the movement. "How did they know where we were?"

"They must've been watching us," Uncle Malik stated firmly. He held Jac in his lap while Nadira curled against his side. The three of them together crowded near Aunt Kiva's pale form where she lay unconscious at their feet. My heart tightened painfully at the sight.

"Where's Aiden?" My voice felt too loud in the silence of the dungeon.

My father sent Mother a look as she pulled Alfie into her lap. His knuckles were white as he clutched his notebook desperately against his chest. "We haven't seen him," she said hesitantly. At my worried expression she added, "I'm sure he's fine."

"Why bring us here?" Cordelia asked as she paced the small remaining space of their cell.

Memories of my time at the castle flashed through my mind as I wrapped my arms around my middle, forcing the cold air of the underground dwelling out of my body. That was a fate I couldn't let my family be damned to endure.

"Esme," my father began, "listen, there's something—"

His words cut off abruptly as the door crashed open again. I jumped at the noise, hating the way it made Amara's small form shake with fresh sobs. I could almost taste my family's fear as I gulped down the stale air.

They opened my cell first, attaching chains to my manacles and yanking me from my cell. I bit down on my lip to keep from crying out as the motion tore through my tender skin.

"Where are you taking her?" my mother demanded as she rattled the bars of their cell.

I couldn't hear the guard's reply as I was escorted up the stairs. My heart pounded frantically in my chest and I was almost sure I could hear it echoing off the stone walls in time to the rattle of my chains.

The hand at my arm tightened as we reached another door. My legs ached from the many stairs as we stepped into the moonlit garden. The charred grass remained near the half-built pyres which appeared to be filled with far more bones than I remembered.

I kept silent as the guard led me through the castle. The painted walls and large windows held little interest as the faint sounds of whispers and heated conversation filtered through the corridors. Guards frowned at me as we passed their stations, and servants refused to meet my eyes. My feet, for once not bare, moved soundlessly across the floor as we rounded corner after corner. It didn't take long for me to understand where we were headed.

The large wooden doors to the throne room loomed ahead and my stomach turned to lead. I knew, no matter what the king wanted with me, I would gladly do it if I could only bargain for my family's freedom. I would spend my life in chains if it meant they would live.

As soon as I caught sight of the full room before me, the whispers stopped. A deadly quiet filled its place as the guard shoved me through the room. Lords and ladies alike stared at me as I passed. Each member of the court sparing me little more than a distasteful glance before turning to whisper silently to their companions. I knew they remembered me. Who could forget the young girl the king kept chained to his throne as a symbol of his false power?

My eyes moved throughout the room, searching for any sign of escape, before settling on the dais. Lady Violette sat just at the prince's shoulder. Her golden hair was tied up in a crown of braids though her eyes yet again remained distant as she stared, unseeing, in my direction. The prince, however, froze at the sight of me. His hands clutched the arms of his throne for support as he shifted to the edge of the seat. I watched as his eyes widened in horror before flickering to his father in pure rage. His dark skin flushed red with anger. And that was the hope I needed.

King Elroy smiled coldly at my arrival. His wife patted his hand, letting her cool gaze sweep over me. The two of them looked every bit the cold, out-of-touch royals they were in their silver robes and gold crowns. I stared at the king, not daring to drop my gaze as he moved to stand at the edge of the dais. The hungry look he wore made my stomach drop further and my heart throb painfully against my ribs. The guard finally yanked me to a stop just a few paces from the dais steps and forced me to my knees. I had to bite the inside of my cheek to keep from wincing as my knees crashed against the marble floor.

A moment of silence passed, causing my breathing to grow more ragged as I waited for news of my fate. Instead, the doors behind me opened again, accompanied by the rattle of chains.

My body tightened as the king stepped closer, letting his gaze turn to the others behind me. Each jostle of their chains seemed like a stab to my heart, unbearably painful, as the king's smile turned cruel. The guards brought my family to a stop on either side of me.

"Not there," King Elroy said into the following silence. His gaze returned to me as he motioned to the floor before him.

I felt my panic growing as the guards forced them to their knees at the base of the dais steps then turned to face me and the crowd at my back. Mousa and Cordelia were placed at one end to my left, Amara and my parents beside them, then Alfie directly before me and my uncle and the others to my right. My body grew numb as I watched tears silently stream down my cousin Jac's face. He was no older than Amara, yet here he appeared to be a young boy far from the age of twelve.

Alfie sobbed softly, his notebook clutched to his chest as his hands shook violently around it. He collected himself with a deep breath as our mother leaned down to whisper words of comfort in his ear.

"The return of the famed wanderer girl," the king bellowed through the hall. I started at the sudden booming of his voice. "It seems a life in shackles at my castle was far more than her poverty-stricken family could provide for her."

The crowd's cackles of cold laughter filled the air at his words. I grit my teeth against a retort I knew would doom us all. The darkness in my chest shifted, beating in time with the pounding of my heart.

King Elroy moved down a step on the dais to frown at my family as if they were merely a dirty stain on his rug. Elias shifted as if to reach out to his father but was stopped by a guard blocking his way.

"As you all know," the king continued simply, "we've been working tirelessly to track down young Esme Loutari. That is why it is my great pleasure to inform you that I have a solution to her corruption. One that will benefit this kingdom greatly."

My stomach threatened to turn violently as he continued. "It has been all too easy to track this wanderer witch." He glanced toward Elias with an unspoken gesture that drained all the color from the prince's face. "Even as my son worked so hard to keep her presence hidden, I knew all I had to do was track him and I would find her."

Elias stiffened, a silent apology in his gaze as he caught my eye.

"I struck a deal, you see," the king continued excitedly, his round belly shaking with silent laughter as he gazed toward my family. "A deal that will provide wealth and safety to those deserving of it in Cordovia.

"A deal not unlike the one Esme's ancestors made with the god of Death generations ago." Gasps erupted through the crowd at the demon's title. My palms began to sweat beneath the king's eager gaze. "A deal that required one female in her family to steal the souls of those who wandered into their grasp and therefore allowed their family to be successful in their earnings at each of their performances. A deal that has ripped so many loved ones from their families. A deal," he continued with a taunting smile, "that has yet to be paid in full."

Amara sobbed then, just once, but loud enough to make Mousa lean over and whisper into her hair. When his eyes met mine, I saw a familiar need reflected there. A need to do whatever necessary to keep this family safe. Yet, unlike the pain in my heart, there was no blame in his eyes.

"However," King Elroy said, regaining my attention, "this deal was not offered by the god of Death himself, but by his son." I looked to my family, silently begging one of them to look at me to confirm if this was true. But they remained stoic, staring at the crowd behind me. "The Prince of Death offered her ancestor a bargain. It is because of him that her family remains in this debt and our kingdom is at this girl's mercy."

But that couldn't be. Aiden and the others said they served the prince. And it was the prince that sent them on their mission to free me from the king's clutches weeks ago… But if I was needed to fulfill the debt to their prince then that would explain why they needed me to be free. Anger burned through my veins as I silently cursed Aiden's true agenda.

"I, too, struck a deal with this prince of the dead," the king continued, though another round of gasps filled the room behind me. "He needs souls, and Esme can provide those for him."

The breath left my body in a rush of air as tears blurred my throat. I was going to be subjected to a life in chains only to damn people. And who knew what would become of my family?

"But where will you get these souls?" someone from the crowd shouted.

The king smiled. "From the filth, of course," he answered as if it were obvious. "The witches and scum who litter our streets and the wanderers who steal our wealth for trickery and deceit. It is through the loss of those souls that our kingdom will remain strong and be restored to the great dynasty it once was. We can all go on to live with full bellies and filled coffers."

"Pigs," Mother muttered under her breath, just loud enough for the king to hear.

He didn't spare her a glance as he continued. "The deal my ancestors struck with the angels has proven forfeit. The Angel of Life promised no demons would walk our realm so long as he provided his protection. Now, we have proof that demons have been among us for decades, possibly centuries." The king paused to let the crowd murmur nervously amongst each other. My mother caught my eye, offering a shallow nod of comfort before the king continued. "The Prince of Death has promised to protect our kingdom against any unnatural beings seeking vengeance or power. As long as we have Miss Loutari in the castle to collect souls, he will ensure our loved ones' safety."

"But where is this prince?" someone shouted from the crowd.

"How do we know we can trust a demon?" another asked as the crowd erupted into nervous chatter.

King Elroy raised his hand, silencing the room. "Perhaps I should let him speak for himself." My hands shook in their chains as he signaled the guards behind me.

The room fell silent again as the doors swung open. I turned stiffly, hatefully anticipating his arrival. When blue-grey eyes met mine, the breath froze in my lungs. The darkness inside me shifted, moving to fill every corner of my being as it thrummed with the prince's arrival.

"Allow me to introduce and welcome Aiden Ozanne, the Prince of Death."

TWENTY-SEVEN

Raven-black feathered wings protruded from his back; a large sword embellished with black markings settled along his spine between them. The crowd leaned away as he moved through the room, chin high and shoulders back, finally revealing the power that he had kept hidden as he walked with comfortable arrogance.

Tarsa and Hakan flanked him on either side, each wearing expressions of cold displeasure. The mortals whispered amongst themselves as the warriors followed their prince through the crowd.

Aiden's gaze bore into mine, making the essence in my chest thrum appreciatively. I couldn't find an ounce of humanity in his gaze—none of the gentleness or kindness I'd learned he possessed was there. Instead, his cold mask sat firmly in place, erasing all traces of emotion. As he walked through the crowd to join the king beside my family, he truly was no more than the Prince of Death.

Elias' gaze matched the horror I felt in mine as he too stared at Aiden with surprise. The room had gone so silent I nearly forgot it was filled with the king's court, people who feared demons above all others and worshipped the angels for their warmth and selflessness.

"Aiden?" my voice rasped on a broken whisper. Tears filled my eyes as he only spared me a brief glance. The wings on his back shifted, expanding slightly before tucking in tightly along his back. All along, it was him. He had damned my family and stolen me from the king only to return me to a life of chains.

I glanced to my family, searching for any sign that I may be hallucinating, but their gazes remained on the demon. Amara and Alfie wore similar expressions of fear and betrayal while my parents and Mousa simply looked bored, unsurprised. That realization sent my chest tightening again with the knowledge that they'd kept more secrets from me.

The king smiled at me, eyes filled with private joy as he watched the horror play out on my face. Aiden shifted, turning to face me head-on as the crowd behind me stirred nervously. My breath caught as I saw him, really saw him. He no longer wore the familiar riding pants and tunic, but instead he wore black pants that hugged the warrior muscles along his legs, and boots that laced up his calf. A dark shirt clung to his broad shoulders beneath a black tunic lined with a black thread that appeared to glow in its own light, like it contained dozens of tiny stars. His hair hung groomed to his shoulders and his hands hung relaxed at his hips where more weapons could be seen in plain view.

"Aiden?" I asked in a broken sob. His face remained impassive with absolutely no hint of emotion as he stared down his nose at me—no sign that he felt remotely guilty for this unimaginable betrayal. I bit the inside of my cheek hard enough to draw blood to keep my sob silent.

"Now," the king bellowed with a smile, "we can begin the first harvesting of souls."

Guards moved as one, lining up behind each member of my family. I jerked against the chains held by my own guard. My knees scraped against the floor as I struggled to free myself.

"No," I cried as one of the guards pulled a knife free from his belt. "Don't hurt them!"

"Father, is this necessary?" Prince Elias demanded as he got to his feet. Anger radiated off of him as he glared between the demon prince and his father. "She's just a girl. She and her family are innocent. Let them go."

The king merely nodded toward a set of guards who moved to pin Elias onto his throne. The prince struggled against their grip, but they didn't dare hurt him further in front of the anxious crowd. Whispers of surprise and unease filtered behind me at the sight of the prince's struggle and stream of curses.

King Elroy nodded to the line of guards standing behind my family. As soon as the knife was placed against my aunt's neck, I reared back against the man holding me, slamming my head into his face with a satisfying crunch.

He cursed and released me immediately. The guard holding the knife smiled as I got to my feet and slid it across my aunt's neck before I could get to her.

Nadira screamed, face reddening with agony as her mother collapsed face-first onto the marble floor, a pool of blood quickly surrounding her.

"Esme," my mother said softly. I tore my gaze from my aunt's body to stare at my mother as my guard forced me to my knees, his hands another set of binds on my arm. My mother, whose face I shared and whose golden, tan skin remained tear free as she offered me a warm smile filled with love. "Be brave, sweetheart. Whatever you do, just follow your heart and it will be okay. I love you, Esme."

Tears flowed in a rush down my cheeks, but I blinked them away, refusing to let them blur this last moment with my family.

Cordelia's spine remained straight as she knelt at the far end of the dais, closest to Aiden who watched me without emotion. I admired the strength my sister possessed as she stared straight ahead, glaring at the crowd who watched eagerly.

Beside her, Mousa remained bloodied and bandaged as he continued to whisper soothing words into Amara's hair. The youngest of us leaned heavily onto our father at her side as she clutched his shirt in her bound hands. I blinked back more tears as I turned to the king.

"Please," I begged. When he only smiled, I turned my pleading gaze on Aiden. The demon stiffened ever so slightly as I trapped him in my gaze, the darkness inside me latching onto him hungrily of its own accord. "Please, not them. Let them go. Please, Aiden."

He didn't move, didn't blink, as he continued to stare at me with emotionless eyes. Beside him, a muscle ticked in Hakan's cheek as he too stared at my family.

King Elroy nodded to the guard again, now standing over Nadira. I watched in muted horror as my cousins and uncle were slaughtered quickly. They each lay face-down in pools of blood that drifted closer to my knees.

Alfie choked on a sob as the guard stepped behind him. My little brother's pants turned wet from his fear as our uncle's blood pooled at his knees. My throat burned as more tears spilled down my own cheeks. I watched that knife press against the small of his throat, dripping blood down his skin. My brother, my dear, sweet, and kind brother looked to me then, his brown eyes lined with tears as his shaking hands clutched his notebook tighter.

"You have all the answers you need," he whispered as the knife remained still against his throat. "It's all just within your grasp."

With a nod from the king the guard slit the throat of my baby brother, tearing a mirroring slice through my heart. A scream erupted from my throat, echoed by my mother who knelt over her dead son. I watched as Alfie's blood spread to puddle at my knees, his notebook still clutched in his hands as he fell into his own blood as I struggled in my guard's grip.

"Esme," my father said urgently as the guard moved toward my mother. The darkness inside my chest opened wide, eagerly searching for the fallen souls as their broken bodies lay crumpled before me. "Esme, look at me." When I did, he nodded encouragement, silently asking me to keep my eyes on him. Tears burned tracks down my cheeks as the guard slid his knife across my mother's throat.

The guard dropped my mother harshly onto the ground. Elias continued to struggle against his own guards' hold but his presence hardly registered now. No one's presence registered within my mind as I continued to stare at my father, not daring to drop my gaze to that of my mother, now lying at my shaking knees.

"It's going to be okay, Esme," my father said gently as the knife moved to his throat. "I am so proud of you." I choked on a sob as he offered me a weak smile. "I love you, Esme. We all do…"

My chains rattled as I placed my shaking hands over my mouth, forcing my sobs to remain silent though they shook through my body.

"Now look away," he said just as the king gave a nod to the guard. "Look away, Esme."

His throat was slit before I could tell him that I loved him too. His blood splattered across my face as the guard dropped him to the ground. Beside his body, Amara cried louder now. Her entire body shook with the force of her sobs as her screams echoed through the room, mirroring the violent protests Elias was displaying as he fought against those holding him in place.

"Essie," Amara begged as sobs shook her small body. "Please, Essie. I don't wanna go to the stars yet." The slices through my heart threatened to break it altogether as I watched helplessly. The guard at my back gripped his hand in my hair, pulling me back when I struggled against the chains.

Amara's throat was cut before I could plead for her escape. My throat burned with the tears I shed as my baby sister's body crumpled to the blood-stained floor.

Mousa and Cordelia remained now. Each staring defiantly ahead, their glowers aimed at those who watched and did nothing. My heart ached for them, for my entire family who now lay in pools of blood before me.

"Stop," King Elroy commanded. The guard stepped away from my older brother with casual grace, his knife dripping in my family's blood. On the dais, Elias too paused his protests as he dared a step toward his father, desperation and anger battling for dominance in his eyes.

Mousa's shoulders sagged with a moment of relief as he looked my way. My heart continued to beat uncontrollably in my chest as I felt the warmth of my family's blood soak through my pants.

"Not these two," the king said with a sly glance my way. "I will let these two go." I nearly collapsed with relief as his words echoed through the room. "But," he said, smiling now. The expression sent my stomach whirling. "Only if they can find their way out of Cordovia by dawn."

I glanced frantically at the small window above the dais. The sky was already lightening with the first signs of dawn. They'd never make it out in time.

Mousa met my stare again, worry in his eyes as he too understood the impossibility of this notion. This was a taunt. Another ploy by the king to wield his power over those he's deemed beneath him. This was his game, and he was enjoying every moment of it.

"If they are caught inside my kingdom once the sun breaks the horizon then they are to be captured by any means necessary and returned to the dungeons," the king commanded as he nodded toward his guards.

I watched as one man moved to release the manacles at their wrists. With a clatter that echoed through my bones, their bindings fell to the floor. Mousa stood, pulling Cordelia to her feet. A fierce determination lit her face as she looked to me, a silent question in her eye.

I shook my head, panic growing as the sky continued to lighten. "Run," I screamed as they remained frozen before me. "What are you waiting for? Run! Get out of here."

Together, they placed their fists over their hearts and dipped their chins. A silent sign of respect. Mousa pulled her away and through the crowd a moment later, their heavy footsteps quickly fading from the room as they disappeared out the door. Whatever remained of my heart left with them.

Blinking away the last of my tears, I turned and found Elias slumped in his seat, chest heaving with frantic breaths. It took only a moment for our gazes to connect and a small dip of his chin to tell me he would help them as best he could.

Aiden shifted slightly, drawing my attention. His gaze remained on the slaughtered members of my family, his expression unreadable. As if he sensed my look, he turned to face me, almost reluctantly. I wanted to spit in his face and curse him for the cold indifference that he displayed. Demons really were cruel of heart; I should've trusted Nonna's stories about them.

The king's laughter filled the hall as he moved to sit on his throne again, seeming bored with the murders he had just committed. Queen Isolde took his hand in hers and gazed at him lovingly.

"Go now," he told his guests. "Drink and be merry, for the celebration of our future fortunes begins now and ends with the dawn, when the last of this girl's family is captured." With echoing cheers, the crowd behind me left the throne room. How easily these people were swayed. I could hear the start of music down the corridor where the musicians waited in the ballroom.

"Let's bring her as many of her friends as we can," King Elroy said to the guards nearby. My shoulders slumped, agony wracking through my bones as I stared at the wreckage that became of my family. "Starting with her siblings."

His words sent a chill whispering down my spine. Slowly, I turned to glare at him. The darkness inside me reared its awful head. The faint traces of my family's souls could be seen in the corner of my vision, but they quickly disappeared as I felt my curse reach for the king. My lungs tightened around a scream as I struggled further against my guard's hold. I bared my teeth in a snarl as a defiant cry burned through my throat.

I lunged forward just as the darkness within unleashed itself. My elbow swung back, colliding with the guard's nose as I rushed forward. Before me, the king collapsed on the dais, face turning purple. The queen cried out in panic while I crawled through my family's blood, in search of the one thing they hadn't taken from me yet.

The warmth of the blood seeped through my fingers, making my stomach turn violently as I pulled Alfie's notebook free from beneath his body and shoved it beneath my tunic.

On the dais the king continued to struggle for air as I watched the dark essence within me wrap its hand around his throat, searching for his scarred soul. From the corner of my eye, I could see the demons watching curiously, but they didn't move to stop me as I got to my feet. Lady Violette watched with interest at Elias' side as he remained frozen on his throne.

Before I could tear his soul from his body, Aiden stepped in front of me. His dark wings were spread wide, blocking me from view. I snarled at him, lunging with blood-soaked hands as he continued to stare at me with his expressionless mask.

"Stop." His voice rang like a sharp command. The darkness inside me answered immediately, drawing back within myself to settle near my heart.

My vision slowly began to darken as his wings collapsed, allowing the growing dawn to fill the space around us in light. The blood soaking my clothes and skin felt hotter now, burning, as exhaustion weighed heavy on my shoulders.

"I hate you," I cursed through my tears. His expression remained unchanged as he stared at me. Behind him, the guards moved to assist their collapsed king. "If I see you again, if anything happens to my brother and sister, I will kill you."

The mask slipped momentarily—so fast I was almost sure I imagined the pain underneath. Anger stoked the fire in my veins as I reached for him again, ready to tear him apart no matter how futile my efforts may be. As soon as his hands gripped my wrists, my vision went black.

TWENTY-EIGHT

THE GUARD SHOVED ME into my old room and slammed the door behind me, leaving me alone. I could hear the muffled sounds of his laughter just on the other side of the door. Fury slammed through me, erasing the heartache I had felt only a moment earlier.

I barreled my body against the door, ignoring the pain that lanced through my shoulder, a cry of rage erupting from my burning throat. My heart began to pound against my ribs as I threw myself at the door again. The door shook with the force of my body as I cried out, refusing to acknowledge the stabbing pain I felt in my chest.

My mind flashed with the fresh memories of my family being slaughtered. One by one I watched again as their throats were slit, and each time I saw one of them die I threw myself at the door. When the door refused to break apart, I turned to my fists. The guards had kept my hands manacled together, my skin already raw beneath the harsh bindings. Again, I screamed in rage as I slammed my fists against the door, again and again as my memory reeled with the deaths of my parents, my little brother, and my baby sister.

Even when the skin broke across my knuckles and my blood spattered on the door, I didn't stop. My heart pounded in my chest in rhythm with the pounding of my fists on the door. Rage, white hot and burning, flooded my veins as tears burned down my cheeks.

When I took a moment to catch my breath, I realized I could no longer hear the guards outside my door. I was alone, again.

The curse in my chest expanded to fill every inch of my body before contracting with the next breath and nearly disappearing entirely, only to hide behind my heart. My rage disappeared with it, leaving me empty and hollow.

My cheeks burned with the heat of my tears. I screamed again. The sound rattled the door on its hinges as I fell to my knees in agony. My hands clutched to my chest, gripping my bloodstained tunic as if I could tear my shattered heart from my chest, just to make the pain stop.

Every part of my body shook with the sobs as I unleashed my pain into the air. My screams echoed through the silent room as the sun rose higher.

"I'm sorry," I croaked as sobs wracked through my body. "I'm so sorry."

I lay there, hands, wrists, and heart bleeding. I shifted, reaching for the notebook that remained tucked into the waistband of my pants, hidden beneath my tunic. My hands shook in pain as I held it before me. How long had I watched my baby brother remain engulfed in the stories he wrote in here as he questioned Aiden and the others about their lives? This was his whole world, and I held it in my hands.

Ignoring the pain in my wrists, I shifted to lean against the door. The rusted smell of my blood dripping down the wood filled my nose as I wiped the tears from my face. I tried to ignore the warm streaks of blood that my hands left behind.

Careful not to tear the pages, I steadied myself with a deep breath and opened the notebook. None of the words were decipherable; the splatters of blood covering so many of the pages were too fresh and too dark. What I could see of Alfie's handwriting appeared more like a bunch of nonsense scribbles I could hardly read. His mind was always so full of ideas I had no doubt he rushed to put them all on paper before he forgot them. My heart sank as I stared at the blood-soaked pages.

Giving up, I tossed the notebook aside with a moan. I might never be able to read the incredible stories my brother found in our dark world.

The skin at my wrists throbbed painfully as I moved. I hugged my hands into my chest as memories I would have rather kept hidden returned. The feel of Aiden's hands along my skin as he bandaged the marred flesh at my ankles. The tenderness with which he cleaned the marks at my wrists, and the cuts and bruises along my face from the king's fists. I swallowed hard against the kindness I'd seen in his eyes as I remembered. My heart stuttered of its own accord, making me curse those moments that had all been a ploy, and lock the memory of them away, far in the depths of my mind. Aiden was a demon; there was nothing kind about him.

I pressed the heels of my hands into my eyes, forcing the thought of Aiden's betrayal away. Beneath the anger and pain I felt from my family's death, I felt hollow. As each of their souls had left for the stars, I felt part of my own soul leave with them.

My eyes closed as the sun moved across the sky. No one came for me. No one brought me food or a change of clothes or thought to tend to my injuries. Instead, I lay there in the quiet of my abandoned corner of the castle. As the sun eventually set in the distance, I felt more of my soul disappear with it until finally, all that was left was a broken shell ready to succumb to the king's cruelty if it meant I'd never have to steal another soul.

When my room fell into darkness, I felt a brush of air along my cheek. Startled, I forced my eyes open, unaware that I had slipped into unconsciousness. What I saw before me stole the breath from my lungs and the warmth from my body.

A tussle of brown hair hung in his eyes as he smiled somberly at me. "Hey, Esme." Warm brown eyes studied me with concern as I pushed myself onto my elbow.

"Kesson?" My voice shook with tears as I stared. His body appeared like a shadow, clear enough to see in the faint trace of moonlight but dim enough to see the empty room through his form.

He flashed his crooked smile that had once made my knees grow weak. "What are you doing on the floor?"

My heart grew heavy as memories flooded me again. "I have nowhere else to go."

"So, you're just giving up?" he said with a slight shake of his head. "You're just going to lay here until the king sends for you? I thought you'd have more fight than that."

"They're all gone, Kesson," I argued half-heartedly. "He killed my entire family. I won't steal another soul for him."

Kesson's soul sighed deeply, the air a chill across my cheeks. "They're not gone, Esme. Not all of them."

My vision blurred with more tears as I forced my gaze to the window and the night sky beyond. "I felt it when they died, Kesson. I felt their souls as I feel yours now."

His hand reached out, brushing along my cheek in a whisper of air. "I'm not talking about them." At my furrowed brow a smile teased his mouth again. "Mousa and Cordelia are still alive, Esme. You are not alone."

"But I am. I am alone."

"I've never known you to give up so easily," he said with false disappointment. "Are you so ready to give yourself over to the mercy of the demon prince and the king that you'd forget there are still people rooting for you? They need you just as you need them. Don't let the king win so soon."

Tears tracked down my cheeks, mixing with the blood smeared there. "What if I can't save them?"

"You won't save them if you don't try," he said softly, brown eyes warming as he knelt before me. "Get up, Esme. Get up and fight back. There is a fire in your soul and it's time you let others see that too. I believe in you. And we both know you are far too stubborn to give up this easily."

I studied the muted form of his soul. He was right. I was tired of being sad, broken. The ache of my family's loss felt like a hole had been ripped from my chest, so I let my rage fill it.

Sensing my rising determination, he smiled at me. "There she is. Show them just how powerful you are."

I returned his smile hesitantly, blinking away tears as I allowed his strength to fill me, erasing the doubt and loss I felt as I reached for his hand.

A chill chased through me as I jolted awake. I blinked into the dark of the room, searching for any sign of Kesson's soul, but all I saw was a brief glimpse of a shadow disappearing through the window and into the night sky.

A sharp scuffle echoed through the dark room, making me jump as I got to my feet. Pain lanced through me as the rigid position I'd taken up for the past day on the floor seemed to bruise my bones.

I shifted closer to the bed, its solid form my only defense against whatever was making such a startling noise.

A loud bang sounded then, almost like someone was throwing their weight against a heavy door, only it seemed to come from the fireplace.

Shock stole my breath as the fireplace shifted with a loud creak, opening up into a narrow tunnel hidden behind the wall. Prince Elias entered, dressed in simple dark traveling clothes that made him appear more like a peasant than the heir to a powerful kingdom.

"Esme," he breathed in relief as he caught sight of me in the dark room. Before I could speak, he took two long strides toward me and wrapped his arms around my shoulders, holding me tightly against himself. "I'm so sorry," he breathed into my hair. "There was nothing I could do."

I refused to let sadness take me again. "Mousa and Cordelia?" I dared ask.

He let me go, holding me at arm's length as he took in the blood soaking nearly every inch of my clothing. "They're fine," he whispered. "I made sure they got on the right ship at Aegan. They're currently out at sea headed toward the Abandoned Desert."

My shoulders sagged with relief. "They're really alive?"

Elias took my hands in his. The stark contrast between his dark, clean hands and the blood staining my own sent a shiver through me. "They are. And they're going to be fine. I have a close friend in the desert that I've sent word to and will keep them safe until you can find them again."

I nodded, blinking away the tears as relief chased away the hollow anger I felt before. As Elias studied my hands I winced against the bindings.

"What did they do to you?" he whispered in horror as he took in the torn skin at my wrists and the swelling of my knuckles. Before I could answer, his gaze shot to the door and I knew what he saw there. I followed his gaze and marveled at the amount of blood staining the wooden paneling.

There were marks in the wood where I slammed my body over and over again, and smaller areas from my fists that were now spattered with blood as it dripped down the door all the way to the floor where I once lay.

"They let you hurt yourself like this?" His voice was filled with horror as he turned back to my hands. My knuckles screamed in protest now that the anger had disappeared, only to be replaced by a strange mixture of relief and exhaustion.

I shrugged but the movement sent an ache through my shoulder. "No one was around to hear," I whispered. "I don't think anyone here would care much anyway."

Elias shot me a look that said otherwise.

"Come on," he said gently, taking a pack off of his back that I hadn't noticed earlier. "Change quickly so we can get out of here."

I stared at the simple pair of men's trousers and black tunic that he pulled out of the bag. "Where am I supposed to go?" I asked as I yanked the boots from my feet. "I can't leave until I find a way to end this debt and free my family—or kill Aiden."

"I know," he said patiently. I waited until he turned his back before I stripped from the blood-soaked clothes and yanked on the clean set he brought me. I had to grit my teeth to keep from groaning at the pain in my hands and shoulder.

"I'm going to help you," he said finally, bending to pick up my brother's notebook. When he turned around, I studied his face.

"If you get caught helping me," I said slowly, "your father may try to kill you too. You'll never be king."

Elias shrugged, taking a key from his pocket and unlocking the shackles that kept me from pulling my arms through the sleeves of the clean tunic. As they fell away, I sighed with relief. My skin shivered at the suddenness of the cool air as it brushed along the wounds.

"There's no point in being king if it means murdering half the kingdom," he said as he hoisted the bag to his back once more. A small patch of blood soaked through where my brother's notebook had been placed at the bottom.

"He'll know you're helping me," I said, not needing to elaborate.

He nodded. "Then let's hope we find a way to kill the demon before he finds us."

"I don't know how to do that," I admitted. "Since he offered my ancestor the debt, his death should end it for my bloodline, but we weren't able to find a way to kill a demon."

"There was a story I was told as a child," he started as he led me toward the hidden passage. "It told of weapons created by the angels that were poisonous for demons or anyone tied to them. The god of Death had most of them destroyed during the war, but there are rumors that the Angel of Life kept one hidden. If we can just get to the angels, maybe we can find that weapon and use it to free your family."

"I don't know," I admitted quietly, doubt filling me as I recalled Nonna's tale of our family's history. "They didn't help my ancestor all those years ago. Who's to say they'll bother helping me now?"

"You won't know until you ask," he replied gently.

Elias led the way through the door behind the fireplace, pulling it closed behind us. Darkness surrounded me on all sides as I waited for my eyes to adjust. I felt the prince's hand gently grip my elbow as he led me through the tunnel.

"This will take us directly to the barn," he said on a quiet breath. "From there we can steal a horse and travel north. The Wood of Rune is about a two week's ride if we travel fast."

I remained silent as he led us through the darkness. My wrists and hands ached from beating on the door for so long, and my back and shoulders ached with the smallest movement. Exhaustion tried to turn my feet to lead, but I refused to stop. For what felt like hours we walked through the narrow tunnel. Every twist and turn and staircase lead us past private chambers of the castle and other dining halls and libraries where the sounds of muffled voices could be heard through the walls.

My heart began to race in my chest as the tunnel broke open to a small room where beams of light filtered through cracks in the wooden walls. The smells of livestock and hay filled my nose as the sounds of a swishing tail and the stomp of a hoof echoed in the quiet.

"Wait here," Elias breathed quietly. A moment later his hand released my elbow as he disappeared through a small door I hadn't noticed. I waited, barely daring to breathe in the quiet room before I finally heard the steady sound of hoofbeats a moment later.

"All right, come on," he whispered a little louder.

Careful not to make too much noise, I left the safety of the darkened tunnel and stepped out into the barn. A single torch lit the walkway where Elias waited atop a black mountain of a horse, hand outstretched toward me.

Ignoring the pain in my bones, I gripped his hand tightly and let him pull me onto the horses back. Settling behind him, I wrapped my arms around his waist and held tightly with my legs around the horse's middle.

Elias clucked his tongue, signaling for the horse to move. Without a moment's hesitation, the horse took off into the night. The air was cool this late in the fall. The moon shone brightly above, lighting our path as we clung to the shadows of the garden.

I barely dared to breathe, let alone hope, as we passed guards stationed throughout the castle grounds. Even though months had passed, I could still smell the remnants of the pyres as the ashes blew in the light breeze.

Squeezing my arms tighter around the prince's middle, I turned my head back to catch a glimpse at the looming fortress that had taken so much from me. With each stride away from the castle, I felt my shoulders lighten and determination fill me. My gaze shot to the stars in time to see a faint shadow shift to blend into the night sky. I sent up a silent thanks to Kesson for finding a way to pull me from the darkness.

A shout sounded then, quickly followed by several others as guards finally took notice of us. Elias urged the horse onward as we took off through the gates and into the night.

The last thing I saw of the castle was the silhouette of a familiar figure in the doorway, his large black wings tucked in tightly as if in restraint.

The guardsmen continued to shout as they sounded the alarm. A bell tolled somewhere in the distance, surely alerting the nearby villages of our escape.

"Hold on," Elias called over his shoulder as he kicked the horse, urging him to move faster.

When I dared a glance over my shoulder, I felt my breath leave my body in fear.

"Elias," I called over the sound of our horse's hooves. "They're coming." Guards moved into view now, all of them mounted on horses of their own. Swords and bows loaded with sharpened arrows glistened in the moonlight.

"How many?" he asked as he turned the horse through a bend in the road, taking us around the nearest northern village.

"All of them."

TWENTY-NINE

THOUGH MILES OF EMPTY road stretched before us, we were surrounded on all other sides by guardsmen on horseback.

"Can't you go any faster?" I cried over the deafening hoofbeats.

Elias grunted. "This horse was not bred for racing, Esme."

My arms squeezed tighter around the prince as I glanced over my shoulder. My heart was beating so hard in my chest I was sure he could feel it against his back.

The king's horses, carrying less weight and clearly trained for this sort of ambush, were able to gain ground as we continued down the winding path. Elias made a sharp turn, nearly throwing me off the back of our horse before weaving his way through the trees.

I could hear the guards behind us calling to one another, making imminent plans to block the path and capture us once and for all.

I glanced over my shoulder again and nearly lost my seat as a guard, only an arm's length away, reached over to grasp onto the end of my cloak.

"Elias," I screeched as I tried to lean away from his grasp.

An arrow breezed past my cheek, close enough to make me wince, before finding its home in the guard's arm. With a cry, he lurched away from me and pulled his horse to a skidding halt. Heart beating for an entirely different reason now, I searched the trees around us. At the sight of a familiar set of blond curls and a head full of fiery red braids, tears threatened to burn my eyes.

But if they were here then...

"Elias, you have to go faster," I called over the angry bellows of the guards.

The prince didn't bother to reply as he kicked the horse forward, already at a breakneck pace. Twin axes appeared then, flying through the air close enough that I had to duck to keep my head on. Two grunts behind us signaled they had found their targets. I swallowed my panic as Hakan appeared, broad sword in hand as he knocked a guard from his horse and sliced him down the middle.

My hands wrapped tighter around Elias' middle as the sounds of battle grew louder behind us, the guards quickly becoming otherwise occupied. Aiden never came out of the shadows, but I could feel his eyes on my back as Elias and I continued to race down the winding path in the trees.

Our horse slowed, either sensing that we were out of immediate danger or too tired to carry on at such a pace. Elias and I panted heavily as we both forced ourselves to keep our gazes on the path ahead. We were well away from the castle now, deep in the forest that occupied the land between the castle and Cimarron, a nearby village.

"I think we'll be okay for now," Elias sighed quietly.

I released my gut-wrenching grip and winced as the movement pulled at my torn skin. "We can't stop yet," I said as I pulled my hands back to look at them. The sight of bloodied and raw flesh sent my stomach turning. I'd barely spent a day in those manacles again and already I would carry new scars from them. "The demons won't be far behind us now if they were able to catch us so quickly."

Elias led the horse off the path and deeper into the overgrown trees. Branches and twigs pulled at my hair and scraped against my cheeks, but I ignored them as I tried to keep my seat centered on the horses back while dodging low-hanging branches.

"We need to get your hands cleaned and bandaged before we continue," he said as he pulled the horse to a stop a hundred yards away from the path we'd been traveling.

I remained still, ears straining to listen to the trees around us for any sign of Aiden or his friends.

"Esme," Elias said gently, regaining my attention. I took his outstretched hand and let him assist me down from the horse.

I held my hands in front of me. The pain of my bloodied knuckles and wrists too great to dig through the bag strapped to Elias' back for the bandages. Elias pulled a wrap of bandages and a tin of medicine from deep within the bag before gently taking my hands in his to study them.

"Was it always like this?" he whispered as he began to slowly apply the medicine. I bit the inside of my cheek to keep from cringing at the sudden sting of the ointment. Whatever this medicine was, it was the expensive kind that was only offered to those of a higher class, like the royal family.

I shrugged as he applied more of the precious ointment to my wrists. "It was worse on my ankles," I said with strain. The stinging from the medicine made me want to claw the skin off my hands. I blinked back the tears that formed in my eyes as he began to wrap the bandages around my wounds.

"I'm sorry," he breathed quietly. I leaned in a little farther to hear. "Had I known, had I bothered to look beyond my own problems, I would've done something."

Aiden's words only days before echoed in my mind. Though Elias vowed to have protected me against his father now, he still allowed the abuse to happen. Aiden, however, wouldn't have let it happen at all. At least the Aiden I thought I knew wouldn't have. Now, I wasn't so sure what the demon might do to me just to get his way.

When the bandages were secure, I pulled my hands gently from his and leaned against a tree. "We should keep moving," I said, watching Elias dig through his bag again. "We can't afford to stop so close to the castle."

"We'll be fine here," he said confidently. "The guards won't come this deep into the trees. They'll stay on the cleared path."

My eyes scanned the small bit of forestry around us. It wasn't the guards I was worried about at the moment.

"Here," he said, forcing an apple into my hand. "Eat while we rest a bit then we can continue to the next village. There's a small place just north of here where we can rest for longer while we figure out our next move."

I sighed, biting into the apple. The crunch of it echoed too loudly through the trees. "You don't have to come with me, you know," I said again. "If we get caught, by the demons or your father's men, then it won't end well for you either. The demons may very well kill you."

Elias only offered a smile—a warm smile that once might've made my stomach flip with the beauty of it. "Want to get rid of me so soon? And here I thought we were having fun." His dark skin glistened with a faint sheen of sweat in the dim moonlight and his tight dark curls settled along his brow in the breeze. The sounds of wildlife around us echoed through the night.

I snorted. "Won't Lady Violette grow to miss her beloved, sleazy groom?"

Elias choked on his bite of bread before turning baffled eyes on me. "I don't think she'll much notice that I'm gone. We hadn't spent much time together anyway."

I smiled, taking another bite of the apple. "Somehow, I get the feeling that's true. Besides," I continued as I sat on the ground beside him. A roll of thunder overhead made my stomach tighten uncomfortably. "I get the feeling there aren't too many thoughts going on in that pretty head of hers."

Elias laughed then. The memory of Lady Violette's blank stare and constant dazed smile lifted a darkness from my shoulders. She was kind, the few times I'd spoken to her, but poor Violette was definitely raised to be nothing more than a pretty face, taught to smile and stand straight for any amiable men. I had no doubt that her parents didn't bother investing much beyond a basic education for the poor girl.

"Amara would've liked her," I noted quietly. The memory of my family burned my throat with tears. "Cordelia would mock her simpleness. But Mousa," I chuckled, taking another bite of the apple, "he would've surely tried to tumble her."

"They'll be okay, you know," he said gently. "Your brother and sister I mean. I've got my men with them now until they arrive to the desert safely. My father's men won't find them."

I offered a nod, not trusting the tears in my eyes to stay hidden as I kept them downcast. "That's all I can hope for until I finish this."

The prince didn't offer a reply as the thunder rolled again, louder this time, making the trees shake slightly. A beginning patter of rain sounded around us, cooling the sweat along my skin.

"We should find cover," Elias cautioned as he got to his feet. The rain came down harder as if hearing his words, blocking my vision beyond a few feet.

I shivered in the sudden temperature drop. All around us the trees went quiet from wildlife, the only sound the loud crack of thunder and the patter of rain. Elias' horse shifted uneasily, feet splashing in the growing mud.

My heart thundered in my chest as the darkness that lived near it shifted, sensing something I couldn't yet see. As the air cooled further my breath came in quick gasps. I shifted, searching through the trees now cast in darkness as the moon remained hidden behind clouds.

I caught sight of a set of dove-grey wings, but as soon as I blinked, they were gone. Fear turned my blood to ice in my veins as I searched the trees to confirm my fear, but I was quickly disproven.

A boulder-sized man stepped into view, blocking my line of sight to the spot where I thought I saw Ephraim. "There they are, fellas," he said. He stood several heads taller than me and looked nearly as wide under his layers of rain-soaked clothes. His boots were coated in mud that looked like he hadn't bothered to clean them in years. I swallowed nervously as others came into view then too, each looking just as menacing as the boulder man.

"Leave us be," Elias snapped as he moved to stand between me and the man. He hadn't yet noticed the others surrounding us on all sides.

The prince held onto my hand tightly, making me wince with the crushing of my swollen knuckles. I spun around, pressing my back against his as I glared at the men creeping forward through the downpour.

"Can't do that, little prince," the large man said. "You see, there's still a large bounty for that girl's head."

"And," a friend of his spoke up from somewhere nearby. Elias and I spun to see him stepping into view on our other side. He was thin and weedy, but his bruised knuckles and missing teeth told me he wasn't afraid to turn this into a fight. "There is now a bounty out for you, too. It seems someone pissed off their dear old father."

My stomach turned leaden as Elias shivered at his words. I'd no idea how well Elias could fight, but I did know we lacked weapons whereas those around us held their knives and clubs at the ready.

"Unfortunately," the boulder man said, making us spin to face him again. Mud splashed up my trousers, soaking them through with each step. "The prince is wanted unharmed. However, you, little girly, are wanted only alive."

"Again, I ask that you leave us be," the prince demanded. I commended Elias for his bravery no matter how foolishly placed. If only we could mount the horse and race off through the trees before these men grabbed us. I took a casual step closer to the horse, not letting go of my grip on Elias' hand.

The men laughed, a chorus of taunting omens. My blood thundered in my ears as a flash of lightening lit the sky over the canopy of trees.

"Take me," Elias said as he spun to face the men surrounding us. He'd finally noticed their slow steps closing the distance around us. "Take me back to my father if you must, but let the girl go. She's done nothing wrong."

The men all laughed, though the boulder of a man scowled at me. "Isn't she the witch that's been cursing our people?"

Fluttering continued in my chest as if confirming the man's words. I grit my teeth to keep the darkness from surfacing and latching onto this man. If I damned him now, there would be no chance of negotiating our way past these men.

Elias leaned into me, pressing the cool hilt of a small knife into my palm. "You can throw them, right?"

"What?" I whispered back in a mixture of fear and surprise.

"Like your parents. You can throw them, can't you?" We whispered quietly as the men shifted around us, slowly growing closer.

"I can't fight," I argued, stepping closer. "I never learned how."

Elias sighed deeply, pulling the knife back into his hand. "Remind me to teach you to fight when this is over."

He stepped away, turning toward the large man who appeared to be the leader. "She is an innocent," Elias retorted harshly. The rain had fully soaked our clothes, making them cling to our skin. My thick curls remained plastered to my face and neck.

The weedy man tilted his head, eyes drifting down to my feet and slowly back up to my face. The hunger that showed there made my knees shake.

"Well, let's find out then," he said mockingly.

They lunged as one. I yelped as Elias was dragged away from me and large arms wrapped around my middle, pulling me further into the depths of the trees.

"Esme!" the prince cried as he fought off his own attackers.

I tried striking out with my feet, but the mud did little to help my footing on the slick ground and my hands were too tender to use. My elbow collided with a snapping sound before the man holding me dropped me straight onto the ground.

"Bitch broke my nose," he spat as he turned, dumbfounded, toward his companions. They all eyed me curiously, some more so than others, before he landed a hard kick to my torso.

Ribs crunched beneath his boot as I rolled away from his towering form. The constant downpour made it difficult to get my feet underneath me on the flooding earth but these men seemed to have little issue with that as they each grabbed onto an ankle and dragged me back through the mud.

I screamed again, loud enough to make my throat catch fire if it hadn't become caked with mud. I choked as my lungs attempted to force the stuff out. Another kick crashed into my back as I pulled myself up onto all fours.

"Esme!" Elias called again.

A quick glance through the rain told me he was further away than I thought. Men surrounded him on all sides, but he mounted an impressive counterattack. His cheek dripped blood, mixing with the rain cascading down his skin.

He held a small knife which he used to strike out against anyone who attempted to close in on him. The prince was quick and steady on his feet despite the rain pooling around his boots.

Something hard crashed into the back of my head then, making my vision go spotty. I gasped as I stumbled, strong hands yanking me off balance.

"I got her," the giant man called over my head. "Let's get out of here, boys."

I blinked through the rain and stars that clouded my vision. His arm wrapped around my throat, tightening enough to make breathing difficult. The man's words waned as he whispered in my ear—the fear of being in these men's care while unconscious the only thing keeping me from passing out.

I clawed at his arm, trying desperately to get it to loosen against my neck.

An arrow shot out of the haze, landing in the man's elbow and just missing my neck. The man screeched and dropped me. I crashed to the mud, coughing as air burned through my deprived lungs.

Killian appeared with his bow loaded and raised at the other man nearby. He looked as I'd never seen him, young face clouded with darkness and pure rage as he shot arrow after arrow at the surrounding men.

Seraphine appeared as nothing more than a spot of bright red hair through the darkness as she spun in a blur, knives in hand as she cut down men like they were stalks of grass. Her scowl was nearly as fierce as Killian's though her eyes registered my presence long enough to soften ever so slightly.

I didn't take the time to decipher the meaning of their arrival as Elias cried out then. I turned to see him going down hard, blood pouring from the cut in his cheek. But it was the dark blood that soaked through the front of his tunic that made me freeze in horror.

My cries cut off abruptly as a familiar set of hands pulled me from the ground and cradled me gently in their grasp.

A mixture of fear and anger made my body turn rigid as I turned to face him. His darkened eyes narrowed in on my face. The sight of his black wings strewn out behind him made a shiver creep along my spine.

His lips turned upward in a crooked smile. I glared at the gentleness of his gaze.

"Hello, princess."

THIRTY

I STRUGGLED IN HIS iron grip, not wanting to be held so close to him after what he did. His smile faltered slightly, as if he too recalled what he'd done.

"Let me go," I cried as I beat my fists against his chest. I tried to ignore the protest from my hands as the jostling tore at my skin.

"As you wish," he breathed against my cheek, making me shiver longingly. I hated him for it.

The demon set me on my feet but refused to release his arm from around my shoulders as he continued to hold me against his side, shielding me from the falling rain. All around us, screams continued as his friends slaughtered the men who'd come to take me and Elias back to the king. My stomach threatened to turn violently as the sounds of flesh being torn by sword and ax echoed through the trees.

The immortals glided through the mud and rain easily as they rounded up all the men and tore their bodies open to bleed on the ground. Elias remained in the center of it all as he clutched a hand to his middle, dark blood still spilling out to stain his clothes. My heart lodged in my throat as I noticed the foreboding paleness lighting his features. Even his eyes appeared glassy through the distance between us as he watched me nervously in the arms of the demon.

Aiden shifted, putting some distance between us and I got a full view of the wreckage. Blood mixed with puddles of mud all around. Trees spattered with blood and flesh held onto the stench of the ruin around me. I pressed a hand to my mouth to keep from succumbing to the nausea.

"Are you all right?" Aiden asked as he studied me through the falling rain.

I glowered at him, ignoring the pain I felt singing through my bones. The moment our eyes met every memory of him flashed behind my eyes. His hands felt too warm against my shoulders as he held me still, the rain a faint touch compared to the searing agony of his own. Tears burned my throat as my mind replaced the tender memories with the bloodstained slaughter of my family. My anger rose quickly, replacing the pain and anguish I felt at being in his presence.

"I hate you," I finally said, voice coming out in a pained whisper. I threw my fists against his chest as the tears burned down my cheeks. "I hate you!" My voice broke on the scream as the sounds of the dying faded behind me.

A muscle tightened along Aiden's cheek as he studied me. There was little emotion in his face, a mask of cold detachment firmly in place, but his eyes were a storm of agony and rage that melded with the gray and blue swirling there. My heart cleaved in two again as he refused to release me from his gaze.

I smacked him hard across the face. The stinging pain across my palm felt stronger compared to the torture it caused my bloodied knuckles.

Again, that muscle twitched in his cheek, his face turned to the side from the force of my slap. Though I knew he could, he hadn't tried to stop me from hitting him. When he slowly turned his eyes back to mine, I felt the connection like an arrow through my heart.

"I hate you," I repeated in a broken whisper. Elias' moans of pain could still be heard behind me. "They're all dead because of you. I thought..." My voice broke as more tears stole my voice. "I thought I meant something to you. You said there were no words...."

Aiden's expression remained cold, hard. "It's true," he finally said in a stilted voice. "There are no words to describe how much you mean to me. Because no matter what sort of poetry I spun, nothing could do my feelings justice."

"Liar!" I screamed against the torrential pour of rain. "I mean nothing to you. I'm nothing more than a tool to bargain with for the god of Death, who you so valiantly serve." My hands balled into fists at my sides as whatever pieces of my heart remained shattered in truth at the words I now spoke. "I'm just a pawn in whatever scheme you're trying to accomplish. As if your mortality wasn't enough, you had to sacrifice my family, my soul, to keep yourself in his favor."

The emotion in his eyes disappeared. There was nothing human in his gaze now. Only an emotionless demon stared back at me, not really seeing. Or possibly really seeing what stood before him for the first time.

I swallowed back more tears. "Was it worth it?" I asked in a faint whisper.

Aiden dropped my gaze, eyes first pausing on the scar at my neck, then settling at the many bruises and bloodied cuts along my hands. The rain continued to fall around us, my clothes entirely soaked through, but I suppressed the shiver against the cold that I felt radiating from his heart.

"There is much you still do not know," he whispered. "You have yet to open your eyes to the truth."

"I know the truth," I snapped angrily. "You cursed my family. You are the reason they're all dead and I am *alone*. You," I said, slamming my fists into his chest again, "lied to me. Everything you said to me was a lie."

His hands caught mine then, forming steel binds around my wrists as he pushed himself out of my reach. "You know nothing," he spat, angry now. "But you will and if you let it, it will break you."

My shoulders slumped, the weight of the last few days pulling me down. "I'm already broken," I breathed quietly.

I wasn't even sure he heard me as Elias let out another moan. The splashing of mud and rain pulled Aiden from whatever he was studying on my face as he turned toward the chaos again. Refusing to let me protest, he wrapped his arm and cloak over my shoulders and pulled me against him once more, wings shifting to shield me from the rain.

I looked at Elias, wishing there was something I could do to ease his agony. There was no way he could continue our journey north. Not in this condition.

"Bring him here," Aiden said with a quiet voice, yet somehow the power and authority it held carried through the rainfall. I allowed myself a moment to marvel at the power radiating from him. His large black wings, feathered like a raven, bristled against the slight wind as he shielded me with them.

Tarsa moved through the wreckage, dragging a man behind her. The weedy man looked to Aiden, eyes widening in horror as he noted the large wings and fierceness in Aiden's face. The demon kept his spine straight and shoulders back as he glared down his nose at the man.

"P-please," the man begged as Tarsa tossed him before the demon prince. "Please. I didn't do nothing, sir."

Aiden didn't so much as breathe as he glowered at the trembling man. I saw Elias shift out of the corner of my eye, trying to drag himself closer to me as I stood with Aiden and the others surrounding me. I lifted my gaze to Seraphine as she stood a few steps away with Killian at her side. Both kept their gazes focused on Aiden, frowns prominent on their usually kind faces.

I felt my brows draw together in confusion as I watched the glance they shared before turning to stare at the trembling man before the demon prince. Hakan stood at my other shoulder, hand gripped tightly onto his sword as he too glared at the man before us.

"You were planning on harming her," Aiden said with false calm. I could hear the strain in his voice as he struggled against his rising anger and felt the slight tremble in his hands which he kept hidden at his sides.

"N-no. We wouldn't have touched her. Honest." His gaze turned to me, pleading.

"I don't believe you," Aiden said with a scoff. "But I will let you live."

The man nearly collapsed with relief, face buried in his hands to sob. "Thank you. Thank you, Your Highness."

I stiffened at the use of Aiden's true title. Though his wing remained over my shoulders, I'd nearly let myself forget who he really was in this world.

"On one condition," Aiden said before the man could scamper off. "You will return to the castle, quickly. And once there, you will tell your king that I have taken Esme into my care, and he will not get her back until she wishes to return to him."

I turned to stare at him in horror before turning back to Elias who continued to crawl in our direction, clothes nearly covered entirely with blood beneath his hands. I watched as his eyes widened at Aiden's words.

"The deal we struck was false," Aiden continued, oblivious to the discomfort of Elias and me. "The only truth to it was that I needed Esme with me. Once your king finds it in himself to get off his useless ass and actually provide for those under his responsibility, then I believe he will see great strides in improving the livelihood of his kingdom. Until then, it will continue to suffer under his greedy hand."

Aiden turned away. His arm wrapped around my shoulders once again in what appeared to be a protective gesture, as if to keep me out of the rain.

"Oh," he said, turning back to the man climbing clumsily to his feet. "Be sure to also let him know of his son's condition and location. It would be a shame for the sole heir of this kingdom to die alone in the woods surrounded by useless brute pigs."

The man bowed low, shaking in his boots before Aiden jerked his chin in dismissal. I watched, frozen, as the man ran back in the direction of the castle. Rain continued to pour from the sky, quickly hiding his retreating figure.

Aiden's arm tightened around my shoulders as I felt his gaze shift in Elias' direction. I dropped my hands to my sides, prepared to aide him in any way I could as he continued to struggle on the ground. The prince's face had gone deathly pale as he kept a hand pressed to his wound. If he didn't get help soon, he would surely die. That weedy bounty hunter wouldn't be able to make it to the castle quickly enough on foot in this weather.

"Don't take her," Elias breathed through his blood loss.

Aiden stiffened almost imperceptibly. Killian and Seraphine shifted uncomfortably from where they stood a few paces away. Tarsa shot them a look that went unnoticed by the two immortals as they watched the prince struggle in the mud.

"You are a fool, princeling," Aiden spat at him. "You are an immature and stupid child for thinking you would be enough to keep her unharmed. To think you could escape with someone as important as Esme and be enough to keep her safe while everyone in your father's kingdom, and my own realm, hunts her. It is by pure luck that she has not been killed tonight."

I fought the urge to defend Elias. It was Aiden's doing that made the king kill my family. It was his fault that I was here to begin with, stuck with this stupid debt owed to his father. I wanted to curse his name and rip his soul from his body, should he even have one.

Elias spat at the demon prince's feet. "You think you're so good for her then?" he snapped. "You're nothing more than a demon. A soulless, heartless demon. As soon as she no longer benefits your motives, you'll kill her. You're no good for her."

Aiden cast a curious look in my direction which I pointedly ignored. His hand tightened at my shoulder. "That may be," he said as he turned to glare at the bleeding prince, "but I would never put her in danger as you did just now. Esme is coming with me. When she's ready, she has every right to return to your realm should she wish it."

"What?" I sputtered. My stomach somersaulted painfully at the thought of traveling into the demon realm with Aiden and his friends. I couldn't leave yet, not until I found a way to end this curse on my family... or kill Aiden.

Aiden offered me a cold smile. "Come," he said, pulling me away from Elias. "We must go before the king's men return." I remained frozen as I watched him paint a set of wings on a nearby tree in blood—the same symbol I saw painted onto the king's throne all those weeks ago at the burning, when Aiden rescued me from the king.

Elias cried out as Aiden pulled me away. My gaze swept over the destruction around me, and I caught sight of Elias struggling on his hands and knees. I needed the weapon from the angels, but we couldn't get to it now. Anger wrapped around my heart in a blanket of comfort as I turned to the immortals. If killing Aiden was what it took to free my family from this curse, then I'd do that. Even if it meant going to his realm instead of the angels.

"Esme," Elias bellowed, shaking the ground with his cry. "Stay alive, Esme. I'll keep them safe. I promise. I promise, Esme."

Tears sprung to my eyes. My heart ached to turn back and ride off on Elias' horse straight to the desert where I knew my remaining family waited. I could hide there, take on a new name and a new persona. I'd forget my life and everyone I knew here if it meant my brother and sister would stay safe and unharmed. But would I be able to live knowing Aiden continued to search for me? No, I couldn't rest until he was dead and I was free of this debt.

Horses came into view; large horses with coats so black they appeared nearly blue, like Aiden's wings. As Elias continued to cry out to me, Aiden's hands gripped my waist as he easily tossed me up onto his horse. I allowed myself to look back, searching through the downpour for Elias.

Hakan mounted his horse, and the others followed. Tarsa shot a glare toward Seraphine and Killian who were whispering quietly to one another as the latter stared after Elias. My heart sank further as I watched him stumble to his feet and lean heavily on a tree. His whole body shook as dark red blood continued to spill out of his gut.

"Esme," he said, breathlessly. Tears burned tracks down my cheeks as I watched him, unable to provide him any help. Seraphine moved then. I watched as she lifted his pack out of the mud, searched through it until a familiar notebook appeared in her hands. She cast me a knowing glance before tucking it into her waistband. I watched as she searched a little longer through his bag until she found whatever she was looking for: a spare tunic, mostly dry though the bag appeared soaked with mud and rain. She held it out to the prince. "Place this against your wound," she said gently. "It'll help stop the bleeding until someone comes."

Elias took it wordlessly, his face remaining cold and hard as he held onto the garment. I watched his face turn a sickly green from the pain as he pressed it against his wounded gut.

"I'm sorry," I called through the rain. Aiden froze on the ground beside me where he'd been readjusting the bags tied to his saddle. "Tell them I'm sorry I couldn't stay."

Elias nodded. "I promise they'll be safe."

Chewing the inside of my lip, I nodded, not trusting my voice any longer. Seraphine tossed the notebook to Aiden who stuffed it unceremoniously into one of his saddlebags. The others had mounted their own horses by now, waiting as Aiden climbed onto the saddle behind me. I froze as his chest pressed warmly into my back, wings tucked around us slightly to keep me out of the rain.

I wiped tears, blood, and rain from my face, smearing it further with mud but not really caring. Aiden watched silently as he wrapped an arm around my middle. I tensed as his hand pressed flat against my stomach, pulling me tighter against him.

He yanked a cloak from another saddle bag, tucking it around my shoulders and pulling the soaked one loose from around my neck.

I glared at the demon prince who merely offered a smile in return. No matter that my heart mirrored the flutter of darkness in my chest at Aiden's closeness. It meant nothing now as I prepared to join him in his realm, only to kill him.

"Ready, princess?" he teased with a wink.

Between one blink and the next his dark wings disappeared, making him appear as he always used to. I closed my eyes against the rain, forcing myself to ignore the way Elias called after me. His voice was pained and broken as I left him alone near death to run off with the demon prince.

THIRTY-ONE

I BLINKED THROUGH THE onslaught of rain. Throughout the night, Aiden and the other immortals raced side by side on horseback until day had come and gone. Somehow, as villages passed in a blur and the rain faded to sunshine, the horses never grew tired.

Throughout it all, tension filled my bones as I waited for Aiden to give the order to send one of his friends to slaughter my remaining family. Surely, he'd known Elias kept them safe and still knew where they were hiding. Instead, he remained a steady beacon of warmth against my back, his arm wrapped around my front to keep his cloak in place while I shivered under my damp clothes.

We stopped only for brief moments at a time. Each time he shoved food into my hands or a flask of water my way, urging me to keep my strength up. But I never took what he offered. Each time he tried to show me kindness, or patience, I cursed him, and every time I did, he gritted his teeth and took it. I couldn't be bothered to even try to understand his patience with me.

"You have to eat something, Esme," he'd said during our last stop hours before.

I narrowed my gaze at him. He'd kept his true form hidden throughout our journey, choosing to hide his wings with the same magic I saw Ephraim use only days before.

"I want nothing from you," I'd snapped.

His hand fell to his side, bread and cheese forgotten as his eyes searched my face for any clue as to what I might be thinking. I scowled and turned my back on him. The others remained uneasy in my presence too. Seraphine and Killian kept to themselves, slightly apart from us, though Tarsa and Hakan kept close, flanking Aiden's sides at all times.

By now, we'd traveled for at least two days. I couldn't sleep and didn't bother to eat anything Aiden offered me. The mountains cast shadows over us now as we entered the Angelwood Forest. My stomach continued to plummet through my body as I sat rigid in front of Aiden, his horse a steady presence beneath us.

"Not long now," he whispered into my hair. I shivered as his breath caressed my neck.

Gritting my teeth, I leaned away from him. "Why bother taking me here?"

His hand shifted slightly across my middle, almost like he wanted to pull me against him but I knew it was only so I wouldn't fall off his large horse. "You'll see," he said with resignation.

Tarsa trotted ahead of us, her large black horse almost an exact replica of Aiden's apart from the slightly smaller frame. As I'd seen her do before, she disappeared into the distance without a trace. Hakan moved up then, keeping pace along our left side while the other two remained a few paces behind us. Neither one had spoken a word to me, let alone looked in my direction. They must have known I hated them as much as I resented Aiden for what happened to my family.

"Are you sure about this?" Hakan asked under his breath. I ignored him as I studied the forest around us. It appeared nothing like I expected.

The trees grew tall and thin in some places and broad and stout in others. The leaves were such vibrant shades of green and yellow that the bark nearly appeared black after all the rain. Even though the canopy of leaves hung menacingly over our heads, enough light from the fading sun peaked through to light the way.

I took a steeling breath to shake the uneasiness growing inside me. Throughout our travels, the strange essence in my chest stirred gradually; not like it usually did in Aiden's presence, but more so now as we entered the forest.

"Yes," Aiden replied with finality. "It's the only way."

"Not for you, it's not," Hakan countered patiently. "There are other options for you, sir."

I felt Aiden shift, shaking his head. "No, not any longer."

Hakan fell silent, but I felt his gaze briefly focus on me. I kept my eyes forward, studying the trees around us until I felt his focus shift. The path ahead widened steadily as we came into view of a small clearing. The sun filled this small space where Tarsa waited, horse left to wander nearby.

"This will do," Aiden sighed. Tarsa nodded, remaining silent. Her tall and lean frame appeared far more menacing now as she turned her steely gaze on me. I knew I'd never been her favorite person, but somehow, in that cold look she sent my way, it felt like I'd grown more troublesome in her eyes.

Aiden pulled his horse to a stop at the edge of the clearing and dismounted. I ignored his outstretched hand and leaped down, surprising myself with my coordination as I stepped away from his horse. Out of the corner of my eye, I saw him give an amused twitch of his lips which I chose to ignore.

"Here," Seraphine said, speaking up for the first time since my capture. "We'll get you cleaned up before."

I started. "Before what?"

Aiden sent her a look before turning his back and moving his horse near Tarsa's. Hakan disappeared, Killian with him. The forest around us had gone silent in the presence of the demons, making my heart race nervously. Surely, they wouldn't kidnap me again just to bring me up here to kill me.

"Doesn't matter," Tarsa snapped as she turned to lead us through a small path in the trees. I was surprised to see two tents already pitched, hidden in the tree line. "There's not much time before dusk anyway."

Tarsa and Seraphine led me into the larger tent, the one I knew to be for Aiden. Inside it was familiar. It was nearly empty apart from the single bed in the far corner and a table in the middle where a candle sat to light the space, only this time, I was surprised to see a small fire beside that table, filling the room with its heated scent.

"Strip her clothes," Tarsa ordered over her shoulder. She bent to grab a couple of towels from beneath the table and kept her back turned.

Seraphine moved closer, her hand on my arm. When I turned to look at her, she offered me a half-hearted smile. "Please undress."

I started. "What? Why?"

"Your clothes are soaked through," she pointed out calmly. "If you don't put on something dry and warm, you'll get ill."

I shrugged. "What does it matter?"

Tarsa scoffed. "I'd rather not have to deal with whatever mortal illness you catch on top of dealing with your presence at all."

My face heated beneath her glare but I obliged. Careful of my hands, still tender beneath what was left of the bandages, I first untied my boots and sighed as they fell to the floor. The trousers were harder as they'd crusted with mud and blood and clung to my skin. I shivered as the cool air kissed my bare skin. My face heated further as I pulled the wet shirt over my head, not meeting their gazes as they collected my wet clothes.

Tarsa handed a towel to Seraphine who then dunked it in the large bucket of water waiting nearby. I hadn't noticed it earlier either. Was this some sort of demon magic? My stomach tightened nervously.

"Here," Seraphine said, offering me the wet towel. "Wipe off the mud and you can dry off with the other one."

Silently, I did as I was told. The white towel darkened with blood that didn't belong to me and streaks of mud. The water turned a murky brown as I rinsed the massacre off of my skin. My hair took longer to clean. I didn't want to think about all the blood that was matted there. I knew some of it was mine as a bruise had formed behind my ear where that man struck me, but too much of it belonged to the dead.

I swallowed my disgust and reached for the dry towel Tarsa held. She frowned as she studied the bandages covering my hands. The raw skin beneath burned from the water soaking into the dirty bandages.

"We'll change those too," she said with a nod to my hands. I wrapped the towel around myself and sat on the edge of the table as she unwrapped my hands.

"He could heal these," Seraphine muttered to Tarsa as she too moved to study my hands.

Tarsa shot her a look. "That won't be a problem."

"What do you mean?" I asked when she didn't elaborate.

"You'll see."

I bit my lip to keep from sighing. I trusted her loyalty to Aiden enough to keep me alive, but not enough to keep track of her patience when it came to my exasperation.

They wrapped my hands quickly, new white bandages contrasting with my golden, tan skin.

"I'll braid your hair," Seraphine offered with a hesitant smile.

My face remained frozen as I merely turned my back. Her hands paused in my hair a moment before working through the tangles. Tarsa moved into view, digging through a large bag that she pulled out from beneath Aiden's bed. I watched as she tossed a pair of simple beige riding pants, a white shirt, and a white cloak onto the bed – each item of clothing containing dark gold trimming. I swallowed nervously as Seraphine worked her fingers through my hair. She braided it in a dark crown atop my head, tucking the end into the braid itself so it remained off of my neck.

With a sigh she stepped back. "There," she said, pleased with her work. "That looks good."

Tarsa looked up from where she continued to dig through the bag and scowled. "It's good enough at least."

I frowned, pulling the towel tighter around my middle. Neither one had bothered to explain what this was all for and I was growing more nervous by the second. My stomach twisted painfully, and my heart beat so chaotically against my ribs I was sure they could hear it in the silence of the tent. This would be easier if we could just get to their realm so I could start looking for ways to kill their prince. Instead, I was in the middle of the forest, naked, with these two immortals. But I'd play whatever part they required of me as long as it meant I would get my revenge in the end.

"Put these on," Tarsa ordered with a nod to the clothes she laid out.

As I dressed, she found a pair of boots and handed them to Seraphine. I tucked my shirt into the waistband of the pants before pulling on the tunic and tying the cloak around my shoulders. The bright colors felt strange. I was used to wearing plain clothes most days, sparing the colorful garb for performances only, but somehow this felt like acceptance of my fate. Acceptance I wasn't sure I was ready for.

Seraphine knelt to lace the boots up my calf while I fidgeted with the ties of my cloak. "Why are we stopping here?" I finally dared to ask.

Tarsa ignored me as she shoved the bag beneath the bed and left the tent. Seraphine watched her retreat before standing with a sigh. Her round face appeared sad now as she studied me.

"There's something Aiden needs to do," she admitted quietly.

I grew nervous as I studied her careful blank expression. "And what is that?"

She didn't answer. Instead, she looped her arm through mine and led me out into the forest. Dusk had begun to fall, casting long shadows through the trees. I swallowed my nerves and let her lead me down the path after Tarsa's retreating figure.

Aiden stepped out in front of us, forcing us to stop. I marveled at the similarities of our clothes as his gaze roamed over me appreciatively.

"What is this?" I asked. My anger and impatience grew steadily.

Aiden smirked. "You'll see soon enough."

I groaned. "Will everyone just stop saying that and answer my damn questions? What the hell do you want with me?" My plan to go along willingly was momentarily forgotten as I glared at him.

His smirk fell away quickly. "I want to keep you safe."

I snorted. "You are the reason my family is dead. You're a demon; you don't have it in you to care for me. You proved that much by letting my family be killed."

A muscle ticked in his jaw as I spoke. Seraphine had gone deathly still at my side, but her focus remained on Aiden, not me. Even the forest around us grew still and quiet at my words.

Aiden stepped forward, warmth radiating against my chest from his closeness as he towered over me. "Your ignorance was once intriguing to witness. Now it is pitiful to watch."

"So then tell me the truth, Aiden," I snapped. "What the hell do you want with me?"

"Esme," Seraphine cautioned gently.

I spun around to her. "What? Are you finally done lying to me too?"

Her face shattered, and for just a moment I saw the sadness she tried to keep hidden. She shook her head, braids falling over her shoulders. "I haven't lied to you, Esme."

I snorted. "You just did." When I turned back around to face Aiden his face was amused, trying to hide the hurt I could still see swirling in his silver-blue eyes. "What?"

He shrugged, annoyingly calm. "One day, you'll look back and realize this was all done for you, to keep you safe, and you'll thank me."

"You killed my family," I barked.

"I did no such thing."

"You were the only one there capable of stopping it," I said, voice breaking with tears I refused to shed. "And you didn't do a damn thing. That's the same as cutting their necks yourself."

"Now tell me the truth," I continued as I shifted to glance at both of them, "What is going on?"

"There's no time," Aiden said, reaching for my hand.

I yanked my hand back and glowered at him, hating the way my heart wanted to reach for him. "Do not touch me," I snapped. Tears burned my throat as I glared at him. The way his face softened in hurt and understanding made me want to scream. "I hate you."

He smirked then. As cold and heartless as it was, I could still see the hurt in his eyes. "Now who's the liar?"

I moved to strike him. Aiden's hand caught mine a moment before it could collide with his cheek where I'd hit him only days before. His grip remained gentle on my wrist though my injured hand stung painfully with the reverberations of the movement. Seraphine stiffened further at my attack but made no move to interfere.

"I will never forgive you for what you did to them." My voice broke with the pain that threatened to crack my chest open.

For a moment he wouldn't look at me, only keeping his eyes downcast as I yanked my hand free. But as he slowly lifted his gaze, I wanted to take it back. The feeling was short lived as determination filled me once again, slowly erasing the force of my anger.

Those blue-grey eyes, filled with such compassion and concern bore into me as I blinked away angry tears. This time when he reached for me, I didn't stop him. As his hand joined with mine the fluttering in my chest spread. The essence that made me the Soul Collector, and caused so much pain for my family, spread throughout my entire body and welcomed Aiden's touch.

"It's time," he said into the silence.

I let him lead me down the path, marveling at the way the setting sun turned his dark hair a shade of red that looked like it was dipped in blood. Fitting for the demon prince.

Tarsa, Hakan, and Killian waited for us in a small clearing, their clothes still caked with blood and mire, but they didn't seem to mind as they watched Aiden and I approach. Seraphine moved to stand at Killian's side.

But it was the tree behind them that stole my breath away. Aiden led me past his friends, his gaze burning into my face as I marveled at the tree. Wide enough to span the width of Aiden's large wings, and tall enough to tower over the entire forest, the white tree appeared to glow in acceptance as we neared.

"Is this…?" my voice drifted off as Aiden pulled us to a stop at the base of the magnificent tree. I craned my neck to look up at the white leaves that seemed frozen, though the breeze shifted the surrounding trees easily.

"Yes," he said, understanding my thoughts. When I turned to look at him questioningly, there was a soft smile on his mouth; pleased in a way that didn't seem fitting for the chaos of our situation. The glow from the tree brightened as he turned to face me, taking both of my hands in his. Awe filled me as I watched the way he seemed to thrive in the tree's presence. A halo of light radiated around him, erasing the shadows from his past and his wings which gave him his dark title.

"Why are we here?" I asked nervously. My heart throbbed against my ribs as I tried, and failed, to find a reason for all of this. My ancestor prayed to this very tree for weeks before Aiden offered him the curse that lives in my chest. Was Nadira's story wrong? Could this be a way to end the curse too?

Aiden hesitated as his gaze flicked to his friends before returning to me, though he wouldn't meet my eyes. "There's something we have to do… to keep you safe."

My brows furrowed as confusion swept through me, nearly overpowering the nerves. "What do you mean?"

He sighed, hands tightening slightly around mine. "It's the only way to keep you and your family alive."

"My family is dead," I deadpanned, glaring at him.

Aiden had the audacity to smirk as he shook his head. "We both know your brother and sister live. If you want them to remain alive, I suggest you follow the instructions."

"What do I need to do?" I asked reluctantly.

His lips twitched toward a smile before being replaced by his mask once again. "The only way to keep you and your family safe is to spread the protection my name and title offer. To do that, we need to be bound together."

"Absolutely not," I said, jerking away.

"It's the only way to keep your family safe," he said patiently. "There are others still hunting you, and if they come across your brother and sister first then we need to make sure they're equally protected."

I grit my teeth but merely offered a stiff nod as he grasped my hands, careful against the bandages. The others grew inhumanly still as the sounds of the forest seemed to quiet further. Whatever I just agreed to do, the forest could sense it as the tree beside us lightened further.

He spoke a strange string of words that would bind my soul to his. I knew them, I could hear them with my ears, but my mind wouldn't work to focus on what they meant. All I could recall was the feel of his hands in mine—the memory of them against my skin. The need I had for him still haunted my heart, though the pain of his betrayal sank its claws deeper into my soul. My breath shuddered through me as a faint burning burst across the back of my left hand and down my third finger.

The clearing fell silent once again. I could feel everyone's focus firmly on me as I stood there, fighting with the emotions raging inside.

Aiden offered me a small smile as he leaned forward slightly. "Esme," he whispered. "You have to repeat the words."

I shook my head to clear it. "What?"

"You have to repeat them," he said patiently. "If you truly want to be reunited with your siblings and keep them safe, then you need to repeat these words. They're for your protection, and theirs as well."

My eyes narrowed, flashing quickly to the tree. If this was where my ancestor came all those years ago to beg for help, then maybe this would help keep them safe too. Until I could find a way to kill Aiden, or his father, then I would need to keep Mousa and Cordelia safe. For them I would do anything.

"What were the words again?" I whispered, cheeks burning in embarrassment.

He smiled, knowing I was too distracted with marveling at his touch. His thumb brushed against the back of my hand in acknowledgment. "Through life and death, with soul and heart. I tie my life to yours from now until we choose to part."

My mouth grew dry as I glanced back to the tree, allowing myself one last moment to silently pray to the stars to watch over my family.

"Esme," he said patiently. "It has to be said, to keep them safe."

I glanced at the others standing by. Tarsa and Hakan remained stoic, blank of emotion as ever. But Killian and Seraphine watched me with pity. Did they know what their prince did to my family?

Aiden frowned slightly. "Esme." The whispered breath of my name from his lips sent a shiver of longing down my spine. I closed my eyes against the tears that threatened.

"Through life and death," I whispered slowly. "With soul and heart. I tie my life to yours, from now until we choose to part."

Before Aiden could so much as offer me a grin, the tree brightened harshly. A white glow erupted around us, forcing me to close my eyes against it. My hand burned further as I yanked it from Aiden's grip with a gasp.

As the pain grew to an unbearable heat, I clawed at the new bandages. They tore away easily as I tossed them to the ground, trying to find the fire that burned my hand. What I found instead made my lungs freeze with shock. Aiden's cool hand reached out to grasp mine gently. The wounds I'd sustained at the castle had closed, still heavily scabbed with much healing left to do, but they no longer bled and appeared to be far less sensitive as I fisted and relaxed my hands repeatedly. My shattered knuckles seemed to have healed entirely along with every other injury that once haunted my body.

Slowly, Aiden turned my left hand over so my palm faced the earth. What I saw there threatened to weaken my knees, for a matching mark showed on the back of Aiden's left hand as well.

Silver vines lined with black thorns covered the back of my left hand and twirled around my third finger, clear to the nail, in a tattooed marking. A single rose bloomed in the middle of it all, a bright silver that appeared nearly white beneath the glow from the tree, topped with a simple black crown embellished with wings.

As the glow slowly dimmed, taking the last of the setting sun with it, we were left in near complete darkness. My hands shook in Aiden's gentle grasp as I stared at the marking that covered my hand, mirroring his own.

My mind whirled with the future that now lay before me, the chaos this might cause to those I love. With shaking knees, I looked up into Aiden's eyes where I hoped to find the answers I desperately needed. Instead, I found a smirk keeping the secrets that lived behind his eyes just out of reach.

"You once said you hated demons," Aiden said softly, though his voice held little warmth. "Well congratulations, princess. You are now married to the Prince of Death."

EPILOGUE

The doors slammed against the walls as the winged male stormed into the castle. The full-bellied king stopped his urgent pacing as he glanced toward the angel. A thin trail of blood could still be noted on the marble flooring, but its victim – the young mortal prince – was nowhere in sight.

"We didn't expect you so soon, Your Holiness." The mortal queen curtsied respectfully as she took her place beside her husband.

The angel glared at them. "You lost the girl." It wasn't a question, and from the sharpness of his tongue the royals knew to tread cautiously.

King Elroy fisted his hands at his sides, hoping the gesture would hide their slight tremble. "The death prince took her."

"You didn't think to stop him." Again, not a question.

The king's mouth flapped open like a fish out of water as he frantically searched for the words that he hoped would extend his miserable mortal life.

The angel raised his hand, signaling the mortal king to hold his tongue. "Your family swore loyalty to me long ago. Am I to believe you have traded your loyalties to another?"

He shook his head harshly. "No. No, of course not, Your Holiness."

"There was no way to stop him." Queen Isolde's voice sounded much more confident than her husband's. The angel appreciated her boldness. "The girl escaped with our son under cover of night. We sent out men after them, but Prince Aiden and his demons took her away."

The angel's jaw tightened painfully as his anger flared through his veins. His wings pulled in tightly across his back in an effort to keep his rage from tearing this castle apart, stone by stone.

"You were to hold her until I could retrieve her," the angel said, voice dangerously soft.

King Elroy's head bobbed nervously. "Yes. We did; we held her for the entire summer. But when the demons first came to take her weeks ago, we thought they had been sent by you."

The angel ran a hand over his face. The movement gave him something to do with his hands other than ring the neck of the king. "Why would I send demons to retrieve what I planned to claim?"

Again, the king was at a loss for words. Typical. His bloodline had grown more foolish with each generation. The only hope for Cordovia's survival would now lie with their dying son.

"Our bargain still stands," the king said boldly. At the angel's quizzical look, he continued hastily. "My family's deal. We remain loyal to you and your angels, and you secure my bloodline to the throne. We've done our part, now you do yours. My kingdom is dying and you're letting it."

The angel tilted his head back and laughed coldly. He couldn't help but admire the king for his brazen tongue.

"Your kingdom is not dying because of me," the angel said coolly. "But you are right. Your family has remained loyal to me all these years. It is time I secure the prosperity of your kingdom and your bloodline to the throne."

The king's shoulders collapsed with relief. The mortal wife at his side sighed as well, offering the angel a thankful smile.

Outside, the storm continued to batter the windows with its harsh rain as lightening lit up the darkened sky. That brief amount of light allowed the angel to see his reflection in the window—a sight he often avoided as his cold eyes had refused to hide the knowledge of his missing soul.

He turned back to the mortals, anger filling his veins again. "Unfortunately," he said coldly, letting his wings spread wide to cast an eerie shadow over the mortal royals, "your kingdom will not prosper under your rule any longer."

The queen looked to her husband, confusion furrowing her groomed brow while the round king appeared just as lost.

"I don't understand. You were supposed to keep my family on the throne." His voice grew shrill with fear and hot anger. The angel drank it in as he stalked through the room. "We captured the Soul Collector for you. All you had to do was take her away from here and leave us be. It is not our fault you came too late."

A smile that held little kindness pulled at the angel's mouth. "I didn't say anything about taking your *family* off of the throne."

Understanding dawned on the king's face for only a moment before the angel plunged his poisoned knife into his throat. The mortal queen cried hysterically as she fell to her knees beside her dying husband. The storm outside did little to silence her cries in the bare room.

Slowly, the angel wiped the blood from his knife before returning it to its sheath between his wings. The guards lining the room did nothing to help their now-dead king or their hysterical queen—a sign that they at least had some sense of self-preservation, unlike their greedy king.

Lightening flashed across the sky outside again, and in that moment, the angel caught his reflection once more. Blue eyes, dead of emotion, haunted his face while pale hair hung around his chin, still dripping from the rain. He knew none of that was what kept the guards glued to the walls, far out of reach. It was the dove-grey wings and sharp horns wrapping around his skull. That, and the knowledge that he—as the Angel of Life—could end their very realm with a simple word to his armies, patiently waiting to claim what should have been theirs all along.

He would get the girl. And when he did, no one was safe from the war igniting the vengeance in his blood.

THANKS FOR READING!

Thank you for giving this indie book a chance. If you enjoyed the adventure with Esme and the rest of the gang, then please consider leaving an online review, sharing with your friends, or following on social media. All of these can help an author's journey more than you know.

THANK YOU!

Acknowledgments

Publishing a book is no easy feat. And I certainly couldn't have done it by myself, so I have a lot of people to thank for helping me get this book to where it is now.

Bucky – Yes, I'm thanking my dog because he deserves a thanks for his endless patience with my long writing hours. Not to mention all the added walks I made him go on just so I could brainstorm story ideas.

Melissa Cole – Your editing expertise and confidence in my work was exactly what I needed at a time I began to doubt every choice in the story. Thank you for helping me bring this story and these characters to life.

Whimsy Book Cover Graphics – You're amazing! Thank you for taking my chaotic notes and ideas to heart and creating a beautiful cover.

EJL Editing - You managed to fit me into your schedule at a fairly late notice and gave such incredible feedback when I needed it most. Thank you!

Melissa Nash – Cartographer extraordinaire. You brought my world to life! I was completely lost as I tried to figure out how to depict this vast world on paper and you did it with such ease and talent. Thank you for turning my poorly drawn map into a beautiful masterpiece.

Luna and Hillary - Thank you so much for your early insight into what was a very chaotic and LONG draft. Your suggestions and words of wisdom kept the story centered around what was important, and not on the many side adventures I added with each draft. Thank you!

Hedaya – For the longest time you were the only person who knew this book existed. Thanks for helping me get to the finish line and keeping me sane!

Mom and Dad – Thank you for your endless support for this book and all the books to come after.

And lastly I have to thank you, the reader, for giving this book a chance. Through many hours of discovering just how challenging writing (and editing) can be, I am glad this book has finally made its way to you. I hope you enjoyed Esme's story and I really hope you stick around for what comes next...wink wink.

From the bottom of my heart, thank you all.

About the Author

Audrey Steves is a fantasy author located in the Midwest. When not writing, or reading, she often spends her time with her dog or horse. The Soul Collector is her debut novel. You can connect with Audrey on her social media pages or her website.

Follow Audrey Steves online.

@audreysteves on TikTok

@author.audreysteves on Instagram

www.ingramcontent.com/pod-product-compliance
Lightning Source LLC
Chambersburg PA
CBHW021228310726
48971CB00006B/1729